A Flann O'Brien Reader

A
Flann O'Brien
Reader

Edited and with an Introduction by

Stephen Jones

A RICHARD SEAVER BOOK

The Viking Press   New York

A Richard Seaver Book / The Viking Press
First published in 1978 by The Viking Press
625 Madison Avenue, New York, N.Y. 10022

Library of Congress Cataloging in Publication Data
O'Nolan, Brian, 1911-1966.
  A Flann O'Brien reader.
  "A Richard Seaver book."
  I. Title.
PR6029.N56F55 1977   828'.9'1209   76-46968
ISBN 0-670-31740-3

Printed in the United States of America
Set in Linotype Fairfield

The editor wishes to acknowledge grateful thanks to Mrs. Evelyn
O'Nolan, Mrs. Seamus Kelly, A.M. Heath, Ltd., MacGibbon and
Kee, The Irish Times, and the Morris Library of Southern Illinois
University for permission to print various material that appeared
in The Journal of Irish Literature.

ACKNOWLEDGMENT
Walker and Company, Inc.: From At Swim-Two-Birds by Flann
O'Brien. Copyright © 1951, 1966 by Brian O'Nolan. From The
Third Policeman by Flann O'Brien. Copyright ©1967 by Evelyn
O'Nolan. Both used by permission of the publisher, Walker
and Company.

ACKNOWLEDGMENTS

I would like to thank the following for helping make "The Potable Flann O'Brien":

David Hanly of Greater Dublin for undertaking numerous scholarly excursions which as often as not seemed to yield more than either he or I had bargained for.

Tim and Anne Magennis for various amenities, books, and David Hanly.

Anne Crowley Kelly of Outer Montville for deciphering and typing a section of my manuscript which looked like a spastic *Book of Kells*.

Helen Petty and Rose York of the University of Connecticut Library at Avery Point for bringing to our outpost shards of civilization from such cultural centers as Carbondale, Chicago, Storrs, and other places less known.

Jessica Murphy Jones for reading the O'Brien canon and offering me her notes. Edward Phillip Jones for transportation into the interior. William Thomas Jones for introducing me at an early age to what might be loosely termed the O'Brien Possibility.

Helen Murphy Preston for recovering some bits of Dublin slang.

David Powell of Western New Mexico University for helpful phone calls and letters. His Ph.D. dissertation, "The English Writings of Flann O'Brien," is still the best source of facts and sane judgments on O'Brien.

Miles Orvell of Temple University for turning over some *Cruiskeen Lawn* materials he and Dr. Powell had amassed. The staff of the Rare Book Room of the Morris Library at Southern Illinois University at Carbondale for help in carrying off their major collection of O'Brien material. The University of Connecticut at Avery Point for use of its copying machine, Scotch tape, and midnight oil. Lee Jacobus of The University of Connecticut at Storrs for some early hints, William Kelly of The University of Connecticut at Avery Point for his knowledge of gallows humor.

Richard Seaver of The Viking Press, who has made a profound commitment to the Resurrection of Flann.

George Connaughton, who cleaned up the mess.

And most of all to Susan Preston, who unearthed good things in Carbondale and put together a great many items in Avery Point, including the editor.

—STEPHEN JONES
The University of Connecticut
Avery Point
Groton, Connecticut

CONTENTS

Introduction

*The chief work of literary men in dealing with language,
and of poets especially, lies in feeling back along the ancient
lines of advance.*

—Fenollosa

Flann O'Brien is the most famous of the pen names employed by the
Irish civil servant Brian O'Nolan (1911–1966). As Flann O'Brien he
wrote several novels that for their exuberant prose and sparkling invention have been proclaimed among the finest of the modern period
by writers such as James Joyce, Dylan Thomas, and Graham Greene
and more recently John Wain, Anthony Burgess, and John Updike.
Philosophic writers such as Vivian Mercier and William Gass have
seen O'Brien as one of the earliest, but more important, one of the
most continually pleasing of the "new novelists."

The commercial fate of O'Brien's works, however, despite brief
flurries, has not been commensurate with his reputation. The first of
his major books, *At Swim-Two-Birds* (1939), although published to
critical success and occasionally enjoying reprints, has never really
recovered from its economic record, caused at least in part by the
fact that it came out on the. eve of World War II. *The Third*

Policeman, another major work, was not published because of the financial showing of *At Swim.* Written a year later, it went the rounds of publishers and was finally returned to the author for safekeeping during the blitz. At this time O'Brien put out a variety of stories announcing that the work had been lost under exotic circumstances, and it was not until a year after his death, some quarter of a century later, that the book was published to the critical acclaim of Benedict Kiely's front page article, "Fun After Death," in *The New York Times Book Review* (November 12, 1967).

In the twenty-five or so years between the publication of these two classic novels, O'Brien occupied his days holding down a responsible job in the bureaucracy of the Irish Government, and his nights, weekends, and holidays turning out a wildly imaginative newspaper column for the conservative *Irish Times.* In this foray, which he entitled *Cruiskeen Lawn* ("The Little Overflowing Jug"), he projected himself as Myles na Gopaleen ("Myles of the Little Ponies"), an irascible pundit who worried such matters as clichés, steam trains, snow gauges, politicians, vacations in remote damps, and conversations at tram stops. As Myles-on-the-way-home, he became a Dublin character. He also managed to write two other novels, *The Hard Life: An Exegesis of Squalor* (1962) and *The Dalkey Archive* (1964); a parody novel in Irish, *An Beál Bocht* (1941), translated by Patrick C. Power as *The Poor Mouth* (1973); a play performed at the Abbey Theatre, *Faustus Kelly* (1943); a batch of short works collected posthumously as *Stories and Plays* (1973); and two collections of *Cruiskeen Lawn,* a cheap wartime edition and the posthumous *The Best of Myles* (1968). In a grim, late phase when he was wracked by illness, he was asked to bring his talents to television and managed, along with less happy efforts, *The Ideas of O'Day.*

He died on April Fool's Day 1966 in Dublin, age fifty-five, from a variety of ailments, leaving various relatives, including his widow, Evelyn, whom he married in 1948, and two literary brothers, Kevin O Nolan and Ciaran O'Nolan, both of whom have written about him.*
He also left what one of his clichémongers could only categorize as "a host of admirers" who refuse to believe that there is not yet another

---

* O'Brien renders an account of most of these illnesses, misfortunes, etc., in "Can a Saint Hit Back?", included here in the introductory material to *The Dalkey Archive.*

posthumous work lurking somewhere, ticking perhaps in a box secreted in "greater Dublin," primed to explode, or more likely implode.

In this Reader are selections from the published works, most of which have been out of print, and some further items that have been, if not ticking, at least reposing nervously under the bronze bust of James Joyce in the Morris Library, which is located in greater Carbondale, Illinois.

* * *

After the manner of a "useful" piece of gear in his Myles na Gopaleen Central Research Bureau, Brian O'Nolan has provided us with a number of deceptively helpful handles by which to pick up his literary remains. A few years ago in America it seemed advisable to talk about the bewildering diversity of pen names, styles, genres, and so forth. Indeed, as Jack White has written, ". . . it was an aspect of his *folie de grandeur* . . . that no connection could ever be provided between Myles na Gopaleen and Brian O'Nolan." There is also an early letter from O'Nolan to *The Irish Press* advising them that, contrary to their note, he "is not the author of the mentioned book [*At Swim-Two-Birds*]." Even late in life, O'Brien brought a laconic listing of equipment a writer needs to a sudden crescendo with, "and the compartmentation of . . . personality for the purpose of literary utterance." Like Joyce's myths, however, these masks, while not without interest to the reader, serve, in Pound's phrase, primarily as scaffolding for the author.

As time has passed, however, these separate guises, transparent to most everyone in the bitterly chummy Dublin literary world, now seem less important than the central unity of the vision of the man the world has come to call Flann O'Brien. It is the purpose of this Reader to display the unity as well as the diversity of this penman who has, without benefit of exile, transcended his island to join Beckett and Joyce (though as Donald O'Hara has said, "Making these writers a trinity by adding O'Brien is a bit like dragging in the Holy Ghost"). Let this Reader then stand as an ancillary document to some future Nicene Creed.

Once people came to see that Myles and Flann and Brian were one, they tried to cling to the old heresy by saying that the promise of Flann, as in the youthful *At Swim-Two-Birds* and *The Third Policeman*, both written before he was thirty, was blighted by either the civil-service career of Brian or the "journalism career" of Myles. That our man died before he was sixty and that he drank helped. While it is true that Flann did not achieve the perfect unity of the Joycean cycle (who has?), there runs through all O'Brien's genres and personae a high level of literateness and perception, and a style that informs everything he touches. He has, in the baseball vernacular, the live arm, and even his pick-off moves to first have something on them.

There are stretches of Myles which are as much "literature" as parts of Flann, and even scraps of the more perishable Brian that may be literature as well. "Over his period of eighteen years in the Civil Service," writes his boss John Garvin, "Brian kept up a constant and delightful correspondence with me, sending me letters from illiterates, nitwits and 'quare fellas' with appropriate comments." Or here is Brian merely walking down the street, where he becomes the occasion of literature in others, in this case publican and Joyce Society secretary John Ryan (see Selected Bibliography):

His legs seemed to be taking off on independent courses—unrelated to the desired destination of the rest of the body. In later years, when somewhat the worse for wear, I have seen him 'hove-to', that is to say, maintaining a position but making slight headway in the sea of pedestrians, while apparently going astern.

In trying to account for, or even just describe, the liveliness of O'Brien's style, many have seen only ferocity. Flann-as-Myles especially has the reputation of being fierce. That word and variations occur in commentaries ranging from the man in the street to formal academic discourse. His eyes are said to be fierce; his eyebrows are fierce; with his massive forehead exposed, his face is fierce; with his black hat covering his massive forehead he gains even more ferocity, for the already fierce eyebrows and fiercer eyes are now highlighted. His teeth are seen by Ryan in terms of their small, comic, surprising un-fierceness, but even in this mildness Ryan sees the "odd conjunction of meekness and ferocity in his features."

Classmates at University College saw his chess playing as a "very characteristic" image of "glowering" and "odd hissing." Every move was delivering the *coup de grace*, as Myles cited his mythological matches with Russian masters. Naturally his scholarship is ferocious in all aspects, especially his etymologies. It follows that such a fierce man produces fierce satire, and John Ryan assures us that even twenty years later civil servants still quake in their boots. (One can just see, alongside such Myles Research Bureau designs as the gauge that measures the snows of yesteryear; the glass houses designed for primary stone throwers; the extra lofty garages housing high dudgeons [a vehicle the angry are wont to drive off in]: a new posthumous device: boots for the fearful, built to pass muster in any civil-service corridor, structured to accept high amounts of seismic stress.)

There is an epithet applied to Myles, however, even more than "fierce," though this was more often in the streets than in the press. That word is (gasp) "lovable." One can hear it particularly in the tone of Dubliners today. "Oh, you're putting together 'Myles.' Yes, he did have those other names but, well, I call him [here the face softens, the voice warms] 'Myles.'" Even Ryan, who is aware of the browbeater, begins and ends his chapter on Myles with a tribute to the lovable side of our man. "Brian O'Nolan was three divinely humorous personae in one." Ryan quotes the irascible Patrick Kavanagh, an Irish poet who, among other things, said he could "do without" Yeats. For Kavanagh, our man was "incomparable," a word he linked, according to Ryan, with "irreplaceable":

Paddy survived Myles by a little more than a year, but even in that short period often remarked to me that there was nobody left to talk to in Dublin now that Myles was gone. He was one of the few writers in whose company he was completely at ease; his respect for him was complete; he was his peer.

In summing up his memoir of Dublin writers (Patrick Kavanagh, Brendan Behan, J. P. Donlevy mainly), Ryan chooses our man to come back to for his coda and, contrasting him to Behan and Kavanagh, says:

For all his disappointments, Myles was a happy enough man. . . . He did not believe that being an author conferred the privileges of being rude and offensive to others not of that calling. He expected the ordinary respect that is the right of any honest burgess.

This respect is there in the letters to him at *The Irish Times*. Often these letters were from "victims" of the fierceness. The recipients of Myles's lash would compliment him on "noticing small points" and end by saying they were "devoted fans," as did Tim Pat Coogan of the *Evening Press*. The Royal National Life-Boat Institution thanked him for noticing the not so small thing that "in most cases of ship's sinking a large proportion of the life boats is useless." The Irish House-wives Association wrote, "The lady members of the above association are ardent admirers of your writings in the *Irish Times*." Perhaps the pen name allowed people that extra distance to breathe. Hilton Edwards, writing in behalf of the Dublin Gate Theatre Productions, was interested in Brian O'Nolan doing a local version of Capek's *Insect Play*, but found it "almost impossible to write a letter to you because your friend Miles [*sic*] -na-gCopaleen's dissertations on cliché have so unnerved me."

No doubt this warmth between O'Brien and his readers was made possible by the pen name that started out as a mere dodge to protect his civil-service career but soon flowered into a full persona. He created dozens of outrageous "autobiographies" that had him doing everything from advising Clemenceau to running for President of Ireland (anticipating the United States's resident elf-provocateur, Norman Mailer). *Time* interviewed him and glibly reported that O'Brien had been married to the daughter of a Cologne basketmaker, a marriage that had been tragically blighted after only a year, when the fair young German had faded with consumption. (He actually married a few years later, in 1948, a girl he met in the civil service. Evelyn O'Nolan is still alive.)

Not only was Myles fleshed out in print, but around town Myles was the person people chose to see, not O'Brien. As the years passed, he grew into the role which included a large-brimmed black hat. Late in life, when he had broken with *The Irish Times*, he persuaded a few provincial newspapers to take (and not "mutilate") his column. To these readers he confided: "My hat is disgracefully aged. Its useful life is long since over. It is stained. It is no exaggeration to say it is filthy. But its many years of faithful service has turned it into part of me. To a large extent, I have become something that fits in under the hat."

In short, what we have is not one man beating up another, a victimizing, but a shared experience between the author and his audience by means of the third party, the literary persona. It is the difference between having a pull toy between you and your dog and presenting for his exercise your personal fingers. "I don't care what you say about me as long as it's literature," Oliver St. John Gogarty was supposed to have said when he heard that Joyce was writing him into a book, a statement that is the direct descendant of Dublin wit Oscar Wilde's claim in the dock that the only immoral literature was a piece poorly written. The style then achieves the distance, but with the Irishmen educated by Latin there is always a certain style they have in mind, a certain persona behind that style, and a world behind that: the fierce scholar rebel. But make no mistake, my good man, the rebel is a scholar first and a rebel later. In fact, he is a rebel only because he was a scholar, and his studies have shown him a better way.

Beneath the Latin in our man was not only the English but the Irish language. The remote O'Nolan House in Tullamore, the family temperament that included uncles educated in Latin, Greek, and Irish, and a father who wrote an unpublished mystery novel, combined to permit the three older brothers the intermittent formal schooling in the lower grades which can often produce the most original scholars later on. The O'Nolans played tricks in Irish, made inventions out of it, and educated themselves by means of it. Brother Ciaran (who to further confuse matters uses the Irish form of his name Ciarán O'Nualláin) is editor of an Irish weekly and has written an account of the County Tyrone childhood in Irish which is being translated as *The Youth of the Brother*. Brother Kevin, professor of classics at Trinity College, Dublin, writes in his memoir:

We, as we grew up, with our book-biased training, were constantly delighted at the vividness and economy of language casually practised by our Strabane elders, and at a great range of strange words like 'hochle' and 'boke' which seemed more expressive than the ordinary words to be found in books.

Unlike Joyce, who was spooked off Irish, Flann O'Brien reveled in the old language, and after moving to Dublin and enduring the Christian Brothers' Synge St. School (see *The Hard Life*), and two years at Blackrock College, he went on to University College, Dublin, where in spite of later disclaimers that he did nothing but play pool and cards, fool, and drink, he wrote much of the student magazine, employing there a barrage of pseudonymns, styles, and languages, including not only modern Irish, but Old Irish. It was in this ancient tongue that the young scholar danced an obscene epic that put the school in an unprecedented legal situation, for almost no one, including the president, could read the chief exhibit. "His humour was original and many-sided," wrote Kevin, "his command of language formidable, and there was an assurance and maturity in what he wrote that is not easily matched among undergraduates."

He took a master's degree, with a thesis on "Nature in Modern Irish Poetry." This is a side often overlooked in O'Brien's verbal stunts and structural tricks but which makes a texture through which these other maneuvers may exist in a palpable way, unlike many modern artists who may build stunts as mere stunts. Certainly what makes all the Chinese-box moves of *The Third Policeman* is the saturation of the opening in a genuine Irish countryside reminiscent of the author's country childhood. Or take this from his last novel, *The Dalkey Archive:*

... Mick began to muse and think of country places he had known in his younger days. He thought of one place he had been fond of.

Brown bogs and black bogs were neatly arranged on each side of the road with rectangular boxes carved out of them here and there, each with a filling of yellow-brown brown-yellow water. Far away near the sky tiny people were stooped at their turf-work, cutting out precisely-shaped sods with their patent spades and building them into a tall memorial the height of a horse and cart. Sounds came from them, delivered to his ears without charge by the west wind, sounds of laughing and whistling and bits of verses from the old bog-songs. Nearer, a house stood attended by three trees and surrounded by the happiness of a coterie of fowls, all of them picking and rooting and disputating loudly in the unrelenting manufacture of their eggs. The house was quiet in itself and silent but a canopy of lazy smoke had been erected over the chimney to indicate that people were within engaged on tasks. Ahead of him went the road, running swiftly across the flat land and pausing slightly to climb slowly up a hill that was waiting for it in a place where there was tall grass, grey boulders and rank stunted trees. The whole overhead was occupied by the sky, translucent, impenetrable, ineffable and incomparable, with a fine island of cloud anchored in the calm two yards to the right of Mr Jarvis's outhouse.

The Debating Society seemed to take up the place that music did in Joyce's schooling, and O'Brien first gained his reputation for fierceness in formal exchanges that packed the halls and overflowed into a loud, crammed vestibule that our man alone had the eloquence to control. As for music, many of the O'Nolan children received training, but none, writes Kevin, as far as he knows was ever heard to utter a note.

It was while at University College that he met Niall Sheridan, who was to play Ezra Pound to his T. S. Eliot, and then some; Sheridan not only cut wads out of *At Swim-Two-Birds* for the author but served as one of the major characters as well. Sheridan and O'Brien romped through those impromptu exercises of parody, satire, and pure invention that bright boys in college do in many countries, but perhaps best in a land that blends fierce (that word again) scholarship and a fireside tradition for improvising yarns. There was Sheridan's idea for an All-Purpose Opening Speech which began as a communal composition that was to provide politicians, clergymen, educators, and so on with a uniform utterance that would fit all occasions, appear to signify, but offend none. The speech was to be one grammatical sentence, and O'Brien thought that, translated into every known language, it would bring world peace. Even in this youthful jest the future author of *The Dalkey Archive* is at work, for in that last novel O'Brien's persona Mick sees that the hope of averting atomic catastrophe lies only in the construction of some great book along the lines of a James Joyce epic, a book which would so befuddle and assuage the malignant scientist (De Selby) that he would subside from the restlessness which drives him to employ his wicked toy.

In many ways I think *The Dalkey Archive* the test for true Flannites, for it eliminates those engineers who admire *At Swim-Two-Birds* and *The Third Policeman* for the cleverness. *The New York Times* found it a book "about nothing," but not in the sense that Sartre or even Beckett would flavor that thinnest of subjects. No doubt the book is structurally flawed. The author was distracted not only by journalism but by dying. Nevertheless, a beautiful humor suffuses the whole work (maybe out of deference to H. W. Fowler and to maintain just a touch of the old word as used by Ben Jonson and Robert Burton we should spell it "humour"):

	Motive or Aim	Province	Method or Means	Audience
humour	Discovery	Human nature	Observation	The sympathetic
wit	Throwing light	Words & ideas	Surprise	The intelligent
satire	Amendment	Morals & manners	Accentuation	The self-satisfied
sarcasm	Inflicting pain	Faults & foibles	Inversion	Victim & bystander
invective	Discredit	Misconduct	Direct statement	The public
irony	Exclusiveness	Statement of facts	Mystification	An inner circle
cynicism	Self-justification	Morals	Exposure of nakedness	The respectable
The sardonic	Self-relief	Adversity	Pessimism	Self

That old chart of Fowler's stands up, I think, except for the pre-Brooks-and-Warren treatment of irony. Certainly humour is the sort of thing Flann O'Brien is really about, "fierce" though the "satire" may sometimes seem, for so winning is the tone of the persona that the audience shifts over, if uneasily, from the "self-satisfied" to the "sympathetic." Within the framework of recent American politics this shift might seem disastrous to social reform, but O'Brien is not so much after political change as a liberating of the imagination. If O'Brien unleashes Myles on "Bores" it is because he recognizes they are not merely tiresome or even antisocial. "The foregoing samples," he writes, "of course, represent *attitudes*. There are, however, troglodytic specimens who can get their effects by a single and unvarying remark which, injected into thousands of conversations in the course of their lifetime, enables them to take leave of humanity knowing that they have done something important to it. Have you ever heard this: Of course Dan O'Connell Was A Freemason Of Course You Knew That?"

The bore is both pre-human (troglodytic) and of that human type which, under the excuse of modern technology, poisons humanity by "injecting" thousands of conversations. (And what can be more important than a conversation, for it is conversation, as James Stephens used to say, that keeps away death, and what is Irish literature, he added, but that continuing communal conversation that staves off the final oblivion?) The bore's remark about Dan O'Connell may strike us as a bit local, but isn't it the essence of a bore to traffic in inside stuff that promises to liberate us from the mundane, but which merely closes off the world even more? In *The Third Policeman* O'Brien constructs a beautiful hell out of just such a series of inside tips, each inside the other. Boxes they finally are. Coffins. But all the same well made and to be enjoyed for the workmanship:

It was about a foot in height, perfect in its proportions and without fault in workmanship. There were indents and carving and fanciful excoriations and designs on every side of it and there was a bend on the lid that gave the article great distinction. At every corner there was a shiny brass corner-piece and on the lid there were brass corner-pieces beautifully wrought and curved impeccably against the wood. The whole thing had the dignity and the satisfying quality of true art.

What exactly is the pervading tone then in Flann O'Brien? In tragedy—at least successful tragedy—there is but the one tone possible, but in humor, that is the larger category including the whole Fowler contraption from "humour" to "the sardonic," there are possibilities for felicities in the full tonal spectrum from fierce Juvenal to mellow Horace (*comus et urbanus*) or, to put it in terms more local to our man, but by no means more familiar, from that well-known Dublin savage indignitary Swift to the benign, dark-fending Stephens.

Tone has to do, as the American resident fox Frost told us, with how the author takes himself as well as how he takes his material and his audience. Ryan says O'Brien "regarded himself primarily as a citizen." Not that he made himself provincial, for by the very nature of the cosmopolitan audience he posited, assumed, and in a sense then created, he transcended the paralysis of the dear, dirty Dublin Joyce was forced to flee. O'Brien raised even petty squabbles to a larger dimension, which is not quite the same as making a tempest in a teapot or a mountain out of a mole hill. (I'm not sure if there isn't a road grader or bulldozer somewhere parked in *Cruiskeen Lawn*, diesel idling, blade poised for the mountainous task, a task possibly connected with urban planning in Donabate [see "Donabete"]. There assuredly *is* an apparatus already available in Myles's jug for handling large cyclonic disturbances within the confines of culinary utensils.) Unlike many others who thirty-five years after *At Swim-Two-Birds* grind out what we wearily continue to class as "literary innovations," and even unlike some of the French "new novels," O'Brien is really more yarning than musing, more texture than tricks:

Grey carrion soul-mincing hope . . .

That from just a bit of chat about a man looking for directions near College Green in a shard from the "journalism career."

Or this from the last novel "about nothing":

—He is nearly sixty years of age by plain computation, the Sergeant said, and if he is itself, he has spent no less than thirty-five years riding his bicycle over the rocky roadsteads and up and down the pertimious hills and into the deep ditches when the road goes astray in the strain of the winter.

The play Hugh Leonard made with the dying author's approval either eliminated or resolved the structural difficulties of *The Dalkey Archive* and, well performed as it evidently was, *When the Saints Go Cycling In* was no doubt funnier than the novel. The success of the play even allowed O'Brien a foray into the spin-off biz, turning the

Sergeant loose on his own TV series. I can't help thinking, however, that the stage version was less humorous. The newly injected neatness, and the funniness that was a product of this neatness, somehow dissipate, or at least divert, the humor.

Since this humor is cumulative, something like the "power" we gladly attribute to stylistic oafs such as Dostoevski, Dreiser, and Whitman, it is difficult to carry the point in short quotations, and I think the case goes especially hard when Flann is alleged worthy for his style, so that we await once again Bernard Shaw or Wilde, or if not wit-bits to serve with cocktails, at least pungent images à la Joyce or Dylan Thomas, to substitute for the booze.

This humor, then, is somehow an aspect of texture, and not merely another name for wit, or even, God help us, *Irish* wit or gallows humor, though we have Flann commenting on the dark side:

Humour, the handmaid of sorrow and fear, creeps out endlessly in all Joyce's works. He used the thing in the same way as Shakespeare does but less formally, to attenuate the fear of those who have belief and who genuinely think they will be in hell or in heaven shortly, and possibly very shortly. With laughs he palliates the sense of doom that is the heritage of the Irish Catholic. True humor needs this background urgency: Rabelais is funny, but his stuff cloys. His stuff lacks tragedy.

As Ryan says, this "is a better summary of [O'Brien's] own literary self-tragedy than of Joyce." Here is our man in *The Third Policeman*, literally on the gallows:

I arose and started to put on my clothes. Through the window I could see the scaffold of raw timber rearing itself high into the heavens, not as O'Feersa had left it to make his way methodically through the rain, but perfect and ready for its dark destiny. The sight did not make me cry or even sigh. I thought it was sad, too sad. Through the struts of the structure I could see the good country. There would be a fine view from the top of the scaffold on any day but on this day it would be lengthened out by five miles owing to the clearness of the air. To prevent my tears I began to give special attention to my dressing.

Close to tragedy, however, is what O'Brien reveled in calling "squalor," and it is more often this squalor, with its Latin roots in filth and its modern associations with the moral degeneracy of those with their eye on the main chance, that O'Brien sees as the enemy.

His third novel, *The Hard Life*, is subtitled *An Exegesis of Squalor*.

Mrs. Crotty, a slatternly but pathetically kind mother replacement for the orphaned young narrator, has just died after an obscene illness, which includes the collapse of her bed just off the kitchen, owing to her kidney trouble. Mr. Collopy, a compulsive disputer and lay-about intellectual with pretensions to social reform among Dublin women, lives with Mrs. Crotty in a nebulous but clearly squalid relationship. The narrator's sister Annie has been seen with corner boys on the canal bank. The brother is a big schemer in small rackets. It is raining. They are all in a cab:

The hearse elected to take the route along Merrion Road by the sea, where a sort of hurricane was in progress. The cabs following stumbled on the exposed terrain. Mr. Collopy, showing some signs of genuine grief, spoke little.

—Poor Mrs. Crotty was very fond of the sea, he said at last.

—Seemingly she was, Annie remarked. She told me once that when she was a girl, nothing could keep her out of the sea at Clontarf. She could swim and all.

—Yes, a most versatile woman, Mr. Collopy said. And a saint.

A burial on a wet day, with the rain lashing down on the mourners, is a matter simply of squalor...

But squalor is not a simple matter with Flann. There is always the redeeming touch, as in the nuances of the dialogue above. Read in context, the passage produces that weird sort of delicious glee that so often frightens non-Irishmen and sometimes even Irishmen themselves. To see by oblique means what O'Brien is getting at in a passage such as the above, it might be best to see again what Flann sees in James Joyce. It is not the sort of thing that the American structural engineers and symbol hunters bother with at all. John Ryan, who tried to get O'Brien to write a piece on Joyce and instead got "A Bash in the Tunnel," did finally manage to capture some criticism by O'Brien, albeit on the wing:

Myles allowed that Joyce had a keener ear for dialogue than he. To illustrate his point, he gave me this example: In the Cyclops sequence of *Ulysses*, when our hero is emerging from Barney Kiernan's pub in Little Britain Street, one of the bystanders yells after him, 'Eh, mister! Your fly is open, mister!' It was the use of the *second* 'mister' that showed Joyce for the subtle artificer that he was. Myles admitted that his ear couldn't have taken in so quintessentially a piece of Dublinese as that nuance. Another example he gave was in the Hades episode from the same book. To comfort the mourners at Paddy Dignam's funeral, the caretaker of Glasnevin cemetery (Mr John O'Connell) is telling them a funny yarn about the two Dubliners who visit the cemetery at night and drunkenly set out to find the tomb of an old crony of theirs, 'Mulcahy of the Coombe'. In time, and by dint of lighting many matches, they find the grave. The inscription on the tombstone confirms the fact that it is indeed the grave of their friend. However, looking up at the statue above, which happens to be that of the Sacred Heart, but failing to find corroboration therein, one of them opines, 'Not a bloody bit like the man. That's not Mulcahy,' says he, 'whoever done it.' 'Whoever done it' is high Dublin idiom at its most hilarious. Again Myles was ready to acknowledge that he could not have essayed that one either.

Marianne Moore in her "Idiosyncrasy and Technique" quotes William Archer as saying that "when we impart distinctiveness to ordinary talk and make it still seem ordinary," what we have is literature.

More obviously "Irish" and therefore available to Americans, as opposed to the sinker/slider deliveries of O'Brien, is the big, blazing stuff that hops and hooks, popping the catcher's mitt so you can hear it from well back of third base. Take a breath, go open the cellar door, and read this out loud down to the roaring furnace. All of it.

I will relate, said Finn. When the seven companies of my warriors are gathered together on the one plain and the truant clean-cold loud-voiced wind goes through them, too sweet to me is that. Echo-blow of a goblet-base against the tables of the palace, sweet to me is that. I like gull-cries and the twittering together of line cranes. I like the surf-roar at Tralee, the songs of the three sons of Meadhra and the whistle of Mac Lughaidh. These also please me, man-shouts at a parting, cuckoo-call in May. I incline to like pig-grunting in Magh Eithne, the bellowing of the stag of Ceara, the whinging of fauns in Derrynish. The low warble of water-owls in Loch Barra also, sweeter than life that. I am fond of wing-beating in dark belfries, cow-cries in pregnancy, trout-spurt in a lake-top. Also the whining of small otters in nettle-beds at evening, the croaking of small-jays behind a wall, these are heart-pleasing. I am friend to the pilibeen, the red-necked chough, the parsnip land-rail, the pilibeen móna, the bottle-tailed tit, the common marsh-coot, the speckle-toed guillemot, the pilibeen sléibhe, the Mohar gannet, the peregrine plough-gull, the long-eared bush-owl, the Wicklow small-fowl, the bevil-beaked chough, the hooded tit, the pilibeen uisce, the common corby, the fish-tailed mud-piper, the crúiskeen lawn, the carrion sea-cock, the green lidded parakeet, the brown bog-martin, the martime wren, the dove-tailed wheatcrake, the beaded daw, the Galway hill-bantam and the pilibeen cathrach. A satisfying ululation is the contending of a river with the sea. Good to hear is the chirping of little red-breasted men in bare winter and distant hounds giving tongue in the secrecy of god. The lamenting of a wounded otter in a black hole, sweeter than harpstrings that. There is no torture so narrow as to be bound and beset in a dark cavern without food or music, without the bestowing of gold on bards. To be chained by night in a dark pit without company of chessmen—evil destiny! Soothing to my ear is the shout of a hidden blackbird, the squeal of a troubled mare, the complaining of wild-hogs caught in snow.

.There is no point in saying that there are excesses in the above passage. The entire passage is excessive, as is the whole book, *At Swim*. Gratuitous. To us with our Puritan heritage there are to be no gifts, however. Beady-eyed we tend to see the shift in the word "gratuitous," meaning not so much "given freely" as "without reason." Things done without reason are a waste of time, the devil's workbench, and so on. In Irish literature we sense a cruelty to this unreason, the gratuitous smack of the drunken father. With Joyce, of course, there was always a reason. With patience we can have explained to us the method in his madness, the father's ultimate love for the son. O'Brien's attitude toward Joyce through the years is complex. There are many reasons for the negative side of his ambivalence, from sibling author rivalry to a sexual puritanism in O'Brien. But there is a legitimate objection. "Joyce was too much in love with the tour de force," he wrote. That is maybe as close as Myles gets to it, but we can tell more by what Joycean maneuvers he avoided in making his own books. Taking the ancient appellation of the Isle of Saints and Scholars too literally, professors descended upon Ireland to sanctify by explication the absent Joyce. They found what they were looking for. Everything in Joyce had a meaning. This is not to say O'Brien wrote dada. As Myles, he denounced the avant-garde from surrealism on down. What then is the significance of those maneuvers that seem "free"? The books themselves? Are they merely little "hey-what-ifs" and "did-you-ever-notices" shyly left on our doorsteps at dawn by coy authors stealing off through the drying dew to join Salinger, Brautigan, Charles Schultz, and other purveyors of benign prepubescent whimsy?

The answer does not lie, I think, in looking for American New Criticism approaches that work such profits out of Joyce. One must go back to the Irish tradition of storytelling, a move that at first may seem provincial, but which if followed far enough comes out with the old universal tradition of storytelling. "Oh, dear, sighs my mother, née Murphy, this man you have taken up tells stories just like your Uncle Bill, or worse your grandfather who also liked that Mr. Dooley Says business in the paper and used to make us sit quiet for all of it and there was never any point. I think his father used to tell stories like that without even having Mr. Dooley Says, just himself doing all the saying."

My mother, of course, was brought up in America in the twenties with the Hard-Hitting Short Story. She's got boxes of idea cards down by the furnace. Stacks of *Writer* magazine down there, too. "How to Get to the Point Quickly." "Grab the Reader and Hold Him." "Tell 'Em What You're Going to Tell 'Em; Tell 'Em; Then Tell 'Em What You Told 'Em." Our idea of the digression is a radial tire ad on a cop-chase show. We might well paraphrase a line from Villiers de l'Isle-Adam's *Axël* that Yeats admired: "As for our texture, we'll let our advertisers do the living."

This may be modern. It certainly is American. It may even become the Way of the World. Here, however, are descriptions of classic storytelling. The first is by a lady magazine editor and begins just as you'd think one of those formulas for appeasing that greatest of all fiction maws would begin:

What is the best way of telling a story? Since the standard must be the interest of the audience . . .

American "media" people would at this point, of course, conclude that there would be only one way of telling a story, i.e., geared to junior high school. This is not what this successful lady magazine editor says, though. She concludes quite the opposite: ". . . there must be several or many good ways rather than the best." Using this pluralism, she goes on to plea for the acceptance of stories not necessarily told in what she calls the "orderly" way:

Why should a story not be told in the most irregular fashion that an author's idiosyncrasy may prompt, provided that he gives us what we can enjoy? The objections to Sterne's wild way of telling *Tristram Shandy* lie more solidly in the quality of the interrupting matter than in the fact of interruption. The dear public would do well to reflect that they are often bored from the want of flexibility in their own minds. They are like the topers of "one liquor."

It should perhaps be noted that the lady above was not merely a magazine editor, but one of the classic storytellers of the nineteenth century, Mary Ann Evans, known to Dear Public as George Eliot. Perhaps our impatient notion of narrative began in the eighteenth century with all those "rises" of this and that, though one could hardly classify Fielding or Smollett, to say nothing of Sterne, as straight-ahead drives. Even Doctor Johnson, that great Commoner of Sense, is suspect. It is no accident that our own great digressor, Nabokov, should begin his baroque masterpiece *Pale Fire* with an epigraph in which Johnson cries out for his cat Hodge. When Johnson and Boswell were tempest-tossed off the Hebrides, the Scotch mariners were finally forced to give the hysterically babbling lexicographer a dead rope tied to the mast in order that he might continually pull upon it and thus hold up the ship from plummeting to the bottom of the horrible wordless sea. As for the Elizabethans, Hamlet may warn his players to get right on, and his mother may wish Polonius had more matter and less art, but the whole play stands for an era in which the art of digressing while on the gallows reached an unprecedented perfection. In classical storytelling we have our contemporaries Borges and Barth to remind us of what Scheherazade was up to, and here is poet Robert Graves boiling his pot by defending the wandering "high and dark" style of the Latin classic *The Golden Ass*:

Apuleius ... was parodying the extravagant language which the 'Milesian' story-tellers used, like barkers at country fairs today, as a means of impressing simple-minded audiences. The professional story-teller, or *sqéalai*, is still [1947] found in the West of Ireland. I have heard one complimented as 'speaking such fine hard Irish that Devil two words together in it would any man understand.'

One of the devices most used by the extravagant storyteller is the pun. To most of us puns are either serious (as in Joyce) or inexcusable (yours and mine). Even Oliver Wendell Holmes, a kind of nineteenth-century American Gogarty, attacked puns in his delightfully rambling *The Autocrat of the Breakfast-Table*: "I shall henceforth consider any interruption by a pun," says his Johnsonian persona, "as a hint to change my boarding house." In the case of a pun by James Joyce, of course, we have profound revelations of truth either emanating from some cryptographic system sanctified by the

New Criticism's Neo-Platonic enabling act or a Freudian goody out of the "Psychopathology of Everyday Strife," or is it "Wife"?

Actually, Holmes has something to say which I find more interesting from a literary point of view. He has his man charge that puns "collapse language," rob it of its possibilities, dry it up. No doubt some do, and his examples from the breakfast table indeed leave one reaching for the decanter. At this point I think Myles would see his fellow morning columnist as a comrade. "Life and language," says the Autocrat, "are alike sacred." Many is the column Myles devotes to this principle, and Joyce's language in the late phase comes in for harsh treatment. For Myles, as for the novelist Flann O'Brien, there is no Platonic reverberation beyond or through the word. Rather there is the spirit of play around the word, or with the word. The word becomes the occasion not for metaphysical systems but for a story.

Enter Vivian Mercier. He has written two books that mention O'Brien briefly, but that serve to establish the two major traditions in which O'Brien writes. The first is the one out of which he grows, *The Irish Comic Tradition*, and the second is the tradition toward which he points, *The New Novel* (*le nouveau roman*). In the first, Mercier says, ". . . the Irish reputation for wit, in so far as it is deserved, is in the last analysis a reputation for playing with words rather than ideas. Word play is as old as Gaelic literature. . . ." Mercier goes on to point out what more solemn significance play itself may have and cites the Dutch philosopher Johan Huizinga, who sees the meaning of play not so much as Freud does as standing for something else but as a universal principle underlying all human activities from law to war, and therefore serving as much as any other single concept to define man: *homo ludens,* man the player.

Enter Keats and Chapman. But in their own due time (see "Myles's Best"). Suffice it to say now that the "pun," which is the occasion for a Keats and Chapman episode, probably does very little for or against the key word, but does serve as the excuse for a delightful outing. In fact sometimes the outing does so well without the excuse one might wish that the picnic basket had been left at home by the time the pun is sprung. At other times the pun seems to serve much as the dead rope that Samuel Johnson was invited to pull on so that common sense would shut up long enough for the mariners to get on with maintaining the illusion that man was born to float.

It is not only in the minor forays, however, that O'Brien plays but in the major "works" as well. In *At Swim-Two-Birds* he has a persona writing a novel about a man writing a novel, and so on. Where he gets a turn on the old Huxley-Gide machine is in having the characters revolt against one of the "authors" and overthrow him, something that perhaps John Fowles, in *The French Lieutenant's Woman*, should have allowed his "new woman" to do on the Chelsea Embankment. In a passage that seems to stand as the basis for the book's method, O'Brien has one character "write" that "a satisfactory novel should be a self-evident sham to which the reader could regulate at will the degree of his credulity." What we are talking about here may be "pure reading," not quite the "good read" of the detective addict or even the "pure poetry" of the French symbolists, but storytelling (and listening) for its own sake. Kipling has an old Indian yarn-spinner give him some advice in the preface to one of his collections. Kipling complains that English readers want new tales, "and when all is written they rise up and declare that the tale were better told in such and such a manner, and doubt either the truth or the invention thereof." To which the old teller replies:

"But what folly is theirs!" said Gobind, throwing out a knotted hand. "A tale that is told is a true tale as long as the telling lasts."

In his exploration of the "new" French novel, Mercier demonstrates that not only were Joyce and Beckett precursors, even practitioners, but so was Flann:

In [Raymond Queneau's] *Le Vol d'Icare* ("The Flight of Icarus"), as in Part I of Pinget's *Mahu*, we encounter a world where novelists' characters literally come to life. Since there is nothing new under the sun, one hesitates to grant priority in this kind of fantasy to the Irish writer Flann O'Brien, whose *At Swim-Two-Birds* appeared in 1939 with a partial cast of such characters. What is certain is that Queneau knew O'Brien's book, for the French translation, *Kermesse irlandaise* (1964), was published by Gallimard.

While Mercier moves away from Huizinga and closer to Sartre, Husserl, and Heidegger, he warns that even among the notoriously metaphysical French one should "beware of assuming that the rare works of fantasy written by the New Novelists—Pinget's *Graal Flibuste*, for instance—must be moral allegories; they are far more likely to be sheer storytelling for its own sake." Of course, the question of ultimate purpose of any act is one of infinite regress, a conundrum that O'Brien does not question in either Freudian or Jesuitical spirit so much as worry, as a dog worries a bone. He growls, cavorts, chews, deriving nourishment of divers sorts, from caloric to clerical. Art for art's sake? Art for humor's sake? Humor for Freud's sake? (Flann also spoke German and would have enjoyed the possibilities of that last one.)

In any case, it is all boxes within boxes. O'Brien was doing that sort of carpentry long before our recent "experimentalists," even before most of what we consider the mature Borges and Nabokov. In 1939's *The Third Policeman* is a passage that stands for the method of the whole book: " 'I decided to myself,' said MacCruiskeen, 'that the only sole correct thing to contain in the chest was another chest of the same make but littler in cubic dimension.' "

But is there not some direct statement O'Brien made himself about what his aims, goals, motives, and so forth, were in writing? Some clue as to how we were to *take him*, as the phrase runs with ominous ambiguity.

In the "O'Bitter Dicta" section of this volume (I'm afraid O'Brien was often not so much gamboling as snapping when worried by questions of Art) are assorted statements made over the years by the civil servant who wrote. These all appeared somewhere in print, except for two which are in two separate notebooks now part of the Flann O'Brien deposit in Carbondale, Illinois. The first is in a notebook manufactured in 1953 and seems in response to some sort of external urging such as the kind that produced the oblique "Bash In The Tunnel." It is, however, straightforward enough and even uplifting:

What is the artist's place in society?
He must head the common people to an appreciation of taste, decency, fair-play—as a counterweight to the squalor of day-to-day existence.

The next is from a diary printed for 1943, and the entry is located under the printed heading February 18. However, the next item on the page, continuing in the same exact hand, is dated by the writer April 6, 1963. Both entries seem to be about the composing of *The Dalkey Archive,* a book that evokes (and invokes) the shade of Saint Augustine. At the time O'Brien was also suffering from the baroque combination of illnesses that killed him. After an illegible phrase ending ". . . and the fires of whiskey," O'Brien writes:

(There is more than an alcoholic nexus between humankind and books. There is an unending accretion to the sum of men and books as time passes, and an ever growing deposit of people dead and books destroyed, forgotten, lost, or out of print). Danger of an undrunken kind can attend the writer of today who presumes to exhume a dead writer and examine the books he left behind him. I tell here of the retribution which overtook myself, though by no means sure just now that the threat is ended.

In 1964 he published this dedication to the last book he saw through the press. Though it is addressed to an Angel, these lines, uncharacteristically arranged as verse, call to mind no mythological passing horseman, but the challenge of pub talk, and the eye that is cast, while cold, is not without a twinkle. That is, *fierce* twinkle.

> I dedicate these pages
> to my Guardian Angel,
> impressing upon him
> that I'm only fooling
> and warning him
> to see to it that
> there is no misunderstanding
> when I go home.

> —S. J.

A Flann O'Brien Reader

At Swim-Two-Birds

'I do not often look at boxes or, chests,' I said, simply, 'but
this is the most beautiful box I have ever seen and I will always remember it. There might be something inside?'
'There might be,' said MacCruiskeen.
—The Third Policeman

INTRODUCTION

Although Flann O'Brien was later to repudiate his first novel, *At
Swim-Two-Birds*, calling it upon numerous occasions "juvenile
blather" and worse, the book has stood by its creator through the
years, refusing to mutiny after the manner of the products of Dermot
Trellis, the creation of the author-narrator of *At Swim*. That Brian
O'Nolan was in the process of forging his most enduring literary
mask at this time, Flann O'Brien, lends another cycle to the series
of infinite regress which he plays with so savagely in his next novel,
The Third Policeman.

There had been, of course, novels within novels before. One could
make a case for *Don Quixote*'s being a kind of happening within a
chivalric novel. Certainly in O'Brien's own lifetime there had been
Gide's *The Counterfeiters* and the one mentioned as being on the
narrator's shelf in *At Swim*, Huxley's *Point Counter Point*. Certainly

there have been boxes within boxes of them since. But as William Gass says in *Fiction and the Figures of Life:*

I don't mean merely those drearily predictable pieces about writers who are writing about what they are writing, but those, like some of the work of Borges, Barth, and Flann O'Brien, for example, in which the forms of fiction serve as the material upon which further forms can be imposed. Indeed, many of the so-called antinovels are really metafictions.

As interesting as Barth and Borges are, however, it is O'Brien who has the old exuberance of the Elizabethan plays and the eighteenth-century novels, along with the metaphysical sophistication of the contemporary "new" and "anti" novels. It is hard to imagine Dylan Thomas, for instance, writing of a Robbe-Grillet novel, as he did of *At Swim,* "This is just the book to give your sister if she's a loud, dirty, boozy girl." Graham Greene, then a reader at Longmans, the British house that published the novel in 1939, wrote:

I read it with continual excitement, amusement and the kind of glee one experiences when people smash china on the stage.

It is in the line of *Tristram Shandy* and *Ulysses:* its amazing spirits do not disguise the seriousness of the attempt to present, simultaneously as it were, all the literary traditions of Ireland—the Celtic legend (in the stories of Finn), the popular adventure novels (of a Mr. Tracy), the nightmare element as you get in Joyce, the ancient poetry of Bardic Ireland and the working-class poetry of the absurd Harry Casey. On all these the author imposes the unity of his own humorous vigour, and the technique he employs is as efficient as it is original. We have had books inside books before now, and characters who are given life outside their fiction, but O'Nolan takes Pirandello and Gide a long way further: the screw is turned until you have, (a) the narrator writing a book about a man called Trellis who is, (b) writing a book about certain characters who, (c) are turning the tables on Trellis by writing about him. . . .

In spite of good reviews, which included a favorable comment by James Joyce, *At Swim* was born at a bad time and did not sell well enough for the publishers to gamble on the "even more fantastic" *The Third Policeman* a year later. Nevertheless, the book was re-issued in England in 1960 and in New York in 1951, 1967, and most recently in 1976.

O'Brien asked his boss in the civil service, John Garvin, for a Greek epigraph, and Garvin, who had read the manuscript, offered some Euripides, *Hercules Furens:* "For all things go out and give place one to another."

There follows a batch of letters by O'Brien on *At Swim*, beginning with the author's submission letter, ranging through responses to editor's queries, a reader's reaction, and even a denial that he wrote the book at all. The last letter, written during the outset of O'Brien's fatal illness, finds him only slightly reconciled to the authorship of the book that made him famous.

To C. H. Brooks, Esq.
31 January, 1938.

About a year ago a friend of mine mentioned your name to me, saying that you would be glad to have a look at manuscripts with a view to placing them with publishers for enormous sums if you thought they were saleable. I do not know whether this is correct but I have just finished a piece of writing and it occurs to me that perhaps you would like to read through it and see what the prospects of selling it are. I haven't sent it to any publisher or agent yet. It is called "At Swim-two-birds" and is a very queer affair, unbearably queer, perhaps. For all its many defects, I feel it has the time-honoured ingredients that make the work of writers from this beautiful little island so acceptable. I would be glad to hear from you on this matter.

[Morris Library]*

A. M. Heath & Co. became O'Brien's British agents.

To Mr. Heath
25 September, 1938.

Thanks for your letter of the 22nd. Of course I agree with the observation of Longman's reader. They are unexpectedly mild. As regards the "Coarseness" I will undertake a decarbonising process immediately and take steps to elucidate the obscurity of the ending and elsewhere. I hope to send you a corrected copy in about a week.

I think I said in my original covering letter that "At Swim-two-birds" was only a provisional label. I will have to think of something more suitable.

To Mr. Heath
3 October, 1938.

I send herewith a further copy of the book, definitive edition. Before I heard Longmans' views, I had intended to make a lot of far-reaching

* All subsequent letters are from the Morris Library collection, Southern Illinois University, Carbondale, Illinois, unless otherwise indicated.

changes, mainly structural. I thought better of this, however, because Longmans did not seem to see the necessity for anything drastic and also because the loosenesses and obscurities I would be remedying would probably be replaced by others. Actually the changes I have made are slight but I think they should meet the publishers' suggestions. Briefly they are as follows:

1. Coarse words and references have been deleted or watered down and made innocuous.

2. "Good spirit" (which was originally "Angel") has been changed to "Good Fairy". I think this change is desirable because "Fairy" corresponds more closely to "Pooka", removes any suggestion of the mock-religious and establishes the thing on a mythological plane.

3. I suggest the deletion of the "Memoir", p. 327. It seems to me feeble stuff and unnecessary. I do not mind if it remains, however.

4. I have made a change at p. 333, substituting a page or so of more amusing material as an extract from the Conspectus. I do not know whether these extracts at this stage of the book are too long.

5. The Trellis ending ("penultimate") has been extended and clarified to show that the accidental burning of Trellis's MS solves a lot of problems and saves the author's life. I think this will go a long way to remove obscurity.

6. I have scrapped the inferior "Mail from M. Byrne" as the final ending and substituted a passage which typifies, I think, the erudite irresponsibility of the whole book.

7. I have given a lot of thought to the question of a title and think *Sweeny in The Trees* quite suitable. Others that occurred to me were *The Next Market Day* (verse reference); Sweet-Scented Manuscript; Truth is an Odd Number; Task-Master's Eye; Through an Angel's eyelid; and dozens of others.

If any further minor changes are deemed necessary, I am quite content to leave them to the discretion of yourselves or the publishers. I would be interested to hear whether Longman's consider the above changes adequate.

When is the book likely to appear?

12 March, 1939.*

"At Swim-Two-Birds"

Thank you for your letter of the 10th.

My full name is Brian O'Nolan.

As regards nationality, I am "Irish" or a "citizen of Eire". While this

* Correspondent is unknown.

is my description according to the law of this country, the position is rather obscure inasmuch as Britain does not recognize any such nationality internationally and simply regards Irishmen, whether of north or south, as "British subjects". I think I should be described as "Irish" with anything it may imply. I understand the word is commonly used in such circumstances.

To Mr. Gillett
1 May, 1939.

. . . a friend of mine brought a copy of "At Swim-Two-Birds" to Joyce in Paris recently. Joyce, however, had already read it. Being now nearly blind, he said it took him a week with a magnifying glass and that he had not read a book of any kind for five years, so this may be taken to be a compliment from the fuehrer. He was delighted with it—although he complained that I did not give the reader much of chance, "Finnegan's Wake" in his hand as he spke—and has promised to push it quietly in his own international Paris sphere. In this connexion he wants a copy sent to Maurice Denhoff, who writes in "Mercure de France". Denhoff's address is Rue de Sureen, Paris viii. I wonder would you be good enough to have a copy sent to him. If a review copy is not possible please debit me with the cost of it. Joyce was very particular that there should be no question of reproducing his unsolicited testimonial for publicity purposes anywhere and got an undertaking to this effect. I think the reviews of the book were satisfactory enough but they were not the sort that sell copies. I am curious to know how it is going.

To *The Irish Press*
4 January, 1939.*

I have been shown an entry in your College Notes in Monday's "Irish Press" in which the authorship of a book called "Swim Two Birds" is attributed to me. Your information apparently derives from a rumour spread by two gentlemen called Sheridan and O'Brien who charge me with the authorship of a book of this name or something similar. The cream of this elaborate "joke" is that the supposed book is anti-clerical, blasphemous and licentious and various lengthy extracts from it have been concocted to show the obscenity of the work. I have joined in the joke to some extent myself but I naturally take strong exception to the publicity given by your paragraph, which associates me by name with something which is objectionable, even if nonexistent. I must therefore ask you to

---

* This whole game of the pseudonym must have seemed strange to those who actually saw the dust jacket of the first edition. On the front the by-line reads "Flann O'Brien," but the long blurb on the back by Graham Greene refers to the author as O'Nolan.

withdraw the statement. I would be satisfied if you merely mentioned that a graduate mentioned in your last Notes is not the author of the book mentioned and has in fact no intention of publishing any book.

[*The Journal of Irish Literature*]

To Ethel Mannin*
10 July, 1939.

A friend of mine Mr. Kevin O'Connor mentioned to me that you might read a book I have written so I have asked the publishers to send you a copy. It is a belly-laugh or high-class literary pretentious slush, depending on how you look at it. Some people say it is harder on the head than the worst whiskey, so do not hesitate to burn the book if you think that's the right thing to do.

[*The Journal of Irish Literature*]

To Ethel Mannin
14 July, 1939.

(Re At Swim-Two-Birds)

Many thanks for your letter and cards....

It is a pity you did not like my beautiful book. As a genius, I do not expect to be readily understood but you may be surprised to know that my book is a definite milestone in literature, completely revolutionises the English novel and puts the shallow pedestrian English writers in their place. Of course I know you are prejudiced against me on account of the IRA bombings.

To be serious, I can't quite understand your attitude to stuff like this. It is not a pale-faced sincere attempt to hold the mirror up and has nothing in the world to do with James Joyce. It is supposed to be a lot of belching, thumb-nosing and belly-laughing and I honestly believe that it is funny in parts. It is also by way of being a sneer at all the slush which has been unloaded from this country on the credulous English although they, it is true, manufacture enough of their own odious slush to make the import unnecessary. I don't think your dictum about "making your meaning clear" would be upheld in any court of law. You'll look a long time for clear meaning in the Marx Brothers or even Karl Marx. In a key I am preparing in collaboration with Mr. Kevin O'Connor, it is explained that the reader should begin on p. 145 and then start at the beginning when he reaches the end like an up-&-down straight in Poker. The fantastic title (which has brought a lot of fatuous inquiries to bird-fanciers) is

* Ethel Mannin is the author of at least thirty-six novels, six collections of short stories, a dozen travel books, two books on politics and ethics, and one biography. Her titles include: *Women Also Dream, Venetian Blinds, Rolling in the Dew,* and *Christianity or Chaos.*

explained on p. 95 and is largely the idea of my staid old-world publishers. My own title was "Sweeny in the Trees". Search me for the explanation of this wilful obscurity. I am negotiating at present for a contract to write 6 Sexton Blake stories (25 to 30,000 words for £25 a time, so please do not send me any more sneers at my art.) Sorry, Art.

To Timothy O'Keeffe of MacGibbon and Kee, London
18 December, 1965.

Many thanks for your encouraging letter of the 14th December. That gland trouble in my neck is still bothering me and my surgeon is insisting on a blood transfusion every three weeks or so, but all that makes the situation seem worse than it is. On the whole I feel all right and am determined to get to real grips with *Slattery's Sago Saga* from 1 January 1966....

[After expressing pleasure at the reissue of *At Swim-Two-Birds* in the U.S. the author closes:] Honestly, if I get sufficiently drunk over Christmas I'm going to read that damned book for the first time. Those birds must have some unsuspected stuffing in them.

Have a happy and fluid feast...

FROM *AT SWIM-TWO-BIRDS*

Having placed in my mouth sufficient bread for three minutes' chewing, I withdrew my powers of sensual perception and retired into the privacy of my mind, my eyes and face assuming a vacant and preoccupied expression. I reflected on the subject of my spare-time literary activities. One beginning and one ending for a book was a thing I did not agree with. A good book may have three openings entirely dissimilar and inter-related only in the prescience of the author, or for that matter one hundred times as many endings.

Examples of three separate openings—the first: The Pooka MacPhellimey, a member of the devil class, sat in his hut in the middle of a firewood meditating on the nature of the numerals and segregating in his mind the odd ones from the even. He was seated at his diptych

8

or ancient two-leaved hinged writing-table with inner sides waxed. His rough long-nailed fingers toyed with a snuff-box of perfect rotundity and through a gap in his teeth he whistled a civil cavatina. He was a courtly man and received honour by reason of the generous treatment he gave his wife, one of the Corrigans of Carlow.

The second opening: There was nothing unusual in the appearance of Mr. John Furriskey but actually he had one distinction that is rarely encountered—he was born at the age of twenty-five and entered the world with a memory but without a personal experience to account for it. His teeth were well-formed but stained by tobacco, with two molars filled and a cavity threatened in the left canine. His knowledge of physics was moderate and extended to Boyle's Law and the Parallelogram of Forces.

The third opening: Finn Mac Cool was a legendary hero of old Ireland. Though not mentally robust, he was a man of superb physique and development. Each of his thighs was as thick as a horse's belly, narrowing to a calf as thick as the belly of a foal. Three fifties of fosterlings could engage with handball against the wideness of his backside, which was large enough to halt the march of men through a mountain-pass.

I hurt a tooth in the corner of my jaw with a lump of the crust I was eating. This recalled me to the perception of my surroundings.

It is a great pity, observed my uncle, that you don't apply yourself more to your studies. The dear knows your father worked hard enough for the money he is laying out on your education. Tell me this, do you ever open a book at all?

I surveyed my uncle in a sullen manner. He speared a portion of cooked rasher against a crust on the prongs of his fork and poised the whole at the opening of his mouth in a token of continued interrogation.

Description of my uncle: Red-faced, bead-eyed, ball-bellied. Fleshy about the shoulders with long swinging arms giving ape-like effect to gait. Large moustache. Holder of Guinness clerkship the third class.

I do, I replied.

He put the point of his fork into the interior of his mouth and withdrew it again, chewing in a coarse manner.

Quality of rasher in use in household: Inferior, one and two the pound.

Well faith, he said, I never see you at it. I never see you at your studies at all.

I work in my bedroom, I answered.

Whether in or out, I always kept the door of my bedroom locked. This made my movements a matter of some secrecy and enabled me to spend an inclement day in bed without disturbing my uncle's assumption that I had gone to the College to attend to my studies. A contemplative life has always been suitable to my disposition. I was accustomed to stretch myself for many hours upon my bed, thinking and smoking there. I rarely undressed and my inexpensive suit was not the better for the use I gave it, but I found that a brisk application with a coarse brush before going out would redeem it somewhat without quite dispelling the curious bedroom smell which clung to my person and which was frequently the subject of humorous or other comment on the part of my friends and acquaintances.

Aren't you very fond of your bedroom now, my uncle continued. Why don't you study in the dining-room here where the ink is and where there is a good book-case for your books? Boys but you make a great secret about your studies.

My bedroom is quiet, convenient and I have my books there. I prefer to work in my bedroom, I answered.

My bedroom was small and indifferently lighted but it contained most of the things I deemed essential for existence—my bed, a chair which was rarely used, a table and a washstand. The washstand had a ledge upon which I had arranged a number of books. Each of them was generally recognized as indispensable to all who aspire to an appreciation of the nature of contemporary literature and my small collection contained works ranging from those of Mr. Joyce to the widely-read books of Mr. A. Huxley, the eminent English writer. In my bedroom also were certain porcelain articles related more to utility than ornament. The mirror at which I shaved every second day was of the type supplied gratis by Messrs. Watkins, Jameson and Pim and bore brief letterpress in reference to a proprietary brand of ale between the words of which I had acquired considerable skill in inserting the reflection of my countenance. The mantelpiece contained forty buckskin volumes comprising a Conspectus of the Arts and Natural Sciences. They were published in 1854 by a reputable Bath house for a guinea the volume. They bore their years bravely and retained in their interior the kindly seed of knowledge intact and without decay.

I know the studying you do in your bedroom, said my uncle. Damn the studying you do in your bedroom.

I denied this.

Nature of denial: Inarticulate, of gesture.

My uncle drained away the remainder of his tea and arranged his cup and saucer in the centre of his bacon plate in a token that his meal was at an end. He then blessed himself and sat for a time drawing air into his mouth with a hissing sound in an attempt to extract food-stuff from the crevices of his dentures. Subsequently he pursed his mouth and swallowed something.

A boy of your age, he said at last, who gives himself up to the sin of sloth—what in God's name is going to happen to him when he goes out to face the world? Boys but I often wonder what the world is coming to, I do indeed. Tell me this, do you ever open a book at all?

I open several books every day, I answered.

You open your granny, said my uncle. O I know the game you are at above in your bedroom. I am not as stupid as I look, I'll warrant you that.

He got up from the table and went out to the hall, sending back his voice to annoy me in his absence.

Tell me this, did you press my Sunday trousers?

I forgot, I said.

What?

I forgot, I shouted.

Well that is very nice, he called, very nice indeed. Oh, trust you to forget. God look down on us and pity us this night and day. Will you forget again today?

No, I answered.

As he opened the hall-door, he was saying to himself in a low tone:

Lord save us!

The slam of the door released me from my anger. I finished my collation and retired to my bedroom, standing for a time at the window and observing the street-scene arranged below me that morning. Rain was coming softly from the low sky. I lit my cigarette and then took my letter from my pocket, opened it and read it. . . .

[He reads a long letter from a "Turf Correspondent" (bookie) which is written in the manner of the brother in *The Hard Life*.]

I put the letter with care into a pocket at my right buttock and went to the tender trestle of my bed, arranging my back upon it in an indolent horizontal attitude. I closed my eyes, hurting slightly my right stye, and retired into the kingdom of my mind. For a time there was complete darkness and an absence of movement on the part of the cerebral mechanism. The bright square of the window was faintly evidenced at the juncture of my lids. One book, one opening, was a principle with which I did not find it possible to concur. After an interval Finn Mac Cool, a hero of old Ireland, came out before me from his shadow, Finn the wide-hammed, the heavy-eyed, Finn that could spend a Lammas morning with girdled girls at far-from-simple chess-play.

Extract from my typescript descriptive of Finn Mac Cool and his people, being humorous or quasi-humorous incursion into ancient mythology: Of the musics you have ever got, asked Conán, which have you found the sweetest?

I will relate, said Finn. When the seven companies of my warriors are gathered together on the one plain and the truant clean-cold loud-voiced wind goes through them, too sweet to me is that. Echo-blow of a goblet-base against the tables of the palace, sweet to me is that. I like gull-cries and the twittering together of fine cranes. I like the surf-roar at Tralee, the songs of the three sons of Meadhra and the whistle of Mac Lughaidh. These also please me, man-shouts at a parting, cuckoo-call in May. I incline to like pig-grunting in Magh Eithne, the bellowing of the stag of Ceara, the whinging of fauns in Derrynish. The low warble of water-owls in Loch Barra also, sweeter than life that. I am fond of wing-beating in dark belfries, cow-cries in pregnancy, trout-spurt in a lake-top. Also the whining of small otters in nettle-beds at evening, the croaking of small-jays behind a wall, these are heart-pleasing. I am friend to the pilibeen, the red-necked chough, the parsnip landrail, the pilibeen móna, the bottle-tailed tit, the common marsh-coot, the speckled-toed guillemot, the pilibeen sléibhe, the Mohar gannet, the peregrine plough-gull, the long-eared bush-owl, the Wicklow small-fowl, the bevil-beaked chough, the hooded tit, the pilibeen uisce, the common corby, the fish-tailed mud-piper, the crúiskeen lawn, the carrion sea-cock, the green-lidded parakeet, the brown bog-martin, the maritime wren, the dove-tailed wheatcrake, the beaded daw, the Galway hill-bantam and the pilibeen cathrach. A satisfying ululation is the contending of a river with the sea. Good to hear is the chirping of little red-breasted men in bare winter and distant hounds giving tongue in the secrecy of fog. The lamenting of a wounded otter in a black hole, sweeter than harp-strings that. There is no torture so narrow as to be bound and beset in a dark cavern without food or music, without the bestowing of gold on bards. To be chained by night in a dark pit without company of chessmen—evil destiny! Soothing to my ear is the shout of a hidden blackbird, the squeal of a troubled mare, the complaining of wild-hogs caught in snow.

Relate further for us, said Conán.

It is true that I will not, said Finn.

With that he rose to a full tree-high standing, the sable cat-guts which held his bog-cloth drawers to the hems of his jacket of pleated fustian clanging together in melodious discourse. Too great was he for standing. The neck to him was as the bole of a great oak, knotted and seized together with muscle-humps and carbuncles of tangled sinew, the better for good feasting and contending with the bards. The chest to him was wider than the poles of a good chariot, coming now out, now in, and pastured from chin to navel with meadows of black man-hair and meated with layers of fine man-meat the better to hide his bones and fashion the semblance of his twin bubs. The arms to him were like the necks of beasts, ball-swollen with their bunched-up brawnstrings and blood-veins, the better for harping and hunting and contending with the bards. Each thigh to him was to the thickness of a horse's belly, narrowing to a green-veined calf to the thickness of a foal. Three fifties of fosterlings could engage with handball against the wideness of his backside, which was wide enough to halt the march of warriors through a mountain-pass.

I am a bark for buffeting, said Finn,
I am a hound for thornypaws.
I am a doe for swiftness.
I am a tree for wind-siege.
I am a windmill:
I am a hole in a wall.

On the seat of the bog-cloth drawers to his fork was shuttled the green alchemy of mountain-leeks from Slieve an Iarainn in the middle of Erin; for it was here that he would hunt for a part of the year with his people, piercing the hams of a black hog with his spears, birds-nesting, hole-drawing, vanishing into the fog of a small gully, sitting on green knolls with Fergus and watching the boys at ball-throw.

On the kerseymere of the gutted jacket to his back was the dark tincture of the ivory sloes and the pubic gooseberries and the mani-varied whortles of the ditches of the east of Erin; for it was here that he would spend a part of the year with his people, courting and rummaging generous women, vibrating quick spears at the old stag of Slieve Gullian, hog-baiting in thickets and engaging in sapient dialectics with the bag-eyed brehons.

The knees and calves to him, swealed and swathed with soogawns and Thomond weed-ropes, were smutted with dungs and dirt-daubs of every hue and pigment, hardened by stainings of mead and trickles of metheglin and all the dribblings and drippings of his medher, for it was the custom of Finn to drink nightly with his people.

I am the breast of a young queen, said Finn,
I am a thatching against rains.
I am a dark castle against bat-flutters.
I am a Connachtman's ear.
I am a harpstring.
I am a gnat.

The nose to his white wheyface was a headland against white seas with height to it, in all, the height of ten warriors man on man and with breadth to it the breadth of Erin. The caverns to the butt of his nose had fulness and breadth for the instanding in their shade of twenty arm-bearing warriors with their tribal rams and dove-cages together with a generous following of ollavs and bards with their law-books and their verse-scrolls, their herb-pots and their alabaster firkins of oil and unguent.

Relate us further, said Diarmuid Donn, for the love of God.

Who is it? said Finn.

It is Diarmuid Donn, said Conán, even Diarmuid O'Diveney of Ui bhFailghe and of Cruachna Conalath in the west of Erin, it is Brown Dermot of Galway.

It is true, said Finn, that I will not.

The mouth to his white wheyface had dimensions and measure-ments to the width of Ulster, bordered by a red lip-wall and inhabited unseen by the watchful host of his honey-yellow teeth to the size, each with each, of a cornstack; and in the dark hollow to each tooth was there home and fulness for the sitting there of a thorny dog or for the lying there of a spear-pierced badger. To each of the two eyes in his head was there eye-hair to the fashion of a young forest, and the colour to each great eyeball was as the slaughter of a host in snow. The lid to each eye of them was limp and cheese-dun like ship-canvas in harbour at evening, enough eye-cloth to cover the whole of Erin.

Sweet to me your voice, said Caolcrodha Mac Morna, brother to sweet-worded sweet-toothed Goll from Sliabh Riabhach and Bros-nacha Bladhma, relate then the attributes that are to Finn's people.

Who is it? said Finn.

It is Caolcrodha Mac Morna from Sliabh Riabhach, said Conán, it is Calecroe MacMorney from Baltinglass.

I will relate, said Finn. Till a man has accomplished twelve books of poetry, the same is not taken for want of poetry but is forced away. No man is taken till a black hole is hollowed in the world to the depth of his two oxters and he put into it to gaze from it with his lonely head and nothing to him but his shield and a stick of hazel. Then must nine warriors fly their spears at him, one with the other and together. If he be spear-holed past his shield, or spear-killed, he is not taken for want of shield-skill. No man is taken till he is run by warriors through the woods of Erin with his hair bunched-loose about him for bough-tangle and briar-twitch. Should branches disturb his hair or pull it forth like sheep-wool on a hawthorn, he is not taken but is caught and gashed. Weapon-quivering hand or twig-crackling foot at full run, neither is taken. Neck-high sticks he must pass by vaulting, knee-high sticks by stooping. With the eyelids to him stitched to the fringe of his eye-bags, he must be run by Finn's people through the bogs and the marsh-swamps of Erin with two odorous prickle-backed hogs ham-tied and asleep in the seat of his hempen drawers. If he sink beneath a peat-swamp or lose a hog, he is not accepted of Finn's people. For five days he must sit on the brow of a cold hill with twelve-pointed stag-antlers hidden in his seat, without food or music or chessmen. If he cry out or eat grass-stalks or desist from the constant recital of sweet poetry and melodious Irish, he is not taken but is wounded. When pursued by a host, he must stick a spear in the world and hide behind it and vanish in its narrow shelter or he is not taken for want of sorcery. Likewise he must hide beneath a twig, or behind a dried leaf, or under a red stone, or vanish at full speed into the seat of his hempen drawers without changing his course or abating his pace or angering the men of Erin. Two young fosterlings he must carry under the armpits to his jacket through the whole of Erin, and six arm-bearing warriors in his seat together. If he be delivered of a warrior or a blue spear, he is not taken. One hundred head of cattle he must accommodate with wisdom about his person when walking all Erin, the half about his armpits and the half about his trews, his mouth never halting from the discoursing of sweet poetry. One thousand rams he must sequester about his trunks with no offence to the men of Erin, or he is unknown to Finn. He must swiftly milk a fat cow and carry milk-pail and cow for twenty years in the seat of his drawers. When pursued in a chariot by the men of Erin he must dismount, place horse and chariot in the slack of his seat and hide behind his spear, the same being stuck upright in Erin. Unless he accomplishes these feats, he is not wanted of Finn. But if he do them all and be skilful, he is of Finn's people.

What advantages are to Finn's people? asked Liagan Luaimneach O Luachair Dheaghaidh.

Who is it? said Finn.

It is Liagan Luaimneach O Luachair Dheaghaidh, said Conán, the third man of the three cousins from Cnoc Sneachta, Lagan Lumley O'Lowther-Day from Elphin Beg.

I will relate three things and nothing above three, said Finn. Myself I can get wisdom from the sucking of my thumb, another (though he knows it not) can bring to defeat a host by viewing it through his fingers, and another can cure a sick warrior by judging the smoke of the house in which he is.

Wonderful for telling, said Conán, and I know it. Relate for us, after, the tale of the feast of Bricriú.

I cannot make it, said Finn.

Then the tale of the Bull of Cooley.

It goes beyond me, said Finn, I cannot make it.

Then the tale of the Giolla Deacar and his old horse of the world, said Gearr mac Aonchearda.

Who is it? said Finn.

Surely it is Gearr mac Aonchaerda, said Conán, the middle man of the three brothers from Cruach Conite, Gar MacEncarty O'Hussey from Phillipstown.

I cannot make it, said Finn.

Recount then for the love of God, said Conán, the Tale of the Enchanted Fort of the Sally Tree or give shanachy's tidings of the Little Brawl at Allen.

They go above me and around me and through me, said Finn. It is true that I cannot make them.

Oh then, said Conán, the story of the Churl in the Puce Great-coat.

Evil story for telling, that, said Finn, and though itself I can make it, it is surely true that I will not recount it. It is a crooked and dis-honourable story that tells how Finn spoke honey-words and peace-words to a stranger who came seeking the high-rule and the high-rent of this kingdom and saying that he would play the sorrow of death and small-life on the lot of us in one single day if his wish was not given. Surely I have never heard (nor have I seen) a man come with high-deed the like of that to Erin that there was not found for him a man of his own equality. Who has heard honey-talk from Finn before strangers, Finn that is wind-quick, Finn that is a better man than God? Or who has seen the like of Finn or seen the living semblance of him standing in the world, Finn that could best God at ball-throw or wrestling or pig-trailing or at the honeyed discourse of sweet Irish with jewels and gold for bards, or at the listening of distant harpers in a black hole at evening? Or where is the living human man who could beat Finn at the making of generous cheese, at the spearing of ganders, at the magic of thumb-suck, at the shaving of hog-hair, or at the unleashing of long hounds from a golden thong in the full chase, sweet-fingered corn-yellow Finn, Finn that could carry an armed host from Almha to Slieve Luachra in the craw of his gut-hung knickers.

Good for telling, said Conán.
Who is it? said Finn.
It is I, said Conán.
I believe it for truth, said Finn.
Relate further then.

I am an Ulsterman, a Connachtman, a Greek, said Finn,
I am Cuchulainn, I am Patrick.
I am Carbery-Cathead, I am Goll.
I am my own father and my son.
I am every hero from the crack of time.

Melodious is your voice, said Conán.

Small wonder, said Finn, that Finn is without honour in the breast
of a sea-blue book, Finn that is twisted and trampled and tortured
for the weaving of a story-teller's book-web. Who but a book-poet
would dishonour the God-big Finn for the sake of a gap-worded story?
Who could have the saint Ceallach carried off by his four acolytes and
he feeble and thin from his Lent-fast, laid in the timbers of an old
boat, hidden for a night in a hollow oak tree and slaughtered without
mercy in the morning, his shrivelled body to be torn by a wolf and a
scaldcrow and the Kite of Cluain-Eo? Who could think to turn the
children of a king into white swans with the loss of their own bodies,
to be swimming the two seas of Erin in snow and ice-cold rain without bards or chess-boards, without their own tongues for discoursing
melodious Irish, changing the fat white legs of a maiden into plumes
and troubling her body with shameful eggs? Who could put a terrible
madness on the head of Sweeney for the slaughter of a single Lent-
gaunt cleric, to make him live in tree-tops and roost in the middle of
a yew, not a wattle to the shielding of his mad head in the middle of
the wet winter, perished to the marrow without company of women
or strains of harp-pluck, with no feeding but stag-food and the green
branches? Who but a story-teller? Indeed, it is true that there has been
ill-usage to the men of Erin from the book-poets of the world and
dishonour to Finn, with no knowing the nearness of disgrace or the
sorrow of death, or the hour when they may swim for swans or trot
for ponies or bell for stags or croak for frogs or fester for the wounds
on a man's back.

True for telling, said Conán.
Conclusion of the foregoing.

Biographical reminiscence, part the first: It was only a few months before composing the foregoing that I had my first experience of intoxicating beverages and their strange intestinal chemistry. I was walking through the Stephen's Green on a summer evening and conducting a conversation with a man called Kelly, then a student, hitherto a member of the farming class and now a private in the armed forces of the King. He was addicted to unclean expressions in ordinary conversation and spat continually, always fouling the flowerbeds on his way through the Green with a mucous deposit dislodged with a low grunting from the interior of his windpipe. In some respects he was a coarse man but he was lacking in malice or ill-humour. He purported to be a medical student but he had failed at least once to satisfy a body of examiners charged with regulating admission to the faculty. He suggested that we should drink a number of *jars* or pints of plain porter in Grogan's public house. I derived considerable pleasure from the casual quality of his suggestion and observed that it would probably do us no harm, thus expressing my whole-hearted concurrence by a figure of speech.

Name of figure of speech: Litotes (or Meiosis).

He turned to me with a facetious wry expression and showed me a penny and a sixpence in his rough hand.
I'm thirsty, he said. I have sevenpence. Therefore I buy a pint.
I immediately recognized this as an intimation that I should pay for my own porter.
The conclusion of your syllogism, I said lightly, is fallacious, being based on licensed premises.
Licensed premises is right, he replied, spitting heavily. I saw that my witticism was unperceived and quietly replaced it in the treasury of my mind.
We sat in Grogan's with our faded overcoats finely disarrayed on easy chairs in the mullioned snug. I gave a shilling and two pennies to a civil man who brought us in return two glasses of black porter, imperial pint measure. I adjusted the glasses to the front of each of us and reflected on the solemnity of the occasion. It was my first taste

of porter. Innumerable persons with whom I had conversed had represented to me that spirituous liquors and intoxicants generally had an adverse effect on the senses and the body and that those who became addicted to stimulants in youth were unhappy throughout their lives and met with death at the end by a drunkard's fall, expiring ingloriously at the stair-bottom in a welter of blood and puke. Indian tonic-waters had been proposed to me by an aged lay-brother as an incomparable specific for thirst. The importance of the subject had been impressed upon me in a school-book which I read at the age of twelve.

Extract from Literary Reader, the Higher Class, by the Irish Christian Brothers: And in the flowers that wreathe the sparkling bowl, fell adders hiss and poisonous serpents roll—Prior. What is alcohol? All medical authorities tell us it is double poison—an irritant and a narcotic poison. As an irritant it excites the brain, quickens the action of the heart, produces intoxication and leads to degeneration of the tissues. As a narcotic, it chiefly affects the nervous system; blunts the sensibility of the brain, spinal cord and nerves; and when taken in sufficient quantity, produces death. When alcohol is taken into the system, an extra amount of work is thrown on various organs, particularly the lungs. The lungs, being overtaxed, become degenerated, and this is why so many inebriates suffer from a peculiar form of consumption called alcoholic phthisis—many, many cases of which are, alas, to be found in our hospitals, where the unhappy victims await the slow but sure march of an early death. It is a well-established fact that alcohol not only does not give strength but lessens it. It relaxes the muscles or instruments of motion and consequently their power decreases. This muscular depression is often followed by complete paralysis of the body, drink having unstrung the whole nervous system, which, when so unstrung leaves the body like a ship without sails or ropes—an unmovable or unmanageable thing. Alcohol may have its uses in the medical world, to which it should be relegated; but once a man becomes its victim, it is a terrible and a merciless master, and he finds himself in that dreadful state when all will-power is gone and he becomes a helpless imbecile, tortured at times by remorse and despair.* Conclusion of the foregoing.

---

* This is a verbatim exerpt from the Christian Brothers' pamphlet, a copy of which resides among O'Brien's papers at the Morris Library.

On the other hand, young men of my acquaintance who were in the habit of voluntarily placing themselves under the influence of alcohol had often surprised me with a recital of their strange adventures. The mind may be impaired by alcohol, I mused, but withal it may be pleasantly impaired. Personal experience appeared to me to be the only satisfactory means to the resolution of my doubts. Knowing it was my first one, I quietly fingered the butt of my glass before I raised it. Lightly I subjected myself to an inward interrogation.

Nature of interrogation: Who are my future cronies, where our mad carousals? What neat repast shall feast us light and choice of Attic taste with wine whence we may rise to hear the lute well touched or artful voice warble immortal notes or Tuscan air? What mad pursuit? What pipes and timbrels? What wild ecstasy?

Here's to your health, said Kelly.
Good luck, I said.
The porter was sour to the palate but viscid, potent. Kelly made a long noise as if releasing air from his interior.
I looked at him from the corner of my eye and said:
You can't beat a good pint.
He leaned over and put his face close to me in an earnest manner.
Do you know what I am going to tell you, he said with his wry mouth, a pint of plain is your only man.
Notwithstanding this eulogy, I soon found that the mass of plain porter bears an unsatisfactory relation to its toxic content and I became subsequently addicted to brown stout in bottle, a drink which still remains the one that I prefer the most despite the painful and blinding fits of vomiting which a plurality of bottles has often induced in me.
I proceeded home one evening in October after leaving a gallon of half-digested porter on the floor of a public-house in Parnell Street and put myself with considerable difficulty into bed, where I remained for three days on the pretence of a chill. I was compelled to secrete my suit beneath the mattress because it was offensive to at least two of the senses and bore an explanation of my illness contrary to that already advanced.

The two senses referred to: Vision, smell.

On the evening of the third day, a friend of mine, Brinsley, was admitted to my chamber. He bore miscellaneous books and papers. I complained on the subject of my health and ascertained from him that the weather was inimical to the well-being of invalids. . . . He remarked that there was a queer smell in the room.

Description of my friend: Thin, dark-haired, hesitant; an intellectual Meath-man; given to close-knit epigrammatic talk; weak-chested, pale.

I opened wide my windpipe and made a coarse noise unassociated with the usages of gentlemen.

I feel very bad, I said.

By God you're the queer bloody man, he said.

I was down in Parnell Street, I said, with the Shader Ward, the two of us drinking pints. Well, whatever happened to me, I started to puke and I puked till the eyes nearly left my head. I made a right haimes of my suit. I puked till I puked air.

Is that the way of it? said Brinsley.

Look at here, I said.

I arose in my bed, my body on the prop of an elbow.

I was talking to the Shader, I said, talking about God and one thing and another, and suddenly I felt something inside me like a man trying to get out of my stomach. The next minute my head was in the grip of the Shader's hand and I was letting it out in great style. O Lord save us. . . .

Here Brinsley interposed a laugh.

I thought my stomach was on the floor, I said. Take it easy, says the Shader, you'll be better when you **get** that off. Better? How I got home at all I couldn't tell you.

Well you did get home, said Brinsley.

I withdrew my elbow and fell back again as if exhausted by my effort. My talk had been forced, couched in the accent of the lower or working classes. Under the cover of the bed-clothes I poked idly with a pencil at my navel. Brinsley was at the window giving chuckles out.

Nature of chuckles: Quiet, private, averted.

What are you laughing at? I said.

You and your book and your porter, he answered.

Did you read that stuff about Finn, I said, that stuff I gave you?

Oh, yes, he said, that was the pig's whiskers. That was funny all right.

This I found a pleasing eulogy. The God-big Finn. Brinsley turned from the window and asked me for a cigarette. I took out my "butt" or half-spent cigarette and showed it in the hollow of my hand.

That is all I have, I said, affecting a pathos in my voice.

By God you're the queer bloody man, he said.

He then brought from his own pocket a box of the twenty denomination, lighting one for each of us.

There are two ways to make big money, he said, to write a book or to make a book.

It happened that this remark provoked between us a discussion on the subject of Literature—great authors living and dead, the character of modern poetry, the predilections of publishers and the importance of being at all times occupied with literary activities of a spare-time or recreative character. My dim room rang with the iron of fine words and the names of great Russian masters were articulated with fastidious intonation. Witticisms were canvassed, depending for their utility on a knowledge of the French language as spoken in the medieval times. Psycho-analysis was mentioned—with, however, a somewhat light touch. I then tendered an explanation spontaneous and unsolicited concerning my own work, affording an insight as to its aesthetic, its daemon, its argument, its sorrow and its joy, its darkness, its sun-twinkle clearness.

Nature of explanation offered: It was stated that while the novel and the play were both pleasing intellectual exercises, the novel was inferior to the play inasmuch as it lacked the outward accidents of illusion, frequently inducing the reader to be outwitted in a shabby fashion and caused to experience a real concern for the fortunes of illusory characters. The play was consumed in wholesome fashion by large masses in places of public resort; the novel was self-administered in private. The novel, in the hands of an unscrupulous writer, could be despotic. In reply to an inquiry, it was explained that a satisfactory novel should be a self-evident sham to which the reader could regulate at will the degree of his credulity. It was undemocratic to compel characters to be uniformly good or bad or poor or rich. Each should be allowed a private life, self-determination and a decent standard of living. This would make for self-respect, contentment and better service. It would be incorrect to say that it would lead to chaos. Characters should be interchangeable as between one book and another. The entire corpus of existing literature should be regarded as a limbo from which discerning authors could draw their characters as required, creating only when they failed to find a suitable existing puppet. The modern novel should be largely a work of reference. Most authors spend their time saying what has been said before— usually said much better. A wealth of references to existing works would acquaint the reader instantaneously with the nature of each character, would obviate tiresome explanations and would effectively preclude mountebanks, upstarts, thimbleriggers and persons of inferior education from an understanding of contemporary literature. Conclusion of explanation.

That is all my bum, said Brinsley.

But taking precise typescript from beneath the book that was at my side, I explained to him my literary intentions in considerable detail— now reading, now discoursing, oratio recta and oratio obliqua.

Extract from Manuscript as to nature of Red Swan premises, oratio recta: The Red Swan premises in Lower Leeson Street are held in fee farm, the landlord whosoever being pledged to maintain the narrow lane which marks its eastern boundary unimpeded and free from nuisance for a distance of seventeen yards, that is, up to the intersection of Peter Place. New Paragraph. A terminus of the Cornelscourt coach in the seventeenth century, the hotel was rebuilt in 1712 and afterwards fired by the yeomanry for reasons which must be sought in the quiet of its ruined garden, on the three-perch stretch that goes by Croppies' Acre. To-day, it is a large building of four stories. The title is worked in snow-white letters along the circumference of the fanlight and the centre of the circle is concerned with the delicate image of a red swan, pleasantly conceived and carried out by a casting process in Birmingham delf. Conclusion of the foregoing.

Further extract descriptive of Dermot Trellis rated occupier of the Red Swan Hotel, oratio recta: Dermot Trellis was a man of average stature but his person was flabby and unattractive, partly a result of his having remained in bed for a period of twenty years. He was voluntarily bed-ridden and suffered from no organic or other illness. He occasionally rose for very brief periods in the evening to pad about the empty house in his felt slippers or to interview the slavey in the kitchen on the subject of his food or bedclothes. He had lost all physical reaction to bad or good weather and was accustomed to trace the seasonal changes of the year by inactivity or virulence of his pimples. His legs were puffed and affected with a prickly heat, a result of wearing his woollen undertrunks in bed. He never went out and rarely approached the windows.

Tour de force by Brinsley, vocally interjected, being a comparable description in the Finn canon: The neck to Trellis is house-thick and house-rough and is guarded by night and day against the coming of enemies by his old watchful boil. His bottom is the stern of a sea-blue schooner, his stomach is its mainsail with a filling of wind. His face is a snowfall on old mountains, the feet are fields.

There was an interruption, I recall, at this stage. My uncle put his head through the door and looked at me in a severe manner, his face flushed from walking and an evening paper in his hand. He was about to address me when he perceived the shadow of Brinsley by the window.

Well, well, he said. He came in in a genial noisy manner, closed the door with vigour and peered at the form of Brinsley. Brinsley took his hands from his pockets and smiled without reason in the twilight.

Good evening to you, gentlemen, said my uncle.

Good evening, said Brinsley.

This is Mr. Brinsley, a friend of mine, I said, raising my shoulders feebly from the bed. I gave a low moan of exhaustion.

My uncle extended an honest hand in the grip of friendship.

Ah, Mr. Brinsley, how do you do? he said. How do you do, Sir? You are a University man, Mr. Brinsley?

Oh, yes.

Ah, very good, said my uncle. It's a grand thing, that—a thing that will stand to you. It is certainly. A good degree is a very nice thing to have. Are the masters hard to please, Mr. Brinsley?

Well, no. As a matter of fact they don't care very much.

Do you tell me so! Well it was a different tale in the old days. The old schoolmasters believed in the big stick. Oh, plenty of that boyo.

He gave a laugh here in which we concurred without emotion.

The stick was mightier than the pen, he added, laughing again in a louder way and relapsing into a quiet chuckle. He paused for a brief interval as if examining something hitherto overlooked in the interior of his memory.

And how is our friend? he inquired in the direction of my bed.

Nature of my reply: Civil, perfunctory, uninformative.

My uncle leaned over towards Brinsley and said to him in a low, confidential manner:

Do you know what I am going to tell you, there is a very catching cold going around. Every second man you meet has got a cold. God preserve us, there will be plenty of 'flu before the winter's out, make no mistake about that. You would need to keep yourself well wrapped up.

As a matter of fact, said Brinsley in a crafty way, I have only just recovered from a cold myself.

You would need to keep yourself well wrapped up, rejoined my uncle, you would, faith.

Here there was a pause, each of us searching for a word with which it might be broken.

Tell me this, Mr. Brinsley, said my uncle, are you going to be a doctor?

I am not, said Brinsley.

Or a schoolmaster?

Here I interposed a shaft from my bed.

He hopes to get a job from the Christian Brothers, I said, when he gets his B.A.

That would be a great thing, said my uncle. The Brothers, of course, are very particular about the boys they take. You must have a good record, a clean sheet.

Well I have that, said Brinsley.

Of course you have, said my uncle. But doctoring and teaching are two jobs that call for great application and love of God. For what is the love of God but the love of your neighbour?

He sought agreement from each of us in turn, reverting a second to Brinsley with his ocular inquiry.

It is a grand and a noble life, he said, teaching the young and the sick and nursing them back to their Godgiven health. It is, faith. There is a special crown for those that give themselves up to that work.

It is a hard life, but, said Brinsley.

A hard life? said my uncle. Certainly so, but tell me this: Is it worth your while?

Brinsley gave a nod.

Worth your while and well worth it, said my uncle. A special crown is a thing that is not offered every day of the week. Oh, it's a grand thing, a grand life. Doctoring and teaching, the two of them are marked out for special graces and blessings.

He mused for a while, staring at the smoke of his cigarette. He then looked up and laughed, clapping his hand on the top of the washstand.

But long faces, he said, long faces won't get any of us very far. Eh, Mr. Brinsley? I am a great believer in the smile and the happy word.

A sovereign remedy for all our ills, said Brinsley.

A sovereign remedy for all our ills, said my uncle. Very nicely put. Well . . .

He held out a hand in valediction.

Mind yourself now, he said, and mind and keep the coat buttoned up. The 'flu is the boy I'd give the slip to.

He was civilly replied to. He left the room with a pleased smile but was not gone for three seconds till he was back again with a grave look, coming upon us suddenly in the moment of our relaxation and relief.

Oh, that matter of the Brothers he said in a low tone to Brinsley, would you care for me to put in a word for you?

Thanks very much, said Brinsley, but—

No trouble at all, said my uncle. Brother Hanley, late of Richmond Street, he is a very special friend of mine. No question of pulling strings, you know. Just a private word in his ear. He is a special friend.

Well, that is very good of you, said Brinsley.

Oh, not in the least, said my uncle. There is a way of doing things, you understand. It is a great thing to have a friend in court. And

Brother Hanley, I may tell you privately, is one of the best—Oh, one of the very best in the world. It would be a pleasure to work with a man like Brother Hanley. I will have a word with him to-morrow.

The only thing is, but, said Brinsley, it will be some time before I am qualified and get my parchment.

Never mind, said my uncle, it is always well to be in early. First come, first called.

At this point he assembled his features into an expression of extreme secrecy and responsibility:

The Order, of course, is always on the look-out for boys of education and character. Tell me this, Mr. Brinsley, have you ever . . .

I never thought of that, said Brinsley in surprise.

Do you think would the religious life appeal to you?

I'm afraid I never thought much about it.

Brinsley's tone was of a forced texture as if he were labouring in the stress of some emotion.

It is a good healthy life and a special crown at the end of it, said my uncle. Every boy should consider it very carefully before he decides to remain out in the world. He should pray to God for a vocation.

Not everybody is called, I ventured from the bed.

Not everybody is called, agreed my uncle, perfectly true. Only a small and a select band.

Perceiving then that the statement had come from me, he looked sharply in the direction of my corner as if to verify the honesty of my face. He turned back to Brinsley.

I want you to make me a promise. Mr. Brinsley, he said. Will you promise me that you will think about it?

I will certainly, said Brinsley.

My uncle smiled warmly and held out a hand.

Good, he said. God bless you.

Description of my uncle: Rat-brained, cunning, concerned-that-he-should-be-well-thought-of. Abounding in pretence, deceit. Holder of Guinness clerkship the third class.

In a moment he was gone, this time without return. Brinsley, a shadow by the window, performed perfunctorily the movements of a mime, making at the same time a pious ejaculation.

Nature of mime and ejaculation: Removal of sweat from brow; holy God.

I hope, said Brinsley, that Trellis is not a replica of the uncle.

I did not answer but reached a hand to the mantelpiece and took down the twenty-first volume of my *Conspectus of the Arts and Natural Sciences*. Opening it, I read a passage which I subsequently embodied in my manuscript as being suitable for my purpose. The passage had in fact reference to Doctor Beatty (now with God) but boldly I took it for my own.

The Third Policeman

Not a few of the critical commentators confess to a doubt as to whether de Selby was permitting himself a modicum of unwonted levity in connection with this theory but he seems to argue the matter seriously enough and with no want of conviction.

—The Third Policeman

We realise the author's ability but think that he should become less fantastic and in this new novel he is more so.

—Longmans' reader to A. M. Heath & Co.

INTRODUCTION

O'Brien began work on *The Third Policeman* in 1939, the year that *At Swim-Two-Birds* was published, and completed it in time to send to his agent in January 1940. The history of the manuscript from then until it was published in 1967 is a story worthy of the recycling theme of the novel itself. The agent passed the manuscript on to Longmans, publisher of *At Swim*, who replied as quoted above. The agent tried a few other places, then returned it owing to the danger in the London office during the Battle of Britain. William Saroyan, who had met O'Brien in Dublin (see his *Places Where I've Done Time*), took up his friend's cause and tried to get his own agent to place the book in New York. This agent mislaid the book and asked O'Brien for a copy. It is not clear what happened next, but O'Brien gave the book a kind of oral life of its own, not only saying that it was lost, but spinning elaborate yarns of just how it was lost. To Jack White he said that the manuscript had been in the boot of his car while he was taking a tour to the West of Ireland and that during an especially rocky section of road the lid had commenced a series of sporadic openings each of which had spewed forth its quota of pages across the bleak landscape of Connemara and Donegal. The fact is that at least one copy survived and is now in the Rare Book Room of the Morris Library at Southern Illinois University at Carbondale, where it may be examined under the dim gaze of a bust of James Joyce. Whether this is the copy that was used in printing the post-humous 1967 edition I do not know, but the pages are suspiciously without any editorial markings whatsoever.

The real story of what happened to *The Third Policeman*, how-ever, is not so much what occurred to the paper upon which it was written, but where the ideas from it went in its author's head and how the rejection affected his literary life in the years to come. After all, here was a man who had written two of the best books in modern literature before he was thirty, and as far as modern literature was concerned he did not exist. Among the things that happened to the author was the continuing of the civil-service career, the excursion into being Myles, and the late novel *The Dalkey Archive*. In this work O'Brien rehires such *Third Policeman* employees as de Selby (awarding him a capital D), comic policemen involved in the "molly-cule" theory, and a baffled protagonist. The Doomsday atmosphere re-emerges. Resurrection, posthumous publication, waking up dead without knowing it, and other recyclings were on O'Brien's mind, however, even before *The Third Policeman* went into its limbo. His father had written a detective story that received encouragement from a publisher's reader, but was returned to a box in the family house, where Flann came across it for the first time after his father's death. There is the juvenilia "Scenes In A Novel" by "Brother Barnabas"—one of Flann's early incarnations—which begins:

I am penning these lines, dear reader, under conditions of great emotional stress, being engaged, as I am, in the composition of a posthumous article.
[*The Journal of Irish Literature*]

The posthumous publication of *The Third Policeman* began a gen-eral revival of O'Brien's work, signaled by the Irish novelist and short story writer Benedict Kiely, whose "Fun After Death" ran on the front page of *The New York Times Book Review*, November 12, 1967. In addition to the hardback there have been at least two paperback editions in America. Because of the availability of this work, I have presented less of it than of some of the other novels, but by no means do I intend to slight a work that ranks with Malcolm Lowry's *Under the Volcano* and Joyce Cary's *The Horse's Mouth*.

Like Borges, O'Brien had read J. W. Dunne, and in *Cruiskeen Lawn* one finds him quoting A. N. Whitehead's *Science and the Modern World*. The following excerpt from Myles's column appeared on December 17, 1941:

"There are less than a thousand people in the world who really understand the Einstein theory of relativity, and less than a 100 people who can discuss it intelligently."

This disturbing statement was made recently by Sir Arthur Eddington. It is nice news for those of us who have to fork out every year to maintain our grandiose university establishments. We have perhaps 30 or 40 well-paid savants whom we have always taken to know all about physics or mathematics or whatever kindred subject they profess. Now we are told that these people know nothing about Einstein's discoveries, and cannot make head or tail of his sums. What would we say if a similar situation obtained in relation to, say, plumbers?...whereas Einstein's discoveries entail the radical revision of conventional concepts of time, space and matter, and a person who undertakes to discourse on such subjects while ignorant of Einstein, must necessarily rely on premises shown to be inadmissable...It is now accepted everywhere without much show of reserve that the earth is a sphere, but these university professors I am talking about are still (in a relative sense) teaching their students that it is flat. That is a fair and perfect analogy, because there is practically no limit to the mistakes you will make if the flatness of the earth is your fundamental *credo,* and you will fare no better if you choose to make pronouncements on the nature of the universe as if Einstein never existed.

And half a year later he wrote:

It was my good fortune to be present at the meeting of the Royal Society in London when the Astronomer Royal for England announced that the photographic plates of the famous eclipse, as measured by his colleagues in Greenwich Observatory, had verified the prediction of Einstein that rays of light are bent as they pass in the neighbourhood of the sun. The whole atmosphere of tense interest was exactly that of the Greek drama: we were the chorus commenting on the decree as disclosed in the development of a supreme incident. There was a dramatic quality in the very staging: the traditional ceremonial, and in the background the picture of

Newton to remind us that the greatest of scientific generalisations was now, after more than two centuries, to receive its first modification.

One might also add he inhaled James Stephens. The last line of the book is:

'Is it a bicycle?' he asked.

Bicycles, it might be noted are not in Ireland quite what they are in America. As a prolonged transition from horse to petrol gobbler, they have held a more utilitarian function in Ireland, which is not to say that their more comic, even metaphysical transports have gone unnoticed. In *The Portable Irish Reader* A.F.'s son Diarmuid Russell has chosen to include in the full sweep of Irish literature a speech by the master rhetorician Tim Healy on bicycles (July 7, 1898), which commences," . . . but we are now dealing with an important matter upon the Report stage," and goes on to discuss just how a bicycle might be lit so that its rights might not suffer beneath the wheels of milk carts. Readers of the novels of Samuel Beckett will also see the literary potency of these two-wheeled extensions of man's body. If there is an entire gentry in Ireland known as "The Horse Protestant," it would seem only fitting to say there is a genre, "The Bike Novelist."

The first of the following two letters from O'Brien was written while he was still working on *The Third Policeman*. The second, to William Saroyan, was written after he had completed the novel.

To Mr. Gillett
1 May, 1939.
    Thanks for your letter of the 21st April.
    I have not yet done anything about another novel beyond turning over some ideas in my head. My difficulty is to find time to get down to work of this kind. My bread-and-butter occupation keeps me busy until very late in the evenings at this time of the year and I do not expect to be able to start anything until rather late in the summer and cannot see it finished until perhaps November or so. I should like to hear from you as to whether whatever is forthcoming should come quickly from the point of view or continuity in whatever fragment I have of the public mind or whether a longish interval is unobjectionable.
    Briefly, the story I have in mind opens as a very orthodox murder mystery in a rural district. The perplexed parties have recourse to the

local barrack which, however, contains some very extraordinary policemen who do not confine their investigations or activities to this world or to any known planes or dimensions. Their most casual remarks create a thousand other mysteries but there will be no question of the difficulty or "fireworks" of the last book. The whole point of my plan will be the perfectly logical and matter-of-fact treatment of the most brain-staggering imponderables of the policemen. I should like to do this rather carefully and spend some time on it. . . .

To William Saroyan
Saint Valentine's Day, 1940.

Thanks a lot for your letter which I got a few weeks ago. I do not know how you write and keep on writing those plays. I don't understand the way you make ordinary things uproarious and full of meaning and sentiment and make yourself appear saner than everybody else merely by being crazy. I've just been reading *The Time Of Your Life* and I think it is what we here call the business. It is fearfully funny. There is great freshness in all your stuff. It's given me a lot of ideas but I can't use them for a while because that would be copying and anyway I'm beginning to think that I can't write at all—I mean, write something that will appeal to people everywhere because they're people, the way you do it. I keep wondering what that new play of yours is like and just how the title works into it. Has Hollywood started smelling round your plays yet?? I've just finished another bum book. I don't think it is much good and haven't sent it anywhere yet. The only thing good about it is the plot and I've been wondering whether I could make a crazy Saroyan play out of it. When you get to the end of this book you realise that my hero or main character (he's a heel and a killer) has been dead throughout the book and that all the queer ghastly things which have been happening to him are happening in a sort of hell which he has earned for the killing. Towards the end of the book (before you know he's dead) he manages to get back to his own house where he used to live with another man who helped in the original murder. Although he's been away 3 days, this other fellow is 20 years older and dies of fright when he sees the other lad standing in the door. Then the two of them walk back along the road to the hell place and start going through all the same terrible adventures again, the first fellow being surprised and frightened at everything just as he was the first time and as if he'd never been through it before. It is made clear that this sort of thing goes on forever—and there you are. It's supposed to be very funny but I don't know about that either. If it's ever published I'll send you a copy. I envy you the way you write just what you want to and like it when it's finished. I can never seem to get anything just right. Nevertheless, I think the idea of a man being dead all the time is pretty new. When you are writing about the world of the dead—and the damned—where none of the rules and laws (not even the law of gravity) holds good, there is any amount of scope for back-chat and funny cracks. . . .

[*The Journal of Irish Literature*]

FROM *THE THIRD POLICEMAN*

I

Not everybody knows how I killed old Phillip Mathers, smashing his jaw in with my spade; but first it is better to speak of my friendship with John Divney because it was he who first knocked old Mathers down by giving him a great blow in the neck with a special bicycle-pump which he manufactured himself out of a hollow iron bar. Divney was a strong civil man but he was lazy and idle-minded. He was personally responsible for the whole idea in the first place. It was he who told me to bring my spade. He was the one who gave the orders on the occasion and also the explanations when they were called for.

I was born a long time ago. My father was a strong farmer and my mother owned a public house. We all lived in the public house but it was not a strong house at all and was closed most of the day because my father was out at work on the farm and my mother was always in the kitchen and for some reason the customers never came until it was nearly bed-time; and well after it at Christmas-time and on other unusual days like that. I never saw my mother outside the kitchen in my life and never saw a customer during the day and even at night I never saw more than two or three together. But then I was in bed part of the time and it is possible that things happened differently with my mother and with the customers late at night. My father I do not remember well but he was a strong man and did not talk much except on Saturdays when he would mention Parnell with the customers and say that Ireland was a queer country. My mother I can recall perfectly. Her face was always red and sore-looking from bending at the fire; she spent her life making tea to pass the time and singing snatches of old songs to pass the meantime. I knew her well but my father and I were strangers and did not converse much; often indeed when I would be studying in the kitchen at night I could hear him through the thin door to the shop talking there from his seat under the oil-lamp for hours on end to Mick the sheepdog. Always it was only the drone of his voice I heard, never the separate bits of words. He was a man who understood all dogs thoroughly and treated them like human beings. My mother owned a cat but it was a foreign outdoor animal and was rarely seen and my mother never took any notice of it. We were all happy enough in a queer separate way.

Then a certain year came about the Christmas-time and when the year was gone my father and mother were gone also. Mick the sheepdog was very tired and sad after my father went and would not do his work with the sheep at all; he too went the next year. I was young and foolish at the time and did not know properly why these people had all left me, where they had gone and why they did not give explanations beforehand. My mother was the first to go and I can remember a fat man with a red face and a black suit telling my father that there was no doubt where she was, that he could be as sure of that as he could of anything else in this vale of tears. But he did not mention where and as I thought the whole thing was very private and that she might be back on Wednesday, I did not ask him where. Later, when my father went, I thought he had gone to fetch her with an outside car but when neither of them came back on the next Wednesday, I felt sorry and disappointed. The man in the black suit was back again. He stayed in the house for two nights and was continually washing his hands in the bedroom and reading books. There were two other men, one a small pale man and one a tall black man in leggings. They had pockets full of pennies and they gave me one every time I asked them questions. I can remember the tall man in the leggings saying to the other man:

'The poor misfortunate little bastard.'

I did not understand this at the time and thought that they were talking about the other man in the black clothes who was always working at the wash-stand in the bedroom. But I understood it all clearly afterwards.

After a few days I was brought away myself on an outside car and sent to a strange school. It wast a boarding school filled with people I did not know, some young and some older. I soon got to know that it was a good school and a very expensive one but I did not pay over any money to the people who were in charge of it because I had not any. All this and a lot more I understood clearly later.

My life at this school does not matter except for one thing. It was here that I first came to know something of de Selby. One day I picked up idly an old tattered book in the science master's study and put it in my pocket to read in bed the next morning as I had just earned the privilege of lying late. I was about sixteen then and the date was the seventh of March. I still think that day is the most important in my life and can remember it more readily than I do my birthday. The book was a first edition of *Golden Hours* with the two last pages missing. By the time I was nineteen and had reached the end of my education I knew that the book was valuable and that in keeping it I was stealing it. Nevertheless I packed it in my bag without a qualm and would probably do the same if I had my time again. Perhaps it is important in the story I am going to tell to remember that it was for de Selby I committed my first serious sin. It was for him that I committed my greatest sin.

I had long-since got to know how I was situated in the world. All my people were dead and there was a man called Divney working the farm and living on it until I should return. He did not own any of it and was given weekly cheques of pay by an office full of solicitors in a town far away. I had never met these solicitors and never met Divney but they were really all working for me and my father had paid in cash for these arrangements before he died. When I was younger I thought he was a generous man to do that for a boy he did not know well.

I did not go home direct from school. I spent some months in other places broadening my mind and finding out what a complete edition of de Selby's works would cost me and whether some of the less important of his commentators' books could be got on loan. In one of the places where I was broadening my mind I met one night with a bad accident. I broke my left leg (or, if you like, it was broken for me) in six places and when I was well enough again to go my way I had one leg made of wood, the left one. I knew that I had only a little money, that I was going home to a rocky farm and that my life would not be easy. But I was certain by this time that farming, even if I had to do it, would not be my life work. I knew that if my name was to be remembered, it would be remembered with de Selby's.

I can recall in every detail the evening I walked back into my own house with a travelling-bag in each hand. I was twenty years of age; it was an evening in a happy yellow summer and the door of the public house was open. Behind the counter was John Divney, leaning forward on the lowdown porter dash-board with his fork, his arms neatly folded and his face looking down on a newspaper which was spread upon the counter. He had brown hair and was made handsomely enough in a small butty way; his shoulders were broadened out with work and his arms were thick like little tree-trunks. He had a quiet civil face with eyes like cow's eyes, brooding, brown, and patient. When he knew that somebody had come in he did not stop his reading but his left hand strayed out and found a rag and began to give the counter slow damp swipes. Then, still reading, he moved his hands one above the other as if he was drawing out a concertina to full length and said:

'A schooner?'

A schooner was what the customers called a pint of Coleraine black-jack. It was the cheapest porter in the world. I said that I wanted my dinner and mentioned my name and station. Then we closed the shop and went into the kitchen and we were there nearly all night, eating and talking and drinking whiskey.

The next day was Thursday. John Divney said that his work was now done and that he would be ready to go home to where his people were on Saturday. It was not true to say that his work was done because the farm was in a poor way and most of the year's work had not even been started. But on Saturday he said there were a few things to finish and that he could not work on Sunday but that he would be in a position to hand over the place in perfect order on Tuesday evening. On Monday he had a sick pig to mind and that delayed him. At the end of the week he was busier than ever and the passing of another two months did not seem to lighten or reduce his urgent tasks. I did not mind much because if he was idle-minded and a sparing worker, he was satisfactory so far as company was concerned and he never asked for pay. I did little work about the place myself, spending all my time arranging my papers and re-reading still more closely the pages of de Selby.

A full year had not passed when I noticed that Divney was using the word 'we' in his conversation and worse than that, the word 'our'. He said that the place was not everything that it might be and talked of getting a hired man. I did not agree with this and told him so, saying that there was no necessity for more than two men on a small farm and adding, most unhappily for myself, that we were poor. After that it was useless trying to tell him that it was I who owned everything. I began to tell myself that even if I did own everything, he owned me.

Four years passed away happily enough for each of us. We had a good house and plenty of good country food but little money. Nearly all my own time was spent in study. Out of my savings I had now bought the complete works of the two principal commentators, Hatch-jaw and Bassett, and a photostat of the de Selby Codex. I had also embarked upon the task of learning French and German thoroughly in order to read the works of other commentators in those languages. Divney had been working after a fashion on the farm by day and talking loudly in the public house by night and serving drinks there. Once I asked him what about the public house and he said he was losing money on it every day. I did not understand this because the customers, judging by their voices through the thin door, were plentiful enough and Divney was continually buying himself suits of clothes and fancy tiepins. But I did not say much. I was satisfied to be left in peace because I knew that my own work was more important than myself.

One day in early winter Divney said to me:

'I cannot lose very much more of my own money on that bar. The customers are complaining about the porter. It is very bad porter be-cause I have to drink a little now and again myself to keep them company and I do not feel well in my health over the head of it. I will have to go away for two days and do some traveling and see if there is a better brand of porter to be had.'

He disappeared the next morning on his bicycle and when he came back very dusty and travel-worn at the end of three days, he told me that everything was all right and that four barrels of better porter could be expected on Friday. It came punctually on that day and was well bought by the customers in the public house that night. It was manufactured in some town in the south and was known as 'The Wrastler'. If you drank three or four pints of it, it was nearly bound to win. The customers praised it highly and when they had it inside them they sang and shouted and sometimes lay down on the floor or on the roadway outside in a great stupor. Some of them complained afterwards that they had been robbed while in this state and talked angrily in the shop the next night about stolen money and gold watches which had disappeared off their strong chains. John Divney did not say much on this subject to them and did not mention it to me at all. He printed the words—BEWARE OF PICKPOCKETS—in large letters on a card and hung it on the back of shelves beside another notice that dealt with cheques. Nevertheless a week rarely passed without some customer complaining after an evening with 'The Wrastler'. It was not a satisfactory thing.

As time went on Divney became more and more despondent about what he called 'the bar'. He said that he would be satisfied if it paid its way but he doubted seriously if it ever would. The Government were partly responsible for the situation owing to the high taxes. He did not think that he could continue to bear the burden of the loss without some assistance. I said that my father had some old-fashioned way of management which made possible a profit but that the shop should be closed if now continuing to lose money. Divney only said that it was a very serious thing to surrender a license.

It was about this time, when I was nearing thirty, that Divney and I began to get the name of being great friends. For years before that I had rarely gone out at all. This was because I was so busy with my work that I hardly ever had the time; also my wooden leg was not very good for walking with. Then something very unusual happened to change all this and after it had happened, Divney and I never parted company for more than one minute either night or day. All day I was out with him on the farm and at night I sat on my father's old seat under the lamp in a corner of the public house doing what work I could with my papers in the middle of the blare and the crush and the hot noises which went always with 'The Wrastler'. If Divney went for a walk on Sunday to a neighbour's house I went with him and came home with him again, never before or after him. If he went away to a town on his bicycle to order porter or seed potatoes or even 'to see a certain party', I went on my own bicycle beside him. I brought my bed into his room and took the trouble to sleep only after he was sleeping and to be wide-awake a good hour before he stirred. Once I nearly failed in my watchfulness. I remember waking up with a start in the small hours of a black night and finding him quietly dressing himself in the dark. I asked him where he was going and he said he could not sleep and that he thought a walk would do him good. I said I was in the same condition myself and the two of us went for a walk together into the coldest and wettest night I ever experienced. When we returned drenched I said it was foolish for us to sleep in different beds in such bitter weather and got into his bed beside him. He did not say much, then or at any other time. I slept with him always after that. We were friendly and smiled at each other but the situation was a queer one and neither of us liked it. The neighbours were not long noticing how inseparable we were. We had been in that condition of being always together for nearly three years and they said that we were the best two Christians in all Ireland. They said that human friendship was a beautiful thing and that Divney and I were the noblest example of it in the history of the world. If other people fell out or fought or disagreed, they were asked why they could not be like me and Divney. It would have been a great shock for everybody if Divney had appeared in any place at any time without myself beside him. And it is not strange that two people never came to dislike each other as bitterly as did I and Divney. And two people were never so polite to each other, so friendly in the face.

I must go back several years to explain what happened to bring about this peculiar situation. The 'certain party' whom Divney went to visit once a month was a girl called Pegeen Meers. For my part I had completed my definitive 'De Selby Index' wherein the views of all known commentators on every aspect of the savant and his work had been collated. Each of us therefore had a large thing on the mind. One day Divney said to me:

'That is a powerful book you have written I don't doubt.'

'It is useful,' I admitted, 'and badly wanted.' In fact it contained much that was entirely new and proof that many opinions widely held about de Selby and his theories were misconceptions based on misreadings of his works.

'It might make your name in the world and your golden fortune in copyrights?'

'It might.'

'Then why do you not put it out?'

I explained that money is required to 'put out' a book of this kind unless the writer already has a reputation. He gave me a look of sympathy that was not usual with him and sighed.

'Money is hard to come by these days,' he said, 'with the drink trade on its last legs and the land starved away to nothing for the want of artificial manures that can't be got for love or money owing to the trickery of the Jewmen and the Freemasons.'

I knew that it was not true about the manures. He had already pretended to me that they could not be got because he did not want the trouble of them. After a pause he said:

'We will have to see what we can do about getting money for your book and indeed I am in need of some myself because you can't expect a girl to wait until she is too old to wait any longer.'

I did not know whether he meant to bring a wife, if he got one, into the house. If he did and I could not stop him, then I would have to leave. On the other hand if marriage meant that he himself would leave I think I would be very glad of it.

It was some days before he talked on this subject of money again. Then he said:

'What about old Mathers?'

'What about him?'

I had never seen the old man but knew all about him. He had spent a long life of fifty years in the cattle trade and now lived in retirement in a big house three miles away. He still did large business through agents and the people said that he carried no less than three thousand pounds with him every time he hobbled to the village to lodge his money. Little as I knew of social proprieties at the time, I would not dream of asking him for assistance.

'He is worth a packet of potato-meal,' Divney said.

'I do not think we should look for charity,' I answered.

'I do not think so either,' he said. He was a proud man in his own way, I thought, and no more was said just then. But after that he took to the habit of putting occasionally into conversations on other subjects some irrelevant remark about our need for money and the amount of it which Mathers carried in his black cash-box; sometimes he would revile the old man, accusing him of being in 'the artificial manure ring' or of being dishonest in his business dealings. Once he said something about 'social justice' but it was plain to me that he did not properly understand the term.

I do not know exactly how or when it became clear to me that Divney, far from seeking charity, intended to rob Mathers; and I cannot recollect how long it took me to realise that he meant to kill him as well in order to avoid the possibility of being identified as the robber afterwards. I only know that within six months I had come to accept this grim plan as a commonplace of our conversation. Three further months passed before I could bring myself to agree to the proposal and three months more before I openly admitted to Divney that my misgivings were at an end. I cannot recount the tricks and wiles he used to win me to his side. It is sufficient to say that he read portions of my 'De Selby Index' (or pretended to) and discussed with me afterwards the serious responsibility of any person who declined by mere reason of personal whim to give the 'Index' to the world.

Old Mathers lived alone. Divney knew on what evening and at what deserted stretch of road near his house we would meet him with his box of money. The evening when it came was in the depth of winter; the light was already waning as we sat at our dinner discussing the business we had in hand. Divney said that we should bring our spades tied on the crossbars of our bicycles because this would make us look like men out after rabbits; he would bring his own iron pump in case we should get a slow puncture.

There is little to tell about the murder. The lowering skies seemed to conspire with us, coming down in a shroud of dreary mist to within a few yards of the wet road where we were waiting. Everything was very still with no sound in our ears except the dripping of the trees. Our bicycles were hidden. I was leaning miserably on my spade and Divney, his iron pump under his arm, was smoking his pipe contentedly. The old man was upon us almost before we realised there was anybody near. I could not see him well in the dim light but I could glimpse a spent bloodless face peering from the top of the great black coat which covered him from ear to ankle. Divney went forward at once and pointing back along the road said:

'Would that be your parcel on the road?'

The old man turned his head to look and received a blow in the back of the neck from Divney's pump which knocked him clean off his feet and probably smashed his neck-bone. As he collapsed full-length in the mud he did not cry out. Instead I heard him saying something softly in a conversational tone—something like 'I do not care for celery' or 'I left my glasses in the scullery'. Then he lay very still. I had been watching the scene rather stupidly, still leaning on my spade. Divney was rummaging savagely at the fallen figure and then stood up. He had a black cash-box in his hand. He waved it in the air and roared at me:

'Here, wake up! Finish him with the spade!'

I went forward mechanically, swung the spade over my shoulder and smashed the blade of it with all my strength against the protruding chin. I felt and almost heard the fabric of his skull crumple up crisply like an empty eggshell. I do not know how often I struck him after that but I did not stop until I was tired.

I threw the spade down and looked around for Divney. He was nowhere to be seen. I called his name softly but he did not answer. I walked a little bit up the road and called again. I jumped on the rising of a ditch and peered around into the gathering dusk. I called his name once more as loudly as I dared but there was no answer in the stillness. He was gone. He had made off with the box of money, leaving me alone with the dead man and with a spade which was now probably tinging the watery mud around it with a weak pink stain.

My heart stumbled painfully in its beating. A chill of fright ran right through me. If anybody should come, nothing in the world would save me from the gallows. If Divney was with me still to share my guilt, even that would not protect me. Numb with fear I stood for a long time looking at the crumpled heap in the black coat.

Before the old man had come Divney and I had dug a deep hole in the field beside the road, taking care to preserve the sod of grass. Now in a panic I dragged the heavy sodden figure from where it lay and got it with a tremendous effort across the ditch into the field and slumped it down into the hole. Then I rushed back for my spade and started to throw and push the earth back into the hole in a mad blind fury.

The hole was nearly full when I heard steps. Looking round in great dismay I saw the unmistakable shape of Divney making his way carefully across the ditch into the field. When he came up I pointed dumbly to the hole with my spade. Wtihout a word he went to where our bicycles were, came back with his own spade and worked steadily with me until the task was finished. We did everything possible to hide any trace of what had happened. Then we cleaned our boots with grass, tied the spades and walked home. A few people who came against us on the road bade us good evening in the dark. I am sure they took us for two tired labourers making for home after a hard day's work. They were not far wrong.

On our way I said to Divney:

'Where were you that time?'

'Attending to important business,' he answered. I thought he was referring to a certain thing and said:

'Surely you could have kept it till after.'

'It is not what you are thinking of,' he answered.

'Have you got the box?'

He turned his face to me this time, screwed it up and put a finger on his lip.

'Not so loud,' he whispered. 'It is in a safe place.'

'But where?'

The only reply he gave me was to put the finger on his lip more firmly and make a long hissing noise. He gave me to understand that mentioning the box, even in a whisper, was the most foolish and reckless thing it was possible for me to do.

When we reached home he went away and washed himself and put on one of the several blue Sunday suits he had. When he came back to where I was sitting, a miserable figure at the kitchen fire, he came across to me with a very serious face, pointed to the window and cried:

'Would that be your parcel on the road?'

Then he let out a bellow of laughter which seemed to loosen up his whole body, turn his eyes to water in his head and shake the whole house. When he had finished he wiped the tears from his face, walked into the shop and made a noise which can only be made by taking the cork quickly out of a whiskey bottle.

In the weeks which followed I asked him where the box was a hundred times in a thousand different ways. He never answered in the same way but the answer was always the same. It was in a very safe place. The least said about it the better until things quietened down. Mum was the word. It would be found all in good time. For the purpose of safe-keeping the place it was in was superior to the Bank of England. There was a good time coming. It would be a pity to spoil everything by hastiness or impatience.

And that is why John Divney and I became inseparable friends and why I never allowed him to leave my sight for three years. Having robbed me in my own public house (having even robbed my customers) and having ruined my farm, I knew that he was sufficiently dishonest to steal my share of Mathers' money and make off with the box if given the opportunity. I knew that there was no possible necessity for waiting until 'things quietened down' because very little notice was taken of the old man's disappearance. People said he was a queer mean man and that going away without telling anybody or leaving his address was the sort of thing he would do.

I think I have said before that the peculiar terms of physical intimacy upon which myself and Divney found ourselves had become more and more intolerable. In latter months I had hoped to force him to capitulate by making my company unbearably close and unrelenting but at the same time I took to carrying a small pistol in case of accidents. One Sunday night when both of us were sitting in the kitchen —both, incidentally, on the same side of the fire—he took his pipe from his mouth and turned to me:

'Do you know,' he said, 'I think things have quietened down.'

I only gave a grunt.

'Do you get my meaning?' he asked.

'Things were never any other way,' I answered shortly.

He looked at me in a superior way.

'I know a lot about these things,' he said, 'and you would be surprised at the pitfalls a man will make if he is in too big a hurry. You cannot be too careful but all the same I think things have quietened down enough to make it safe.'

'I am glad you think so.'

'There are good times coming. I will get the box tomorrow and then we will divide the money, right here on this table.'

'We will get the box,' I answered, saying the first word with great care. He gave me a long hurt look and asked me sadly did I not trust him. I replied that both of us should finish what both had started.

'All right,' he said in a very vexed way. 'I am sorry you don't trust me after all the work I have done to try to put this place right but to show you the sort I am I will let you get the box yourself, I will tell you where it is tomorrow.'

I took care to sleep with him as usual that night. The next morning he was in a better temper and told me with great simplicity that the box was hidden in Mathers' own empty house, under the floorboards of the first room on the right from the hall.

'Are you sure?' I asked.

'I swear it,' he said solemnly, raising his hand to heaven.

I thought the position over for a moment, examining the possibility that it was a ruse to part company with me at last and then make off himself to the real hiding-place. But his face for the first time seemed to wear a look of honesty.

'I am sorry if I injured your feelings last night,' I said, 'but to show that there is no ill-feeling I would be glad if you would come with me at least part of the way. I honestly think that both of us should finish what the two of us started.'

'All right,' he said. 'It is all the same but I would like you to get the box with your own hands because it is only simple justice after not telling you where it was.'

As my own bicycle was punctured we walked the distance. When we were about a hundred yards from Mathers' house, Divney stopped by a low wall and said that he was going to sit on it and smoke his pipe and wait for me.

'Let you go alone and get the box and bring it back here. There are good times coming and we will be rich men tonight. It is sitting under a loose board in the floor of the first room on the right, in the corner forenenst the door.'

Perched as he was on the wall I knew that he need never leave my sight. In the brief time I would be away I could see him any time I turned my head.

'I will be back in ten minutes,' I said.

'Good man,' he answered. 'But remember this. If you meet anybody, you don't know what you're looking for, you don't know in whose house you are, you don't know anything.'

'I don't even know my own name,' I answered.

This was a very remarkable thing for me to say because the next time I was asked my name I could not answer. I did not know.

II

De Selby has some interesting things to say on the subject of houses.[1] A row of houses he regards as a row of necessary evils. The softening and degeneration of the human race he attributes to its progressive predilection for interiors and waning interest in the art of going out and staying there. This in turn he sees as the result of the rise of such pursuits as reading, chess-playing, drinking, marriage and the like, few of which can be satisfactorily conducted in the open. Elsewhere[2] he defines a house as 'a large coffin', 'a warren', and 'a box'. Evidently his main objection was to the confinement of a roof and four walls. He ascribed somewhat far-fetched therapeutic values—chiefly pulmonary —to certain structures of his own design which he called 'habitats', crude drawings of which may still be seen in the pages of the Country Album. These structures were of two kinds, roofless 'houses' and 'houses' without walls. The former had wide open doors and windows with an extremely ungainly superstructure of tarpaulins loosely rolled on spars against bad weather—the whole looking like a foundered sailing-ship erected on a platform of masonry and the last place where one would think of keeping even cattle. The other type of 'habitat' had the conventional slated roof but no walls save one, which was to be erected in the quarter of the prevailing wind; around the other sides were the inevitable tarpaulins loosely wound on rollers suspended from the gutters of the roof, the whole structure being surrounded by a diminutive moat or pit bearing some resemblance to military latrines. In the light of present-day theories of housing and hygiene, there can be no doubt that de Selby was much mistaken in these ideas but in his own remote day more than one sick person lost his life in an ill-advised quest for health in these fantastic dwellings.[3]

My recollections of de Selby were prompted by my visit to the home

[1] Golden Hours, ii, 261. [This and the following are O'Brien's footnotes.]
[2] Country Album, p. 1,034.
[3] Le Fournier, the reliable French commentator (in De Selby—l'Énigme de l'Occident) has put forward a curious theory regarding these 'habitats'. He suggests that de Selby, when writing the Album, paused to consider some point of difficulty and in the meantime engaged in the absent-minded practice known generally as 'doodling', then putting his manuscript away. The next time he took it up he was confronted with a mass of diagrams and drawings which he took to be the plans of a type of dwelling he always had in mind and immediately wrote many pages explaining the sketches. 'In no other way,' adds the severe Le Fournier, 'can one explain so regrettable a lapse.'

of old Mr Mathers. As I approached it along the road the house appeared to be a fine roomy brick building of uncertain age, two storeys high with a plain porch and eight or nine windows to the front of each floor.

I opened the iron gate and walked as softly as I could up the weed-tufted gravel drive. My mind was strangely empty. I did not feel that I was about to end successfully a plan I had worked unrelentingly at night and day for three years. I felt no glow of pleasure and was unexcited at the prospect of becoming rich. I was occupied only with the mechanical task of finding a black box.

The hall-door was closed and although it was set far back in a very deep porch the wind and rain had whipped a coating of gritty dust against the panels and deep into the crack where the door opened, showing that it had been shut for years. Standing on a derelict flower-bed, I tried to push up the sash of the first window on the left. It yielded to my strength, raspingly and stubbornly. I clambered through the opening and found myself, not at once in a room, but crawling along the deepest window-ledge I have ever seen. When I reached the floor and jumped noisily down upon it, the open window seemed very far away and much too small to have admitted me.

The room where I found myself was thick with dust, musty and deserted of all furniture. Spiders had erected great stretchings of their web about the fireplace. I made my way quickly to the hall, threw open the door of the room where the box was and paused on the threshold. It was a dark morning and the weather had stained the windows with blears of grey wash which kept the brightest part of the weak light from coming in. The far corner of the room was a blur of shadow. I had a sudden urge to have done with my task and be out of this house forever. I walked across the bare boards, knelt down in the corner and passed my hands about the floor in search of the loose board. To my surprise I found it easily. It was about two feet in length and rocked hollowly under my hand. I lifted it up, laid it aside and struck a match. I saw a black metal cash-box nestling dimly in the hole. I put my hand down and crooked a finger into the loose reclining handle but the match suddenly flickered and went out and the handle of the box, which I had lifted up about an inch slid heavily off my finger. Without stopping to light another match I thrust my hand bodily into the opening and just when it should be closing about the box, something happened.

I cannot hope to describe what it was but it had frightened me very much long before I had understood it even slightly. It was some change which came upon me or upon the room, indescribably subtle, yet momentous, ineffable. It was as if the daylight had changed with unnatural suddenness, as if the temperature of the evening had altered greatly in an instant or as if the air had become twice as rare or twice as dense as it had been in the winking of an eye; perhaps all of these and other things happened together for all my senses were bewildered all at once and could give me no explanation. The fingers of my right hand, thrust into the opening of the floor, had closed mechanically, found nothing at all and came up again empty. The box was gone!

I heard a cough behind me, soft and natural yet more disturbing than any sound that could ever come upon the human ear. That I did not die of fright was due, I think, to two things, the fact that my senses were already disarranged and able to interpret to me only gradually what they had perceived and also the fact that the utterance of the cough seemed to bring with it some more awful alteration in everything, just as if it had held the universe standstill for an instant, suspending the planets in their courses, halting the sun and holding in mid-air any falling thing the earth was pulling towards it. I collapsed weakly from my kneeling backwards into a limp sitting-down upon the floor. Sweat broke upon my brow and my eyes remained open for a long time without a wink, glazed and almost sightless.

In the darkest corner of the room near the window a man was sitting in a chair, eyeing me with a mild but unwavering interest. His hand had crept out across the small table by his side to turn up very slowly an oil-lamp which was standing on it. The oil-lamp had a glass bowl with the wick dimly visible inside it, curling in convolutions like an intestine. There were tea things on the table. The man was old Mathers. He was watching me in silence. He did not move or speak and might have been still dead save for the slight movement of his hand at the lamp, the very gentle screwing of his thumb and forefinger against the wick-wheel. The hand was yellow, the wrinkled skin draped loosely upon the bones. Over the knuckle of his forefinger I could clearly see the loop of a skinny vein.

It is hard to write of such a scene or to convey with known words the feelings which came knocking at my numbed mind. How long we sat there, for instance, looking at one another I do not know. Years or minutes could be swallowed up with equal ease in that indescribable and unaccountable interval. The light of morning vanished from my sight, the dusty floor was like nothingness beneath me and my whole body dissolved away, leaving me existing only in the stupid spellbound gaze that went steadily from where I was to the other corner.

I remember that I noticed several things in a cold mechanical way as if I was sitting there with no worry save to note everything I saw. His face was terrifying but his eyes in the middle of it had a quality of chill and horror which made his other features look to me almost friendly. The skin was like faded parchment with an arrangement of puckers and wrinkles which created between them an expression of fathomless inscrutability. But the eyes were horrible. Looking at them I got the feeling that they were not genuine eyes at all but mechanical dummies animated by electricity or the like, with a tiny pinhole in the centre of the 'pupil' through which the real eye gazed out secretively and with great coldness. Such a conception, possibly with no foundation at all in fact, disturbed me agonisingly and gave rise in my mind to interminable speculations as to the colour and quality of the real eye and as to whether, indeed, it was real at all or merely another dummy with its pinhole on the same plane as the first one so that the real eye, possibly behind thousands of these absurd disguises, gazed out through a barrel of serried peep-holes. Occasionally the heavy cheese-like lids would drop down slowly with great languor and then rise again. Wrapped loosely around the body was an old wine-coloured dressing-gown.

In my distress I thought to myself that perhaps it was his twin brother but at once I heard someone say:

Scarcely. If you look carefully at the left-hand side of his neck you will notice that there is sticking-plaster or a bandage there. His throat and chin are also bandaged.

Forlornly, I looked and saw that this was true. He was the man I had murdered beyond all question. He was sitting on a chair four yards away watching me. He sat stiffly without a move as if afraid to hurt the gaping wounds which covered his body. Across my own shoulders a stiffness had spread from my exertions with the spade.

But who had uttered these words? They had not frightened me. They were clearly audible to me yet I knew they did not ring out across the air like the chilling cough of the old man in the chair. They came from deep inside me, from my soul. Never before had I believed or suspected that I had a soul but just then I knew I had. I knew also that my soul was friendly, was my senior in years and was solely concerned for my own welfare. For convenience I called him Joe. I felt a little reassured to know that I was not altogether alone. Joe was helping me.

I will not try to tell of the space of time which followed. In the terrible situation I found myself, my reason could give me no assistance. I knew that old Mathers had been felled by an iron bicycle-pump, hacked to death with a heavy spade and then securely buried in a field. I knew also that the same man was now sitting in the same room with me, watching me in silence. His body was bandaged but his eyes were alive and so was his right hand and so was all of him. Perhaps the murder by the roadside was a bad dream.

There is nothing dreamy about your stiff shoulders. No, I replied, but a nightmare can be as strenuous physically as the real thing.

I decided in some crooked way that the best thing to do was to believe what my eyes were looking at rather than to place my trust in a memory. I decided to show unconcern, to talk to the old man and to test his own reality by asking about the black box which was responsible, if anything could be, for each of us being the way we were. I made up my mind to be bold because I knew that I was in great danger. I knew that I would go mad unless I got up from the floor and moved and talked and behaved in as ordinary a way as possible. I looked away from old Mathers, got carefully to my feet and sat down on a chair that was not far away from him. Then I looked back at him, my heart pausing for a time and working on again with slow heavy hammer-blows which seemed to make my whole frame shudder. He had remained perfectly still but the live right hand had gripped the pot of tea, raised it very awkwardly and slapped a filling into the empty cup. His eyes had followed me to my new position and were now regarding me again with the same unwavering languorous interest.

Suddenly I began to talk. Words spilled out of me as if they were produced by machinery. My voice, tremulous at first, grew hard and loud and filled the whole room. I do not remember what I said at the beginning. I am sure that most of it was meaningless but I was too pleased and reassured at the natural healthy noise of my tongue to be concerned about the words.

Old Mathers did not move or say anything at first but I was certain that he was listening to me. After a while he began to shake his head and then I was sure I had heard him say No. I became excited at his responses and began to speak carefully. He negatived my inquiry about his health, refused to say where the black box had gone and even denied that it was a dark morning. His voice had a peculiar jarring weight like the hoarse toll of an ancient rusty bell in an ivy-smothered tower. He had said nothing beyond the one word No. His lips hardly moved; I felt sure he had no teeth behind them.

'Are you dead at present?' I asked.

'I am not.'

'Do you know where the box is?'

'No.'

He made another violent movement with his right arm, slapping hot water into his teapot and pouring forth a little more of the feeble brew into his cup. He then relapsed into his attitude of motionless watching. I pondered for a time.

'Do you like weak tea?' I asked.

'I do not,' he said.

'Do you like tea at all?' I asked, 'strong or weak or half-way tea?'

'No,' he said.

'Then why do you drink it?'

He shook his yellow face from side to side sadly and did not say anything. When he stopped shaking he opened up his mouth and poured the cupful of tea in as one would pour a bucket of milk into a churn at churning-time.

Do you notice anything?

No, I replied, nothing beyond the eeriness of this house and the man who owns it. He is by no means the best conversationalist I have met.

I found I spoke lightly enough. While speaking inwardly or outwardly or thinking of what to say I felt brave and normal enough. But every time a silence came the horror of my situation descended upon me like a heavy blanket flung upon my head, enveloping and smothering me and making me afraid of death.

But do you notice nothing about the way he answers your questions?

No.

Do you not see that every reply is in the negative? No matter what you ask him he says No.

That is true enough, I said, but I do not see where that leads me.

Use your imagination.

When I brought my whole attention back to old Mathers I thought he was asleep. He sat over his teacup in a more stooped attitude as if he were a rock or part of the wooden chair he sat on, a man completely dead and turned to stone. Over his eyes the limp lids had drooped down, almost closing them. His right hand resting on the table lay lifeless and abandoned. I composed my thoughts and addressed to him a sharp noisy interrogation.

'Will you answer a straight question?' I asked. He stirred somewhat, his lids opening slightly.

'I will not,' he replied.

I saw that this answer was in keeping with Joe's shrewd suggestion. I sat thinking for a moment until I had thought the same thought inside out.

'Will you refuse to answer a straight question?' I asked.

'I will not,' he replied.

This answer pleased me. It meant that my mind had got to grips with his, that I was now almost arguing with him and that we were behaving like two ordinary human beings. I did not understand all the terrible things which had happened to me but I now began to think that I must be mistaken about them.

'Very well,' I said quietly, 'Why do you always answer No?'

He stirred perceptibly in his chair and filled the teacup up again before he spoke. He seemed to have some difficulty in finding words.

' "No" ' is, generally speaking, a better answer than "Yes",' he said at last. He seemed to speak eagerly, his words coming out as if they had been imprisoned in his mouth for a thousand years. He seemed relieved that I had found a way to make him speak. I thought he even smiled slightly at me but this was doubtless the trickery of the bad morning light or a mischief worked by the shadows of the lamp. He swallowed a long draught of tea and sat waiting, looking at me with his queer eyes. They were now bright and active and moved about restlessly in their yellow wrinkled sockets.

'Do you refuse to tell me why you say that?' I asked.

'No,' he said. 'When I was a young man I led an unsatisfactory life and devoted most of my time to excesses of one kind or another, my principal weakness being Number One. I was also party to the formation of an artificial manure-ring.'

My mind went back at once to John Divney, to the farm and the public house and on from that to the horrible afternoon we had spent on the wet lonely road. As if to interrupt my unhappy thoughts I heard Joe's voice again, this time severe:

No need to ask him what Number One is, we do not want lurid descriptions of vice or anything at all in that line. Use your imagination. Ask him what all this has to do with Yes and No.

'What has that got to do with Yes and No?'

'After a time,' said old Mathers disregarding me, 'I mercifully perceived the error of my ways and the unhappy destination I would reach unless I mended them. I retired from the world in order to try to comprehend it and to find out why it becomes more unsavoury as the years accumulate on a man's body. What do you think I discovered at the end of my meditations?'

I felt pleased again. He was now questioning me.

'What?'

'That No is a better word than Yes,' he replied.

This seemed to leave us where we were, I thought.

On the contrary, very far from it. I am beginning to agree with him. There is a lot to be said for No as a General Principle. Ask him what he means.

'What do you mean?' I inquired.

'When I was meditating,' said old Mathers, 'I took all my sins out and put them on the table, so to speak. I need not tell you it was a big table.'

He seemed to give a very dry smile at his own joke. I chuckled to encourage him.

'I gave them all a strict examination, weighed them and viewed them from all angles of the compass. I asked myself how I came to commit them, where I was and whom I was with when I came to do them.'

This is very wholesome stuff, every word a sermon in itself. Listen very carefully. Ask him to continue.

'Continue,' I said.

I confess I felt a click inside me very near my stomach as if Joe had put a finger to his lip and pricked up a pair of limp spaniel ears to make sure that no syllable of the wisdom escaped him. Old Mathers continued talking quietly.

'I discovered,' he said, 'that everything you do is in response to a request or a suggestion made to you by some other party either inside you or outside. Some of these suggestions are good and praiseworthy and some of them are undoubtedly delightful. But the majority of them are definitely bad and are pretty considerable sins as sins go. Do you understand me?'

'Perfectly.'

'I would say that the bad ones outnumber the good ones by three to one.'

Six to one if you ask me.

'I therefore decided to say No henceforth to every suggestion, request or inquiry whether inward or outward. It was the only simple formula which was sure and safe. It was difficult to practise at first and often called for heroism but I persevered and hardly ever broke down completely. It is now many years since I said Yes. I have refused more requests and negatived more statements than any man living or dead. I have rejected, reneged, disagreed, refused and denied to an extent that is unbelievable.'

An excellent and original régime. This is all extremely interesting and salutary, every syllable a sermon in itself. Very very wholesome.

'Extremely interesting,' I said to old Mathers.

'The system leads to peace and contentment,' he said. 'People do not trouble to ask you questions if they know the answer is a foregone conclusion. Thoughts which have no chance of succeeding do not take the trouble to come into your head at all.'

'You must find it irksome in some ways,' I suggested. 'If, for instance, I were to offer you a glass of whiskey . . .'

'Such few friends as I have,' he answered, 'are usually good enough to arrange such invitations in a way that will enable me to adhere to my system and also accept the whiskey. More than once I have been asked whether I would refuse such things.'

'And the answer is still NO?'

'Certainly.'

Joe said nothing at this stage but I had the feeling that this confession was not to his liking; he seemed to be uneasy inside me. The old man seemed to get somewhat restive also. He bent over his teacup with abstraction as if he were engaged in accomplishing a sacrament. Then he drank with his hollow throat, making empty noises.

A saintly man.

I turned to him again, fearing that his fit of talkativeness had passed.

'Where is the black box which was under the floor a moment ago?'

I asked. I pointed to the opening in the corner. He shook his head and did not say anything.

'Do you refuse to tell me?'

'No.'

'Do you object to my taking it?'

'No.'

'Then where is it?'

'What is your name?' he asked sharply.

I was surprised at this question. It had no bearing on my own conversation but I did not notice its irrelevance because I was shocked to realise that, simple as it was, I could not answer it. I did not know my name, did not remember who I was. I was not certain where I had come from or what my business was in that room. I found I was sure of nothing save my search for the black box. But I knew that the other man's name was Mathers and that he had been killed with a pump and a spade. I had no name.

'I have no name,' I replied.

'Then how could I tell you where the box was if you could not sign a receipt? That would be most irregular. I might as well give it to the west wind or to the smoke from a pipe. How could you execute an important Bank document?'

'I can always get a name,' I replied. 'Doyle or Spaldman is a good name and so is O'Sweeny and Hardiman and O'Gara. I can take my choice. I am not tied down for life to one word like most people.'

'I do not care much for Doyle,' he said absently.

The name is Bari. Signor Bari, the eminent tenor. Five hundred thousand people crowded the great piazza when the great artist appeared on the balcony of St. Peter's Rome.

Fortunately these remarks were not audible in the ordinary sense of the word. Old Mathers was eyeing me.

'What is your colour?' he asked.

'My colour?'

'Surely you know you have a colour?'

'People often remark on my red face.'

'I do not mean that at all.'

Follow this closely, this is bound to be extremely interesting. Very edifying also.

I saw it was necessary to question old Mathers carefully.

'Do you refuse to explain this question about the colours?'

'No,' he said. He slapped more tea in his cup.

'No doubt you are aware that the winds have colours,' he said. I thought he settled himself more restfully in his chair and changed his face till it looked a little bit benign.

'I never noticed it.'

'A record of this belief will be found in the literature of all ancient peoples.[4] There are four winds and eight sub-winds, each with its own colour. The wind from the east is a deep purple, from the south a fine shining silver. The north wind is a hard black and the west is amber. People in the old days had the power of perceiving these colours and could spend a day sitting quietly on a hillside watching the beauty of the winds, their fall and rise and changing hues, the magic of neighbouring winds when they are interweaved like ribbons at a wedding. It was a better occupation than gazing at newspapers. The sub-winds had colours of indescribable delicacy, a reddish-yellow half-way between silver and purple, a greyish-green which was related equally to black and brown. What could be more exquisite than a countryside swept lightly by cool rain reddened by the south-west breeze!'

'Can *you* see these colours?' I asked.

'No.'

'You were asking me what my colour was. How do people get their colours?'

'A person's colour,' he answered slowly, 'is the colour of the wind prevailing at his birth.'

'What is your own colour?'

'Light yellow.'

'And what is the point of knowing your colour or having a colour at all?'

'For one thing you can tell the length of your life from it. Yellow means a long life and the lighter the better.'

This is very edifying, every sentence a sermon in itself. Ask him to explain.

---

4 It is not clear whether de Selby had heard of this but he suggests (*Garcia*, p. 12) that night, far from being caused by the commonly accepted theory of planetary movements, was due to accumulations of 'black air' produced by certain volcanic activities of which he does not treat in detail. See also p. 79 and 945, *Country Album*. Le Fournier's comment (in *Homme ou Dieu*) is interesting. 'On ne saura jamais jusqu'à quel point de Selby fut cause de la Grande Guerre, mais, sans aucun doute, ses théories excentriques—spécialement celle que nuit n'est pas un phénomène de nature, mais dans l'atmosphère un état malsain amené par un industrialisme cupide et sans pitié—auraient l'effet de produire un trouble profond dans les masses.'

'Please explain.'

'It is a question of making little gowns,' he said informatively.

'Little gowns?'

'Yes. When I was born there was a certain policeman present who had the gift of wind-watching. The gift is getting very rare these days. Just after I was born he went outside and examined the colour of the wind that was blowing across the hill. He had a secret bag with him full of certain materials and bottles and he had tailor's instruments also. He was outside for about ten minutes. When he came in again he had a little gown in his hand and he made my mother put it on me.'

'Where did he get this gown?' I asked in surprise.

'He made it himself secretly in the backyard, very likely in the cow-house. It was very thin and slight like the very finest of spider's muslin. You would not see it at all if you held it against the sky but at certain angles of the light you might at times accidentally notice the edge of it. It was the purest and most perfect manifestation of the outside skin of light yellow. This yellow was the colour of my birth-wind.'

'I see,' I said.

A very beautiful conception.

'Every time my birthday came,' old Mathers said, 'I was presented with another little gown of the same identical quality except that it was put on over the other one and not in place of it. You may appreciate the extreme delicacy and fineness of the material when I tell you that even at five years old with five of these gowns together on me, I still appeared to be naked. It was, however, an unusual yellowish sort of nakedness. Of course there was no objection to wearing other clothes over the gown. I usually wore an overcoat. But every year I got a new gown.'

'Where did you get them?' I asked.

'From the police. They were brought to my own home until I was big enough to call to the barracks for them.'

'And how does all this enable you to predict your span of life?'

'I will tell you. No matter what your colour is, it will be represented faithfully in your birth-gown. With each year and each gown, the colour will get deeper and more pronounced. In my own case I had attained a bright full-blown yellow at fifteen although the colour was so light at birth as to be imperceptible. I am now nearing seventy and the colour is a light brown. As my gowns come to me through the years ahead, the colour will deepen to dark brown, then a dull mahogany and from that ultimately to that very dark sort of brownness one associates usually with stout.'

'Yes?'

'In a word the colour gradually deepens gown by gown and year by year until it appears to be black. Finally a day will come when the addition of one further gown will actually achieve real and full blackness. On that day I will die.'

Joe and I were surprised at this. We pondered it in silence, Joe, I thought, seeking to reconcile what he had heard with certain principles he held respecting morality and religion.

'That means,' I said at last, 'that if you get a number of these gowns and put them all on together, reckoning each as a year of life, you can ascertain the year of your death?'

'Theoretically, yes,' he replied, 'but there are two difficulties. First of all the police refuse to let you have the gowns together on the ground that the general ascertainment of death-days would be contrary to the public interest. They talk of breaches of the peace and so forth. Secondly, there is a difficulty about stretching.'

'Stretching?'

'Yes. Since you will be wearing as a grown man the tiny gown that fitted you when you were born, it is clear that the gown has stretched until it is perhaps one hundred times as big as it was originally. Naturally this will affect the colour, making it many times rarer than it was. Similarly there will be a proportionate stretch and a corresponding diminution in colour in all the gowns up to manhood—perhaps twenty or so in all.'

I wonder whether it can be taken that this accretion of gowns will have become opaque at the incidence of puberty.

I reminded him that there was always an overcoat.

'I take it, then,' I said to old Mathers, 'that when you say you can tell the length of life, so to speak, from the colour of your shirt, you mean that you can tell roughly whether you will be long-lived or short-lived?'

'Yes,' he replied. 'But if you use your intelligence you can make a very accurate forecast. Naturally some colours are better than others. Some of them, like purple or maroon, are very bad and always mean an early grave. Pink, however, is excellent, and there is a lot to be said for certain shades of green and blue. The prevalence of such colours at birth, however, usually connote a wind that brings bad

weather—thunder and lightning, perhaps—and there might be difficulties such, for instance, as getting a woman to come in time. As you
know, most good things in life are associated with certain disadvan-
tages.'

Really very beautiful, everything considered.

'Who are these policemen?' I asked.

'There is Sergeant Pluck and another man called MacCruiskeen
and there is a third man called Fox that disappeared twenty-five years
ago and was never heard of after. The first two are down in the barracks and so far as I know they have been there for hundreds of years.
They must be operating on a very rare colour, something that ordinary
eyes could not see at all. There is no white wind that I know of. They
all have the gift of seeing the winds.

A bright thought came to me when I heard of these policemen. If
they knew so much they would have no difficulty in telling me where
I would find the black box. I began to think I would never be happy
until I had that box again in my grip. I looked at old Mathers. He had
relapsed again to his former passivity. The light had faded from his
eyes and the right hand resting on the table looked quite dead.

'Is the barracks far?' I asked loudly.

'No.'

I made up my mind to go there with no delay. Then I noticed a
very remarkable thing. The lamplight, which in the beginning had
been shining forlornly in the old man's corner only, had now grown
rich and yellow and flooded the entire room. The outside light of
morning had faded away almost to nothingness. I glanced out of the
window and gave a start. Coming into the room I had noticed that
the window was to the east and that the sun was rising in that quarter
and firing the heavy clouds with light. Now it was setting with last
glimmers of feeble red in exactly the same place. It had risen a bit,
stopped, and then gone back. Night had come. The policemen would
be in bed. I was sure I had fallen among strange people. I made up
my mind to go to the barracks the first thing on the morrow. Then I
turned again to old Mathers.

'Would you object,' I said to him, 'if I went upstairs and occupied
one of your beds for the night? It is too late to go home and I think it
is going to rain in any case.'

'No,' he said.

I left him bent at his teaset and went up the stairs. I had got to like him and thought it was a pity he had been murdered. I felt relieved and simplified and certain that I would soon have the black box. But I would not ask the policemen openly about it at first. I would be crafty. In the morning I would go to the barracks and report the theft of my American gold watch. Perhaps it was this lie which was responsible for the bad things that happened to me afterwards. I had no American gold watch.

V

The long and unprecedented conversation I had with Policeman Mac-Cruiskeen after I went in to him on my mission with the cigarette brought to my mind afterwards several of the more delicate speculations of de Selby, notably his investigation of the nature of time and eternity by a system of mirrors.[1] His theory as I understand it is as follows:

If a man stands before a mirror and sees in it his reflection, what he sees is not a true reproduction of himself but a picture of himself when he was a younger man. De Selby's explanation of this phenomenon is quite simple. Light, as he points out truly enough, has an ascertained and finite rate of travel. Hence before the reflection of any object in a mirror can be said to be accomplished, it is necessary that rays of light should first strike the object and subsequently impinge on the glass, to be thrown back again to the object—to the eyes of a man, for instance. There is therefore an appreciable and calculable interval of time between the throwing by a man of a glance at his own face in a mirror and the registration of the reflected image in his eye.

So far, one may say, so good. Whether this idea is right or wrong, the amount of time involved is so negligible that few reasonable people

[1] Hatchjaw remarks (unconfirmed, however, by Bassett) that throughout the whole ten years that went to the writing of *The Country Album* de Selby was obsessed with mirrors and had recourse to them so frequently that he claimed to have two left hands and to be living in a world arbitrarily bounded by a wooden frame. As time went on he refused to countenance a direct view of anything and had a small mirror permanently suspended at a certain angle in front of his eyes by a wired mechanism of his own manufacture. After he had resorted to this fantastic arrangement, he interviewed visitors with his back to them and with his head inclined towards the ceiling; he was even credited with long walks backwards in crowded thoroughfares. Hatchjaw claims that his statement is supported by the MS. of some three hundred pages of the *Album*, written backwards, 'a circumstance that made necessary the extension of the mirror principle to the bench of the wretched printer.' (*De Selby's Life and Times*, p. 221.) This manuscript cannot now be found.

would argue the point. But de Selby ever loath to leave well enough alone, insists on reflecting the first reflection in a further mirror and professing to detect minute changes in this second image. Ultimately he constructed the familiar arrangement of parallel mirrors, each reflecting diminishing images of an interposed object indefinitely. The interposed object in this case was de Selby's own face and this he claims to have studied backwards through an infinity of reflections by means of 'a powerful glass'. What he states to have seen through his glass is astonishing. He claims to have noticed a growing youthfulness in the reflections of his face according as they receded, the most distant of them—too tiny to be visible to the naked eye—being the face of a beardless boy of twelve, and, to use his own words, 'a countenance of singular beauty and nobility'. He did not succeed in pursuing the matter back to the cradle 'owing to the curvature of the earth and the limitations of the telescope.'

So much for de Selby. I found MacCruiskeen with a red face at the kitchen table panting quietly from all the food he had hidden in his belly. In exchange for the cigarette he gave me searching looks. 'Well, now,' he said.

He lit the cigarette and sucked at it and smiled covertly at me.

'Well, now,' he said again. He had his little lamp beside him on the table and he played his fingers on it.

'That is a fine day,' I said. 'What are you doing with a lamp in the white morning?'

'I can give you a question as good as that,' he responded. 'Can you notify me of the meaning of a bulbul?'

'A bulbul?'

'What would you say a bulbul is?'

This conundrum did not interest me but I pretended to rack my brains and screwed my face in perplexity until I felt it half the size it should be.

'Not one of those ladies who take money?' I said.

'No.'

'Not the brass knobs on a German steam organ?'

'Not the knobs.'

'Nothing to do with the independence of America or such-like?'

'No.'

'A mechanical engine for winding clocks?'

'No.'

'A tumour, or the lather in a cow's mouth, or those elastic articles that ladies wear?'

'Not them by a long chalk.'

'Not an eastern musical instrument played by Arabs?'

He clapped his hands.

'Not that but very near it,' he smiled, 'something next door to it. You are a cordial intelligible man. A bulbul is a Persian nightingale. What do you think of that now?'

'It is seldom I am far out,' I said dryly.

He looked at me in admiration and the two of us sat in silence for a while as if each was very pleased with himself and with the other and had good reason to be.

'You are a B.A. with little doubt?' he questioned.

I gave no direct answer but tried to look big and learned and far from simple in my little chair.

'I think you are a sempiternal man,' he said slowly.

He sat for a while giving the floor a strict examination and then put his dark jaw over to me and began questioning me about my arrival in the parish.

'I do not want to be insidious,' he said, 'but would you inform me about your arrival in the parish? Surely you had a three-speed gear for the hills?'

'I had no three-speed gear,' I responded rather sharply, 'and no two-speed gear and it is also true that I had no bicycle and little or no pump and if I had a lamp itself it would not be necessary if I had no bicycle and there would be no bracket to hang it on.'

'That may be,' said MacCruiskeen, 'but likely you were laughed at on the tricycle?'

'I had neither bicycle nor tricycle and I am not a dentist,' I said with severe categorical thoroughness, 'and I do not believe in the penny-farthing or the scooter, the velocipede or the tandem-tourer.'

MacCruiskeen got white and shaky and gripped my arm and looked at me intensely.

'In my natural puff,' he said at last, in a strained voice, 'I have never encountered a more fantastic epilogue or a queerer story. Surely you are a queer far-fetched man. To my dying night I will not forget this today morning. Do not tell me that you are taking a hand at me?'

'No,' I said.

'Well Great Crikes!'

He got up and brushed his hair with a flat hand back along his skull and looked out of the window for a long interval, his eyes popping and dancing and his face like an empty bag with no blood in it.

Then he walked around to put back the circulation and took a little spear from a place he had on the shelf.

'Put your hand out,' he said.

I put it out idly enough and he held the spear at it. He kept putting it near me and nearer and when he had the bright point of it about half a foot away, I felt a prick and gave a short cry. There was a little bead of my red blood in the middle of my palm.

'Thank you very much,' I said. I felt too surprised to be annoyed with him.

'That will make you think,' he remarked in triumph, 'unless I am an old Dutchman by profession and nationality.'

He put his little spear back on the shelf and looked at me crookedly from a sidewise angle with a certain quantity of what may be called *roi-s' amuse.*

'Maybe you can explain that?' he said.

'That is the limit,' I said wonderingly.

'It will take some analysis,' he said, 'intellectually.'

'Why did your spear sting when the point was half a foot away from where it made me bleed?'

'That spear,' he answered quietly, 'is one of the first things I ever manufactured in my spare time. I think only a little of it now but the year I made it I was proud enough and would not get up in the morning for any sergeant. There is no other spear like it in the length and breadth of Ireland and there is only one thing like it in Amurikey but I have not heard what it is. But I cannot get over the no-bicycle. Great Crikes!'

'But the spear,' I insisted, 'give me the gist of it like a good man and I will tell no one.'

'I will tell you because you are a confidential man,' he said, 'and a man that said something about bicycles that I never heard before. What you think is the point is not the point at all but only the beginning of the sharpness.'

'Very wonderful,' I said, 'but I do not understand you.'

'The point is seven inches long and it is so sharp and thin that you cannot see it with the old eye. The first half of the sharpness is thick and strong but you cannot see it either because the real sharpness runs into it and if you saw the one you could see the other or maybe you would notice the joint.'

'I suppose it is far thinner than a match?' I asked.

'There *is* a difference,' he said. 'Now the proper sharp part is so thin that nobody could see it no matter what light is on it or what eye is looking. About an inch from the end it is so sharp that sometimes— late at night or on a soft bad day especially—you cannot think of it or try to make it the subject of a little idea because you will hurt your box with the excruciation of it.'

I gave a frown and tried to make myself look like a wise person who was trying to comprehend something that called for all his wisdom.

'You cannot have fire without bricks,' I said, nodding.

'Wisely said,' MacCruiskeen answered.

'It was sharp sure enough,' I conceded, 'it drew a little bulb of the red blood but I did not feel the pricking hardly at all. It must be very sharp to work like that.'

MacCruiskeen gave a laugh and sat down again at the table and started putting on his belt.

'You have not got the whole gist of it at all,' he smiled. 'Because what gave you the prick and brought the blood was not the point at all; it was the place I am talking about that is a good inch from the reputed point of the article under our discussion."

'And what is this inch that is left?' I asked. 'What in heaven's name would you call that?'

'That is the real point,' said MacCruiskeen, 'but it is so thin that it could go into your hand and out in the other extremity externally and you would not feel a bit of it and you would see nothing and hear nothing. It is so thin that maybe it does not exist at all and you could spend half an hour trying to think about it and you could put no thought around it in the end. The beginning part of the inch is thicker than the last part and is nearly there for a fact but I don't think it is if it is my private opinion that you are anxious to enlist.'

I fastened my fingers around my jaw and started to think with great concentration, calling into play parts of my brain that I rarely used. Nevertheless I made no progress at all as regards the question of the points. MacCruiskeen had been at the dresser a second time and was back at the table with a little black article like a leprechaun's piano with diminutive keys of white and black and brass pipes and circular revolving cogs like parts of a steam engine or the business end of a thrashing-mill. His white hands were moving all over it and feeling it as if they were trying to discover some tiny lump on it, and his face was looking up in the air in a spiritual attitude and he was paying no attention to my personal existence at all. There was an overpowering tremendous silence as if the roof of the room had come down half-way to the floor, he at his queer occupation with the instrument and myself still trying to comprehend the sharpness of the points and to get the accurate understanding of them.

After ten minutes he got up and put the thing away. He wrote for a time in his notebook and then lit his pipe.

'Well now,' he remarked expansively.

'Those points,' I said.

'Did I happen to ask you what a bulbul is?'

'You did,' I responded, 'but the question of those points is what takes me to the fair.'

'It is not today or yesterday I started pointing spears,' he said, 'but maybe you would like to see something else that is a medium fair example of supreme art?'

'I would indeed,' I answered.

'But I cannot get over what you confided in me privately *sub-rosa* about the no-bicycle, that is a story that would make your golden fortune if you wrote down in a book where people could pursue it literally.'

He walked back to the dresser, opened the lower part of it, and took out a little chest till he put it on the table for my inspection. Never in my life did I inspect anything more ornamental and well-made. It was a brown chest like those owned by seafaring men or lascars from Singapore, but it was diminutive in a very perfect way as if you were looking at a full-size one through the wrong end of a spy-glass. It was about a foot in height, perfect in its proportions and without fault in workmanship. There were indents and carving and fanciful excoriations and designs on every side of it and there was a bend on the lid that gave the article great distinction. At every corner there was a shiny brass corner-piece and on the lid there were brass corner-pieces beautifully wrought and curved impeccably against the wood. The whole thing had the dignity and the satisfying quality of true art.

'There now,' said MacCruiskeen.

'It is nearly too nice,' I said at last, 'to talk about it.'

'I spent two years manufacturing it when I was a lad,' said Mac-Cruiskeen, 'and it still takes me to the fair.'

'It is unmentionable,' I said.

'Very nearly,' said MacCruiskeen.

The two of us then started looking at it and we looked at it for five minutes so hard that it seemed to dance on the table and look even smaller that it might be.

'I do not often look at boxes or chests,' I said, simply, 'but this is the most beautiful box I have ever seen and I will always remember it. There might be something inside it?'

'There might be,' said MacCruiskeen.

He went to the table and put his hands around the article in a fawning way as if he were caressing a sheepdog and he opened the lid with a little key but shut it down again before I could inspect the inside of it.

'I will tell you a story and give you a synopsis of the ramification of the little plot,' he said. 'When I had the chest made and finished, I tried to think what I would keep in it and what I would use it for at all. First I thought of them letters from Bridie, the ones on the blue paper with the strong smell but I did not think it would be anything but a sacrilege in the end because there was hot bits in them letters. Do you comprehend the trend of my observations?'

'I do,' I answered.

'Then there was my studs and the enamel badge and my presentation iron-pencil with a screw on the end of it to push the point out, an intricate article full of machinery and a Present from Southport. All these things are what are called Examples of the Machine Age.'

'They would be contrary to the spirit of the chest,' I said.

'They would be indeed. Then there was my razor and the spare plate in case I was presented with an accidental bash on the gob in the execution of me duty . . .'

'But not them.'

'Not them. Then there was my certificates and me cash and the picture of Peter the Hermit and the brass thing with straps that I found on the road one night near Matthew O'Carahan's. But not them either.'

'It is a hard conundrum,' I said.

'In the end I found there was only one thing to do to put myself right with my private conscience.'

'It is a great thing that you found the right answer at all,' I countered.

'I decided to myself,' said MacCruiskeen, 'that the only sole correct thing to contain in the chest was another chest of the same make but littler in cubic dimension.'

'That was very competent masterwork,' I said, endeavouring to speak his own language.

He went to the little chest and opened it up again and put his hands down sideways like flat plates or like the fins on a fish and took out of it a smaller chest but one resembling its mother-chest in every particular of appearance and dimension. It almost interfered with my breathing, it was so delightfully unmistakable. I went over and felt it and covered it with my hand to see how big its smallness was. Its brasswork had a shine like the sun on the sea and the colour of the wood was a rich deep richness like a colour deepened and toned only by the years. I got slightly weak from looking at it and sat down on a chair and for the purpose of pretending that I was not disturbed I whistled *The Old Man Twangs His Braces.*

MacCruiskeen gave me a smooth inhuman smile.

'You may have come on no bicycle,' he said, 'but that does not say that you know everything.'

'Those chests,' I said, 'are so like one another that I do not believe they are there at all because that is a simpler thing to believe than the contrary. Nevertheless the two of them are the most wonderful two things I have ever seen.'

'I was two years manufacturing it,' MacCruiskeen said.

'What is in the little one?' I asked.

'What would you think now?'

'I am completely half afraid to think,' I said, speaking truly enough.

'Wait now till I show you,' said MacCruiskeen, 'and give you an exhibition and a personal inspection individually.'

He got two thin butter-spades from the shelf and put them down into the little chest and pulled out something that seemed to me remarkably like another chest. I went over to it and gave it a close examination with my hand, feeling the same identical wrinkles, the same proportions and the same completely perfect brasswork on a smaller scale. It was so faultless and delightful that it reminded me forcibly, strange and foolish as it may seem, of something I did not understand and had never even heard of.

'Say nothing,' I said quickly to MacCruiskeen, 'but go ahead with what you are doing and I will watch here and I will take care to be sitting down.'

He gave me a nod in exchange for my remark and got two straight-handled teaspoons and put the handles into his last chest. What came out may well be guessed at. He opened this one and took another one out with the assistance of two knives. He worked knives, small knives and smaller knives, till he had twelve little chests on the table, the last of them an article half the size of a matchbox. It was so tiny that you would not quite see the brasswork at all only for the glitter of it in the light. I did not see whether it had the same identical carvings upon it because I was content to take a swift look at it and then turn away. But I knew in my soul that it was exactly the same as the others. I said no word at all because my mind was brimming with wonder at the skill of the policeman.

'That last one,' said MacCruiskeen, putting away the knives, 'took me three years to make and it took me another year to believe that I had made it. Have you got the convenience of a pin?'

I gave him my pin in silence. He opened the smallest of them all with a key like a piece of hair and worked with the pin till he had another little chest on the table, thirteen in all arranged in a row upon the table. Queerly enough they looked to me as if they were all the same size but invested with some crazy perspective. This idea surprised me so much that I got my voice back and said:

'These are the most surprising thirteen things I have ever seen together.'

'Wait now, man,' MacCruiskeen said.

All my senses were now strained so tensely watching the policeman's movements that I could almost hear my brain rattling in my head when I gave a shake as if it was drying up into a wrinkled pea. He was manipulating and prodding with his pin till he had twenty-eight little chests on the table and the last of them so small that it looked like a bug or a tiny piece of dirt except that there was a glitter from it. When I looked at it again I saw another thing beside it like something you would take out of a red eye on a windy dry day and I knew then that the strict computation was then twenty-nine.

'Here is your pin,' said MacCruiskeen.

He put it into my stupid hand and went back to the table thought-fully. He took a something from his pocket that was too small for me to see and started working with the tiny black thing on the table beside the bigger thing which was itself too small to be described.

At this point I became afraid. What he was doing was no longer wonderful but terrible. I shut my eyes and prayed that he would stop while still doing things that were at least possible for a man to do. When I looked again I was happy that there was nothing to see and that he had put no more of the chests prominently on the table but he was working to the left with the invisible thing in his hand on a bit of the table itself. When he felt my look he came over to me and gave me an enormous magnifying-glass which looked like a basin fixed to a handle. I felt the muscles around my heart tightening painfully as I took the instrument.

'Come over here to the table,' he said, 'and look there till you see what you see infra-ocularly.'

When I saw the table it was bare only for the twenty-nine chest articles but through the agency of the glass I was in a position to re-port that he had two more out beside the last ones, the smallest of all being nearly half a size smaller than ordinary invisibility. I gave him back the glass instrument and took to the chair without a word. In order to reassure myself and make a loud human noise I whistled the *Corncrake Plays the Bagpipes*.

'There now,' said MacCruiskeen.

He took two wrinkled cigarettes from his fob and lit the two at the same time and handed me one of them.

'Number Twenty-Two,' he said, 'I manufactured fifteen years ago and I have made another different one every year since with any amount of nightwork and overtime and piece-work and time-and-a-half incidentally.'

'I understand you clearly,' I said.

'Six years ago they began to get invisible, glass or no glass. Nobody has ever seen the last five I made because no glass is strong enough to make them big enough to be regarded truly as the smallest things ever made. Nobody can see me making them because my little tools are invisible into the same bargain. The one I am making now is nearly as small as nothing. Number One would hold a million of them at the same time and there would be room left for a pair of woman's horse-breeches if they were rolled up. The dear knows where it will stop and terminate.'

'Such work must be very hard on the eyes,' I said, determined to pretend that everybody was an ordinary person like myself.

'Some of these days,' he answered, 'I will have to buy spectacles with gold ear-claws. My eyes are crippled with the small print in the newspapers and in the offeecial forms.'

'Before I go back to the day-room,' I said, 'would it be right to ask you what you were performing with that little small piano-instrument, the article with the knobs, and the brass pins?'

'That is my personal musical instrument,' said MacCruiskeen, 'and I was playing my own tunes on it in order to extract private satisfaction from the sweetness of them.'

'I was listening,' I answered, 'but I did not succeed in hearing you.'

'That does not surprise me intuitively,' said MacCruiskeen, 'because it is an indigenous patent of my own. The vibrations of the true notes are so high in their fine frequencies that they cannot be appreciated by the human ear-cup. Only myself has the secret of the thing and the intimate way of it, the confidential knack of circumventing it. Now what do you think of that?'

I climbed up to my legs to go back to the day-room, passing a hand weakly about my brow.

'I think it is extremely acatalectic,' I answered.

IX

I was awakened the following morning by sounds of loud hammering[1]

[1] Le Clerque (in his almost forgotten *Extensions and Analyses*) has drawn attention to the importance of percussion in the de Selby dialectic and shown that most of the physicist's experiments were extremely noisy. Unfortunately the hammering was always done behind locked doors and no commentator has hazarded even a guess as to what was being hammered and for what purpose. Even when constructing the famous water-box, probably the most delicate and fragile instrument ever made by human hands, de Selby is known to have smashed three heavy coal-hammers and was involved in undignified legal proceedings with his landlord (the notorious Porter) arising from an allegation of strained floor-joists and damage to a ceiling. It is clear that he attached considerable importance to 'hammerwork' (v. *Golden Hours*, p. 48–9). In *The Layman's Atlas* he publishes a rather obscure account of his inquiries into the nature of hammering and boldly attributes the sharp sound of percussion to the bursting of 'atmosphere balls' evidently envisaging the air as being composed of minute balloons, a view scarcely confirmed by later scientific research. In his disquisitions elsewhere on the nature of night and darkness, he refers in passing to the straining of 'air-skins', *al.* 'air-balls' and 'bladders'. His conclusion was

outside the window and found myself immediately recalling—the recollection was an absurd paradox—that I had been in the next world yesterday. Lying there half awake, it is not unnatural that my thoughts should turn to de Selby. Like all the great thinkers, he has been looked to for guidance on many of the major perplexities of existence. The commentators, it is to be feared, have not succeeded in extracting from the vast store-house of his writings any consistent, cohesive or comprehensive corpus of spiritual belief and praxis. Nevertheless, his ideas of paradise are not without interest. Apart from the contents of the famous de Selby 'Codex',[2] the main references are to

---

that 'hammering is anything but what it appears to be'; such a statement, if not open to explicit refutation, seems unnecessary and unenlightening.

Hatchjaw has put forward the suggestion that loud hammering was a device resorted to by the savant to drown other noises which might give some indication of the real trend of the experiments. Bassett has concurred in this view, with, however, two reservations.

[2] The reader will be familiar with the storms which have raged over this most tantalising of holograph survivals. The 'Codex' (first so-called by Bassett in his monumental *De Selby Compendium*) is a collection of some two thousand sheets of foolscap closely hand-written on both sides. The signal distinction of the manuscript is that not one word of the writing is legible. Attempts made by different commentators to decipher certain passages which look less formidable than others have been characterised by fantastic divergencies, not in the meaning of the passages (of which there is no question) but in the brand of nonsense which is evolved. One passage, described by Bassett as being 'a penetrating treatise on old age' is referred to by Henderson (biographer of Bassett) as 'a not unbeautiful description of lambing operations on an unspecified farm'. Such disagreement, it must be confessed, does little to enhance the reputation of either writer.

Hatchjaw, probably displaying more astuteness than scholastic acumen, again advances his forgery theory and professes amazement that any person of intelligence could be deluded by 'so crude an imposition'. A curious contretempts arose when, challenged by Bassett to substantiate this cavalier pronouncement, Hatchjaw casually mentioned that eleven pages of the 'Codex' were all numbered '88'. Bassett, evidently taken by surprise, performed an independent check and could discover no page at all bearing this number. Subsequent wrangling disclosed the startling fact that both commentators claimed to have in their personal possession the 'only genuine Codex'. Before this dispute could be cleared up, there was a further bombshell, this time from far-off Hamburg. The Norddeutsche Verlag published a book by the shadowy Kraus purporting to be an elaborate exegesis based on an authentic copy of the 'Codex' with a transliteration of what was described as the obscure code in which the document was written. If Kraus can be believed, the portentously-named 'Codex' is simply a collection of extremely puerile maxims on love, life, mathematics and the like, couched in poor ungrammatical English and entirely lacking de Selby's characteristic reconditeness and obscurity. Bassett and many of the other commentators, regarding this extraordinary book as merely another manifestation of the mordant du Garbandier's spleen, pretended never to have heard of it notwithstanding the fact that Bassett is known to have obtained, presumably by questionable means, a proof of the work many months before it appeared. Hatchjaw alone did not ignore the book. Remarking dryly in a newspaper article that Kraus's 'aberration' was due to a foreigner's confusion of the two English words code and codex, he declared his intention

be found in the *Rural Atlas* and in the so-called 'substantive' appendices to the *Country Album*. Briefly he indicates that the happy state is 'not unassociated with water' and that 'water is rarely absent from any wholly satisfactory situation'. He does not give any closer definition of this hydraulic elysium but mentions that he has written more fully on the subject elsewhere.[3] It is not clear, unfortunately, whether the reader is expected to infer that a wet day is more enjoyable than a dry one or that a lengthy course of baths is a reliable method of achieving peace of mind. He praises the equilibrium of water, its circumambiency, equiponderance and equitableness, and declares that water, 'if not abused,'[4] can achieve 'absolute superiority.' For the rest, little remains save the record of his obscure and unwitnessed experiments. The story is one of a long succession of prosecutions for water wastage at the suit of the local authority. At one hearing it was shown that he

---

of publishing 'a brief brochure' which would effectively discredit the German's work and all similar 'trumpery frauds'. The failure of this work to appear is popularly attributed to Kraus's machinations in Hamburg and lengthy sessions on the transcontinental wire. In any event, the wretched Hatchjaw was again arrested, this time at the suit of his own publishers who accused him of the larceny of some of the firm's desk fittings. The case was adjourned and subsequently struck out owing to the failure to appear of certain unnamed witnesses from abroad. Clear as it is that this fantastic charge was without a vestige of foundation, Hatchjaw failed to obtain any redress from the authorities.

It cannot be pretended that the position regarding this 'Codex' is at all satisfactory and it is not likely that time or research will throw any fresh light on a document which cannot be read and of which four copies at least, all equally meaningless, exist in the name of being the genuine original.

An amusing diversion in this affair was unwittingly caused by the mild Le Clerque. Hearing of the 'Codex' some months before Bassett's authoritative 'Compendium' was published, he pretended to have read the 'Codex' and in an article in the *Zuercher Tageblatt* made many vague comments on it, referring to its 'shrewdness', 'compelling if novel arguments', 'fresh viewpoint', etc. Subsequently he repudiated the article and asked Hatchjaw in a private letter to denounce it as a forgery. Hatchjaw's reply is not extant but it is thought that he refused with some warmth to be party to any further hanky-panky in connection with the ill-starred 'Codex'. It is perhaps unnecessary to refer to du Garbandier's contribution to this question. He contented himself with an article in *l'Avenir* in which he professed to have decyphered the 'Codex' and found it to be a repository of obscene conundrums, accounts of amorous adventures and erotic speculation, 'all too lamentable to be repeated even in broad outline'.

3 Thought to be a reference to the 'Codex'.

4 Naturally, no explanation is given of what is meant by 'abusing' water but it is noteworthy that the savant spent several months trying to discover a satisfactory method of 'diluting' water, holding that it was 'too strong' for many of the novel uses to which he desired to put it. Bassett suggests that the de Selby Water Box was invented for this purpose although he cannot explain how the delicate machinery is set in motion. So many fantastic duties have assigned to this inscrutable mechanism (witness Kraus's absurd sausage theory) that Bassett's speculation must not be allowed the undue weight which his authoritative standing would tend to lend it.

had used 9,000 gallons in one day and on another occasion almost 80,000 gallons in the course of a week. The word 'used' in this context is the important one. The local officials, having checked the volume of water entering the house daily from the street connection, had sufficient curiosity to watch the outlet sewer and made the astonishing discovery that *none of the vast quantity of water drawn in ever left the house.* The commentators have seized avidly on this statistic but are, as usual, divided in their interpretations. In Bassett's view the water was treated in the patent water-box and diluted to a degree that made it invisible—in the guise of water, at all events—to the untutored watchers at the sewer. Hatchjaw's theory in this regard is more acceptable. He tends to the view that the water was boiled and converted, probably through the water-box, into tiny jets of steam which were projected through an upper window into the night in an endeavor to wash the black 'volcanic' stains from the 'skins' or 'air-bladders' of the atmosphere and thus dissipate the hated and 'insanitary' night. However far-fetched this theory may appear, unexpected colour is lent to it by a previous court case when the physicist was fined forty shillings. On this occasion, some two years before the construction of the water-box, de Selby was charged with playing a fire hose out of one of the upper windows of his house at night, an operation which resulted in several passers-by being drenched to the skin. On another occasion[5] he had to face the curious charge of hoarding water, the police testifying that every vessel in his house, from the bath down to a set of three ornamental egg-cups, was brimming with the liquid. Again a trumped-up charge of attempted suicide was preferred merely because the savant had accidentally half-drowned himself in a quest for some vital statistics of celestial aquatics.

It is clear from contemporary newspapers that his inquiries into water were accompanied by persecutions and legal pin-prickings un-

[5] Almost all of the numerous petty litigations in which de Selby was involved afford a salutary example of the humiliations which great minds may suffer when forced to have contact with the pedestrian intellects of the unperceiving laity. On one of the water-wastage hearings the Bench permitted itself a fatuous inquiry as to why the defendant did not avail himself of the metered industrial rate 'if bathing is to be persisted in so immoderately'. It was on this occasion that de Selby made the famous retort that 'one does not readily accept the view that paradise is limited by the capacity of a municipal waterworks or human happiness by water-meters manufactured by unemancipated labour in Holland.' It is some consolation to recall that the forcible medical examination which followed was characterised by an enlightenment which redounds to this day to the credit of the medical profession. De Selby's discharge was unconditional and absolute.

paralleled since the days of Galileo. It may be some consolation to the minions responsible to know that their brutish and barbaric machinations succeeded in denying posterity a clear record of the import of these experiments and perhaps a primer of esoteric water science that would banish much of our worldly pain and unhappiness. Virtually all that remains of de Selby's work in this regard is his house where his countless taps[6] are still as he left them, though a newer generation of more delicate mind has had the water turned off at the main.

Water? The word was in my ear as well as in my brain. Rain was beginning to beat on the windows, not a soft or friendly rain but large angry drops which came spluttering with great force upon the glass. The sky was grey and stormy and out of it I heard the harsh shouts of wild geese and ducks labouring across the wind on their coarse pinions. Black quails called sharply from their hidings and a swollen stream was babbling dementedly. Trees, I knew, would be angular and ill-tempered in the rain and boulders would gleam coldly at the eye.

I would have sought sleep again without delay were it not for the loud hammering outside. I arose and went on the cold floor to the window. Outside there was a man with sacks on his shoulders hammering at a wooden framework he was erecting in the barrack yard. He was red-faced and strong-armed and limped around his work with enormous stiff strides. His mouth was full of nails which bristled like steel fangs in the shadow of his moustache. He extracted them one by one as I watched and hammered them perfectly into the wet wood. He paused to test a beam with his great strength and accidentally let the hammer fall. He stooped awkwardly and picked it up.

Did you notice anything?

No.

The Hammer, man.

It looks like an ordinary hammer. What about it?

---

[6] Hatchjaw (in his invaluable *Conspectus of the de Selby Dialetic*) has described the house as 'the most water-piped edifice in the world.' Even in the living-rooms there were upwards of ten rough farmyard taps, some with zinc troughs and some (as those projecting from the ceiling and from converted gas-brackets near the fireplace) directed at the unprotected floor. Even on the stairs a three-inch main may still be seen nailed along the rail of the balustrade with a tap at intervals of one foot, while under the stairs and in every conceivable hiding-place there were elaborate arrangements of cisterns and storage-tanks. Even the gas pipes were connected up with this water system and would gush strongly at any attempt to provide the light.

Du Garbandier in this connection has permitted himself some coarse and cynical observations bearing upon cattle lairages.

You must be blind. It fell on his foot.

Yes?

And he didn't bat an eyelid. It might have been a feather for all the sign he gave.

Here I gave a sharp cry of perception and immediately threw up the sash of the window and leaned out into the inhospitable day, hailing the workman excitedly. He looked at me curiously and came over with a friendly frown of interrogation on his face.

'What is your name?' I asked him.

'O'Feersa, the middle brother,' he answered. 'Will you come out here,' he continued, 'and give me a hand with the wet carpentry?'

'Have you a wooden leg?'

For answer he dealt his left thigh a mighty blow with the hammer. It echoed hollowly in the rain. He cupped his hand clownishly at his ear as if listening intently to the noise he had made. Then he smiled.

'I am building a high scaffold here,' he said, 'and it is lame work where the ground is bumpy. I could find use for the assistance of a competent assistant.'

'Do you know Martin Finnucane?'

He raised his hand in a military salute and nodded.

'He is almost a relation,' he said, 'but not completely. He is closely related to my cousin but they never married, never had the time.'

Here I knocked my own leg sharply on the wall.

'Did you hear that?' I asked him.

He gave a start and then shook my hand and looked brotherly and loyal, asking me was it the left or the right?

Scribble a note and send him for assistance. There is no time to lose.

I did so at once, asking Martin Finnucane to come and save me in the nick of time from being strangled to death on the scaffold and telling him he would have to hurry. I did not know whether he could come as he had promised he would but in my present danger anything was worth trying.

I saw Mr O'Feersa going quickly away through the mists and threading his path carefully through the sharp winds which were racing through the fields, his head down, sacks on his shoulders and resolution in his heart.

Then I went back to bed to try to forget my anxiety. I said a prayer that neither of the other brothers was out on the family bicycle because it would be wanted to bring my message quickly to the captain of the one-legged men [Martin Finnucane]. Then I felt a hope kindling fitfully within me and I fell asleep again.

X

When I awoke again two thoughts came into my head so closely together that they seemed to be stuck to one another; I could not be sure which came first and it was hard to separate them and examine them singly. One was a happy thought about the weather, the sudden brightness of the day that had been vexed earlier. The other was suggesting to me that it was not the same day at all but a different one and maybe not even the next day after the angry one. I could not decide that question and did not try to. I lay back and took to my habit of gazing out of the window. Whichever day it was, it was a gentle day—mild, magical and innocent with great sailings of white cloud serene and impregnable in the high sky, moving along like kingly swans on quiet water. The sun was in the neighbourhood also, distributing his enchantment unobtrusively, colouring the sides of things that were unalive and livening the hearts of living things. The sky was a light blue without distance, neither near nor far. I could gaze at it, through it and beyond it and see still illimitably clearer and nearer the delicate lie of its nothingness. A bird sang a solo from nearby, a cunning blackbird in a dark hedge giving thanks in his native language. I listened and agreed with him completely.

Then other sounds came to me from the nearby kitchen. The policemen were up and about their incomprehensible tasks. A pair of their great boots would clump across the flags, pause and then clump back. The other pair would clump to another place, stay longer and clump back again with heavier falls as if a great weight were being carried. Then the four boots would clump together solidly far away to the front door and immediately would come the long slash of thrown-water on the road, a great bath of it flung in a lump to fall flat on the dry ground.

I arose and started to put on my clothes. Through the window I could see the scaffold of raw timber rearing itself high into the heavens, not as O'Feersa had left it to make his way methodically through the rain, but perfect and ready for its dark destiny. The sight did not make me cry or even sigh. I thought it was sad, too sad. Through the struts of the structure I could see the good country. There would be a fine view from the top of the scaffold on any day but on this day it would be lengthened out by five miles owing to the clearness of the air. To prevent my tears I began to give special attention to my dressing.

When I was nearly finished the Sergeant knocked very delicately at the door, came in with great courtesy and bade me good morning.

'I noticed the other bed has been slept in,' I said for conversation. 'Was it yourself or MacCruiskeen?'

'That would likely be Policeman Fox. MacCruiskeen and I do not do our sleeping here at all, it is too expensive, we would be dead in a week if we played that game.'

'And where do you sleep then?'

'Down below—over there—beyant.'

He gave my eyes the right direction with his brown thumb. It was down the road to where the hidden left turn led to the heaven full of doors and ovens.

'And why?'

'To save our lifetimes, man. Down there you are as young coming out of a sleep as you are going into it and you don't fade when you are inside your sleep, you would not credit the time a suit or a boots will last you and you don't have to take your clothes off either. That's what charms MacCruiskeen—that and the no shaving.' He laughed kindly at the thought of his comrade. 'A comical artist of a man,' he added.

'And Fox? Where does he live?'

'Beyant, I think.' He jerked again to the place that was to the left. 'He is down there beyant somewhere during the daytime but we have never seen him there, he might be in a distinctive portion of it that he found from a separate ceiling in a different house and indeed the unreasonable jumps of the lever-reading would put you in mind that there is unauthorised interference with the works. He is as crazy as bedamned, an incontestable character and a man of ungovernable inexactitudes.'

'Then why does he sleep here?' I was not at all pleased that this ghostly man had been in the same room with me during the night.

'To spend it and spin it out and not have all of it forever unused inside him.'

'All what?'

'His lifetime. He wants to get rid of as much as possible, undertime and overtime, as quickly as he can so that he can die as soon as possible. MacCruiskeen and I are wiser and we are not yet tired of being ourselves, we save it up. I think he has an opinion that there is a turn to the right down the road and likely that is what he is after, he thinks the best way to find it is to die and get all the leftness out of his blood. I do not believe there is a right-hand road and if there is it would surely take a dozen active men to look after the readings alone, night and morning. As you are perfectly aware the right is much more tricky than the left, you would be surprised at all the right pitfalls there are. We are only at the beginning of our knowledge of the right, there is nothing more deceptive to the unwary.'

'I did not know that.'

The Sergeant opened his eyes wide in surprise.

'Did you ever in your life,' he asked, 'mount a bicycle from the right?'

'I did not.'

'And why?'

'I do not know. I never thought about it.'

He laughed at me indulgently.

'It is nearly an insoluble pancake,' he smiled, 'a conundrum of inscrutable potentialities, a snorter.'

He led the way out of the bedroom to the kitchen where he had already arranged my steaming meal of stirabout and milk on the table. He pointed to it pleasantly, made a motion as if lifting a heavily-laden spoon to his mouth and then made succulent spitty sounds with his lips as if they were dealing with the tastiest of all known delicacies. Then he swallowed loudly and put his red hands in ecstasy to his stomach. I sat down and took up the spoon at this encouragement.

'And why is Fox crazy?' I inquired.

'I will tell you that much. In MacCruiskeen's room there is a little box on the mantelpiece. The story is that when MacCruiskeen was away one day that happened to fall on the 23rd of June inquiring about a bicycle, Fox went in and opened the box and looked into it from the strain of his unbearable curiosity. From that day to this . . .'

The Sergeant shook his head and tapped his forehead three times with his finger. Soft as porridge is I nearly choked at the sound his finger made. It was a booming hollow sound, slightly tinny, as if he had tapped an empty watering-can with his nail.

'And what was in the box?'

'That is easily told. A card made of cardboard about the size of a cigarette-card, no better and no thicker.'

'I see,' I said.

I did not see but I was sure that my easy unconcern would sting the Sergeant into an explanation. It came after a time when he had looked at me silently and strangely as I fed solidly at the table.

'It was the colour,' he said.

'The colour?'

'But then maybe it was not that at all,' he mused perplexedly.

I looked at him with a mild inquiry. He frowned thoughtfully and looked up at a corner of the ceiling as if he expected certain words he was searching for to be hanging there in coloured lights. No sooner had I thought of that than I glanced up myself, half expecting to see them there. But they were not.

'The card was not red,' he said at last doubtfully.

'Green?'

'Not green. No.'

'Then what colour?'

'It was not one of the colours a man carries inside his head like nothing he ever looked at with his eyes. It was ... different. Mac-Cruiskeen says it is not blue either and I believe him, a blue card would never make a man batty because what is blue is natural.'

'I saw colours often on eggs,' I observed, 'colours which have no names. Some birds lay eggs that are shaded in a way too delicate to be noticeable to any instrument but the eye, the tongue could not be troubled to find a noise for anything so nearly not-there. What I would call a green sort of complete white. Now would that be the colour?'

'I am certain it would not,' the Sergeant replied immediately, 'because if birds could lay eggs that would put men out of their wits, you would have no crops at all, nothing but scarecrows crowded in every field like a public meeting and thousands of them in their top hats standing together in knots on the hillsides. It would be a mad world completely, the people would be putting their bicycles upside down on the roads and pedalling them to make enough mechanical movement to frighten the birds out of the whole parish.' He passed a hand in consternation across his brow. 'It would be a very unnatural pancake,' he added.

I thought it was a poor subject for conversation, this new colour.

Apparently its newness was new enough to blast a man's brain to imbecility by the surprise of it. That was enough to know and quite sufficient to be required to believe. I thought it was an unlikely story but not for gold or diamonds would I open that box in the bedroom and look into it.

The Sergeant had wrinkles of pleasant recollection at his eyes and mouth.

'Did you ever in your travels meet with Mr Andy Gara?' he asked me.

'No.'

'He is always laughing to himself, even in bed at night he laughs quietly and if he meets you on the road he will go into roars, it is a most enervating spectacle and very bad for nervous people. It all goes back to a certain day when MacCruiskeen and I were making inquiries about a missing bicycle.'

'Yes?'

'It was a bicycle with a criss-cross frame,' the Sergeant explained, 'and I can tell you that it is not every day in the week that one like that is reported, it is a great rarity and indeed it is a privilege to be looking for a bicycle like that.'

'Andy Gara's bicycle?'

'Not Andy's. Andy was a sensible man at the time but a very curious man and when he had us gone he thought he would do a clever thing. He broke his way into the barrack here in open defiance of the law. He spent valuable hours boarding up the windows and making MacCruiskeen's room as dark as night time. Then he got busy with the box. He wanted to know what the inside of it felt like, even if it could not be looked at. When he put his hand in he let out a great laugh, you could swear he was very amused at something.'

'And what did it feel like?'

The Sergeant shrugged himself massively.

'MacCruiskeen says it is not smooth and not rough, not gritty and not velvety. It would be a mistake to think it is a cold feel like steel and another mistake to think it blankety. I thought it might be like the damp bread of an old poultice but no, MacCruiskeen says that would be a third mistake. And not like a bowl-full of dry withered peas, either. A contrary pancake surely, a fingerish atrocity but not without a queer charm all its own.'

'Not hens' piniony under-wing feeling?' I questioned keenly. The Sergeant shook his head abstractedly.

'But the criss-cross bicycle,' he said, 'it is no wonder it went astray. It was a very confused bicycle and was shared by a man called Barbery with his wife and if you ever laid your eye on big Mrs Barbery I would not require to explain this thing privately to you at all.'

He broke off his utterance in the middle of the last short word of it and stood peering with a wild eye at the table. I had finished eating and had pushed away my empty bowl. Following quickly along the line of his stare, I saw a small piece of folded paper lying on the table where the bowl had been before I moved it. Giving a cry **the** Sergeant sprang forward with surpassing lightness and snatched the paper up. He took it to the window, opened it out and held it far away from him to allow for some disorder in his eye. His face was puzzled and pale and stared at the paper for many minutes. Then he looked out of the window fixedly, tossing the paper over at me. I picked it up and read the roughly printed message:

ONE-LEGGED MEN ON THEIR WAY TO RESCUE PRISONER. MADE A CALCULATION ON TRACKS AND ESTIMATE NUMBER IS SEVEN. SUBMITTED PLEASE.—FOX.

My heart began to pound madly inside me. Looking at the Sergeant I saw that he was still gazing wild-eyed into the middle of the day, which was situated at least five miles away, like a man trying to memorise forever the perfection of the lightly clouded sky and the brown and green and boulder-white of the peerless country. Down some lane of it that ran crookedly through the fields I could see inwardly my seven true brothers hurrying to save me in their lame walk, their stout sticks on the move together.

The Sergeant still kept his eye on the end of five miles away but moved slightly in his monumental standing. Then he spoke to me.

'I think,' he said, 'we will go out and have a look at it, it is a great thing to do what is necessary before it becomes essential and unavoidable.'

The sounds he put on these words were startling and too strange. Each word seemed to rest on a tiny cushion and was soft and far away from every other word. When he had stopped speaking there was a

warm enchanted silence as if the last note of some music too fascinating almost for comprehension had receded and disappeared long
before its absence was truly noticed. He then moved out of the house
before me to the yard, I behind him spellbound with no thought of
any kind in my head. Soon the two of us had mounted a ladder with
staid unhurrying steps and found ourselves high beside the sailing
gable of the barrack, the two of us on the lofty scaffold, I the victim
and he my hangman. I looked blankly and carefully everywhere,
seeing for a time no difference between any different things, inspect-
ing methodically every corner of the same unchanging sameness.
Nearby I could hear his voice murmuring again:

'It is a fine day in any case,' he was saying.

His words, now in the air and out of doors, had another warm
breathless roundness in them as if his tongue was lined with furry
burrs and they came lightly from him like a string of bubbles or like
tiny things borne to me on thistledown in very gentle air. I went forward
to a wooden railing and rested by weighty hands on it, feeling perfectly the breeze coming chillingly at their fine hairs. An idea came
to me that the breezes high above the ground are separate from those
which play on the same level as men's faces: here the air was newer
and more unnatural, nearer the heavens and less laden with the
influences of the earth. Up here I felt that every day would be the
same always, serene and chilly, a band of wind insolating the earth of
men from the far-from-understandable enormities of the girdling universe. Here on the stormiest autumn Monday there would be no
wild leaves to brush on any face, no bees in the gusty wind. I sighed
sadly.

'Strange enlightenments are vouchsafed,' I murmured, 'to those
who seek the higher places.'

I do not know why I said this strange thing. My own words were
also soft and light as if they had no breath to liven them. I heard the
Sergeant working behind me with coarse ropes as if he were at the
far end of a great hall instead of at my back and then I heard his
voice coming back to me softly called across a fathomless valley:

'I heard of a man once,' he said, 'that had himself let up into the
sky in a balloon to make observations, a man of great personal charm
but a devil for reading books. They played out the rope till he was
disappeared completely from all appearances, telescopes or no telescopes, and then they played out another ten miles of rope to make

sure of first-class observations. When the time-limit for the observations was over they pulled down the balloon again but lo and behold there was no man in the basket and his dead body was never found afterwards lying dead or alive in any parish ever afterwards.'

Here I heard myself give a hollow laugh, standing there with a high head and my two hands still on the wooden rail.

'But they were clever enough to think of sending up the balloon again a fortnight later and when they brought it down the second time lo and behold the man was sitting in the basket without a feather out of him if any of my information can be believed at all.'

Here I gave some sound again, hearing my own voice as if I was a bystander at a public meeting where I was myself the main speaker. I had heard the Sergeant's words and understood them thoroughly but they were no more significant than the clear sounds that infest the air at all times—the far cry of gulls, the disturbance a breeze will make in its blowing and water falling headlong down a hill. Down into the earth where dead men go I would go soon and maybe come out of it again in some healthy way, free and innocent of all human perplexity. I would perhaps be the chill of an April wind, an essential part of some indomitable river or be personally concerned in the ageless perfection of some rank mountain bearing down upon the mind by occupying forever a position in the blue easy distance. Or perhaps a smaller thing like movement in the grass on an unbearable breathless yellow day, some hidden creature going about its business —I might well be responsible for that or for some important part of it. Or even those unaccountable distinctions that make an evening recognisable from its own morning, the smells and sounds and sights of the perfected and matured essences of the day, these might not be innocent of my meddling and my abiding presence.

'So they asked where he was and what had kept him but he gave them no satisfaction, he only let out a laugh like one that Andy Gara would give and went home and shut himself up in his house and told his mother to say he was not at home and not receiving visitors or doing any entertaining. That made the people very angry and inflamed their passions to a degree that is not recognised by the law. So they held a private meeting that was attended by every member of the general public except the man in question and they decided to get out their shotguns the next day and break into the man's house and give him a severe threatening and tie him up and heat pokers in the fire to make him tell what happened in the sky the time he was up inside it. That is a nice piece of law and order for you, a terrific indictment of democratic self-government, a beautiful commentary on Home Rule.'

Or perhaps I would be an influence that prevails in water, something sea-borne and far away, some certain arrangement of sun, light and water unknown and unbeheld, something far-from-usual. There are in the great world whirls of fluid and vaporous existences obtaining in their own unpassing time, unwatched and uninterpreted, valid only in their essential un-understandable mystery, justified only in their eyeless and mindless immeasurability, unassailable in their actual abstraction; of the inner quality of such a thing I might well in my own time be the true quintessential pith. I might belong to a lonely shore or be the agony of the sea when it bursts upon it in despair.

'But between that and the next morning there was a stormy night in between, a loud windy night that strained the trees in their deep roots and made the roads streaky with broken branches, a night that played a bad game with root-crops. When the boys reached the home of the balloon-man the next morning, lo and behold the bed was empty and no trace of him was ever found afterwards dead or alive, naked or with an overcoat. And when they got back to where the balloon was, they found the wind had torn it up out of the ground with the rope spinning loosely in the windlass and it invisible to the naked eye in the middle of the clouds. They pulled in eight miles of rope before they got it down but lo and behold the basket was empty again. They all said that the man had gone up in it and stayed up but it is an insoluble conundrum, his name was Quigley and he was by all accounts a Fermanagh man.'

Parts of this conversation came to me from different parts of the compass as the Sergeant moved about at his tasks, now right, now left and now aloft on a ladder to fix the hang-rope on the summit of the scaffold. He seemed to dominate the half of the world that was behind my back with his presence—his movements and his noises—filling it up with himself to the last farthest corner. The other half of the world which lay in front of me was beautifully given a shape of sharpness or roundness that was faultlessly suitable to its nature. But the half behind me was black and evil and composed of nothing at all except the menacing policeman who was patiently and politely arranging the mechanics of my death. His work was now nearly finished and my eyes were faltering as they gazed ahead, making little sense of the distance and taking a smaller pleasure in what was near.

There is not much that I can say.

No.

Except to advise a brave front and a spirit of heroic resignation.

That will not be difficult. I feel too weak to stand up without support.

In a way that is fortunate. One hates a scene. It makes things more difficult for all concerned. A man who takes into consideration the feelings of others even when arranging the manner of his own death shows a nobility of character which compels the admiration of all classes. To quote a well-known poet, 'even the ranks of Tuscany could scarce forbear to cheer'. Besides, unconcern in the face of death is in itself the most impressive gesture of defiance.

I told you I haven't got the strength to make a scene.

Very good. We will say no more about it.

A creaking sound came behind me as if the Sergeant was swinging red-faced in mid-air to test the rope he had just fixed. Then came the clatter of his great hobs as they came again upon the boards of the platform. A rope which would stand his enormous weight would never miraculously give way with mine.

You know, of course, that I will be leaving you soon?

That is the usual arrangement.

I would not like to go without placing on record my pleasure in having been associated with you. It is no lie to say that I have always received the greatest courtesy and consideration at your hands. I can only regret that it is not practicable to offer you some small token of my appreciation.

Thank you. I am very sorry also that we must part after having been so long together. If that watch of mine were found you would be welcome to it if you could find some means of taking it.

But you have no watch.

I forgot that.

Thank you all the same. You have no idea where you are going . . . when all this is over?

No, none.

Nor have I. I do not know, or do not remember, what happens to

*the like of me in these circumstances. Sometimes I think that perhaps
I might become part of . . . the world, if you understand me?*

I know.

*I mean—the wind, you know. Part of that. Or the spirit of the
scenery in some beautiful place like the Lakes of Killarney, the inside
meaning of it if you understand me.*

I do.

*Or perhaps something to do with the sea. 'The light that never was
on sea or land, the peasant's hope and the poet's dream.' A big wave
in mid-ocean, for instance, it is a very lonely and spiritual thing. Part
of that.*

I understand you.

Or the smell of a flower, even.

Here from my throat bounded a sharp cry rising to a scream. The
Sergeant had come behind me with no noise and fastened his big hand
into a hard ring on my arm, started to drag me gently but relentlessly
away from where I was to the middle of the platform where I knew
there was a trapdoor which could be collapsed with machinery.

Steady now!

My two eyes, dancing madly in my head, raced up and down the
country like two hares in a last wild experience of the world I was
about to leave for ever. But in their hurry and trepidation they did
not fail to notice a movement that was drawing attention to itself in
the stillness of everything far far down the road.

'The one-legged men!' I shouted.

I know that the Sergeant behind me had also seen that the far
part of the road was occupied for his grip, though still unbroken, had
stopped pulling at me and I could almost sense his keen stare running
out into the day parallel with my own but gradually nearing it till the
two converged a quarter of a mile away. We did not seem to breathe
or be alive at all as we watched the movement approaching and becoming clearer.

'MacCruiskeen, by the Powers!' the Sergeant said softly.

My lifted heart subsided painfully. Every hangman has an assistant.
MacCruiskeen's arrival would make the certainty of my destruction
only twice surer.

When he came nearer we could see that he was in a great hurry
and that he was travelling on his bicycle. He was lying almost prostrate
on top of it with his rear slightly higher than his head to cut a passage

through the wind and no eye could travel quickly enough to understand the speed of his flying legs as they thrashed the bicycle onwards in a savage fury. Twenty yards away from the barrack he threw up his head, showing his face for the first time, and saw us standing on the top of the scaffold engaged in watching him with all our attention. He leaped from the bicycle in some complicated leap which was concluded only when the bicycle had been spun round adroitly to form a seat for him with its bar while he stood there, wide-legged and diminutive, looking up at us and cupping his hands at his mouth to shout his breathless message upwards:

'The lever—nine point six nine!' he called.

For the first time I had the courage to turn my head to the Sergeant. His face had gone instantly to the colour of ash as if every drop of blood had left it, leaving it with empty pouches and ugly loosenesses and laxities all about it. His lower jaw hung loosely also as if it were a mechanical jaw on a toy man. I could feel the purpose and the life running out of his gripping hand like air out of a burst bladder. He spoke without looking at me.

'Let you stay here till I come back reciprocally,' he said.

For a man of his weight he left me standing there alone with a speed that was astonishing. With one jump he was at the ladder. Coiling his arms and legs around it, he slid to the ground out of view with a hurry that was not different in any way from an ordinary fall. In the next second he was seated on the bar of MacCruiskeen's bicycle and the two of them were disappearing into the end of a quarter of a mile away.

When they had gone an unearthly weariness came down upon me so suddenly that I almost fell in a heap on the platform. I called together all my strength and made my way inch by inch down the ladder and back into the kitchen of the barrack and collapsed helplessly into a chair that was near the fire. I wondered at the strength of the chair for my body seemed now to be made of lead. My arms and legs were too heavy to move from where they had fallen and my eyelids could not be lifted higher than would admit through them a small glint from the red fire.

For a time I did not sleep, yet I was far from being awake. I did not mark the time that passed or think about any question in my head. I did not feel the ageing of the day or the declining of the fire or even the slow return of my strength. Devils or fairies or even bicycles could have danced before me on the stone floor without perplexing me or altering by one whit my fallen attitude in the chair. I am sure I was nearly dead.

But when I did come to think again I knew that a long time had passed, that the fire was nearly out and that MacCruiskeen had just come into the kitchen with his bicycle and wheeled it hastily into his bedroom, coming out again without it and looking down at me.

'What has happened?' I whispered listlessly.

'We were just in time with the lever,' he replied, 'it took our combined strengths and three pages of calculations and rough-work but we got the reading down in the nick of zero-hour, you would be surprised at the coarseness of the lumps and the weight of the great fall.'

'Where is the Sergeant?'

'He instructed me to ask your kind pardon for his delays. He is lying in ambush with eight deputies that were sworn in as constables on the spot to defend law and order in the public interest. But they cannot do much, they are outnumbered and they are bound to be outflanked into the same bargain.'

'Is it for the one-legged men he is waiting?"

'Surely yes. But they took a great rise out of Fox. He is certain to get a severe reprimand from headquarters over the head of it. There is not seven of them but fourteen. They took off their wooden legs before they marched and tied themselves together in pairs so that there were two men for every two legs, it would remind you of Napoleon on the retreat from Russia, it is a masterpiece of military technocratics.'

This news did more to revive me than would a burning drink of finest brandy. I sat up. The light appeared once more in my eyes.

'Then they will win against the Sergeant and his policemen?' I asked eagerly.

MacCruiskeen gave a smile of mystery, took large keys from his pocket and left the kitchen. I could hear him opening the cell where the Sergeant kept his bicycle. He reappeared almost at once carrying a large can with a bung in it such as painters use when they are distempering a house. He had not removed his sly smile in his absence but now wore it more deeply in his face. He took the can into his bedroom and came out again with a large handkerchief in his hand and his smile still in use. Without a word he came behind my chair and bound the handkerchief tightly across my eyes, paying no attention to my movements and my surprise. Out of my darkness I heard his voice:

'I do not think the hoppy men will best the Sergeant,' he said, 'because if they come to where the Sergeant lies in secret ambush with his men before I have time to get back there, the Sergeant will delay them with military manoeuvres and false alarms until I arrive down the road on my bicycle. Even now the Sergeant and his men are all blindfolded like yourself, it is a very queer way for people to be when they are lying in an ambush but it is the only way to be when I am expected at any moment on my bicycle.'

I muttered that I did not understand what he had said.

'I have a private patent in that box in my bedroom,' he explained, 'and I have more of it in that can. I am going to paint my bicycle and ride it down the road in full view of the hoppy lads.'

He had been going away from me in my darkness while saying this and now he was in his bedroom and had shut the door. Soft sounds of work came to me from where he was.

I sat there for half an hour, still weak, bereft of light and feebly wondering for the first time about making my escape. I must have come back sufficiently from death to enter a healthy tiredness again for I did not hear the policeman coming out of the bedroom again and crossing the kitchen with his unbeholdable and brain-destroying bicycle. I must have slept there fitfully in my chair, my own private darkness reigning restfully behind the darkness of the handkerchief. . . .

The Poor Mouth

Oftentimes now there were gentlemen to be seen about the roads, some young and others aged, addressing the poor Gaels in awkward unintelligible Gaelic and delaying them on their way to the field. The gentlemen had fluent English from birth but they never practised this noble tongue in the presence of the Gaels lest, it seemed, the Gaels pick up an odd word of it as a protection against the difficulties of life.

—*The Poor Mouth*

INTRODUCTION

It is usually said of a parody that it loses its value unless we are familiar with the original. Perhaps one might add, more than familiar, saturated in it. If we add to this, paraphrasing Frost, that style is what is lost in translation, we have what may be a holepess case for presenting a translation of a parody of a genre that flourished in Irish in the first half of our century, especially when what appeals to the parodist in this case is not so much the broad mythic possibilities in the original (though there is humor broad enough in what he does), but the sense that "Irish is a precise, elegant and cultivated language, with a most unusual and curious literature." Nevertheless I think enough of the fun survives in Patrick C. Power's translation to include some here.

O'Brien had been, as we have seen, fooling around in Irish for some time. It should be remembered that after the undergraduate foray into Old Irish by means of the obscene epic, he went on to do his master thesis on Irish nature poetry (*Tráchtas ar Nádúr—Fhilíocht na Gaeilge*—Lúnasa 1934), which took the form of an essay accompanying an anthology. This interest was carried forward in *At Swim-Two-Birds* and emerged again in a more combative form in the first Myles columns for *The Irish Times,* which were written in modern Irish. He continued to alternate columns in Irish and English for several years before subsiding entirely into the tongue of the conqueror.

More to our purpose, the working knowledge of another language which he had had since childhood gave him a mind outside of the often petty culture of dear dirty Dublin. When this other world was moved in on by politicians eager to sound chauvinistic, O'Brien, through his Irish mask of Myles of the Little Horses, attacked "the bucklepping antics of the Gaelic League type of moron (few of whom know Irish properly at all)." His assault on the mindless collecting of any sort of drivel as long as it "was in Irish" reaches a high point in the following selection, and his remark that every Irish-speaking family includes a mother, father, child, and Gaelic scholar anticipates the great *bon mot* of America's Indian Revival, Dee Brown's remark that every Red family contains brave, squaw, papoose, and anthropologist.

Anne Clissmann and David Powell (see Selected Bibliography) have sections on the book, but Breandan O Conaire goes into the background more thoroughly in "Flann O'Brien, *An Béal Bocht* and Other Irish Matters."*

In January 1975 *The New York Times* blessed the book in Power's translation, as did *Time* and *Newsweek* earlier, all using the occasion to "rerediscover" our man, as the *Times*'s Brian O'Doherty put it:

The recurring case of Flann O'Brien alias Brian Nolan, a civil servant, alias Myles na Gopaleen, a newspaper columnist, seems to end up with the same verdict—quite possibly a major comic writer. But a forgettable one, apparently, who has to be rediscovered every time a book of his swims into our ken.

As for the targets: Tomás Ó Crohan's (Criomhthainn) *The Island-man,* available in Robin Flower's translation, and *Twenty Years A-Growing* by Maurice O'Sullivan, translated by Moya Llewelyn Davis and George Thomson with an introductory note by E. M.

* *Irish University Review,* Vols. 3–4 (1973–74), pp. 121–41.

Forster. Those failing, Synge will do, especially *Riders to the Sea* and *Playboy of the Western World*. (His prose book on the Aran Islands is too sophisticated for the kind of parody O'Brien aims at here.)

The phrase "poor mouth" survives in our culture more in the verb form as in: *That bastard Uncle Dick driving around in his Caddie spattering all over everyone, poor mouthing about how he can't afford a new mud flap.* O'Brien is not attacking poor people, but the sentimental uses rural poverty is put to by people who should know better, in order to advance their own spiritual worth. The log-cabin syndrome in American presidents after Lincoln. Lyndon Johnson barefoot on the banks of the whatever it was. John Kennedy or Richard M. Nixon tearful and bareheaded before a thatched cottage in the West of Ireland. Incidentally, the view with which O'Brien opens the book—from Connemara to the Great Blasket from the Rosses to Kilronan—is a little like the view from Johnson's river to Springfield, Illinois. (Actually the Irish original had endpaper maps by Seán O'Sullivan which showed, after the manner of early navigators, just where everything seemed. America takes up at least a third of the world and is composed of: three cities, New York, Boston, and Springfield, Massachusetts; the rest is devoted to assorted money-order officers and at least three cows, although these may stand for herds, or units of Texas. In O'Brien's last work, the rather flat *Slattery's Sago Saga,* much is made of Texas's potential for giving succor to Ireland.)

Power explains some of the nuances he encountered in making his translation in 1973.

The third edition, which contains many interpolations and emendations, is the text translated here. Wherever this particular edition presented difficulties or ambiguities, the earlier editions have been consulted. In this text the author included some humorous 'translations' of single words which he added to the ends of the pages as footnotes. They occur only in the first chapter of the third edition and have been included here in notes at the back of the book.

In *The Poor Mouth* Myles comments mercilessly on Irish life and not only on the Gaeltacht. Words such as 'hard times', 'poverty', 'drunkenness', 'spirits' and 'potatoes' recur in the text with almost monotonous regularity. The atmosphere reeks of the rain and the downpour and with relentless insistence he speaks of people who are 'facing for eternity' and the like. The key-words in this work are surely 'downpour', 'eternity' and 'potatoes' set against a background of squalor and poverty.

In his edition Power also uses footnotes to hassle the subtleties, but I have omitted them here in the spirit of restaurants that hang out signs announcing: CLOSED FOR YOUR CONVENIENCE.

Myles himself had much to say about *The Poor Mouth*, working his way into it from his columns, boosting it after its publication, defending it, worrying it, finally abandoning the possibilities of translation into English. Translation as a kind of stylistic filter always intrigued him, and he dreamed of seeing his books translated out of English into, say, German, then back again by some literal-minded hacks. He actually began *The Poor Mouth* by pretending to translate literally from *The Islandman*. Clissmann, in her book on O'Brien, lines up the passage translated by Robin Flower, then quotes the "literal translation" that Myles published in *Cruiskeen Lawn*. First Flower:

A while after this my brother Pats came over from America to me. I was amazed at his coming over this second time, for his two sons were grown up by this; and I fancied they were on the pig's back since they were on the other side. When I saw my brother after his return, anybody would have conjectured from his ways that it was in the woods he had spent his time in America. He was hardly clothed; he had an ill appearance; there wasn't a red farthing in his pocket; and two of his brothers in America paid for his passage across with their own money.

Then Myles-Flann:

A time after that my brother Paddy moved towards me from being over there in Ameriky. There was great surprise on me he is coming from being over there the second time, because the two sons who were at him were strong hefty ones at that time; and my opinion was that they were on the pig's back to be over there at all. On my seeing my brother on his arrival, there was no get-up on him—as would appear to any person who threw an opinion with him—save that it was in the woods he had spent his years yonder. There was no cloth on him, there was no shape on his person itself, there was not a dun-colored penny in his pocket, and it was two sisters to him yonder who had sent him across at their own expense.

Myles next reported to his readers in *The Irish Times* that he had actually written a whole book of this sort of thing, but that a publisher's reader had rejected it with the following note. No one has yet been able to establish the non-Mylesian reality of this "reader":

I can safely assert that in an experience of sixty years this is quite the craziest piece of Irish I have ever met.

What most surprises me is the self-assurance of its author—a man who demonstrates twenty times on every page that he is the veriest tyro in the Irish language. For want of knowledge he cannot begin, or continue or finish a sentence properly. Constructions such as he writes have never before been seen in Irish, and one earnestly hopes that nothing of the kind will ever be repeated.

The late Stephen McKenna at one time proposed to write a book:

HOW TO WRITE IRISH

BY

ONE WHO CAN'T

and here, I am convinced, we have an author who could take up his project with every hope of success.

Chapter II of the typescript is devoted, almost entirely, to a description of a sickly and stinking pig whose odoriferousness was such as to cause a horse to turn back, and to drive a certain family into exile The author may reply that the whole thing is an extravaganza, but if every word of his text were a *genuine* pearl, jem, or jewel, the inferiority of the Irish would damn the production.

At first I put a pencil mark against every solecism of his, but the marks became so numerous that I was obliged to give up the idea and to erase those I had made.

My advice to you is—to spend none of the firm's money on his work.

When the book came out Myles did a piggyback column, exaggerating, however, the sale of the book:

I am rather pleased at the reception given to my book, 'An Béal Bocht'. It is gratifying to know that an important work of literature receives in this country the recognition that is its due. Scholars, students, men-about-town, clerics, TDs ladies of fashion, and even the better-class corner-boys have vied with one another in grabbing the copies as they pour from the giant presses. How long will the strictly limited edition of 50,000 copies last? A week? A month? Who can tell? Suffice it to say that you cannot order your copy too soon. Paper difficulties make it doubtful whether another edition of 50,000 will be possible, in our own generation at any rate.

Critics liked the book. Sean O'Casey wrote him, "There is, I think, the wish of Swift's scorn in it, bred well into the genial laughter of Mark Twain." O'Brien wrote back:

It is by no means all you say but it is an honest attempt to get under the skin of a certain type of 'Gael', which I find the most nauseating phenomenon in Europe. I mean the baby-brained dawnburst brigade who are ignorant of everything, including the Irish language itself. I'm sure they were plentiful enough in your own day. I cannot see any real prospect of reviving Irish at the present rate of going and way of working. I agree absolutely with you when you say it is essential, particularly for any sort of a literary worker. It supplies that unknown quantity in us that enables us to transform the English language and this seems to hold of people who know little or no Irish, like Joyce. It seems to be an inbred thing.

In defending *The Poor Mouth*, Myles revealed the sort of thing that interested him, the kind of linguistic awareness that makes the novels of Flann O'Brien what they are:

There is scarcely a single word in Irish (barring, possibly Sasanach) that is simple and explicit. Apart from words with endless shades of cognate meaning, there are many with so complete a spectrum of graduated ambiguity that each of them can be made to express two directly contrary meanings, as well as a plethora of intermediate concepts that have no bearing on either. And all this strictly within the linguistic field. Superimpose on all that the miasma of ironic usage, poetic licence, oxymoron, plamás, Celtic evasion, Irish bullery and Paddy Whackery, and it is a safe bet that you will find yourself very far from home.

Twenty years later he wrote his literary editor Timothy O'Keeffe:

I don't think there is any point about translating stuff I have written in Irish into English. The significance of most of it is verbal or linguistic or tied up with a pseudo Gaelic mystique and this would be quite lost in translation. However, I had published here in 1941 a book called *An Béal Bocht* (*The Poor Mouth*) which was, for this country, an amazing success, close to 3,000 copies being sold in a matter of a few weeks. It was an enormous jeer at the Gaelic morons here with their bicycle clips and handball medals but in language and style was an ironical copy of a really fine autobiographical book written by a man from the Great Blasket island off Kerry (long dead and island now uninhabited).

The "editor" who wrote the Preface to the First Edition and the Foreword is, of course, Myles.

FROM *THE POOR MOUTH*

PREFACE TO THE FIRST EDITION

I believe that this is the first book ever published on the subject of Corkadoragha. It is timely and opportune, I think. Of great advantage both to the language itself and to those studying it is that a little report on the people who inhabit that remote Gaeltacht should be available after their times and also that some little account of the learned smooth Gaelic which they used should be obtainable.

This document is exactly as I received it from the author's hand except that much of the original matter has been omitted due to pressure of space and to the fact that improper subjects were included in it. Still, material will be available ten-fold if there is demand from the public for the present volume.

It is understandable that anything mentioned here concerns only Corkadoragha and it is not to be understood that any reference is intended to the Gaeltacht areas in general; Corkadoragha is a distinctive place and the people who live there are without compare.

It is a cause of jubilation that the author, Bonaparte O'Coonassa, is still alive today, safe in jail and free from the miseries of life.

The Editor
The Day of Want, 1941

FOREWORD

It is sad to relate that neither praise nor commendation is deserved by Gaelic folk—those of them who are moneyed gentle-folk or great bucks (in their own estimation)—because they have allowed a fascicle such as *The Poor Mouth* to remain out of print for many years; without young or old having an opportunity to see it, nor having any chance of milking wisdom, shrewdness and strength from the deeds of the unusual community that lives west in Corkadoragha—the seed of the strong and the choicest of paupers.

They live there to this day, but they are not increasing in numbers and the sweet Gaelic dialect, which is oftener in their mouths than a scrap of food, is not developing but rather declining like rust. Apart from this fact, emigration is thinning out the remote areas, the young folk are setting their faces toward Siberia in the hope of better weather and relief from the cold and tempest which is natural to them.

I recommend that this book be in every habitation and mansion where love for our country's traditions lives at this hour when, as Standish Hayes O'Grady says 'the day is drawing to a close and the sweet wee maternal tongue has almost ebbed'.

The Editor
The Day of Doom, 1964

CHAPTER I

Why I speak ♣ my birth ♣ my mother and the Old-Grey-Fellow ♣ our house ♣ the glen where I was born ♣ the hardships of the Gaels in former times

I am noting down the matters which are in this document because the next life is approaching me swiftly—far from us be the evil thing and may the bad spirit not regard me as a brother!—and also because our likes will never be there again. It is right and fitting that some testimony of the diversions and adventures of our times should be provided for those who succeed us because our types will never be there again nor any other life in Ireland comparable to ours who exists no longer.

O'Coonassa is my surname in Gaelic, my first name is Bonaparte and Ireland is my little native land. I cannot truly remember either the day I was born or the first six months I spent here in the world. Doutbless, however, I was alive at that time although I have no memory of it, because I should not exist now if I were not there then and to the human being, as well as to every other living creature, sense comes gradually.

The night before I was born, it happened that my father and Martin O'Bannassa were sitting on top of the hen-house, gazing at the sky to judge the weather and also chatting honestly and quietly about the difficulties of life.

Well, now, Martin, said my father, the wind is from the north and there's a forbidding look about the White Bens; before the morning there'll be rain and we'll get a dirty tempestuous night of it that will knock a shake out of us even if we're in the very bed. And look here! Martin, isn't it the bad sign that the ducks are in the nettles? Horror and misfortune will come on the world tonight; the evil thing and sea-cat will be a-foot in the darkness and, if 'tis true for me, no good destiny is ever in store for either of us again.

Well, indeed, Michelangelo, said Martin O'Bannassa, 'tis no little thing you've said there now and if you're right, you've told nary a lie but the truth itself.

I was born in the middle of the night in the end of the house. My father never expected me because he was a quiet fellow and did not understand very accurately the ways of life. My little bald skull so astounded him that he almost departed from this life the moment I entered it and, indeed, it was a misfortune and harmful thing for him that he did not, because after that night he never had anything but misery and was destroyed and rent by the world and bereft of his health as long as he lived. The people said that my mother was not expecting me either and it is a fact that the whisper went around that I was not born of my mother at all but of another woman. All that, nevertheless, is only the neighbours' talk and cannot be checked now because the neighbours are all dead and their likes will not be there again. I never laid eyes on my father until I was grown up but that is another story and I shall mention it at another time in this document.

I was born in the West of Ireland on that awful winter's night—may we all be healthy and safe!—in the place called Corkadoragha and in the townland named Lisnabrawshkeen. I was very young at the time I was born and had not aged even a single day; for half a year I did not perceive anything about me and did not know one person from the other. Wisdom and understanding, nevertheless, come steadily, solidly and stealthily into the mind of every human being and I spent that year on the broad of my back, my eyes darting here and there at my environment. I noticed my mother in the house before me, a decent, hefty, big-boned woman; a silent, cross, big-breasted woman. She seldom spoke to me and often struck me when I screamed in the end of the house. The beating was of little use in stopping the tumult because the second tumult was worse than the first one and, if I received a further beating, the third tumult was worse than the second one. However, my mother was sensible, level-headed and well-fed; her like will not be there again. She spent her life cleaning out the house, sweeping cow-dung and pig-dung from in front of the door, churning butter and milking cows, weaving and carding wool and working the spinning-wheel, praying, cursing and setting big fires to boil a houseful of potatoes to stave off the day of famine.

There was another person in the house in front of me—an old crooked, stooped fellow with a stick, half of whose face and all of whose chest were invisible because there was a wild, wool-grey beard blocking the view. The hairless part of his face was brown, tough and wrinkled like leather and two sharp shrewd eyes looked out from it at the world with a needle's sharpness. I never heard him called anything but the Old-Grey-Fellow. He lived in our house and very often my mother and he were not of the same mind and, bedad, it was an incredible thing the amount of potatoes he consumed, the volume of speech which issued from him and what little work he performed around the house. At first in my youth I thought he was my father. I remember sitting in his company one night, both of us gazing peacefully into the great red mass of the fire where my mother had placed a pot of potatoes as big as a barrel a-boiling for the pigs—she herself was quiet in the end of the house. It happened that the heat of the fire was roasting me but I was not able to walk at that time and had no means of escape from the heat on my own. The Old-Grey-Fellow cocked an eye at me and announced:

– 'Tis hot, son!

– There's an awful lot of heat in that fire truly, I replied, but look, sir, you called me son for the first time. It may be that you're my father and that I'm your child, God bless and save us and far from us be the evil thing!

– 'Tisn't true for you, Bonaparte, said he, for I'm your grandfather. Your father is far from home at the present but his name and surname in his present habitation are Michelangelo O'Coonassa.

– And where is he?

– He's in the jug! said the Old-Grey-Fellow.

At that time I was only about in the tenth month of my life but when I had the opportunity I looked into the jug. There was nothing in it but sour milk and it was a long time until I understand the Old-Grey-Fellow's remark, but that is another story and I shall mention it in another place in this document. . . .

The Old-Grey-Fellow often provided accounts such as this of the old times and from him I received much of the sense and wisdom which is now mine. However, concerning the house where I was born, there was a fine view from it. It had two windows with a door between them. Looking out from the right-hand window, there below was the bare hungry countryside of the Rosses and Gweedore; Bloody Foreland yonder and Tory Island far away out, swimming like a great ship where the sky dips into the sea. Looking out of the door, you could see the West of County Galway with a good portion of the rocks of Connemara, Aranmore in the ocean out from you with the small bright houses of Kilronan, clear and visible, if your eyesight were good and the Summer had come. From the window on the left you could see the Great Blasket, bare and forbidding as a horrible otherworldly eel, lying languidly on the wave-tops; over yonder was Dingle with its houses close together. It has always been said that there is no view from any house in Ireland comparable to this and it must be admitted that this statement is true. I have never heard it said that there was any house as well situated as this on the face of the earth. And so this house was delightful and I do not think that its like will ever be there again. At any rate, I was born there and truly this cannot be stated concerning any other house, whether that fact be praise or blame!

CHAPTER 3

♣ One

of our pigs missing ♣ the shanachee and the gramophone

. . . On the following day, when we counted the pigs while divest-
ing them of their breeches, it appeared that we were missing one.
Great was the lamentation of the Old-Grey-Fellow when he noticed
that both pig and suit of clothes had been snatched privily from him
in the quiet of the night. It is true that he often stole a neighbour's
pig and he often stated that he never slaughtered one of his own but
sold them all, although we always had half-sides of bacon in our
house. Night and day there was constant thieving in progress in the
parish—paupers impoverishing each other—but no one stole a pig
except the Old-Fellow. Of course, it was not joy which flooded his
heart when he found another person playing his own tune.

— Upon me soul, said he to me, I'm afraid they're not all just and
honest around here. I wouldn't mind about the young little pig but
there was a fine bit of stuff in that breeches.

— Everyone to his own opinion, my good man, said I, but I don't
think that anyone took that pig or the breeches either.

— Do you think, said he, that fear would keep them from doing the
stealing?

— No, I replied, but the stench would.

— I don't know, son, said he, but that you're truly in the right. I
don't know but that the pig is off rambling?

— It's an unfragrant rambling if 'tis true for you, my good man,
said I.

That night the Old-Fellow stole a pig from Martin O'Bannassa
and killed it quietly in the end of the house. It happened that the
conversation had reminded him that our bacon was in short supply.
No further discussion concerning the lost pig took place then.

A new month called March was born; remained with us for a
month and then departed. At the end of that time we heard a loud
snorting one night in the height of the rain. The Old-Fellow thought
that yet another pig was being snatched from him by force and went
out. When he returned, his companion consisted of none other than
our missing pig, drenched and wet, the fine breeches about him in

saturated rags. The creature seemed by his appearance to have trudged quite an area of the earth that night. My mother arose willingly when the Old-Fellow stated that it was necessary to prepare a large pot of potatoes for the one who had after all returned. The awakening of the household did not agree too well with Charlie and, having lain awake, looking furious during the talking and confusion, he suddenly arose and charged out into the rain. The poor creature never favoured socialising much. God bless him!

The return in darkness of the pig was amazing but still more amazing was the news which he imparted to us when he had partaken of the potatoes, having been stripped of the breeches by the Old-Grey-Fellow. The Old-Fellow found a pipe with a good jot of tobacco in one pocket. In another he found a shilling and a small bottle of spirits.

– Upon me soul, said he, if 'tis hardship that's always in store for the Gaels, it's not that way with this creature. Look, said he, directing his attention to the pig, where did you get these articles, sir?

The pig threw a sharp glance out of his two little eyes at the Old-Fellow but did not reply.

– Leave the breeches on him, said my mother. How do we know but that he'll be coming to us every week and wonderful precious things in his pockets—pearls, necklaces, snuff and maybe a money-note—wherever in Ireland he can get them. Isn't it a marvellous world today altogether?

– How do we know, said the Old-Grey-Fellow in reply to her, that he will ever again return but live where he can get these good things and we'd be for ever without the fine suit of clothes that he has?

– True for you, indeed, alas! said my mother.

The pig was now stark naked and was put with the others.

A full month went by before we received an explanation of the complicated matter of that night. The Old-Fellow heard a whisper in Galway, half a word in Gweedore and a phrase in Dunquin. He synthesised them all and one afternoon, when the day was done and the nocturnal downpour was mightily upon us, he told the following interesting story.

There was a gentleman from Dublin travelling through the country who was extremely interested in Gaelic. The gentleman understood that in Corkadoragha there were people alive who were unrivalled in any other region and also that their likes would never be there again. He had an instrument called a gramophone and this instrument was capable of memorising all it heard if anyone narrated stories or old lore to it; it could also spew out all it had heard whenever one desired it. It was a wonderful instrument and frightened many people in the area and struck others dumb; it is doubtful whether its like will ever be there again. Since folks thought that it was unlucky, the gentleman had a difficult task collecting the folklore tales from them.

For that reason, he did not attempt to collect the folklore of our ancients and our ancestors except under cover of darkness when both he and the instrument were hidden in the end of a cabin and both of them listening intently. It was evident that he was a wealthy person because he spent much money on spirits every night to remove the shyness and disablement from the old people's tongues. He had that reputation throughout the countryside and whenever it became known that he was visiting in Jimmy's or Jimmy Tim Pat's house, every old fellow who lived within a radius of five miles hastened there to seek tongue-loosening from this fiery liquid medicine; it must be mentioned that many of the youths accompanied them.

On the night of which we speak, the gentleman was in the house of Maximilian O'Penisa quietly resting in the darkness and with the hearing-machine by him. There were at least a hundred old fellows gathered in around him, sitting, dumb and invisible, in the shadow of the walls and passing around the gentleman's bottles of spirits from one to the other. Sometimes a little spell of weak whispering was audible but generally no sound except the roar of the water falling outside from the gloomy skies, just as if those on high were emptying buckets of that vile wetness on the world. If the spirits loosened the men's tongues, it did not result in talk but rather in rolling and tasting on their lips the bright drops of spirits. Time went by in that manner and it was rather late in the night. As a result of both the heavy silence inside and the hum of the rain outside, the gentleman was becoming a little disheartened. He had not collected one of the gems of our ancients that night and had lost spirits to the value of five pounds without result.

Suddenly he noticed a commotion at the doorway. Then, by the weak light of the fire, he saw the door being pushed in (it was never equipped with a bolt) and in came a poor old man, drenched and wet, drunk to the full of his skin and creeping instead of walking upright because of the drunkenness. The creature was lost without delay in the darkness of the house but wherever he lay on the floor, the gentleman's heart leaped when he heard a great flow of talk issuing from that place. It really was rapid, complicated, stern speech —one might have thought that the old fellow was swearing drunkenly—but the gentleman did not tarry to understand it. He leaped up and set the machine near the one who was spewing out Gaelic. It appeared that the gentleman thought the Gaelic extremely difficult and he was overjoyed that the machine was absorbing it; he understood that good Gaelic is difficult but that the best Gaelic of all is wellnigh unintelligible. After about an hour the stream of talk ceased. The gentleman was pleased with the night's business. As a token of his gratitude he put a white pipe, a jot of tobacco and a little bottle of spirits in the old fellow's pocket who was now in an inebriated slumber where he had fallen. Then the gentleman departed homewards in the rain with the machine, leaving them his blessing quietly but no one responded to it because drunkenness had come in a flood-tide now through the skull of everyone of them who was present.

It was said later in the area that the gentleman was highly praised for the lore which he had stored away in the hearing-machine that night. He journeyed to Berlin, a city of Germany in Europe, and narrated all that the machine had heard in the presence of the most learned ones of the Continent. These learned ones said that they never heard any fragment of Gaelic which was so good, so poetic and so obscure as it and that were sure there was no fear for Gaelic while the like was audible in Ireland. They bestowed fondly a fine academic degree on the gentleman and, something more interesting still, they appointed a small committee of their own members to make a detailed study of the language of the machine to determine whether any sense might be made of it.

I do not know whether it was Gaelic or English or a strange irregular dialect which was in the old speech which the gentleman collected from among us here in Corkadoragha but it is certain that whatever was uttered that night came from our rambling pig.

CHAPTER 4

The comings and goings of the Gaeligores ♣ the Gaelic college ♣ a

Gaelic feis in our countryside ♣ the gentlemen from Dublin ♣ sorrow

follows the jollity

One afternoon I was reclining on the rushes in the end of the house considering the ill-luck and evil that had befallen the Gaels (and would always abide with them) when the Old-Grey-Fellow came in the door. He appeared terrified, a severe fit of trembling throughout his body and limbs, his tongue between his teeth dry and languid and bereft of vigour. I forget whether he sat or fell but he alighted on the floor near me with a terrible thump which set the house dancing. Then he began to wipe away the large beads of sweat which were on his face.

– Welcome, my good man! said I gently, and also may health and longevity be yours! I've just been thinking of the pitiable situation of the Gaels at present and also that they're not all in the same state; I perceive that yourself are in a worse situation than any Gael since the commencement of the reign of Gaelicism. It appears that you're bereft of vigour?

– I am, said he.

– You're worried?

– I am.

– And is it the way, said I, that new hardships and new calamities are in store for the Gaels and a new overthrow is destined for the little green country which is the native land of both of us?

The Old-Grey-Fellow heaved a sigh and a sad withdrawn appearance spread over his face, leading me to understand that he was meditating on eternity itself. He did not reply to me but his lips were dry and his voice weak and feeble.

– Little son, said he, I don't think that the coming night's rain will drench anyone because the end of the world will arrive before that very night. The signs are there in plenty through the firmament. Today I saw the first ray of sunshine ever to come to Corkadoragha, an unworldly shining a hundred times more venomous than the fire and it glaring down from the skies upon me and coming with a needle's sharpness at my eyes. I also saw a breeze going across the grass of a field and returning when it reached the other side. I heard a crow screeching in the field with a pig's voice, a blackbird bellowing and a bull whistling. I must say that these frightening things don't predict good news. Bad and all as they were, I heard another thing that put a hell of fright in my heart . . .

– All that you say is wonderful, loving fellow, said I honestly, and a little account of that other sign would be nice.

The Old-Fellow was silent for a while and when he withdrew from that taciturnity, he did not produce speech but a hoarse whispering into my ears.

– I was coming home today from Ventry, said he, and I noticed a strange, elegant, well-dressed gentleman coming towards me along the road. Since I'm a well-mannered Gael, into the ditch with me so as to leave all the road to the gentleman and not have me there before him, putrifying the public road. But alas! there's no explaining the world's wonders! When he came as far as me and I standing there humbly in the dung and filth of the bottom of the ditch, what would you say but didn't he stop and, looking fondly at me, *didn't he speak to me!*

Amazed and terrified, I exhaled all the air in my lungs. I was then dumb with terror for a little while.

– But...said the Old-Fellow, laying a trembling hand upon my person, dumb also but making the utmost endeavour to regain his power of speech, but ... wait! *He spoke to me in Gaelic!*

When I had heard all this, I became suspicious. I thought that the Old-Fellow was romancing or raving in a drunken delirium ... There are things beyond the bounds of credibility.

– If 'tis true for you, said I, we'll never live another night and without a doubt, the end of the world is here today.

It is, however, mysterious and bewildering how the human being comes free from every peril. That night arrived both safely and punctually and in spite of all, we were safe. Another thing: as the days went by, it was evident that the Old-Fellow spoke the truth about the gentleman who addressed him in Gaelic. Oftentimes now there were gentlemen to be seen about the roads, some young and others aged, addressing the poor Gaels in awkward unintelligible Gaelic and delaying them on their way to the field. The gentlemen had fluent English from birth but they never practised this noble tongue in the presence of the Gaels lest, it seemed, the Gaels might pick up an odd word of it as a protection against the difficulties of life. That is how the group, called the Gaeligores nowadays, came to Corkadoragha for the first time. They rambled about the countryside with little black notebooks for a long time before the people noticed that they were not *peelers* but gentle-folk endeavouring to learn the Gaelic of our ancestors and ancients. As each year went by, these folk became more numerous. Before long the place was dotted with them. With the passage of time, the advent of spring was no longer judged by the flight of the first swallow but by the first Gaeligore seen on the roads. They brought happiness and money and high revelry with them when they came; pleasant and funny were these creatures, God bless them! and I think that their likes will not be there again!

When they had been coming to us for about ten years or thereabouts, we noticed that their number among us was diminishing and that those who remained faithful to us were lodging in Galway and in Rannafast while making day-trips to Corkadoragha. Of course, they carried away much of our good Gaelic when they departed from us each night but they left few pennies as recompense to the paupers who waited for them and had kept the Gaelic tongue alive for such as them a thousand years. People found this difficult to understand; it had always been said that accuracy of Gaelic (as well as holiness of spirit) grew in proportion to one's lack of worldly goods and since we had the choicest poverty and calamity, we did not understand why the scholars were interested in any half-awkward, perverse Gaelic which was audible in other parts. The Old-Grey-Fellow discussed this matter with a noble Gaeligore whom he met.

– Why and wherefore, said he, are the learners leaving us? Is it the way that they've left so much money with us in the last ten years that they have relieved the hunger of the countryside and that for this reason, our Gaelic has declined?

– I don't think that Father Peter has the word *decline* in any of his works, said the Gaeligore courteously.

The Old-Grey-Fellow did not reply to this sentence but he probably made a little speech quietly for his own ear. . . .

The Hard Life

As usual the subject under discussion was never named.
                                        —The Hard Life

"I said nothing, of course."
                                        —the brother in *The Hard Life*

INTRODUCTION

As *At Swim-Two-Birds* was a masterpiece of extravagance, *The Hard Life*, if not a masterpiece, is at least an amusing excursion in reticence. The main character, Mr. Collopy, is eternally (one feels that this will be literal) engaged on important business that is discussed for most of the novel, yet never named. (Dare one whisper what it is? He wants to have the Dublin Corporation [city government] install toilets for ladies in public places. . . . Oh . . . well, listen now. When my father, a man about O'Brien's age, was young in rural Connecticut, the outhouse was behind the grape arbor and all females, winter and summer, were ostensibly going to gather grapes.)

Even the simple, by God, *legal* relationships between characters are not spelled out in the usual way. The narrator makes various guesses, but is never sure if Mr. Collopy is actually married to Mrs. Crotty. In his one orthodox attempt at an explanation of "the nature and standing of the persons present" the narrator says, "an ill-disposed person might suspect that they were not married at all. . . ." After suggesting just what notorious possibilities are left for Mrs. Crotty, he decides these alternatives are "quite unthinkable" and concludes that his account has not "illuminated the situation or made it more reasonable." Illness, sex, alcoholism, unemployment, bodily functions, crime, and other staples of *the hard life* are merely alluded to while matters such as Church history, tightrope walking, and the properties of Gravid Water are exposed relentlessly.

Reticence, many would say, is just the more silent form of extravagance, Irishmen moving between the two not so much as two sides of the same coin, but more after the manner of an Oriental with his yin and yang. Flann O'Brien was hard on empty rhetoric. His canon bristles with parodies. Yet like the greatest parodists—Petronius, Cervantes, Scott Fitzgerald—he is half in love with the subjects he seeks to correct. Because of Myles's scorn for pedants, politicians, and other abusers of language, critics often see O'Brien as writing a simple, corrective satire or parody in the novels. Given this intent, he seems to go way beyond the "point." Anne Clissmann, in her chapter on *The Hard Life*, says:

The satire of all kinds of jargon in *Cruiskeen Lawn* had revealed clearly enough that O'Brien was intolerant of any language which tended to obscure rather than reveal its subject. He was equally intolerant about mental sloppiness of any kind, and the prejudiced arguments of Father Fahrt and Mr Collopy are therefore satirised as essentially the squalid products of untrained mentalities. Yet, that said, it is still necessary to point out that there are a large number of these conversations and an equally large number of letters from the brother full of pedantic detail. The result is that the devices fail to hold the attention for very long. Pedantry is apt material for satire, yet it does not remain amusing in itself. . . .

She brings up the charge again in discussing the miscellany of plays for TV O'Brien was forced into writing toward the end of his life:

The dialogue in the plays and the series was always convincing, if sometimes tedious. O'Brien found the speech habits of the Dubliner an unending source of amusement and was very concerned to portray them accurately. He forgot, however, that speech which is repetitious, misinformed and trivial will eventually bore if the content is not significant.

Without denying that O'Brien had his bad days and even hangs a few curves on his better ones, I think it important to see that O'Brien is not simply using pedantry for the sake of correcting a social abuse. He is rather, in the manner of Cervantes (incidentally, one of the brother's rackets), making something else. Not all parody is mockery after the mode of the soldiers crowning Christ with thorns. Some parody is, as the etymology suggests, *a song alongside of*. In all the talk of Joyce and O'Brien there seems little recognition of this sense of singing the song alongside of. One thinks especially of Joyce's Gerty MacDowell or, in America, Randall Jarrell's Bat-Poet, who seems to be finding a new genre as well as a species for Yeats's dancer:

> A mockingbird can sound like anything.
> He imitates the world he drove away
> So well that for a minute, in the moonlight,
> Which one's the mockingbird? which one's the world?

In the following selection I have of necessity cheated and cut much of what Clissmann finds excessive. More than any of the other novels, however, *The Hard Life* depends upon a cumulative sense of its characters and their milieu. There are some potential set pieces, but extracted from the deliciously greasy paste of the context, these mincemeat balls lose their flavor. I have therefore tried to provide at least the illusion of having presented the entire 156-page novella. It is only fair to admit that I have thrown the balance somewhat in favor of the brother and away from Mr. Collopy and his work. As for the narrator's love life, I have yielded even less than the girl herself.

The book was published in 1961, twenty years and more after the publication of *At Swim-Two-Birds* and the writing of *The Third Policeman*. Because of the fate of *The Third Policeman*, the special audience for the Irish *The Poor Mouth* and the play *Faustus Kelly*, the novel was greeted as O'Brien's second full-length work, and he was welcomed back after what the critics could only assume was a strangely long absence.

Just why did O'Brien write this "exegesis of squalor" after the two bright inventions of the earlier novels, and why did he write it at this interval? The reissue of *At Swim-Two-Birds* may account for some of the motivation to write another book, but the choice of subject would on the surface seem inexplicable. O'Brien, however, thought of the book as "very important and very funny" and warned its editor, Tim

O'Keeffe, that it's "apparently pedestrian style is delusive." O'Brien fans will also see that many earlier and later interests emerge in this book, which seems most untypical of any of his longer works. The brother is not only a frequenter of *Cruiskeen Lawn,* but a minor-league de Selby. Mrs. Crotty is the basic Flann mother. Mr. Collopy is much like *At Swim's* uncle, and, as Clissmann points out, the Uncle Andy of the late TV series *Th' Oul Lad of Kilsalaher.* The Gravid Water is an anticipation of *The Dalkey Archive's* lethal D.M.P., and so forth. Perhaps more important for him was not the recognition of the squalor level, which had always been in O'Brien's longer works, but the ability in this work to hang in there, reveling in the grayness without recourse to tempting flights. Gravid Water wins out over tightrope walking and theology.

To keep our feet sticking to the ground, O'Brien uses a point of view that holds us closer to conventional realism than does that of any of the preceding works. In spite of the scheming by the brother and Mr. Collopy, there is no threat that the narrative itself will rise up and do us in after the manner of *At Swim* or *The Third Policeman.* In this sense, the book represents a technical step backward. O'Brien had, of course, been warned that he "should become less fantastic." The book sold well enough to justify such advice, although much of its commercial appeal might have been due to its naughtiness. O'Brien himself was aware of this potential, as his letters demonstrate.

The book leads off with dedication, caveat, and epigraph—three conventions that in ordinary writers may often go unnoticed. The dedication presents to the man who discovered *At Swim-Two-Birds,* Graham Greene, "whose own forms of gloom I admire, this misterpiece." O'Brien reverses the usual warning found in novels of the period, "All the persons in this book are real and none is fictitious even in part." The epigraph in French is from Pascal, the famous remark that all the trouble in the world comes from our not knowing how to sit still in our room.

The Hard Life was a favorite of O'Brien, and since it marked his return as a novelist, he was eager to talk about it not only to his British and American editors but to the librarian of the National Library of Ireland in the early 1960s. The topics ranged from the censorship O'Brien anticipated, even welcomed (but did not get), through tub-thumping and technical quibbles. In the letter to New York editor Gerald Gross, O'Brien tosses off as important a statement concerning how he wishes to be taken as he ever makes.

To Mark Hamilton of A. M. Heath & Co., London
20 February, 1961.

Many thanks for your letter of 17 February regarding *The Hard Life*. I am very pleased with the terms offered by MacGibbon and Kee and accept them. I would be glad if you would draw up an appropriate contract as soon as possible.

A few changes are called for in the MS, mostly minor verbal and textual changes and a few brief interpolations. I am getting to work on those. Until I have a final "definitive" copy, I cannot get the extra copies typed.

I feel that the doubts you personally had will turn out to be mistaken. Everything was done with deliberation, the characters illuminating themselves and each other by their outlandish behavior and preposterous conversations. The plot, episodically evolved, is sternly consecutive and conclusive and makes the book compact and short. Digression and expatiation would be easy but I feel would injure the book's spontaneity. You are right in saying that I deliberately avoided direct narrative or description. The "I" narrator or interlocutor, is himself a complete ass. A few people here whose opinion I value have seen the MS and are all really impressed, particularly by the Collopy-Father Fahrt dialogues, which are set down in absolutely accurate Dublinese. One suggestion was that Father Fahrt was not objectionable enough and that he should have some disease. I absolutely turned down TB, which is never funny, but there is a lot to be said for some scaly skin disease (psoriasis?) which need not appear on the face but be conveyed by itching and scratching. . . .

It may sound rash and silly to say so but I am convinced that this book will be a resounding success, though possibly after a slow start. The greatest living European arbiter of literature said first that the book paralysed him and finally confessed it was "a gem." I mean Brendan Behan. . . .

To Timothy O'Keeffe of MacGibbon and Kee, London
1 September, 1961.

Many thanks for your letter of 30 August about *The Hard Man* [*sic*].

It is deplorable if it is genuinely too late to do anything about that picture. (What's wrong with a hatchet?) I hold it is not a picture of me at all.

With local knowledge I am looking further ahead than you are. You have probably only a very sketchy idea of the situation here as regards

the censorship of books. Many years ago a confederation of pious hum-
bugs who never read and certainly never buy a book caused an act to be
passed outlawing filthy publications. In practice this means (i) that the
Board, composed exclusively of ignorant balloxes, ban any book they do
not like, and (ii) that any intelligent person can get any book he wants.
Two reputable bookshops keep banned books under the counter, like
cigarettes in war-time. If the assistant knows you, you can have anything
under the sun, including (for students) continental magazines full of
pictures of women without a stitch on them.

There are two statutory grounds for banning a book, namely (a) plain
obscenity, and (b) advocating the unnatural prevention of birth. The
censors pursue their purpose with the single-mindedness of Gadarene
swine. About ten years ago Dr. Halliday Sutherland published a book
called "The Laws of Life". Sutherland is a Catholic and his book dealt
with the scientific theme of calculating the intervals within which a
respectable, married woman can have intercourse (preferably with her
husband) without the possibility of pregnancy. This book was banned.
It was nothing to the censors that it bore the *imprimatur* of the Arch-
diocese of Westminster. See where you are?

For these reasons I *know* that *The Hard Life* will be banned here.
True, the book doesn't offend under heads a) or b) above, but the mere
name of Father Kurt Fahrt, S.J., will justify the thunder clap. The ban
will be improper and illegal and when it comes, I will challenge it in the
High Court here. I will seek not only a declaration that the book is one
to be properly on sale but also damages from those who imposed the ban
and who will be shown in court to be incapable of quoting a line that
contravenes what is provided for in the Acts.

The foregoing is admittedly hypothetical but it would be pretty awful
if the jacket of the book gratuitously afforded ammunition to those most
reverend spivs. I think the book in appearance should be utterly colourless,
anonymous (pseudonymous), neutral. All biographical matter should be
cut right out. Our bread and butter depends on being one jump ahead
of the other crowd. Please do what you can in this interest.

I accept what you say about publication date. What's a week or a
month when one is dealing with immortal literature?

To Timothy O'Keeffe
5 November, 1961.

A letter from me concerning *The Hard Life* is overdue; I was away
for some weeks though not on holiday.

I am truly pleased with the book and think you deserve profound con-
gratulation. It is precisely right that elegance should attach to a volume

which contains a treatise on piss and vomit. The price, too, is a great achievement, for I do know something about production costs. Friends to whom I showed the book were also appreciative and every one of them said that Mr. Collopy on the cover was an excellent portrait of a former Vice-President of our empire here, to whom once upon a time I was private secretary. This sort of thing helps enormously.

I lent the book to two persons who hadn't heard of it, deliberately chosen for what we will call their incongruity of temperament and judgement. The first found it very, very funny—uproarious. The second (a lady) handed it back to me sadly. She said she did not understand me and now doubted whether she ever had. But of one thing I could be sure. Not one night would pass but she would say a Hail Mary for me. And wasn't it a good job that my poor mother wasn't still alive?

I gathered that she had been shocked, not so much by Mr. Collopy's "words" but by the name of the good Jesuit father. That was exactly what I thought would happen. The name will cause holy bloody ructions here. It will lead to wire-pulling behind the scenes here to have the book banned as obscene (for there is no other statutory ground for a ban than advocating birth control). If this happens I will seriously consider taking an action for libel in the High Court against the Censorship Board. The upper justiciary here are quite intelligent and in fact I know most of them but the fact that it would be a jury case would be the complication. That's all premature, however. Anyway, it's the British and Commonwealth market that matters, subject to their majesties the reviewers being reasonably well-behaved. I'm still very confident but am sorry I didn't take more time and trouble on the job. . . .

I had a letter from Graham Greene expressing what seemed to be genuine thanks. I don't think he'd read the book. At all events he made no comment. . . .

To Gerald Gross of Pantheon Books, New York
16 January, 1962.

Many thanks for your friendly letters of Dec. 19 and Jan. 11 regarding *The Hard Life*. This book seems to have had an immense sale (here in Dublin, I mean) but, though most reviews were excellent, I'm not so sure of the British and ancillary markets. Those people are very hard to amuse—they look for overtones, undertones, subtones, grunts and "philosophy", they assume something very serious is afoot. It's disquieting for a writer is only, for the moment, clowning. That is one feeling that makes me glad of U.S. publication, because the people of the U.S. and the Irish are really brothers under the skin. Only the Italians could match the Irish for leadership in crime, for instance, in the Prohibition era, but we have also been prominent in many somewhat better spheres (politics?)....

To Timothy O'Keeffe
3 October, 1962

Thanks for your letter of 30th September....

There has been an awful Theatre Festival here. Last Saturday at midnight in the ballroom of the Shelbourne Hotel, completely crammed, Siobhan McKenna (the Irish Bernhardt) gave readings from the Irish immortals—Joyce, James Stephens, GBS, Moore, etc. That morning she rang to ask whether she might include *The Hard Life*. It was very funny to see this fashionable crowd hearing of fucking on the banks of the Grand Canal, gonorrhea, the Pope threatening to silence Father Fahrt, and so on.

To the Librarian,
National Library of Ireland, Dublin
[no date]

I had occasion to consult the Index of your Library recently on another matter and took the occasion to see the entry in relation to myself. Writing is my main source of livelihood and for good but personal reasons never in this country write under my own name. I found under O'BRIEN, FLANN the reference "Pseud. O NUALLAIN". I looked under this head and found several works listed but not *The Hard Life*, published in London in November, 1961. I would draw your attention to the following matters:

1) The gratuitous attempt at the destruction of a pseudonym or pseudonyms may be presumed to be damaging and can in fact seriously damage or even destroy an individual's livelihood.

2) In fact my name is not O Nuallain; as my birth certificate attests, it is O'Nolan.

3) I am aware that according to law you have in fact in your possession a copy of *The Hard Life*. Its exclusion from the index and refusal of access to it by the public would mean, in the mind of a fair-minded person, that the book is obscene, advocates birth control, is banned under statute or is otherwise unfit for circulation. None of such conclusions would be true.

I would be happy to receive your comments on the foregoing.

FROM *THE HARD LIFE*

[In the opening paragraphs the narrator looks back on his Edwardian childhood in Dublin when he was one of two orphaned brothers.]

My memory is a bit mixed about what exactly happened after the mammy went away but a streel of a girl with long lank fair hair arrived to look after myself and the brother. She did not talk very much and seemed to be in a permanent bad temper. We knew her as Miss Annie. At least that is what she ordered us to call her. She spent a lot of time washing and cooking, specializing in boxty and kalecannon and eternally making mince balls covered with a greasy paste. I got to hate those things. . . .

How long this situation—a sort of interregnum, lacuna or hiatus—lasted I cannot say, but I do remember that when myself and the brother noticed that Miss Annie was washing more savagely, mangling and ironing almost with ferocity, and *packing*, we knew something was afoot. And we were not mistaken.

One morning after breakfast (stirabout and tea with bread and jam) a cab arrived and out of it came a very strange elderly lady on a stick. I saw her first through the window. Her hair peeping from under her hat was grey, her face very red, and she walked slowly as if her sight was bad. Miss Annie let her in, first telling us that here was Mrs Crotty and to be good. She stood in silence for a moment in the kitchen, staring rather blankly about her.

—These are the two rascals, Mrs Crotty, Miss Annie said.

—And very well they're looking, God bless them, Mrs Crotty said in a high voice. Do they do everything they're told?

—Oh, I suppose they do, but sometimes it's a job to make them take their milk.

—Well, faith now, Mrs Crotty said in a shocked tone, did you ever hear of such nonsense? When I was their age I could never get *enough* milk. Never. I could drink jugs of it. Buttermilk too. Nothing in the wide world is better for the stomach or the nerves. Night and day I am telling Mr Collopy that but you might as well be talking to *that table!*

Here she struck the table with her stick. Miss Annie looked startled that her trivial mention of milk should induce such emphasis. She took off her apron. . . .

* * *

There is something misleading but not dishonest in this portrait of Mr Collopy. It cannot be truly my impression of him when I first saw him but rather a synthesis of all the thoughts and experiences I had of him over the years, a long look backwards. But I do remember clearly enough that my first glimpse of him was, so to speak, his absence: Mrs Crotty, having knocked imperiously on the door, immediately began rooting in her handbag for the key. It was plain she did not expect the door to be opened.

—There is a clap of rain coming, she remarked to Miss Annie.

—Seemingly, Miss Annie said.

Mrs Crotty opened the door and led us in single file into the front kitchen, semi-basement, Mr Hanafin [the cabby] bringing up the rear with some bags.

He was sitting there at the range in a crooked, collapsed sort of cane armchair, small reddish eyes looking up at us over the rims of steel spectacles, the head bent forward for closer scrutiny. Over an ample crown, long grey hair was plastered in a tattered way. The whole mouth region was concealed by a great untidy dark brush of a moustache, discoloured at the edges, and a fading chin was joined to a stringy neck which disappeared into a white celluloid collar with no tie. Nondescript clothes contained a meagre frame of low stature and the feet wore large boots with the laces undone.

—Heavenly fathers, he said in a flat voice, but you are very early. Morning, Hanafin.

—Morra, Mr Collopy, Mr Hanafin said.

—Annie here had everything infastatiously in order, Mrs Crotty said, thanks be to God.

—I wonder now, Miss Annie said.

—Troth, Mr Collopy, Mr Hanafin beamed, but I never seen you looking better. You have a right bit of colour up whatever you are doing with yourself at all.

The brother and myself looked at Mr Collopy's slack grey face and then looked at each other.

—Well, the dear knows, Mr Collopy said, I don't think hard work ever hurt anybody. Put that stuff in the back room for the present, Hanafin. Well now, Mrs Crotty, are these the two pishrogues out of the storm? They are not getting any thinner from the good dinners you have been putting into them, Annie, and that's a fact.

—Seemingly, Miss Annie said.

—Pray introduce me if you please, Mrs Crotty.

We went forward and had our names recited. Without rising, Mr Collopy made good an undone button at the neck of the brother's jersey and then shook hands with us solemnly. From his waistcoat he extracted two pennies and presented one to each of us.

—I cross your hands with earthly goods, he said, and at the same time I put my blessing on your souls.

—Thanks for the earthly goods, the brother said.

—Manus and Finbarr are fine names, fine Irish names, Mr Collopy said. In the Latin Manus means big. Remember that. Ecce Sacerdos Manus comes into the Missal, and that Manus is such an uplifting name. Ah but Finbarr is the real Irish for he was a saint from the County Cork. Far and wide he spread the Gospel thousands of years ago for all the thanks he got, for I believe he died of starvation at the heel of the hunt on some island on the river Lee, down fornenst Queenstown.

—I always heard that St Finbarr was a Protestant, Mrs Crotty snapped. Dug with the other foot. God knows what put it into the head of anybody to put a name the like of that on the poor *bookul*.

—Nonsense, Mrs Crotty. His heart was to Ireland and his soul to the Bishop of Rome. What is sticking out of that bag, Hanafin? Are they brooms or shovels or what?

Mr Hanafin had reappeared with a new load of baggage and followed Mr Collopy's gaze to one item.

—Faith now, Mr Collopy, he replied, and damn the shovels. They are hurling sticks. Best of Irish ash and from the County Kilkenny, I'll go bail.

—I am delighted to hear it. From the winding banks of Nore, ah? Many a good puck I had myself in the quondam days of my nonage. I could draw on a ball in those days and clatter in a goal from midfield, man.

—Well it's no wonder you are never done talking about the rheumatism in your knuckles, Mrs Crotty said bleakly.

—That will do you, Mrs Crotty. It was a fine manly game and I am not ashamed of any wounds I may still carry. In those days you were damn nothing if you weren't a hurler. Cardinal Logue is a hurler and a native Irish speaker, revered by Pope and man. Were *you* a hurler, Hanafin?

—In my part of the country—Tinahely—we went in for the football.

—Michael Cusack's Gaelic code, I hope?

—Oh, certaintly, Mr Collopy.

—That's good. The native games for the native people. By dad and I see young thullabawns of fellows got out in baggy drawers playing this new golf out beyond on the Bull Island. For pity's sake sure that isn't a game at all.

—Oh you'll always find the fashionable jackeen in Dublin and that's a certainty, Mr Hanafin said. They'd wear nightshirts if they seen the British military playing polo in nightshirts above in the park. Damn the bit of shame they have.

—And then you have all this talk about Home Rule, Mr Collopy asserted. Well how are you! We're as fit for Home Rule here as the blue men in Africa if we are to judge by those Bull Island looderamawns.

—Sit over here at the table, Mrs Crotty said. Is that tea drawn, Annie?

—Seemingly, Miss Annie said.

We all sat down and Mr Hanafin departed, leaving a shower of blessings on us.

It is seemly for me to explain here, I feel, the nature and standing of the persons present. Mr Collopy was my mother's half-brother and was therefore my own half-uncle. He had married twice, Miss Annie being his daughter by his first marriage. Mrs Crotty was his second wife but she was never called Mrs Collopy, why I cannot say. She may have deliberately retained the name of her first husband in loving memory of him or the habit may have grown up through the absence of mind. Moreover, she always called her second husband by the formal style of Mr Collopy as he also called her Mrs Crotty, at least in the presence of other parties; I cannot speak for what usage obtained in private. An ill-disposed person might suspect that they were not married at all and that Mrs Crotty was a kept-woman or resident prostitute. But that is quite unthinkable, if only because of Mr Collopy's close interest in the Church and in matters of doctrine and dogma, and also his long friendship with the German priest from Leeson Street, Father Kurt Fahrt, S.J., who was a frequent caller.

It is seemly, as I have said, to give that explanation but I cannot pretend to have illuminated the situation or made it more reasonable.

*   *   *

The years passed slowly in this household where the atmosphere could be described as a dead one. The brother, five years older than myself, was first to be sent to school, being marched off early one morning by Mr Collopy to see the Superior of the Christian Brothers' school at Westland Row. A person might think the occasion was one merely of formal introduction and enrolment, but when Mr Collopy returned, he was alone.

—By God's will, he explained, Manus's foot has been placed today on the first rung of the ladder of learning and achievement, and on yonder pinnacle beckons the lone star.

—The unfortunate boy had no lunch, Mrs Crotty said in a shrill voice.

—You might consider, Mrs Crotty, that the Lord would provide, even as He does for the birds of the air. I gave the bosthoon a tuppence. Brother Cruppy told me that the boys can get a right bag of broken biscuits for a penny in a barber's shop there up the lane.

—And what about milk?

—Are you out of your wits, woman? You know the gorawars you have to get him to drink his milk in this kitchen. He thinks milk is poison, the same way *you* think a drop of malt is poison. That reminds me—I think I deserve a smahan. Where's my crock? . . .

* * *

And still the years kept rolling on, and uneventfully enough, thank God. I was now about eleven, the brother sixteen and convinced he was a fully grown man.

One day in spring about half-three I was trudging wearily home from school at Synge Street. I was on the remote, or canal side of the roadway near home. I happened to glance up at the house when about fifty yards away and, turned to cold stone, stopped dead in my tracks. My heart thumped wildly against my ribs and my eyes fell to the ground. I blessed myself. Timidly I looked up again. Yes!

To the left of the house entrance and perhaps fifteen yards from it a tallish tree stood in the front garden. Head and shoulders above the tree but not quite near it was the brother. I stared at the apparition in the manner fascinated animals are reputed to stare at deadly snakes about to strike. He began waving his arms in a sickening way, and the next prospect I had of him was his back. He was returning towards the house *and he was walking on air!* Now thoroughly scared, I thought of Another who had walked on water. I again looked away helplessly, and after a little time painfully stumbled into the house. I must have looked very pale but went in and said nothing.

Mr Collopy was not in his usual chair at the range. Annie—we had now learned to drop the 'Miss'—placed potatoes and big plate of stew before me. I thought it would be well to affect a casual manner.

—Where's Mr Collopy? I asked.

She nodded towards the back room.

—He's inside, she said. I don't know what father's at. He's in there with a tape taking measurements. I'm afraid poor Mrs Crotty's getting worse. She had Dr Blennerhassett again this morning. God look down on us all!

Mrs Crotty was certainly sick. She had taken to the bed two months before and insisted that the door between her bedroom and the kitchen should be always left slightly ajar so that her cries, often faint, could be heard either by Mr Collopy or Annie. Neither myself nor the brother ever entered the room but all the same I had accidentally seen her on several occasions. This was when she was coming down the stairs leaning on Mr Collopy and clutching the banister with one frail hand, her robe or nightdress of fantastic shape and colour and a frightening pallor on her spent face.

—I'm afraid she *is* pretty sick, I said.

—Seemingly.

I finished with a cup of tea, then casually left the kitchen and went upstairs, my heart again making its excitement known. I entered the bedroom.

The brother, his back to me, was bending over a table examining some small metal objects. He looked up and nodded abstractedly.

—Do you mind, I said nervously, do you mind answering a question?

—What question? I have got a great bit of gear here.

—Listen to the question. When I was coming in a while back, did I see you walking on the air?

He turned again to stare at me and then laughed loudly.

—Well, by damn, he chuckled, I suppose you did, in a manner of speaking.

—What do you mean?

—Your question is interesting. Did it look well?

—If you want to know, it looked unnatural and if you are taking advantage of a power not of God, if you are dealing in godless things of darkness, I would strongly advise you to see Father Fahrt, because these things will lead to no good.

Here he sniggered.

—Have a look out of the window, he said.

I went and did so very gingerly. Between the sill and a stout branch near the top of the tree stretched a very taut wire, which I now saw came in at the base of the closed window and was anchored with some tightening device to the leg of the bed, which was in against the wall.

—My God Almighty! I exclaimed.

—Isn't it good?

—A bloody wire-walker, by cripes!

—I got the stuff from Jem out of the Queen's. There's nothing at all to it. If I rigged the wire across this room tomorrow and only a foot from the floor, you'd walk it yourself with very little practice. What's the difference? What's the difference if you're an inch or a mile up?

The only trouble is what they call psychological. It's a new word but I know what it means. The balancing part of it is child's play, and the trick is to put all idea of height out of your mind. It *looks* dangerous, of course, but there's money in that sort of danger. Safe danger.

—What happens if you fall and break your neck?

—Did you ever hear of Blondin? He died in his bed at the age of seventy-three, and fifty years ago he walked on a wire across Niagara Falls, one hundred and sixty feet above the roaring water. And several times—carrying a man on his back, stopping to fry eggs, a great man altogether. And didn't he appear once in Belfast?

—I think you are going off your head.

—I'm going to make money, for I have . . . certain schemes, certain very important schemes. Look what I have here. A printing machine. I got it from one of the lads at Westland Row, who stole it from his uncle. It's simple to operate, though it's old.

But I could not detach my mind from that wire.

—So you're to be the Blondin of Dublin?

—Well, why not?

—Niagara is too far away, of course. I suppose you'll sling a wire over the Liffey?

He started, threw down some metal thing, and turned to me wide-eyed.

—Well, sweet, God, he said, you have certainly said something. *You have certainly said something*. Sling a wire over the Liffey? The Masked Daredevil from Mount Street! There's a fortune there—*a fortune!* Lord save us, why didn't I think of it?

—I was only joking, for goodness' sake.

—*Joking?* I hope you'll keep on joking like that. I'll see Father Fahrt about this.

—To bless you before you risk your life?

—Balls! I'll need an organizer, a manager. Father Fahrt knows a lot of those young teachers and I'll get him to put me on to one of them. They're a sporty crowd. Do you remember Frank Corkey, N.T.? He was in this house once, a spoilt Jesuit. That man would blow up the walls of Jerusalem for two quid. He'd be the very man.

—And get sacked from his school for helping a young madman to kill himself?

—I'll get him. You wait and see.

That ended that day's surprising disputation. I was secretly amused at the idea of the brother getting on to Father Fahrt about organizing a walk across the Liffey on a tight-wire, with Mr Collopy sprawled in his cane armchair a few feet away listening to the appeal. I had heard of earthquakes and the devastation attending them. Here surely would be a terrible upheaval.

But once more I reckoned without the brother. Without saying a word he slipped off one day up to 35, Lower Leeson Street and saw Father Fahrt privately. He said so when he returned that evening, looking slightly daunted.

—The holy friar, he said, won't hear of it. Asked did I think I was a cornerboy or had I no respect for my family. Public pranks is what he called walking the high wire. Threatened to tell ould Collopy if I didn't put the idea out of my head. Asked me to promise. I promised, of course. But I'll find Corkey on my own and we'll make a damn fine day of it, believe you me. Had I no respect for my family, ah? What family?

—No Jesuit likes being mistaken for a Barnum, I pointed out.

Rather bitterly he said: You'll hear more about this.

I felt sure I would.

*   *   *

It had become evident to me that one of the brother's schemes was in operation, for a considerable stream of letters addressed to him began to arrive at the house, and he had become more secretive than ever. I refused to give him the satisfaction of asking him what he had been up to. I will tell all about that later but just now I wish to give an account of the sort of evening we had in our kitchen, not once but very many times, and the type of talk that went on. As usual, the subject under discussion was never named.

The brother and myself were at the table, struggling through that wretched homework, cursing Wordsworth and Euclid and Christian Doctrine and all similar scourges of youth. Mr Collopy was slumped in his cane armchair, the steel-rimmed glasses far down his nose. In an easy chair opposite was Father Kurt Fahrt who was a very tall man, thin, ascetic, grey-haired, blue about the jaws with a neck so slender that there would be room, so to speak, for two of them inside his priestly collar. On the edge of the range, handy to the reach of those philosophers, was a glass. On the floor beside Mr Collopy's chair was what was known as 'the crock'. It was in fact a squat earthenware container, having an ear on each side, in which the Kilbeggan Distill-ery marketed its wares. The Irish words for whiskey—*Uisge Beatha*—were burnt into its face. This vessel was, of course, opaque and there-fore mysterious; one could not tell how empty or full it was, nor how much Mr Collopy had been drinking. The door of Mrs Crotty's bed-room was, as usual, very slightly ajar.

—What the devil ails you, Father, Mr Collopy asked almost ir-ritably.

—Oh it's nothing much, Collopy, Father Fahrt said.

—But heavens above, this scrabbling and scratching—

—Forgive me. I have a touch of psoriasis about the back and chest.

—The sore *what*?

—Psoriasis. A little skin ailment.

—Lord save us, I thought you said you had sore eyes. Is there any question of scabs or that class of thing?

—Oh not at all. I am taking treatment. An ointment containing stuff known as chrysarobin.

—Well, this sore-whatever-it-is causes itching?

Father Fahrt laughed softly.

—Sometimes it feels more like etching, he smiled.

—The man for that is sulphur. Sulphur is one of the great sovereign remedies of the world. Bedamn but a friend of mine uses a lot of sulphur even in his garden.

Here Father Fahrt unconsciously scratched himself.

—Let us forget about such trivial things, he said, and thank God it is not something serious. So you're getting worked up again about your plan?

—It's a shame, Father, Mr Collopy said warmly. It's a bloody shame and that's what it is.

—Well, Collopy, what are we for in this world? We are here to suffer. We must sanctify ourselves. That's what suffering is for.

—Do you know, Father, Mr Collopy said testily, I am getting a bit sick in my intesteens at all this talk of yours about suffering. You seem to be very fond of suffering when other people do it. What would you do if you had the same situation in your own house?

—In my own house I would do what my Superior instructs me to do. My Order is really an army. We are under orders.

—Give me your glass, Your Holiness.

—Not much now, Collopy.

There was a small silence here that seemed portentous, though I did not raise my head to look.

—Father, said Mr Collopy at last, you would go off your bloody head if you had the same situation in your own house. You would make a show of yourself. You would tell Father Superior to go to hell, lep out the front door and bugger off down to Stephen's Green. Oh, I'm up to ye saints. Well up to ye. Do you not think that women have enough suffering, as you call it, bringing babbies into the world? And why do they do that? Is it because they're mad to sanctify themselves? Well faith no! It's because the husband is one great torch ablaze with the fires of lust!

—Collopy, please, Father Fahrt said in mild remonstrance. That attitude is quite wrong. Procreation is the *right* of a married man. Indeed it is his duty for the greater glory of God. It is a duty enjoined by the sacrament of marriage.

—Oh is that so, Mr Collopy said loudly, is that so indeed. To bring unfortunate new bosthoons into this vale of tears for more of this suffering of yours, ah? Another woman maybe. Sweet Lord!

—Now, now, Collopy. . . .

*   *   *

It had been a dull autumn day and in the early evening I decided that the weather would make it worth while looking for roach in the canal. My rod was crude enough but I had hooks of a special size which I had put away in a drawer in the bedroom. I got out the rod and went up for a hook. To my surprise the drawer was littered with sixpenny postal orders and also envelopes addressed to the brother describing him as 'Director, General Georama Gymnasium'. I decided to leave this strange stuff alone, took a hook and went off up along the canal. Perhaps my bait was wrong but I caught nothing and was back home in about an hour. The brother was in the bedroom when I returned, busy writing at the smaller table.

—I was out looking for roach, I remarked, and had to get a hook in that drawer. I see it's full of sixpenny postal orders.

—Not full, he said genially. There are only twenty-eight. But keep that under your hat.

—Twenty-eight is fourteen bob.

—Yes, but I expect a good few more.

—What's all this about General Georama Gymnasium?

—Well, it's my name for the moment, he said.

—What's Georama?

—If you don't know what a simple English word means, the Brothers in Synge Street can't be making much of a hand of you. A georama is a globe representing the earth. Something like what they have in schools. The sound of it goes well with general and gymnasium. That's why I took it. Join the GGG.

—And where did all those postal orders come from?

—From the other side. I put a small ad. in one of the papers. I want to teach people to walk the high wire.

—Is that what the General Georama Gymnasium is for, for heaven's sake?

—Yes. And it's one of the cheapest courses in the world. A great number of people want to walk the high wire and show off. Some of them may be merely mercenary and anxious to make an easy, quick fortune with some great circus.

—And are you teaching them this by post?

—Well, yes.

—What's going to happen if one of them falls and gets killed?

—A verdict of death by misadventure, I suppose. But it's most unlikely because I don't think any of them will dare to get up on the wire any distance from the ground. If they're young their parents will stop them. If they're old, rheumatism, nerves and decayed muscles will make it impossible.

—Do you mean you're going to have a correspondence course with those people?

—No. They get a copy of my four-page book of instructions. Price sixpence only. It's for nothing. A packet of fags and a box of matches would cost you nearly that, and no fag would give you the thrill of thinking about the high wire.

—This looks to me like a swindle.

—Rubbish. I'm only a bookseller. The valuable instructions and explanations are given by Professor Latimer Dodds. And he has included warnings of the danger as well.

—Who is Professor Latimer Dodds?

—A retired trapeze and high wire artist.

—I never heard of him.

—Here, take a look at the course yourself. I'm posting off copies just now to my clients.

I took the crudely-printed folder he handed me and put it in my pocket, saying that I would look over it later and make sure that Mr Collopy didn't see it. I didn't want the brother to appraise my reactions to his handiwork, for already I had a desire to laugh. Downstairs, Mr Collopy was out and Annie was in the bedroom colloguing with Mrs Crotty. I lit the gas and there and then had a sort of free lesson on how to walk the high wire. The front page or cover read 'THE HIGH WIRE—Nature Held at Bay—Spine-chilling Spectacle Splenetises Sporting Spectators—By Professor H. Q. Latimer Dodds'.

Lower down was the title of the Gymnasium and our own address. There was no mention of the brother by name but a note said 'Consultations with the Director by appointment only'. I was horrified to think of strangers calling and asking Mr Collopy to be good enough to make an appointment for them with the Director of the Gymnasium.

The top of the left inside page had a Foreword which I think I may quote:

'It were folly to asseverate that periastral peripatesis on the *aes ductile,* or wire, is destitute of profound peril not only to sundry *membra,* or limbs, but to the back and veriest life itself. Wherefore is the reader most graciously implored to abstain from *le risque majeur* by first submitting himself to the most perspicacious scrutiny by highly-qualified physician or surgeon for, in addition to anatomical verifications, evidence of Ménière's Disease, caused by haemorrhage into the equilibristic labyrinth of the ears, causing serious nystagmus and insecurity of gait. If giddiness is suspected to derive from gastric disorder, resort should be had to bromide of potassium, acetanilide, bromural or chloral. The aural labyrinth consists of a number of membranous chambers and tubes immersed in fluid residing in the cavity of the inner ear, in mammals joined to the cochlea. The membranous section of the labyrinth consists of two small bags, the saccule and the utricle, and three semi-circular canals which open into it. The nerves which supply the labyrinth end with a number of cells attired in hair-like projections which, when grouped, form the two otolith organs in the saccule and utricle and the three *cristae* of the semi-circular canals. In the otolith organs the hair-like protruberances are embedded in a gelatinous mess containing calcium carbonate. The purpose of this grandiose apparatus, so far as *homo sapiens* is concerned, is the achievement of remaining in an upright posture, one most desirable in the case of a performer on the high wire who is aloft and far from the ground.'

I found that conscientiously reading that sort of material required considerable concentration. I do not know what it means and I have no doubt whatever that the brother's 'clients' will not know either.

The actual instructions as to wire-walking were straightforward enough. Perhaps it was the brother's own experience (for he was undoubtedly Professor Latimer Dodds) which made him advise a bedroom as the scene of opening practices. The wire was to be slung about a foot from the floor between two beds very heavily weighted 'with bags of cement, stone, metal safes or other ponderous objects'. When the neophyte wire-walker was ready to begin practice, the massive bedsteads were to be dragged apart by 'friends', so that the necessary tension of the wire would be established and maintained. 'If it happens that the weight on a bed turns out to be insufficient to support the weight of the performer on the wire, the friends should sit or lie on the bed.' Afterwards practice was transferred to 'the orchard' where two stout adjacent fruit trees were to be the anchors of the wire, the elevation of which was to be gradually increased. The necessity for daily practice was emphasized and (barring accidents) a good result was promised in three months. A certain dietetic regimen was prescribed, with total prohibition of alcohol and tobacco, and it was added that even if the student proved absolutely hopeless in all attempts at wire-walking, he would in any event feel immensely improved in health and spirits at the end of that three months.

I hastily put the treatise in my pocket as I heard the steps of Mr Collopy coming in the side-door. He hung his coat up on the back of the door and sat down at the range.

—A man didn't call about the sewers? he asked.

—The sewers? I don't think so.

—Ah well, please God he'll be here tomorrow. He's going to lay a new connection in the yard, never mind why. He is a decent man by the name of Corless, a great handball player in his day. Where's that brother of yours?

—Upstairs.

—Upstairs, faith! What is he doing upstairs? Is he in bed?

—No. I think he's writing.

—Writing? Well, well. Island of Saints and Scholars. Upstairs

writing and burning the gas. Tell him to come down here if he wants
to write.

Annie came out of the back room.

—Mrs Crotty would like to see you, Father.

—Oh, certainly.

I went upstairs to warn the brother. He nodded grimly and stuffed
a great wad of stamped envelopes, ready for the post, under his coat.
Then he put out the gas. . . .

*   *   *

About the time of Mrs Crotty's death, the brother's 'business' had
grown to a surprising size. He had got a box—fitly enough, a soap-box
—from Davies the grocers, and went down to the hall every morning
very early to collect the little avalanche of letters awaiting him there
before they should come to the notice of Mr Collopy. Still using our
home address, he had become, in addition to Professor Latimer Dodds,
The Excelsior Turf Bureau. He operated, I suspect, on the old system
of dividing clients into groups equal to the number of runners in a given
race, and sending a different horse with any chance to each group. No
matter which horse won, a group of clients would have backed it, and
one of the brother's rules of business was that a winning client should
send him the odds to five shillings. He was by now smoking openly in
the house and several times I saw him coming out of or going into a
public house, usually with a rather down-at-heel character. He had
money to spend.

He also operated the Zenith School of Journalism, which claimed
to be able to explain how to make a fortune with the pen in twelve
'clear, analytical, precise and unparagoned lessons'. As well he was
trying to flood Britain with a treatise on cage-birds, published by the
Simplex Nature Press, which also issued a Guide to Gardening, both
works obviously composed of material looted from books in the National Library. He had put away his little press and now had printing
done by an impoverished back-lane man with some small semblance of
machinery. He once asked me to get stamps for him, giving me two
pounds; this gives some idea of the volume of his correspondence.

He seemed in a bad temper the evening the remains of Mrs Crotty
were brought to the church at Haddington Road; he did not come
home afterwards but walked off without a word, possibly to visit a

public house. Next morning dawned dark, forbidding and very wet, suitable enough, I thought, for a funeral. I thought of Wordsworth and his wretched 'Pathetic Fallacy'. The brother, still in a bad temper, went down as usual to collect his mail.

—To hell with this house and this existence, he said when he came back. Now we will have to trail out to Deansgrange in this dirty downpour.

—Mrs Crotty wasn't the worst, I said. Surely you don't begrudge her a funeral? You'll need one yourself some day.

—She was all right, he conceded. It's her damned husband I'm getting very tired of . . .

Mr Hanafin called with his cab for myself, the brother, Mr Collopy and Annie. The hearse and two other cabs were waiting at the church, the cabs accommodating mysterious other mourners who hurried to Mr Collopy and Annie with whispers and earnest handshakes. Myself and the brother were ignored. As the Mass was about to begin, a third cab arrived with three elderly ladies and a tall, emaciated gentleman in severe black. These, I gather later, were members of the committee assisting Mr Collopy in his work, whatever that was.

The hearse elected to take the route along Merrion Road by the sea, where a sort of hurricane was in progress. The cabs following stumbled on the exposed terrain. Mr Collopy, showing some signs of genuine grief, spoke little.

—Poor Mrs Crotty was very fond of the sea, he said at last.

—Seemingly she was, Annie remarked. She told me once that when she was a girl, nothing could keep her out of the sea at Clontarf. She could swim and all.

—Yes, a most versatile woman, Mr Collopy said. And a saint.

A burial on a wet day, with the rain lashing down on the mourners, is a matter simply of squalor. The murmured Latin at the graveside seemed to make the weather worse. The brother, keeping well to the back of the assembly, was quietly cursing in an undertone. I was surprised and indeed a bit shocked to see him surreptitiously taking a flat half-pint bottle from his hip pocket and, with grimaces, swallowing deep draughts from it. Surely this was unseemly at the burial of the dead? I think Father Fahrt noticed it.

When all was over and the sodden turgid clay in on top of the deceased, we made for the gate. Mr Collopy was walking with a breathless stout man who had come on foot. When it was made known

to us that this poor man had no conveyance, the brother gallantly
offered his seat in the cab; this was gratefully accepted. The brother
said he could borrow a bicycle near by but I was certain his plan was
to borrow more than a bicycle, for there was a pub at Kill Avenue,
which was also near by. . . .

* * *

During the year that followed Mrs Crotty's death, the atmosphere of
the house changed somewhat. Annie joined some sort of a little club,
probably composed mostly of women who met every afternoon to play
cards or discuss household matters. She seemed to be—heavens!—
coming out of her shell. Mr Collopy returned to his mysterious work
with renewed determination, not infrequently having meetings of his
committee in our kitchen after warning everybody that this deliberative
chamber was out of bounds for that evening. . . .

The brother went from strength to strength and eventually reached
the stage of prosperity that is marked by borrowing money for industrial expansion. From little bits of information and from inference,
I understood that he had borrowed £400 short-term with interest at
twenty per cent. A quick turn-over, no matter how small the profit,
was the brother's business axiom. He happened to read of the discovery
in an old English manor house of 1,500 two-volume sets of a survey in
translation of Miguel de Cervantes Saavaedra, his work and times. . . .

Mr Collopy came in about five o'clock, followed shortly afterwards
by Annie. He seemed in a bad temper. Without a word he collapsed
into his armchair and began reading the paper. The brother came in
about six, loaded with books and small parcels. He naturally perceived
the chill and said nothing. The tea turned out to be a very silent, almost menacing, meal. . . .

When the tea things had been cleared away, Mr Collopy resumed
reading his paper but after a time, he suddenly sat up and glared at
the brother, who was dozing opposite him at the range.

—I want a word with you, mister-me-friend, he said abruptly.

The brother sat up.

—Well? he said. I'm here.

—Do you know a certain party by the name of Sergeant Driscoll of
the D.M.P.?

—I don't know any policemen. I keep far away from them. They're
a dangerous gang, promoted at a speed that is proportionate to the

number of people they manage to get into trouble. And they have one way of getting the most respectable people into very bad trouble.

—Well, is that a fact? And what is the one way?

—Perjury. They'd swear a hole in an iron bucket. They are all the sons of gobhawks from down the country.

—I mentioned Sergeant Driscoll of the D.M.P.————

—The wilds of Kerry, I'll go bail. The banatee up at six in the morning to get ready thirteen breakfasts out of a load of spuds, maybe a few leaves of kale, injun meal, salt and buttermilk. Breakfast for Herself, Himself, the eight babies and the three pigs, all out of the one pot. That's the sort of cods we have looking after law and order in Dublin.

—I mentioned Sergeant Driscoll of the D.M.P. He was here this morning. Gold help me, being interviewed by the police has been *my* cross, and at my time of life.

—Well, it is a good rule never to make any statement. Don't give him the satisfaction. Say that you first must see your solicitor, no matter what he is accusing you of.

—Accusing *me* of? It had nothing to do with me. It was *you* he was looking for. He was making inquiries. There may yet be deleterious ructions, you can take my word for that.

—What, *me*? And what have *I* done?

—A young lad fell into the river at Islandbridge, hurt his head and was nearly drowned. He had to be brought to hospital. Sergeant Driscoll and his men questioned this lad and the other young hooligans with him. And *your* name was mentioned.

—I know nothing about any young lads at Islandbridge.

—Then how did they get your name? They even knew this address, and the Sergeant said they had a little book with this address here on the cover.

—Did you see the book?

—No.

—This is the work of some pultogue that doesn't like me, one that has it in for me over some imaginary grievance. A trouble-maker. This town is full of them. I'm damn glad I'm clearing out. Give me a blood-thirsty and depraved Saxon any day.

—I've never known you not to have an answer. You are the right stainless man.

—I refuse to be worried about what brats from the slums say or think, or at country rozzers either.

—Those youngsters, Sergeant Driscoll said, were experimenting with a frightfully dangerous contraption, a sort of death machine. They had fixed a wire across the Liffey, made fast to lamp-posts or trees on either side. And this young bosthoon gets his feet into a pair of special slippers or something of the kind. What do you think of that?

—Nothing much, except it reminds me of a circus.

—Yes, or The Dance Of Death at the Empire Theatre at Christmas. Lord look down on us but I never heard of such recklessness and sinful extravaganza. It is the parents I pity, the suffering parents that brought them up by wearing their fingers to the bone and going without nourishing food in their old age to give the young poguemahones an education. A touch of the strap, night and morning, is what those boyos badly need.

—And how did one of them get into the water?

—How do you think? He gets out walking on this wire until he's half-way, then he flies into a panic, gets dizzy, falls down into the deep water, hitting his head off a floating baulk of timber. And of course not one of those thoolermawns could swim. It was the mercy of God that a bailiff was within earshot. He heard the screaming and the commotion and hurried up. But an unemployed man was there first. Between the pair of them they got this half-drowned young character out of the river and held him upside-down to drain the water out of him.

—And the pinkeens, the brother interposed.

—It was a direct act of Providence that those men were there. The high-wire genius had to be lurried into hospital, Jervis Street, and there is no need to try to be funny about it. You could be facing murther today, or manslaughter.

—I've told you I had nothing to do with it. I know nothing. I am unaware of the facts.

—I suppose you'd swear that.

—I would.

—And you have the brazen cheek to sit there and accuse the long-suffering D.M.P. of being addicted to perjury.

—And so they are.

—Faith then, and if I was on the jury I would know who to believe about that Islandbridge affair.

—If I was charged with engineering that foolish prank, I would stop at nothing to unmask the low miscreant who has been trying to put stains on my character.

—Yes, I know right well what you mean. One lie would lead to another till you got so bogged down in mendacity and appalling perjury that the Master of the Rolls or the Recorder or whoever it would be would call a halt to the proceedings and send the papers to the Attorney-General. And faith then your fat would be in the fire. You could get five years for perjury and trying to pervert the course of justice. And the same Islandbridge case would be waiting for you when you came out.

—I don't give a goddam about any of those people.

—Do you tell me? Well, *I* do. This is my house.

—You know I'm leaving it very soon.

—And Sergeant Driscoll said you were to call at College Street for an interview.

—I'll call at no College Street. Sergeant Driscoll can go to hell.

—Stop using bad, depraved language in this house or you may leave it sooner than you think. You are very much mistaken if you think I am content to be hounded and pestered by policemen over your low and contemptible schemes to delude simple young people———

—Oh, rubbish!

—And rob them, rob them of money they never earned but filched from the purses of their long-suffering parents and guardians.

—I told you I don't know any simple young people at Islandbridge. And any young people I do know, they're not simple.

—You have one of the lowest and most lying tongues in all Ireland and that's sure fact. You are nothing but a despicable young tramp. May God forgive me if I have been in any way to blame for the way I brought you up.

—Why don't you blame those crows, the holy Christian Brothers? God's Disjointed.

—I have warned you several times to stop desecrating my kitchen with your cowardly blackguarding of a dedicated band of high-minded Christian teachers.

—I hear Brother Cruppy is going to throw off the collar and get married.

—Upon my word, Mr Collopy said shrilly, you are not too old to have a stick taken to. Remember that. A good thrashing would work wonders.

He was clearly very angry. The brother shrugged and said nothing but it was lucky just then that there was a knock at the outer door. . . .

* * *

[The knock is not the D.M.P. but a friend of Mr. Collopy's come to aid the master of the house in carrying on the mysterious good work. The brother realizes, however, that it is time to move on. In the months that follow, Mr. Collopy leaves the house frequently to go into the downpours and high wind. He becomes "a familiar figure, sheltering under a sodden umbrella, on the fringe of the small crowds attending street-corner meetings. . . . He was not in any way concerned with the purpose or message of those meetings. He was there to heckle, and solely from the angle of his own mysterious preoccupation."]

One night he came home very thoroughly drenched, and instead of going straight to bed, he sat at the range taking solace from his crock.

—For heaven's sake go to bed, Father, Annie said. You are drowned. Go to bed and I will make you punch.

—Ah, no, he said brightly. In such situations my early training as a hurler will stand to me.

Sure enough, he had a roaring cold the following morning and did stay in bed for a few days by command of Annie, who did not lack his own martinet quality. Gradually the cold ebbed but when he was about the house again his movements were very awkward and he complained loudly of pains in his bones. Luckily he was saved the excruciation of trying to go upstairs, for he had himself built a lavatory in the bedroom in Mrs Crotty's time. But his plight was genuine enough, and I suggested that on my way to school I should drop in a note summoning Dr Blennerhassett.

Dr Blennerhassett did call and said Mr Collopy had severe rheumatism. He prescribed a medicament which Annie got from the chemist —red pills in a round white box labelled 'The Tablets'. He also said, I believe, that the patient's intake of sugar should be drastically reduced, that alcohol should not in any circumstances be consumed, that an endeavour should be made to take mild exercise, and to have hot baths as often as possible. Whether or not Mr Collopy met those four conditions or any of them, he grew steadily worse as the weeks went by. He took to using a stick but I actually had to assist him in the short distance between his armchair and his bed. He was a cripple, and a very irascible one.

*   *   *

[More squalor follows: One night as our narrator is returning home from another inconsequential date with his inconsequential girl acquaintance Penelope:]

The route I took was by Wilton Place, a triangular shaded nook not much used by traffic. I knew from other experiences that it was haunted by prostitutes of the very lowest cadres, and also by their scruffy clients. A small loutish group of five or six people were giggling in the shadows as I approached but became discreetly silent as I passed. But when I had gone only two yards or so, I heard one solitary word in a voice I swore I knew:

—*Seemingly.*

I paused involuntarily, deeply shocked, but I soon walked on. I had, in fact, been thinking of Penelope, and that one word threw my mind into a whirl. What was the meaning of this thing sex, what was the nature of sexual attraction? Was it all bad and dangerous? What was Annie doing late at night, standing in a dark place with young blackguards? Was I any better myself in my conduct, whispering sly things into the ear of lovely and innocent Penelope? Had I, in fact, at the bottom of my heart dirty intentions, some dark deed postponed only because the opportunity had not yet presented itself.

As I had expected, the kitchen was empty, for I had assisted Mr Collopy to bed before going out earlier. I did not want to be there when Annie came. I got notepaper and an envelope, went upstairs and got into bed.

I lay there with the light on for a long time, reflecting. Then I wrote a confidential and detailed letter to the brother about, first, the very low and painful condition of Mr Collopy; and second, the devastating incident concerning Annie. I paused before signing my name and for a wild few minutes considered writing a little about myself and Penelope. But reason, thank God, prevailed. I said nothing but signed and sealed the letter.

*   *   *

A reply was not long coming, taking the form of a parcel and a letter. I opened the letter first, and here it is:

'Many thanks for your rather alarming communication.

'From what you say it is clear to me that Collopy is suffering from rheumatoid arthritis, very likely of the peri-articular type. If you can persuade him to let you have a look, you will find that the joints are swollen and of fusiform shape and I think you will find that he is afflicted at the hands and feet, knees, ankles and wrists. Probably his temperature is elevated, and total rest in bed is most desirable. The focus of infection for rheumatoid arthritis is usually bad teeth and the presence in the gums of pyorrhoea alveolaris, so that he should order Hanafin's cab and call on a dentist. But happily we have invented here in the Academy a certain cure for the disorder, provided the treatment is sedulously followed. I am sending you under separate cover a bottle of our patent Gravid Water. It will be your own job to make sure that he takes a t/spoonful of it three times a day after meals. See to the first dose before you leave the house in the morning, inquire about the daytime dose when you get back from school, and similarly ensure the evening dose. It would be well to tell Annie of the importance of this treatment and the need for regularity . . .'

At this stage I opened the parcel and under many wrappings uncovered a large bottle which bore a rather gaudy label. Here was its message:

THE GRAVID WATER
The miraculous specific for the
complete   cure   within   one
month   of   the   abominable
scourage known as Rheumatoid
Arthritis.
Dose—one t-spoonful three
times daily after meals.
Prepared at
LONDON ACADEMY LABORATORIES

Well, this might be worth trying, I thought, but immediately soaked the bottle in water and removed the label, for I knew that nothing would induce Mr Collopy to touch the contents if he knew or suspected that they had originated with the brother. I then resumed reading the letter:

'I was certainly shocked to hear that Annie has been consorting with cornerboys up the canal. These are dirty merchants and if she continues, disease will be inevitable. I am sure that neither you nor I could attempt any estimate of how cunning and cute she is or how totally ignorant and innocent. Does she know the Facts of Life? Apart from venereal disease, does she know of the danger of pregnancy? I don't think the arrival of an illegitimate on the doorstep would alleviate Collopy's rheumatoid condition.

'You did not say in your letter that you suspected that she had some infection but if she has, diagnosis without examination at this distance is rather difficult. I think we may rule out Granuloma Inguinale. It takes the form of very red, beefy ulceration. A clear symptom is ever-increasing debility and marked physical wasting, often ending in extreme cachexia and death. It is mostly met with in tropical countries, and almost confined to negroes. We may discount it.

'For similar reasons of rarity, we may discard the possibility of Lymphogranuloma Venereum. This is a disease of the lymph glands and lymph nodes, and one finds a hot, painful group of swollen buboes in the inguinal area. There will be headaches, fever and pains in the joints. The causitive agent is a virus. Here again, however, Lymphogranuloma Venereum is a near-monopoly of the negro.

'The greatest likelihood is that Annie, if infected, labours under the sway of H.M. Gonococcus. In women the symptoms are so mild at the beginning as to be unnoticed but it is a serious and painful invasion. There is usually fever following infection of the pelvic organs. Complications to guard against include endocarditis, meningitis and skin decay. Gonococcal endocarditis can be fatal.

'There remains, of course, the Main Act. This disease is caused by a virus known as *spirochaeta pallida* or *treponema pallidum*. We can have skin rash, lesions of the mouth, enlargement of lymph glands, loss of scalp hair, inflammation of the eyes, jaundice from liver damage, convulsions, deafness, meningitis and sometimes comma. The Last Act, the most serious, in most cases takes a cardiovascular form where the main lesion is seated in the thoracic aorta directly near the heart. The extensible tissue is ruined, the aorta swells and a saccular dilatation or an aneurysm may take shape. Sudden death is quite common. Other results are G.P.I. (paresis), locomotor ataxia, and wholesale contamination of the body and its several organs. My London Academy Laboratories markets a three-in-one remedy "Love's Lullaby" but as this specific involves fits and head-staggers in persons who have in fact not been infected at all, it would be unwise to prescribe for Annie on the blind.

'I would advise that at this stage you would keep her under very minute observation and see if you can detect any symptoms and then get in touch with me again. You might perhaps devise some prophylactic scheming such as remarking apropos of nothing that conditions on the canal bank are nothing short of a scandal with men and women going about there poxed up to the eyes, drunk on methylated spirits, flooding the walks with contaminated puke and making it unsafe for Christians even to take a walk in that area. You could add that you are writing to the D.M.P. urging the arrest at sight of any characters found loitering there. We all know that probably Annie is a cute and cunning handful but very likely she is not proof against a good fright. On the other hand you might consider telling Mr Collopy what you know, for it would be easier for a father to talk straight to his own daughter on this very serious subject, on the off-chance that Annie is innocent and quite uninstructed; in fact it would be his duty to do so. If you see fit to adopt that course, it would be natural to bring Father Fahrt into the picture, for the matter has a self-evident spiritual content. If being on the scene you would feel embarrassed to thus take the initiative, I could write from here to Mr Collopy or Father Fahrt or both, telling of the information I have received (not disclosing the source) and asking that steps should be taken for prevention and/or cure.

'However, I must say that I doubt whether Annie is in trouble at all and the best plan might be to keep wide-awake so far as yourself is concerned, report to me if there are any symptoms or other development, and take no action for the present.'

Well, that was a long and rather turgid letter but I found myself in agreement with the last paragraph. In fact I put the whole subject out of my head and merely dedicated myself to Mr Collopy's rheumatism.

*   *   *

I duly produced the bottle of Gravid Water to Mr Collopy, saying it was a miracle cure for rheumatism which I had got from a chemist friend. I also produced a tablespoon and told him he was to take a spoonful without fail three times a day after meals. And I added that I would keep reminding him.

—Oh well now, I don't know, he said. Are there salts in it?

—No, I don't think so.

—Is there anything in the line of bromide or saltpetre?

—No. I believe the stuff in the fluid is mostly vitamins. I would say it is mainly a blood tonic.

—Ah-Ah? The blood is all, of course. It's like the mainspring on a watch. If a man lets his blood run down, he'll find himself with all classes of boils and rashes. And scabs.

—And rheumatism, I add.

—And who is this chemist when he is at home?

—He's . . . he's a chap I know named Donnelly. He works in Hayes, Conyngham and Robinson. He is a qualified man, of course.

—Oh very well. I'll take a chance. Amn't I nearly crippled? What have I to lose?

—Nothing at all.

There and then he took his first tablespoonful and after a week of the treatment said he felt much better. I was glad of this and emphasized the necessity of persevering in the treatment. From time to time I wrote to the brother for a fresh bottle.

After six weeks I began to notice something strange in the patient's attempts at movement. His walk became most laborious and slow and the floor creaked under him. One night in bed I heard with a start a distant rending crash coming from his bedroom off the kitchen. I hurried down to find him breathless and tangled in the wreckage of his bed. It seems that the wire mattress, rusted and rotted by Mrs Crotty's nocturnal diuresis (or bed-wetting) had collapsed under Mr Collopy's weight.

—Well, the dear knows, he said shrilly, isn't this the nice state of affairs? Help me out of this.

I did so, and it was very difficult.

—What happened? I asked.

—Faith and can't you see? The whole shooting-gallery collapsed under me.

—The fire is still going in the kitchen. Put on your overcoat and rest there. I'll take this away and get another bed.

—Very well. That catastrophe has me rightly shaken. I think a dram or two from the crock is called for.

Not in a very good temper, I took down the whole bed and put the pieces against the wall in the passage outside. Then I dismantled the brother's bed and re-erected it in Mr Collopy's room.

—Your bed awaits, sir, I told him.

—Faith now and that was quick work, he said. I will go in directly I finish this nightcap. You may go back to your own bed.

On the following day, Sunday, I went in next door and borrowed their weighing scales. When I managed to get Mr Collopy to stand on the little platform, the needle showed his weight to be 29 stone! I was flabbergasted. I checked the machine by weighing myself and found it was quite accurate. The amazing thing was that Mr Collopy was still the same size and shape as of old. I could attribute his extraordinary weight only to the brother's Gravid Water, so I wrote to him urgently explaining what had happened. And the letter I got back was surprising enough in itself. Here it is:

'It is not only in Warrington Place that amazing things are happening; they are happening here as well. A week ago the mother of Milton Byron Barnes, my partner, died. In her will, which came to light yesterday, she left him her house and about £20,000 in cash and she left £5,000 TO ME! What do you think of that? It looks like the blessing of God on my Academy.

'I was indeed sorry about what you tell me of Mr Collopy. The cause of it is too obvious—excessive dosage. On the label of the bottle the term 't-spoonful" meant "tea-spoonful", not "tablespoonful". The Gravid Water, properly administered was calculated to bring about a gradual and controlled increase in weight and thus to cause a re-development of the rheumatoid joints by reason of the superior weight and the increased work they would have to do.

'Unfortunately the alarming overweight you report is an irreversible result of the Gravid Water; there is no antidote. In this situation we must put our trust in God. In humble thanks for my own legacy and to help poor Mr Collopy, I have made up my mind to bring him and Father Fahrt on a pilgrimage to Rome. The present Pontiff, Pius X, or Giuseppe Sarto, is a very noble and holy man, and I do not think it is in the least presumptuous to expect a miracle and have Mr Collopy restored to his proper weight. Apart from that, the trip will be physically invigorating, for I intend to proceed by sea from London to the port of Ostia in the Mediterranean, only about sixty miles from the Eternal City. Please advise both pilgrims accordingly and tell them to see immediately about passports and packing clothes.

'You should have ingestion of the Gravid Water discontinued and need not disclose the spiritual aim of the pilgrimage to Mr Collopy. I will write again in a week or so.'

* * *

[The brother somehow pulls off the audience with the Pope. There is an interview between His Holiness and Mr. Collopy which stands somewhere between the kitchen disputes in this novel and the job interview between the Jesuit and James Joyce in *The Dalkey Archive*. The tone at times, however, falls into buffoonery, like a similar scene in the *Doctor Faustus* attributed to Marlowe. There are also gusts of Latin and Italian jokes which blow long enough to make the scene depend upon them somewhat as Henry V's courting in Shakespeare depends on French. The audience in this case comes to an embarrassing halt after a misunderstanding between the Pope and Mr. Collopy. Or rather, one might say, a sudden, shocking undertsanding of Mr. Collopy's life work. The brother, of course, must provide our narrator with the details, including Mr. Collopy's death, which follows shortly after the catastrophic audience.]

I was lying in bed one morning, having already decided I would not go to school that day and thinking that perhaps I would never go back to it. The brother's last extraordinary letter about the Holy Father and Father Fahrt had contained a cheque for twenty-five pounds. I had already trained Annie to bring me some breakfast in bed and was lying there at my ease, smoking and thinking. I could hear men shouting at horses on the tow-path, hauling a barge. It was amazing how quickly life changed. The brother's...miracle was his feat in founding a new sort of university in London. Then you had the three of them inside the Vatican arguing with the Holy Father himself. It would not surprise me if the brother turned out to be appointed Governor of Rome or even came home in the purple of a cardinal, for I knew that in the old days it was common for Popes to appoint mere children to be cardinals. I thought I would join the brother in London. Even if his business did not suit me, there would be plenty of other jobs to be had there. Suddenly Annie came into the room and handed me an orange envelope. It was a cablegram.

COLLOPY DEAD AND FUNERAL IS
TOMORROW HERE IN ROME AM WRITING

The next three or four days were very grim. There was almost total silence in the house. Neither of us could think of anything to say. I went out a bit and drank some stout but not much. In the end a letter did arrive from the brother. This is what he had to say:

'My cablegram must have been a great shock to you, to say nothing of Annie. Let me tell you what happened.

'After the Vatican rumpus, Father Fahrt and Collopy, but particularly Collopy, were very depressed. I was busy thinking about getting back to London and my business. Father Fahrt thought that some distraction and uplift were called for and booked two seats for a violin recital in a small hall near the hotel. He foolishly booked the most expensive seats without making sure they were not in an upstairs gallery. They were, and approached by a narrow wooden stairs. This concert was in the afternoon. Halfway up the first flight of stairs there was a small landing. Collopy painfully led the way up with his stick and the aid of the banister, Father Fahrt keeping behind to save him if he overbalanced and fell backwards. When Collopy got to this landing and stepped on to the middle of it, there was a rending, splintering crash, the whole floor collapsed and with a terrible shriek, Collopy disappeared through the gaping hole. There was a sickening thud and more noise of breakage as he hit bottom. Poor Father Fahrt was distracted, rushed down, alerted the doorman, got the manager and other people and had a message sent to me at the hotel.

'When I arrived the scene was grotesque. There was apparently no access to the space under the stairs and two carpenters using hatchets, saws and chisels were carefully breaking down the woodwork in the hallway below the landing. About a dozen lighted candles were in readiness on one of the steps, casting a ghastly light on the very shaken Father Fahrt, two gendarmes, a man with a bag who was evidently a doctor and a whole mob of sundry characters, many of them no doubt onlookers who had no business there.

'The carpenters eventually broke through and pulled away several boards as ambulance men arrived with a stretcher. The doctor and Father Fahrt pushed their way to the aperture. Apparently Collopy was lying on his back covered with broken timbers and plastering, one leg doubled under him and blood pouring from one of his ears. He was semi-conscious and groaning pitifully. The doctor gave him some massive injection and then Father Fahrt knelt beside him, and hoarse, faltering whispers told us he was hearing a confession. Then, under the shattered stairway of this cheap Roman hall, Father Fahrt administered the Last Rites to Collopy.

'Getting the unfortunate man on the stretcher after the doctor had given him another knock-out injection was an enormous job for the ambulance men, who had to call for assistance from two bystanders. Nobody could understand his prodigious weight. (N.B.—I have changed the label on the Gravid Water bottle to guard strictly against overdosage.) It was fully twenty minutes before Collopy, now quite unconscious, could be got from under the stairs, and four men were manning the stretcher. He was driven off to hospital.

'Father Fahrt and I walked glumly back to the hotel. He told me he was sure the fall would kill Collopy. After an hour or so he got a telephone call from the hospital. A doctor told him that Collopy was dead on admission, from multiple injuries. He, the doctor, would like to see us urgently and would call to the hotel about six.

'When he arrived, he and Father Fahrt had a long conversation in Italian one word of which, I need hardly say, I did not understand.

'When he had gone, Father Fahrt told me the facts. Collopy had a fractured skull, a broken arm and leg and severe rupture of the whole stomach region. Even if none of those injuries was individually fatal, no man of Collopy's age could survive the shock of such an accident. But what had completely puzzled the doctor and his colleagues was the instantaneous onset of decomposition in the body and its extraordinarily rapid development. The hospital had got in touch with the city health authorities, who feared some strange foreign disease and had ordered that the body be buried the next morning. The hospital had arranged for undertakers to attend, at our expense, the following morning at 10 A.M. and a grave had been booked at the cemetery of Campo Verano.

'I was interested in that mention of premature and rapid decomposition of the body. I am not sure but I would say that here was the Gravid Water again. I said nothing of course.'

* * *

[When the brother returns to Dublin he shows the narrator a photograph of Mr. Collopy's headstone, and in doing so allows O'Brien to work in Keats again.]

✠

COLLOPY
of Dublin
1848–1910
Here lies one whose name
is writ in water
R.I.P.

—Isn't it good, he [the brother] chuckled. 'In water' instead of
'on water'?

Myles's Best

The true function of a writer is to produce a masterpiece. No other task is of any consequence.
                    —Cyril Connolly, *Enemies of Promise*

Day after day I receive letters calling for stuff that is more 'popular', 'more in touch with the ordinary people'. 'Give us,' a reader says, 'something that may interest and help us in our daily lives.'
                    —"Hints for Sots" in *Cruiskeen Lawn*

". . . though this knave came something saucily into the world . . . yet . . . there was good sport at his making, and the whoreson must be acknowledged."
                    —Gloucester, in *King Lear*

If you don't think that's funny, write and tell me why.
                    —*The Best of Myles*

INTRODUCTION

As for a serious writer's taking up journalism, we are apt to follow Hemingway's prescription: it is all right for apprentice work, but you have to get out in time; and there are those who say that our man is such a case, a man who did not get out in time. They can point to the first two novels, *At Swim* and *The Third Policeman,* as the masterpieces written pretty much before the Myles thing took hold. Once settled into the column and, more important, settled into the comfortable persona of the column, O'Brien never wrote a book comparable to the first two. Therefore, it may be argued, far from sharpening a technique which, after all, was fully developed in the first novel, the column merely served as a slightly improved version of the Dublin saloon, that notorious dissipator of would-be Irish novels. While it is true that some notions that first appeared in the columns later wandered into novels such as *The Hard Life* and *The Dalkey Archive,* so the argument runs, it is precisely because these

153

ideas were no longer virginal that the novelist lacked the passion to fuse them with the kind of structure that would have made them major novels.

One could cite here as parallels the lives of Truman Capote and Norman Mailer, who never wrote novels as good as *Other Voices, Other Rooms* or *The Naked and the Dead* after the authors embarked, as the phrase always runs, upon a career in journalism. There are many reasons, however, why a novelist who writes original, moving fiction in his twenties might not continue to do so through the next two decades, when one would expect him to be peaking. Some of these reasons have to do with biology, some economics, and some with the kind of novel the writer wrote in his twenties and the kind he is interested in reading in his thirties or forties. O'Brien, for instance, did not ever want to read *At Swim* again, and he came to criticize Joyce more and more for, among other things, being too much in love with the tour de force. *The Hard Life,* however, a book no one ever accused of being a tour de force, was a favorite of his.

Of course, through all this speculation lurks the rejection of *The Third Policeman.* As in the case of Beckett's refusal to write in English after the rejection of *Watt,* people read O'Brien's refusal to write novels as a statement. The fact may well be that as Beckett wrote in French because he was living with French people in France, O'Brien wrote journalism because that was what people spoke where he lived. Yet the rejection of *The Third Policeman* cannot be overlooked entirely, for it was not lost, as O'Brien put out in various fanciful variations, nor was it turned down by Longmans alone, as he confided to a few. It was passed over by a number of houses, and O'Brien's agents let him know that it was in part the commercial failure of *At Swim* which made publishers reluctant to take on the new, "even more fantastic" book. In short, writing a masterpiece was something he'd gotten away with once, but such behavior would not be tolerated again. Having written the best novels he could, and seen that they were not good enough, because in a sense they were too good, O'Brien was not really presented with a choice of going over to journalism so much as an opportunity to use journalism to stay in print.

Something should be said about the sort of "journalism" that went out under the title *Cruiskeen Lawn* by Myles na Gopaleen. It was hardly Hemingway's quai at Smyrna or Capote's trip to Russia or even

Mailer's highly personalized and metaphorical political conventions, movie stars, and other moon shots. Though occupying a role in Irish Journalism somewhere between our H. L. Mencken and Art Buchwald, he was more interested in being a kind of Mark Twain, a man whom he admired as being "derogatory." That word, however, can be misleading if we think of it only as a *taking away from*. In Ireland it seems that the emphasis quickly shifts from what is lost to who is doing the talking. Mark Twain was also handy coin of the realm, for as O'Brien emerged from the obscurities of the fierce Irish satirical tradition into the more public and benign world of English letters, he found it expedient to cite the palatable precedent of Samuel Clemens's lovable insult. In later years, when O'Brien was often irascible on the subject of American Joyce scholars, he used his fondness for Twain to demonstrate that after all some of the best reads were American.

The way in which the *Cruiskeen Lawn* column came about is indicative of the sort of journalism it represented. While his brother Kevin is correct in stating in his introduction to *The Best of Myles* that the author "was for many years a committed newspaperman and it would distort the tone of this book if all indications that these articles were written against a deadline, or that his own column was part of the greater whole, were to be deleted," it is best for us to know enough about that "greater whole" and how Myles fit in it to see in what way he transcended the occasion.

Dublin in the late thirties was in a strange backwater, between two wars in which it was not quite going to participate. It was also at the end of a world depression, which in some ways was no worse than what it was used to since the middle of the previous century. More important, Dublin was out of writers, or at least *good new* writers, or thought it was. The literati were unaware the tipsy young house painter setting up his ladder under the sign and singing a song was going to be Brendan Behan, or that the lank farmer striding in from the north, shoes literally in hand, for he'd waded the streams, was to be Paddy Kavanagh:

When I came to Dublin in 1939 the Irish Literary affair was still booming. It was the notion that Dublin was a literary metropolis and Ireland, as invented and patented by Yeats, Lady Gregory and Synge, a spiritual entity. It was full of writers and poets and I am afraid I thought their work had the Irish quality. The conversation in Poets' Pub had the richness and copiosity that H. W. Nevinson said all Dublin conversation had. To me, even then, it was tiresome drivel between journalists and civil servants. No humour at all. And, of course, they thought so much of poetry they didn't believe in the poet ating. I am not, I assure you, complaining, merely stating a few ridiculous facts. It was all my fault. What was I doing there? Wasn't I old enough to know the differ? Shouldn't I have cottoned on? Ah well, we live and we sometimes learn.*

Our man himself saw the "faded Georgian elegance" of Dublin:

... and drop me a postcard telling me in your own words about the remote faded poignancy of elegant proportions, minute delicacy of architectural detail balanced against the rather charmingly squalid native persons who sort of provide a contrapuntal device in the aesthetic apprehension of the whole.

Of course Brian O'Nolan had been around Dublin for some time, but in a sense had not yet waded into the professional waters. He chose the two leading men of the post-Yeats period, the short-story writers Frank O'Connor (also a pen name) and Sean Ó Faoláin, whom he considered to be playing a kind of literary patty-cake with their affected view of Ireland. With the help of Niall Sheridan (the Brinsley of At Swim), O'Nolan began a controversy in The Irish Times which incidentally served to introduce the name Flann O'Brien, a fact he soon regretted, as At Swim-Two-Birds was also to bear that name and O'Connor was the man who decided as much as anyone what was going to be part of Irish Literature and what was not. (See repercussions in note to "The Martyr's Crown" in the introduction to O'Brien's Stories and Plays.)

John Garvin, who was daily with O'Nolan in those days, thinks the "Brien" came from a combination of O'Nolan's name and that of the doggerel hero Brian O'Lynn:

I do not recall having ever discussed with Brian the origin of his pen-name, Flann O'Brien, but I was and am quite certain that he derived it from the hero of an old ballad, Brian O Lynn, in Irish, Brian O Fhloinn, which he turned backways, taking the nominative of O Floinn, Flann, as a personal name which, indeed, it was—one thousand years previously. Frank O'Connor remarked that the name looked like an Easter egg with a Santa Claus beard on it. The ballad was humorous after the mid-nineteenth-century fashion:

* Patrick Kavanagh, Self-Portrait (Dublin: Dolmen Press, 1964).

Brian O'Lynn, his wife and wife's mother
Were all going over the bridge together
The bridge broke down and they all fell in—
We'll go home by water, says Brian O'Lynn.

Brian O'Nolan had a hotted-up modern version of the ballad to which he treated some staid clerks celebrating a promotion.*

A flan is also a type of pie made in Ireland and would go very well in one's face. Writing to Longmans in 1938 about *At Swim* he adds:

I have been thinking over the question of a pen-name and would suggest FLANN O'BRIEN. I think this invention has the advantage that it contains an unusual name and one that is quite ordinary. 'Flann' is an old Irish name now rarely heard.

He was to be many things in *The Irish Times* before he settled into Myles, just as he had been operating under many names back in his college days when, as his friend the Joyce scholar Niall Montgomery wrote, he came on, "like a shower of paratroopers, deploying a myriad of pseudonymous personalities in the interest of pure destruction." A destruction which, I might add, again makes a construction of something else.

In the *Times* controversy his various personae had soon spread the issue way beyond its original bounds. He was redefining the modern Irish sensibility, not in a hermetic novel of silence, exile, and cunning, but by means of a wild man-in-the-street dialectic. It was from these fictional people generated by the amateur letter-writer O'Nolan that the paid columnist Myles later drew energy in carrying forth such standbys as "The Plain People of Ireland" ("from whom all authority derived"), and "The Brother."

The man who changed civil servant O'Nolan into a paid writer was the editor of the very newspaper the letters attacked. Although the *Times* was traditionally conservative, its editor of the moment was the flamboyant man-about-Dublin R. M. Smyllie. Jack White, who later came to work as a kind of go-between for Myles and the *Times,* saw the paper and its editor at the beginning of the Myles adventure:

It was often said of R. M. Smyllie that he was the last of the great editors. He was an editor, that is, in the sense that Louis XIV was a king: an editor

* In *Myles: Portraits of Brian O'Nolan,* ed. Timothy O'Keeffe (London: Martin Brian & O'Keeffe, 1973).

by divine right, an absolute tyrant, an editor who left the imprint of his personality all over his newspaper. At this time he was about fifty; he had been editor for six years, and he was at the height of his hegemony. The position he occupied in Dublin society is illustrated in a celebrated cartoon by Alan Reeve which depicted the Palace Bar in 1940. Almost every writer and artist then practicing in Dublin is included, and Smyllie's place is in the centre.

In a country with only three national newspapers, no weekly press of any intellectual standing, and only a sporadic mushroom-crop of literary periodicals, Smyllie's *Irish Times* occupied a position of rare significance. It was traditionally Protestant, traditionally conservative, traditionally pro-British, and Smyllie himself shared most of these attitudes. But the very fact that the paper held a minority position gave it a degree of independence that Smyllie was able to exploit.*

Smyllie was to *The Irish Times* then a bit of what Harold Ross was to *The New Yorker,* an eccentric editor whose peculiarities included the idea that journalism might be well enough written upon occasion to approach literature. He spotted the game in the letter-writing farce and arranged a meeting with the main perpetrator. As White points out, "It appealed to Smyllie's sense of fun to engage a columnist whose first contribution was a send-up of one of his own leaders." As for O'Nolan, the civil servant, here was a chance to keep a foot out of the bureaucracy. Employed in the Department of Local Government, wherein lurked somewhere the power for supervising the undertaking by local authorities of waterworks and sewage schemes and the financing of same by government loans and grants, O'Nolan's artistic soul was in mortal danger. He was even becoming a good civil servant. There lingered in the author of *The Hard Life* vestiges as manifest in the rantings of Mr. Collopy:

–We'll see what's in them all in good time, he announced sternly, and if those books are dirty books, lascivious peregrinations on the fringes of filthy indecency, cloacal spewings in the face of Providence. . .

John Garvin, who was not only O'Brien's supervisor in the Department of Local Government but the man he turned to for *At Swim*'s Greek epigraph (only in Irish, English, German, French, and Latin did O'Brien feel comfortable), says of O'Brien's range:

* Ibid.

I once told him that I did not consider him a good critic of his own work because he tended in the one book or even in one article to vary his style from well-knit, recondite prose to sterile word-play and inane conversation pieces.

He replied that he could not argue on the point as he never re-read his published works, but that he had fans for all his different presentations —some readers thought his Keats and Chapman pre-fabs were the last word, while others entreated him to give them more of The Brother.*

There is no way to guarantee the fans of his different presentations all a good time here, but there is a chance to display the persona that was Myles na Gopaleen, and if one were to take the persona of Myles na Gopaleen as a kind of legitimate literary creation in itself, then one might well argue that there are three great works in the O'Brien canon: *At Swim, The Third Policeman,* and *The Best of Myles.* This, at least, is the position of the two best O'Brien scholars in America, Miles Orvell and David Powell, who have read everything in *Cruiskeen Lawn* and make the claim in "Myles na Gopaleen: Mystic, Horse-Doctor, Hackney Journalist and Ideological Catalyst."† Myles himself says:

I DISLIKE LABELS—rather I mean it's not that they aren't terribly useful. *They are, old man.* But do . . . do they sufficiently take account of one as . . . a . . . person? There is my dilemma. (How do you like his horns?) But I . . . I . . . (little indulgent laugh) I know humanity, its foibles, its frailties, its fatuities; I know how the small mind hates what can't be penned into the humiliating five-foot shelf of its 'categories'. And so . . . if you must libel me, sorry, wrong brief, if you must label me, if you must use one epithet to 'describe' a being who in diversity of modes, universality of character and heterogeneity of spatio-temporal continuity transcends your bathetic dialectic, if, in short, one . . . practically algebraic symbol must suffice to cover the world-searing nakedness of that ontological polymorph who is at once immaculate brahmin, austere neo-platonist, motor-salesman, mystic, horse-doctor, hackney journalist and ideological catalyst, call me . . . call me . . . (qu'importe en effet, tout cela?) call me . . . ex-rebel. [The full version of this is in the "O'Bitter Dicta."]

In any case, Cyril Connolly, who wrote better than anyone else on the subject of "Enemies of Promise," makes this distinction in his chapter on journalism:

* Ibid.
† *Eire-Ireland* (Summer 1975).

We have suggested that journalism must obtain its full impact on the first reading while literature can achieve its effect on a second, being intended for an interested and not an indifferent public. Consequently the main difference between them is one of texture. Journalism is loose, intimate, simple and striking; literature formal and compact, not simple and not immediately striking in its effects. Carelessness is not fatal to journalism nor are clichés, for the eye rests lightly on them.*

It is precisely this texture that makes Myles's prose last: the atmosphere of a Keats-Chapman exchange, the very breath of "the Bore," the snap of a cliché clinched. Unlike those newsmen-schoolmasters who merely scold us for sloppy usage, who decry and deplore, bewail and bemoan all that is abominable and atrocious, and go on to mourn the Decline, perhaps even pointing to the political Imps, O'Brien not only ferrets out the abuse, he holds up the wriggling victim and makes us a lifelong present of him:

He is delighted. God forgive you—he stands there with the embalmed profile up to the light, he has raised the hand to stop you and then says: 'How old would you say I am?

You look at him steadily, unsmiling: you know that you are worse than he is and that the whole thing is the price of you.

As Handel would try out a tune with a single horn that he'd later encharge to a whole chorus, Myles would frequently steal from the chamber music that was his column and give to his novels. Sometimes he reversed the process, especially in the case of the seemingly doomed *The Third Policeman*. A minor sport for Flann fans is spotting these appearances and debating their relative effectiveness. Or maybe not judging at all, but just waving hello, in the manner of soap-opera fans, at an old friend. Or opera fans, for that matter, saluting a motif. For instance, the brother's scheme to get his landlady to abandon the building long enough for him to smuggle in a female companion involves an elaborate plot to send the old woman to the Skerries in winter. It is, of course, the Skerries in winter that James Joyce has chosen as his ultimate place of exile in *The Dalkey Archive*.

A piece "For Steam Men" on steam for 1944 is an oboe version of the main theme of *The Dalkey Archive,* in which Joyce's book is to save the world from De Selby's technology. In the column we have Myles "writing a book on steam" even though "the "younger genera-

* Cyril Connolly, *Enemies of Promise, and Other Essays* (New York: Macmillan, 1949).

tion, I find, knows very little of the great art." It is a book that will, if not save the world, at least avoid head-on collisions. And like Joyce's book, it is to be an elaborate, technical tour de force, incomprehensible. In short, art is a kind of metaphysical Rube Goldberg (or Heath Robinson) with social responsibility. Einstein, who at the time was not only receiving credit for the atomic bomb but agonizing publicly over the military uses his equations had been put to, is much on O'Brien's mind and is even mentioned in the above article.

Too heavy a dose? Remember the Gravid Water.

Or as the man said about it himself:

Our aim, by the way, is to give complete satisfaction. If this column is not in good condition when you receive it, return it to this office and your money will be refunded. In addition, you will receive six stouts in a handsome presentation cooper. When the column is written, it weighs exactly 0.03 grammes. Due to heat, evaporation or damp, the contents may become impaired or discoloured. In case of complaint, return it to this office with the rest of the newspaper and we will gladly replace it, or, at your option, return your money in full. Our aim is to make every customer a friend for life. We wish to give you complete satisfaction. We are your obsequious handwashing servants. We are very meek and humble. One frown from you and we feel that we have made a mess of our whole lives....

Think not too ill of me, I am young, my nails are broken and it is years since I amused myself by rubbing them on slates.

Myles's quibbles, conundrums, jokes, and stories began to appear on the leader page of the *Times* just as German bombs began falling on London. Occasionally cussing the annoyance of the War, or suggesting fanciful ways to combat it via such Myles na Gopaleen Research Bureau ideas as conserving midnight oil, the column survived the paper shortage. Initially written in Irish (Myles dedicated *The Poor Mouth* to editor Smyllie), it soon surfaced on alternate days in English, using different material, for much of what Myles had to say early and late was about language. After several years the column was written entirely in English.

Brother Kevin, in his preface to the book *The Best of Myles*, approved *New York Herald Tribune* critic Richard Watts's description of the first five years of the column:

'...a column devoted to magnificently laborious literary puns, remarkable parodies of De Quincey and others, fanciful literary anecdotes, and erudite study of clichés, scornful dissection of the literal meaning of highflown literary phraseology and a general air of shameless irony and high spirits. No one can build up a pun more shamelessly. No one can analyse the exact meaning of a literary flight of fantasy more devastatingly. He is at his best when telling absurd anecdotes, which he usually attributes to Keats and Chapman.'

Later, however, the tone of the column changed. Kevin O Nolan calls it "sombre, more fiercely satirical . . . many passages of savage denunciation." Less charitable critics have seen O'Brien in these years as losing control of the fine balance he had achieved earlier, and it was in the later years that he himself chose to break with the paper, which was no longer run by Smyllie. He farmed out his talents to other papers. This last phase, however, was not a success, according to even sympathetic critics like David Powell, Miles Orvell, and Anne Clissmann. Often O'Brien would rerun old *Times* material in the provincial papers. He even peeped out from behind a few new masks, including one mildly labeled John Doe, a persona he promised any editors buying that he'd keep noncontroversial.

Before O'Brien employed the name, "Myles na Gopaleen" saw service in three other works, including an opera, by three different writers, so that O'Brien was recalling this stock character out of popular (but now obscure) Irish tradition. One of his favorite quibbles was over translating *Gopaleen* as "little horses," his point being that "the autonomy of the pony must not be subjugated by the imperialism of the horse." It might also be recalled that the ball of malt, or highball as we used to call it back in the forties, is usually served in pony glasses, often without benefit of ginger ale as was the custom in America and, of course, without that dreadful American invention the ice cube. While we're on the topic, the alternative to the pony of malt would be the pint of plain (see page 250) or occasionally straight gin (see a death-bed story by John Ryan about our man).* Wine in Ireland, especially in O'Brien, seems to exist only in the Latin tags connecting the grape with metaphysics. The column's name, *Cruiskeen Lawn,* is Irish for "the overflowing jug" or "little overflowing jug" (I do not recall Myles worrying the politics of the diminutive here). The jug presumably could be used in Ireland to

* In *Remembering How We Stood* (Dublin: Gill & Macmillan, 1975).

hold anything, milk in the morning, something stronger by evening. Myles no doubt, however, means this breakfast crock to be emptied more in the spirit of the jug Mr. Collopy keeps by his chair to lubricate dispute in *The Hard Life*. The connection between talk, writing, and booze is one that O'Brien played about with in almost all his works, though never in the mammary Viennese manner.

I

Let the farmer praise his grounds
Let the hunter praise his hounds,
And the shepherd his sweet scented lawn,
But I, more blest than they
Spend each happy night and day
With my charming little cruiskeen lawn, lawn, lawn,
Oh, my charming little cruiskeen lawn!

II

Immortal and divine,
Great Bacchus, god of wine,
Create me by adoption your son;
In hope that you'll comply,
That my glass shall ne'er run dry,
Nor my smiling little cruiskeen lawn, lawn, lawn,
Oh, my charming little cruiskeen lawn!

III

And when grim Death appears,
In a few but pleasant years,
To tell me that my glass has run;
I'll say, "Begone, you knave!
For great Bacchus gave me leave
To take another cruiskeen lawn, lawn, lawn,
To take another cruiskeen lawn!"

Chorus:

The love of my heart is my little jar
Here's a health to my dear
The love of my heart is my fair-headed
    one
O, the love of my heart is my fair-headed
    one.

[Traditional Irish song]

In the past few years selections from the vintage years have reappeared in *The Irish Times* as *The Best of Myles*. The book by that title, edited by Kevin O Nolan, was published in London in 1968 and later in New York. An earlier wartime edition under the title *Cruiskeen Lawn* was made from slightly different material, and a further edition of *"saeva indignatio"* Myles, as well as an entire edition of Keats and Chapman, has just appeared in London.

The pieces in this section are taken mainly from *The Best of Myles*, following the editor's categories. I have extracted some Myles material, however, for the "O'Bitter Dicta" section of this book. "The True Biography of Myles na Gopaleen" is taken directly from *The Irish Times*.

Since I have largely borrowed Kevin O Nolan's selections and categories I might as well stay with his caveats:

The daily contribution was often quite long, and the topic of one day might be resumed on a subsequent day. This serial form was acknowledged in later years where an identical caption was often followed by I, II, III, and so forth.

In the present selection articles are separated by asterisks. Where the topic was continued, the continuation follows the asterisks. Accordingly the asterisks denote the conclusion of an article or a lapse of time before resuming. Apart from single or continued articles the selection includes shorter extracts, also isolated by asterisks.

It seemed worth while, for the convenience of readers, to attempt some classification. But it is not rigid.... the ... compartments [are not] specially reserved. A Keats and Chapman anecdote may be found lurking elsewhere than in their allotted space, or the Plain People of Ireland may find themselves hopelessly embedded in some alien context. But this reflects the reality of the column, where innovation and surprise were no rare ingredients, where the reader was unceremoniously hauled within brackets (for greater privacy), or addressed not in English but in a strangelooking mixture, English through the phonology of the Irish alphabet. In later years some of the author's adventures were related wholly in Latin. [Fear not, *Reader* reader, none of this here.]

In this section I have reversed the usual procedure of introducing a selection of O'Brien's fiction with a sheaf of related letters and have placed two letters from the late phase at the close. It should be remembered, however, that strict chronology has not been kept with any other items in this section.

THE TRUE BIOGRAPHY OF
MYLES NA GOPALEEN

I

Our record is necessarily episodic but large tracts of it will appear
from time to time so that ultimately a massive tome, in effect a part of
the history of Ireland, will have been compiled to be lodged in Santry
Old Place when, in the heel of some bleak year, that venerable tene-
ment becomes a national museum and shrine. For now, it is meet to
say that we deal with an incident arising from his reputed marriage to
Thérèse, *née* Hopkins.

Two strange men had arrived in the neighbourhood, reputed to be
Keats and Chapman, and called, outwardly to inquire about the existence of fairies, pishrogues and journalists in the district but in
reality in quest of drink or money, or both. Myles received them with

exemplary courtesy, bade the "wife" prepare a meal and treated the visitors to generous gulpings of a domestic distillate of his own called IS-KAY BAA.

By the time the meal had been consumed—a splendid repast of black pudding and York cabbage—the host suggested "a turn about the hillside." By this time the visitors were convinced of the existence of at least pishrogues and afterwards claimed to have actually seen them. The party then staggered forth to a foray.

The evidence is that they eventually arrived at a tavern where there occurred the enmixment and consumption of sundry grogs. Keats sang a song named La Belle Dame Sans Merci which Myles, with some heat, resented as an insult to the lady of his house. Tempers were allayed, however, by the enbibulment of further grogs. Finally Keats and Chapman collapsed and were put to bed in an outhouse by the far-a-tee, a shutter being used for transport.

It is not clear how Myles got home but undoubtedly without question a serious uproar followed his return. The terrified wife (if wife she was) and her sister sent an urgent cry for help to the father, who soon arrived in a towering rage.

"What have you been up to, you ruffian?" he bellowed.

"Who are you?" Myles asked.

"I am your father-in-law."

"Zat so? I'm up to you by now. You're Gerard Manley Hopkins. Isn't one poet enough for one day?"

"You low blackguard!"

"That colleen dhat there isn't my wife either. Get yourself a medium of grog from the pantry and keep quiet."

"I will not hesitate for a moment to send for the police. I will not have my daughter assaulted by a tramp."

"You make me laugh. What would the boys in the Scotch House say if they heard my grand-uncle was a Jesuit? Eh?"

"You are a despicable bad-tongued scoundrel."

"Bedahust, acharm. That reminds me. I must go for my constitutional walk. The corpus sanum must be preserved."

He then fell from the room.

TO-MORROW—His return to the tavern and the dreadful upheaval which ensued.

11

It appears that Myles managed to reach the tavern a second time. He was met at the door by the frightened owner, who said he was closing as required by the licensing laws.

"I am not subject to the licensing laws," Myles riposted sternly, "by virtue of a Bull promulgated by Queen Victoria. Furthermore, I am your ground landlord. I will have you and your shanvan on the roadside to-morrow if I hear any more impertinence. Know your station in life and get off at it. Out of my way!"

He curtly brushed past the startled vintner and paused in the hall.

"I seem to hear voices upstairs," he said. "Are you at the after-hours game again?"

"Oh a few personal friends. Relatives, I mean."

"You must come from a very long-tailed family, for you seem to have at least a hundred blood relations. I'll see for myself who's upstairs. Is it a crowd of swaddlers?"

"Certainly not. Just a few uncles and nieces and *their* friends."

"Well tell me this. How are *my* friends? The pair you stored away in the out-house?"

"I don't know."

"Well, find out. Get out your shutters and tell the uncles to bring them upstairs, where I'm going now. And send me a smahan of Tulla-more."

Then Myles gruffly mounted the stairs to find a very motley assortment of customers of all ages and sexes in the back room. Soon rough stumbling noises on the stairs betokened the arrival of Keats on a shutter borne by two strong boys, with the boss in attendance carrying a half-pint of Tullamore. The poet was gingerly lowered onto a chair.

"The other gentleman," the host said, "told me he would kick me to death if I touched him."

"Leave Chapman alone," Keats said. "He has taken a terrible hiding from those pishrogues of yours, Myles. I escaped but must have fallen in with a leprachaun, for I got a terrible blow on the head with a hammer."

"It's our Irish climate, my tourist friend," Myles said. Turning to the far-a-tee, he rapped out: "Another half-pint of Tullamore for my poor friend."

They drank in apparent amity and conversed, notwithstanding the house and coarse language all about them.

"Your father Mathew never visited the hamlet," Keats remarked, "thanks be to God."

"Are you the man who rode the horse Hyperion?" Myles inquired innocently. Keats flushed.

"I am the man who wrote the verse *Hyperion*," he snapped. "This Tullamore grog is very good. Drink is good if not taken to excess. Judging by the reports those ruffians in Moscow issue to the newspapers, they must be in transports of intoxication night and day. Frequently they accidentally tell the truth. . . ."

"I can smell something cooking," Myles said.

"See what I mean? IN VINO VERY TASS."

"That," Myles said, "represents the wit of an out and out 18-carat bowsie."

Keats, unused to Irish banter, flew into a temper, sprang up and hit Miles a severe puck in the stomach. The Santry man, undaunted, squared to action stations but for his pains received a thremendious haymaker which knocked him sprawling. A little girl ran to restrain the enraged poet, the vintner appeared with the boys carrying two shutters, and the two would-be bruisers were borne off to the outhouse.

ON MONDAY—His awakening in the straw beside Chapman to find Keats fled, his enfeebled condition and savage disputation with the vintner's family.

III

When Myles awoke in the unfamiliar straw, he found that Keats was missing and Chapman sprawled some distance from him, vehemently snoring. Feeble though he felt, he managed to hit the good companion with a basket and bring him to life.

"Heavenly fathers," Chapman said limply," those pishrogues of yours are the very devil. Is there any prayer or spell against them itself?"

"There are pookas in these parts as well," Myles sighed, "and puckers too."

"Where is Keats?"

"I don't know. He may be buried in this straw. Heaven help him if he is. It is full of maggots. I now know what people mean when they refer to a man as being maggoty."

"What are we going to do at all?"

"Life," Myles explained, "is merely a system of improvisations. I will think of the appropriate course after I've had my breakfast. Obviously our first problem is to find a means of standing up."

Chapman gave a little cry.

"Did you say *breakfast?*" he said. "Oh dear dear *dear!*"

"I meant a pint a piece of Tullamore to put the blood flowing again in our *cushla machrees.*"

Here he let out a savage *bake,* or phantam howl. He repeated this until finally a young girl peeped in.

"Tell your mother," he rapped out, "to come here like a flash."

She disappeared and came back with a sturdy, rather handsome lady.

"Ah my poor lads," she said, "have you been on the rhodimontando? Isn't it a shame for ye?"

"My good woman," Myles said testily, "we require none of your country blether. We require breakfast consisting of two bottles of Tullamore, two glasses, and *quanto sufficio* of *aqua pura.*"

"Well now, now, I don't know."

"You don't *know?* I'm your ground landlord. If you don't fill that order at once, I'll rise and I'll bate you up and down this stable, and then I'll bate your oul wan."

Here the mother made a signal to the little girl, who ran out. She returned almost at once with the bottles, but was accompanied by her grandmother.

"It has come to my hearing inquisitively," this formidable virago said, "that threats of awful import have been uttered here concerning the integrity of my person?"

"That was merely mildest banter, ma'am," Myles said. "Last night I got the worst of an encounter with a man who would at best be classed as a flyweight. You look to me to be in the super-heavy class. If you fell on me even accidentally, you would kill me. We now have our breakfast and, having consumed it, will make our adieux."

"It is well," the great lady said, turning and departing.

"Make our wills, you mean," Chapman moaned.

Myles took an enormous slug of raw malt from the bottle of Tullamore, with magical result.

"*Nunc is bibendum,*" he chirruped, "*nunc pepulisse, ter pede terram!*"

"There must be an amulet to be got," Chapman said after a drink, "against them pishrogues."

NEXT INSTALMENT—How Myles, bargaining with a jarvey, accidentally encounters Michael Davitt and the two zealous men embark on an outside car to visit Parnell at Avondale.

IV

One day Myles na Gopaleen, who affected the uniform of an admiral of the French Grand Fleet, was down the kays bargaining with a jarvey, and who should come along but Michael Davitt, just home from the U.S. The two men saluted warily.

"Beannacht ort, a sheanóir chóir," said Myles in faultless Gaelic. "How is my segocia?"

"I do not know who or what your segocia is," Davitt replied sternly.

"Never mind. You look very well."

"Do not tell me you are in the forces?"

"I am not. This rig gets me credit in Kavanagh's Wine Rooms. I was talking to this scoundrel of a jarvey with the idea of taking his hackenay with the notion of running down to Avondale to have a collogue with the Chief. Would you think of coming along? Isn't it very hash to-day?"

"Faith then and there is nothing I would like better. He needs a good bawling out. It is indeed hash, very hash."

"We will have nothing to do with this ruffian. He wants a pound, but a pound of gelignite is what he should get. I have a better idea. We will take a tram to Clontarf, for I know a chap by the name of Teague Ogue O'Tuckey who lives on the sloblands there." Davitt, surprised at such a method of getting to County Wicklow, agreed and the two selfless men got the tram.

"That is a very hash day," the conductor said when collecting the fares.

"It is indeed hash," Myles said.

"Tell me," Davitt said, "just WHAT is the meaning of this word 'hash'?"

"I have no idea," Myles replied, "but all Dublin people use it. It is applied to the weather but it appears to have no relevance to the nature of the weather."

"I see. Then tell me this. Why in the name of God should we go to Clontarf in order to get to Avondale?"

"My friend O'Tuckey is the *entrepreneur par excellence*. He keeps a dickie-car at Dalkey Harbour. He will row us across from Contarf to Dalkey and from there drive us hell for leather down to Avondale with the assistance of a spanking cob. We are really taking a short-cut."

"Well, well." Davitt was astonished. "It seems a perilous short-cut."

"Atachall," Myles said. "Teague is a great man with the oars. He is powered by Tullamore."

"Powered by WHAT?"

"Tullamore. If you met him in the street you would be inclined to slip him a few coppers but he never fails to have a bottle of it in the glory-hole of his cabin, wherever he gets it."

Teague's cabin in the slobs was duly reached. He came out and welcomed his visitors, immediately inviting them in for a smahan. The trip, he thought, would be quite straightforward though, he added, "I find it a bit hash to-day."

He in due time attacked the sea and land journey with what may be termed ferocity and landed the travelers at Avondale at one o'clock. Parnell himself opened the door. He bowed in grave welcome.

"Do come in," he said. "I presume you gentlemen find it quite hash to-day?"

TO-MORROW—At luncheon with the Chief. A heated discussion on the peasantry and dangers attending its liberation.

v

The Chief, Parnell, invited his guests to a sumptuous luncheon that was embellished with several decanters of costly clarets. There was, in fact, very little food served.

"Gentlemen," he said, "do you know whom I suspect to be the true enemies of Ireland? Ah, but first let me propose the toast of her four green fields and her mighty hero who now sleeps, Coohoolin of the Red Hand of Ulster. . . ."

"I believe that man is a myth," Myles said. "A hurley pucker muryas, a primeval G.A.A. man."

"You are very foolish," Parnell replied, "to denounce anybody because he is a myth. It is far from established that we are not myths ourselves."

"Very likely," Myles retaliated, "it can be reasonably proved that we are the myths that do be on the bog."

"Who do you say are the true enemies of Ireland?" Davitt growled.

"The excruciated peasantry."

"That's you all over," Davitt barked, "you are still too timid to throw your dirty Irish Party in with the League."

"I never quite understood the word peasant," Myles remarked. "It is the French word *paysan* and merely means a person who lives in the country. There are peasants in the County Meath who have so much fat about their necks and bellies that they look remarkably like their own bullocks. There are sheep farmers in Canada who have grown to be half sheep themselves, they bleat and grow wool on their bodies. I hope we are not occupied with the liberation of the animal kingdom in our movement. For that were veriest folly."

"You think," Davitt said, shaking a finger at the Chief, "that the geographical orthocentre of Ireland is Committee Room 15 in the House of Commons. Bah! You probably drink in the bars with the Liberal ruffians and your butty Gladstone."

"Do not misunderstand me, gentlemen," Parnell said mildly. "Liberation after generations of bondage can be a dangerous intoxicant. Peering into the future, I can foresee a monstrous peasant ascendency after the British have given them up as a bad job and cleared out. Times will come more illiberal than they are now. Clowns from the wilderness will appear wearing boots and garments looking remarkably like trousers. Peasants will vote themselves, perhaps with guns, into high and fabulously remunerated public office notwithstanding that they entirely lack education. I fear gigantic public larcenies. The country will resemble such remote kingdoms as Algeria full of sallow, wicked men praying to Allah or, worse, purple men wrestling with crocodiles in the mighty Congo river. I fear the day here when a rampaging peasantry, surrounded with guns, will put their brutal boots on the necks of the Plain People of Ireland and exterminate them with taxational extravagance, grandiose pathogenic schemes of heavenly development, and make food so dear that most of them will die of galloping consumption."

"If that should happen," Myles said, "can't we always invite the British back?"

"We can't, because we would not be allowed to speak. They would be far too wise to come, anyway."

"We won't have an administration formed by your wretched Irish Party anyway," Davitt bellowed, rising, "and I am going home to my dinner."

Myles rose and bowed.

"Please understand, Chief," he said, "that my pen and sword are ever at your service."

The party then broke up with curt politenesses.

NEXT INSTALMENT: Another accidental encounter with Chapman and a search for Keats, who has been mislaid.

VI

One morning in the billiard room at Santry Myles turned to his cousin, the aged Comptess Statia le Goupelin, and said:

"I am not too happy about this affair they are arranging at Fontenoy. The place is in Belgium, which alone is a bad start. Our own Marshal Saxe is a capital fellow but he is crippled with the dropsy."

"Mon cher enfant," replied the Comptess, "voici le seul soldat qui n'ait pas fait de fautes."

"Hmmm. He may yet unwittingly ruin my friend Louis XV, for every man fights best in his health. And the man on the other side, the Duke of Cumberland, is a fearful bowsie."

He turned and left the room sadly, went to his study and drank a decanter of alcoholic rosewater. Suddenly there came to his ear a great clamour—the baying of hounds and the discharge of gatekeepers' muskets. Unperturbed, he lit a cigar and sat down to read the *Racing Calendar*.

Then there was a crash of shattering glass and a young man had bounded in through the French window. It was none other than Thomas Davis.

"What sort of man are you," he cried, "sitting here scoffing gin while our boys are out there with the French facing the British and the Dutch?"

"Well, where should I be?"

"In the van, of course."

"On a certain Christmas Eve I was in Findlaters' van, if that's what you mean."

"It's not what I mean. You should be leading our men in the field. There they are out there in a land strange to them, like Africa, the Congo. I know I won't fail them. In anticipation I have composed a victory poem from which here is a snatch:

On through the camp the column trod—King Louis turns his rein:
"Not yet, my liege," Myles interposed, "the Irish troops remain."
And Fontenoy, famed Fontenoy, had been a Waterloo,
Were not these exiles ready then, fresh, vehement and true.

"Your dates are a bit mixed, my boy. This is 1745. Waterloo won't be until 1815."

"You talk as if you were on the B.B.C. *Are you coming?*"

"Oh, very well. Get me my cape, shooting stick and shot gun."

The sequel belongs to history. . . .

(Another instalment to-morrow)

VII

An episode in literary history, of absorbing interest but hidden from the public until now, occurred when two earthquakes took place almost simultaneously in the Republic of Letters: these were the completion of *Ulysses* by James Joyce and the emergence of Sean O'Casey at the Abbey Theatre. Both men had worked under the general supervision of Myles na Gopaleen, whose encouragement, it is no harm to say, was occasionally more eleemosynary than literary. He was very pleased with their work, however.

He invited Joyce to visit Dublin and the latter agreed on condition that the visit should be strictly secret. That being so, it was strange that he wore his old yachting cap.

After greeting at Santry, Myles humorously rebuked him: "At the end of the *Portrait,* Jim," he said, "you wrote that your weapons were silence, exile and cunning. Well, I've just read *Ulysses.* I don't mind about exile and cunning . . . but SILENCE?"

"Quod scripsi scripsi," Joyce said.

That night the two men went to the opening of *Juno and the Paycock,* Joyce wearing a heavy black beard and carrying a spurious violin case. At the end of the second act, they were astonished to hear in the foyer the play and O'Casey being furiously denounced by Edward Martyn on the queer grounds that "that Casey fellow hasn't got the guts to deal with incest."

After the last curtain, they went "back" to the Green Room and told O'Casey of the incident. He merely grimaced and said, "Sure that poor fellow is only a sluggawn."

But the great man who had played Captain Boyle happened to be there and was far from willing to let the situation rest on so negative a conclusion. He demanded Edward Martyn's address, which was promptly supplied.

"We'll get a cab," he said.

"Now look here," Myles said, "I wouldn't soil my shoes going into that man's house."

"Can't you take them off," Joyce interposed, "unless you have dirty feet."

The end of the argument was that a cab was got and Martyn run to earth in his Dublin flat. The confrontation was spectacular.

"I demand that you state in plain terms," Captain Boyle roared, "why you publicly denounced and insulted to-night my friend Sean O'Casey."

"His stuff is decrepit and bourgeois," Martyn replied with a show of courage.

"Well now is that so," the Captain said with a fresh intonation of menace.

"There is no incest in his play. Why don't they produce *The Heather Field?*"

"Because it's a lousy play, Mister-Me-Friend," Joyce said.

But Captain Boyle had now come to action stations and hit Martyn an unmerciful box in the right eye which knocked him sprawling, and after he had managed to totter to his feet, gave him a thremondious haymaker to where his stomach should be, sending him down for the count.

The *fracas*, violent as it was, was cut short, for Myles had discovered that old tin tacks were protruding from the floor, and called the party off.

"My feet are killing me," he said simply.

NEXT INSTALMENT—Myles's boundless charity and his visit to the old over-worked foster-mother.

VIII

Myles na Gopaleen's charity—using that last word in its true and broad meaning of *caritas*, "the greatest of these"—had long been a Dublin legend. If an impoverished nobleman should ask for the "loan" of a shilling, the Dean of Santry never in refusal took refuge in the pharisaical phrase that "he would drink it." For no fee at all, he agreed to a request from the Department of Finance to campaign privately to induce young and fresh civil servants to desist from wearing hobnails, a practice which—seemliness apart—was damaging the floors of State offices. In times when this newspaper was somewhat weak, he worked for it *for nothing*. The calls on his boundless heart have been boundless. He lent Jimmy O'Dea ten bob in 1946 and not a whisper about it has he heard since. Does this annoy, embitter him? Good Lord not at all. He still thinks Jimmy le drôle farceur par exyolongs.

An instance of the strange calls on his liberality may be cited. He was one day approached by a respectable, and indeed religious, T.D. who had heard of a harrowing case; the calls on his own purse were so heavy that he could take no personal action. It seemed that an old lady had set up in a garret as foster-mother to strange ragged children of indeterminate origin. The pittance she was paid for each was so miserable that she was constrained to take in a swarm of them, but this solution made her situation worse. Starvation faced the strange household.

Myles took counsel with a friend.

"Where women of any kind are concerned," he said, "one must be careful. But if the case is genuine I must help."

"Yes indeed."

"You see, this place might be a potheen den. Or there might be some attempt at blackmail afoot."

"One must think of these things."

"I certainly would not dream of going there alone. Can you suggest two ladies who might accompany me?"

"Two ladies? Hmm. Let me see. What about Maureen Potter?"

"Capital, my dear fellow—capital. Now if we could only think of another. . . ."

"Yes. Very difficult."

"Ah, I have it," Myles cried, now quite excited. "MARIA CAL-LAS, the great soprano!"

And so it was done and the visit paid. Myles gave the old lady a most generous subvention in notes while his fair companions had great quantities of tuck concealed under their great skirts, true balm for the little ones.

Troublesome? Nonsense! He considers that just being decent.

(NEXT INSTALMENT—The extraordinary affair of the eel and Tim Healy.)

IX

An incident in the life of Myles which might fairly be described as macabre, yet not unrelieved with humor, occurred in the sweet vale of Avoca.

A German gentleman, having obtained from the State a lease of a large tract of County Wicklow for mineral explorations, having particular regard to bauxite, pyrites and copper, had imported a large company of Congolese slaves to do the labouring work, having purchased them at the rate roughly of 6d. a head from the Belgian Government. These poor creatures, knowing no English, lived in a rather barbarous huddle of their own quite apart from the local community, and even made their own liquor, a fact which led to sundry bestialities. The punishment decided upon by the German gentleman for any who got too far out of hand was to shoot them. This system was known as *Arbeitskriegzucht*.

It happened that at this time Myles na Gopaleen was on a fishing holiday in the area, and—wonder of coincidence—the younger Tim Healy, resting from triumphs at the English bar, was bicycling in the area. Clearly this *dramatis personae* would inevitably coalesce into some impossible occurrence.

It happened that Myles, ever the Bohemian, had brushed up an acquaintance of a kind with one of the Congolese slaves. Some will say that his real purpose was to get his hands on a firkin of turnip-whiskey, the most potent distillate known to man, but more likely is the theory that he sought to survey more closely the wider frontiers of humanity.

Communication was mostly by signs but at one session of turnip commerce the slave could swear he heard Myles say HUILE, and repeat the word with gestures. He was flabbergasted. Here they were rooting around for copper and sundry chemicals and here was a lone fisherman who had casually discovered OIL! He leapt up and raced at a steady 20 m.p.h. to the hotel at Woodenbridge, where he knew the sage Tim Healy was staying. He knew better than to share the extraordinary news with his tyrannical German master.

Healy, whose French was excellent, listened enrapt to the tale of the poor savage and at once donned his bicycle clips, notwithstanding that his dress was of the knickerbocker variety, and bade the slave lead the way to Myles's abode. He duly found our hero there.

"I understand, my good friend," he said, "that you have found something that may yet be the salvation economically of our hallowed motherland?"

"What va mane?" said Myles, obviously fluthered.

"Have you found oil?"

"I caught an eel . . . this length."

"Oh, *Huile*, oil, eel. I thought London was a complicated place but Woodenbridge is quite insoluble. See that you eat that eel. I'll go back to-night."

NEXT INSTALMENT— In search of Chapman.

x

The poet Keats had long become Mystery Man No. 1, for he had totally disappeared, leaving no clue as to his destination. This caused a lot of speculation, most of it far from flattering. But Myles managed to retain fairly firm liaison with Chapman.

He was shocked to discover one morning that Chapman too had gone. There was no sign of him high or low. Myles remembered that he had evinced interest in a certain young widow of attractive if rather wild looks, and thought the obvious thing was to make an inquiry at her house.

In this he was mistaken, for the good lady took himself for a preda-tory libertine and pulled a knife on him. He was lucky to escape from the house without serious injury.

His next resort was to try the pubs, for Chapman was notoriously fond of a drink, and it was not the true, the blushful Hippocrene. The quest became a sort of martyrdom for Myles, for he was impelled to take a drink himself in every establishment at which he called. And the quest was vain, for each house was Chapmanless. He considered himself lucky to be able in the end to drag himself home to the lodgings for he was undoubtedly in danger of collapse.

He noted with sad surprise and dismay the form of Chapman slumped on a chair, absolutely floothered and dead to the world. Our hero managed to reach his own bed before passing out.

Meantime the widow who had pulled the knife had regretted her hasty action and called to make tender amends. But all in that room was silence save for the rumble of misdirected mucus.

(FINAL INSTALMENT—He is asked to stand for Parliament.)

XI

At his house in Santry one morning Myles was not feeling very well. Truth to tell, he had the previous day attended the weddings of eight cousins, and weddings are the same the world over. They are really sinful debauches, and properly should be held secretly in crypts, nobody permitted to be present except the parties and the clergy.

Suddenly the benatee announced that a deputation had arrived from the head office of the Fianna Fail Party. Before he had time to say that he could not see them, an astounding phalanx of gurriers filed in. They seemed to have stepped from another century, and clearly they had hired their clothes from Lorcan Bourke. The leader or chairman said Deesmaragut and took a seat.

MYLES: Morra, lads. What has ye up so early?

LEADER: Well, you see, the Party feels that the next election might be pretty close and we were wondering would you stand for South Tipp. The result in a constituency can depend a lot on the calibre of the candidate.

MYLES: Don't let me hear any of your crowd use that word calibre. It reminds me of guns.

LEADER: Sorry.

MYLES: Is it go to Leinster House? Ah no, there's too much barley-corn stirring there.

LEADER: That's the other side. Our people are most abstemious.

MYLES: You are at least four feet away from me and yet I can tell from the smell that you had a bath of hot whiskey this morning and then washed your hair in stout. If I did go forward, I would get a special job?

LEADER: You mean be made Minister?

MYLES: Maybe.

LEADER: Well, you see, the new ruse is that you must be an old Minister's sprout of a son and know next to nothing. A man of your great learning and experience would be out of place. But . . .

MYLES: But what?

LEADER: All your relatives would be fixed up. For instance we would think nothing of making your uncle, if you have one, a director of E.S.B.

MYLES: That is an organisation he particularly detests.

LEADER: Well, the Racing Board, the Sugar Company, the Turf Board, the Central Bank, C.I.E.—these are all run and owned by our lads. That's the importance of this election, you see. We don't want anything to happen.

MYLES: But something is bound to happen some time. People die, for instance. No cure for that disease has been found yet. I don't see that you offer me the precious thing we call *security*.

LEADER: I am sure the Party would generously insure you, and I'm sure a State car could be found any time you want free transport for yourself or relatives.

MYLES: But that would be illegal.

LEADER: It's we who make the law and when it doesn't suit we change it.

MYLES: Let me tell you a secret. I have been convinced for some weeks that there is a large rat hiding somewhere in this bedroom. I want to get him. For that reason I keep a shotgun under my pillow. Now clear out as quick as lightning, ye guts and bowsies!

Exeunt Omnes.

(THIS IS THE CONCLUDING INSTALMENT OF THE PRESENT BIO-GRAPHICAL SERIES. ANOTHER SERIES WILL BE PRESENTED LATER.)

The brother has it all worked out.

—The Best of Myles

Himself and his brother. I would not be surprised to hear that he has no brother at all.

That is a shocking thing to say.

—The Best of Myles

THE BROTHER

Things is movin in great style above in the digs. The brother has the landlady humped down to Skerries.

This is scarcely the season for seaside holidays.

Wait till you hear what happened man. This night, d'y'see, the landlady is for the pictures. Has the black hat and the purple coat on and is standin in the hall havin a screw at the glass and puttin on the gloves. The shoes polished and shinin like an eel's back, of course. All set.

I understand.

Then the key is heard in the hall door and in comes the brother. He's half turnin into the room when he gives a look at her nibs. Then he stops and comes back and starts starin like a man that was seein things. The landlady gets red, of course.

A not unnatural reaction in the circumstances.

Well annyway the brother orders the landlady into the room where

181

he can see her in the light. He puts the finger on the landlady's eye and starts pullin the lids out of her to get a decko at th'inside. Begob the poor landlady gets the windup in right style. Then the brother starts tappin her chest and givin her skelps on the neck. Inside ten minutes he has her stuffed into bed upstairs with himself below in the kitchen makin special feeds of beef-tea and the crowd in the digs told off to take turns sittin up with the landlady all night. That's a quare one for you.

It is undoubtedly a very queer one for you.

And th'unfortunate woman all set for the pictures thinkin' she was as right as rain. Wasn't it the mercy of God the brother put his nose in at that particular minute?

The coincidence has that inscrutable felicity that is usually associated with the more benevolent manifestations of Providence.

Well the next day the brother gives orders for the landlady's things to be packed. What she wanted, the brother said, was a COMPLETE REST, The brother said he wouldn't be responsible if the landlady didn't get a complete rest.

I see.

So what would do him only pack the landlady down to the married sister in Skerries. With strict orders that she was to stop in bed when she got there. And that's where she is since.

To be confined to bed in midwinter in that somewhat remote hamlet is not the happiest of destinies.

Of course the brother does things well, you know. Before he packs the landlady off in a cab for the station, he rings up Foley. And of course Foley puts the landlady on the train and sees her right t'oblige the brother.

I see.

A great man for lookin after other people, the brother. Ah yes. Yes, certainly . . .

I quite agree. And now I fear I must be off.

Ah yes . . . I'll tell you another funny thing that happened. Queer things always happen in pairs. I was goin home late wan night and I was certain sure I was the last in. I'm lying there in the bed when I hear the door been opened below. Then the light is switched on in the sittin-room. Next thing begob I think I hear voices. So not knowin what's goin on, I hop out of bed and run down in me peejamas.

A very proper precaution in these queer times.

I whip open the sittin-room door and march in. What do I see only the brother leppin up to meet me with the face gettin a little bit red. This, says he, is Miss Doy-ull.

A lady?

The brother was with a dame on the sofa. I suppose he was chattin her about banks and money and that class of thing. But . . . do you know . . . if the landlady was there . . . not that it's my place to say anything . . . but her nibs would take a very poor view of women been brought into the digs after lights out. Wouldn't fancy that at all.

That is the fashion with all landladies.

Well the brother does have Miss Doy-ull in every night since. They do work very late into the night at the bankin questions. I couldn't tell you when she leaves. A very hard-workin' genius, the brother. I was askin' him when he's going to let the landlady get up below in Skerries. A thing like this, says he, will take a long time, but I might let her up for half an hour a Sunday.

Care is necessary in these delicate illnesses, of course.

You're right there, but it's not the first breakdown the brother pulled the landlady through. Begob here's me bus!

Good-bye.

* * *

The brother can't look at an egg.

Is that so?

Can't stand the sight of an egg at all. Rashers, ham, fish, anything you like to mention—he'll eat them all and ask for more. But he can't go the egg. Thanks very much all the same but no eggs. The egg is barred.

I see.

I do often hear him talking about the danger of eggs. You can get all classes of disease from eggs, so the brother says.

That is disturbing news.

The trouble is that the egg never dies. It is full of all classes of microbes and once the egg is down below in your bag, they do start moving around and eating things, delighted with themselves. No trouble to them to start some class of an ulcer on the sides of the bag.

I see.

Just imagine all your men down there walking up and down your stomach and maybe breeding families, chawing and drinking and feeding away there, it's a wonder we're not all in our graves man, with all them hens in the country.

I must remember to avoid eggs.

I chance an odd one meself but one of these days I'll be a sorry man. Here's me Drimnagh 'bus, I'll have to lave yeh, don't do anything when your uncle's with you, as the man said.

Good bye.

* * *

I was out in a boat with the brother down in Skerries, where he's stopping with the married sister. On his holliers, you know. A great man for the sea, the brother.

Indeed?

Ah yes. If the brother had his way, of course, it's not here he'd be but off out with real sea-farin men, dressed up in oil-skins, running up and down ropes and all the rest of it.

I see.

The brother was givin out about the seals. 'Tumblers', he called them. The brother says all them lads should be destroyed.

That would be a considerable task.

They do spend the day divin and eatin mackerel. If them lads had their way, they wouldn't leave a mackerel in the sea for you and me or the man in the next street. They do swally them be the hundred, head an' all. And the brother says they do more than that—they do come out of the water in the middle of the night-time and rob gardens. You wouldn't want to leave any fancy tomato-plants around. And you wouldn't want to leave one of your youngsters out after dark, either, because your men would carry it off with them. The brother says they do take a great interest in the chislers. They do be barkin out of them during the day-time at chislers on the beach.

That is most interesting.

The brother says the seals near Dublin do often come up out of the water at night-time and do be sittin above in the trams when they're standin in the stables. And they do be upstairs too. Begob the brother says it's a great sight of a moonlight night to see your men with the big moustaches on them sittin upstairs in the trams lookin out. And they do have the wives and the young wans along with them, of course.

Is that a fact?

Certainly, man. The seals are great family people, always were.

Well then the brother was showin me two queer lookin men with black and white feathers on them and black beaks, out sittin there in the water.

Two birds?

Two of the coolest customers I ever seen, didn't give a damn about us although we went near enough to brain them with the oars. Do you know the funny thing about them lads?

I do not.

Them lads takes a very poor view of dry land. Never ask to go near the land at all. They do spend their lives sittin on the sea, bar an odd lep into the air to fly to another part of it. Well do you know what I'm going to tell you, I wouldn't fancy that class of a life at all. Because how would you put in your time or what would you do with yourself, stuck there out on the water night an mornin? Sure them lads might as well be dead as have a life like that. Anyway, it wouldn't suit me and that's a certainty. Would *you* fancy it?

Scarcely, but then I am not a bird. Birds have ideas of their own.

Begob they've a poor time of it, say what you like, no comfort or right way of livin' at all. Sure they do have to lay their eggs out in the sea.

Do they?

Certainly they do. The brother says the mother-hen has some kind of pocket in under the wing. Nobody knows how she whips the egg into the pocket when she lays it. Do you know what the brother called it? ONE OF THE GREAT UNSOLVED MYSTERIES OF THE SEA.

I understand.

ONE OF THE GREAT UNSOLVED MYSTERIES OF THE SEA. And of course there wouldn't be anny need for anny mystery at all if they had the sense to land on the shore like anny other bird. That's what I'd do to lay me eggs if I had anny. But no, the shore is barred, they do take a very poor view of everything but the water. Begob, here's me 'bus. Cheers!

Good bye.

* * *

Did you ever meet our friend's dog?

Whose dog?

Your man's.

But whose?

The brother's.

No.

Well the animal's an extraordinary genius. Do you know what I'm going to tell you, he could take you out and lose you. There's nothing he can't do bar talk. And do you know what?

What?

Who said he can't talk?

I thought you said so yourself.

Don't believe a word of it man. The dog talks to the brother. He does be yarnin with the brother above in the digs of a Sunday when everybody's out at the first house of the pictures. Believe me or believe me not now.

Upon what subjects does this animal discourse?

Sure luckit. I seen meself on a day's walk with the brother off out in Howth last March. Your man was with us and the three of us went for a ramble.

Who was with you?

Arthur. The dog. Well here was I in front, suckin in the fresh air and exercisin meself and payin no attention. What happens? I hear the brother chattin away behind me and been answered back. Then the brother gives a laugh at some joke d'other lad was after makin'. Then there's more laughin and chattin. I look back but the brother's hidden be a bend. I wait there unbeknownst and I see the brother comin into sight laughin his head off and your man beside him gruntin' and growlin and givin chat out of him for further orders. Course I was too far away to hear what was goin on. And when the pair sees me, the laughin stops and the two gets serious. It wouldn't do, of course, to say anything to the brother about a thing like that. He wouldn't like that, you know. An extraordinary pair, Arthur and the brother.

I see.

But I'll tell you what takes me to the fair. Your men above in the park. The fellas that's tryin to hunt the deer into a cage. Sure the brother and Arthur could take charge of them animals, and walk every wan of them up to Doll Erin of a Monda mornin if there was anny need for them to go there.

I see.

Sure luckit here man, I seen meself out in Santry four years ago when the brother had Arthur out on sheepdog trials and I'll go bail no man ever seen a dog parcel up sheep the way Arthur done it. There was a hundred of them in it if there was wan. Did Arthur start jumpin and scootin about an' roarin out of him? Did he start bitin and snarlin, snawshilin and givin leps in the air with excitement?

I deduce that quite the contrary was the case.

O nothin like that atchall. Not a sound out of him but a short step this way, a step maybe that way, the nose down in the ground, the tail stuck sideways, just enough to put the fear of God into your men the sheep. You'll see the right ear go up. That means a sheep two hundred yards away is thinkin of makin a dash out. Does he do it after Arthur puts up the ear? He certainly does NOT.

I understand.

He stops where he is and he's a sound judge. But I got on to the brother about them deer. Why is it, says I, that you and Arthur don't take a walk up there some fine day and march the deer in instead of having your men above there makin exhibitions of themselves with their lassoos and five bar gates and bicycles? Do you know what the brother said?

I do not.

THE DEER, says the brother, IS MAN'S FRIEND. The deer is man's friend. That's what he said. And he's right. Because when did the deer harm you?

Never, I assure you.

And when did they take a puck at me?

Never.

When did they try to ate your men on the bicycles?

Never.

Then tell me why they're tryin to slaughter them.

I am sorry I do not know. I perceive my large public service vehicle approaching. Good bye.

Your bus? O.K. Cheers.

*   *   *

Do you know that picture by George Roll[1] that was banned be the gallery?

I think I understand your reference.

Well the whole thing was gone into in the digs the other night. The brother was layin' down the law about pictures and art and all this

[1] Rouault.

class of thing. The brother says that any picture done be a Frenchman must be right.

Admittedly there is a widely held opinion that the French excel in artistic pursuits.

The brother says the French do be at the art night and mornin'. They do have it for breakfast, dinner and tea.

Is that a fact?

The brother says some of them lads thinks nothing of being up in the middle of the night-time workin' away at the pictures. Stuck inside a room wearin' the hair off a brush. Very mad-lookin' stuff some of it is too, so the brother says. But very INTERESSTIN' stuff. O very interesstin'. Very . . . very . . . interesstin'.

I see.

Then other lads does be stuck below in cellars makin' statues. There's a quare game for you now. They do be down hammerin' away in the middle of the night-time.

Surely not the most healthy of occupations.

Ah, yes. Well then do you know what goes on in the mornin-time in a French house?

I do not.

They do all come down for breakfast, ready to tuck into a damn fine feed of rashers and black puddin'. Starvin' with the hunger, do you understand, after been up all night workin' at the art. What happens?

I take it they eat their meal.

Notatall. In marches your man of the house with overalls on him. Will yez all come in here, says he, into this room, says he, till I show yez me new picture. This, of course, is something he was after runnin' up in the middle of the night-time. So in they all march and leave the grub there. And be the time they're finished lookin' at that, your man below in the cellar is roarin' out of him for them all to come down and take a look at what HE'S after doin'. Do you understand? No breakfast. But plenty of art, do you know.

That is a rare example of devotion to the things of the intellect.

The brother says it's what they call art for art's sake. Well then do you know what goes on on Sunda?

I do not.

The brother says that beyond in France they have a big palace be the name of the Tweeleries. The Tweeleries was built in the days of the French Revolution be Napoleon Bonipart himself and built be slave labour too. None of your one and fourpence an hour with time and a half on Saherdas. Well annyway all around the Tweeleries they do have fancy gardens and parks. What would you say is in the gardens?

Root crops, one should hope, in keeping with these stern times.

I'll tell you what's in the gardens. The gardens is full of statues. And of a Sunda the Frenchmen do be walkin' around the gardens havin' a screw at the statues.

I see.

They do be up early in the mornin' waitin' for the gates to be opened. And then nothin'll do them all day only gawkin' out of them at the statues. They'll ask nothin' better than that. As happy as Larry lookin' at them first from this side and then that. And talkin' away in French to one another. And do you know why?

I do not.

Because the statues is art too. The brother says the statue is the highest form of art. And he's not far wrong because even look at the height of some of the ones we have ourselves above in the Phoenix Park.

The effigy of Nelson also ranks high.

Ah yes, great men for the art, the French. Sure the brother says a man told him they do be sellin' pictures in the streets. Here's me 'bus. Cheers now.

Cheers.

* * *

I've a quare bit of news for you. The brother's nose is out of order.

What?

A fact. Some class of a leak somewhere.

I do not understand.

Well do you see it's like this. Listen till I tell you. Here's the way he's fixed. He starts suckin the wind in be the mouth. That's OK, there's no damper there. But now he comes along and shuts the mouth. That leaves him the nose to work with or he's a dead man. Fair enough. He starts suckin in through the nose. AND THEN DO YOU KNOW WHAT?

What?

THE—WIND GOES ASTRAY SOMEWHERE. Wherever it goes it doesn't go down below. Do you understand me? There's some class of a leak above in the head somewhere. There's what they call a valve there. The brother's valve is banjaxed.

I see.

The air does leak up into the head, all up around the brother's brains. How would you like that? Of course, his only man is to not use the nose at all and keep workin' on the mouth. O be gob it's no joke to have the valve misfirin'. And I'll tell you a good one.

Yes?

The brother is a very strict man for not treatin' himself. He does have crowds of people up inside in the digs every night lookin for all classes of cures off him, maternity cases and all the rest of it. But he wouldn't treat himself. Isn't that funny? HE WOULDN'T TREAT HIM-SELF.

He is at one there with orthodox medical practice.

So he puts his hat on his head and takes a walk down to Charley's. Charley is a man like himself—not a doctor, of course, but a layman that understands first principles. Charley and the brother do have consultations when one or other has a tough case do you understand me. Well anyway the brother goes in and is stuck inside in Charley's place for two hours. And listen till I tell you.

Yes?

When the brother leaves he has your man Charley in bed with strict orders not to make any attempt to leave it. Ordered to bed and told to stop there. The brother said he wouldn't be responsible if Charley stayed on his feet. What do you think of that?

It is very odd to say the least of it.

Of course Charley was always very delicate and a man that never minded himself. The brother takes a very poor view of Charley's kidneys. Between yourself, meself and Jack Mum, Charley is a little bit given to the glawsheen. Charley's little finger is oftener in the air than anywhere else, shure wasn't he in the hands of doctors for years man. They had him nearly destroyed when somebody put him on to the brother. And the brother'll make a job of him yet, do you know that?

No doubt.

Ah yes. Everybody knows that it's the brother that's keepin Charley alive. But begob the brother'll have to look out for himself now with the nose valve out of gear and your man Charley on his hands into the bargain.

Is there any other person to whom your relative could have recourse?

Ah, well, of course, at the latter end he'll have to do a job on himself. HAVE TO, man, sure what else can he do? The landlady was telling me that he's thinkin of openin himself some night.

What?

You'll find he'll take the razor to the nose before you're much older. He's a man that would understand valves, you know. He wouldn't be long puttin it right if he could get his hands at it. Begob there'll be blood in the bathroom anny night now.

He will probably kill himself.

The brother? O trust him to look after Number One. You'll find he'll live longer than you or me. Shure he opened Charley in 1934.

He did?

He gave Charley's kidneys a thorough overhaul, and that's a game none of your doctors would try their hand at. He had Charley in the bathroom for five hours. Nobody was let in, of course, but the water was goin all the time and all classes of cutthroats been sharpened, you could hear your man working at the strap. O a great night's work. Begob here's me 'bus!

Bye bye.

RESEARCH BUREAU

A Handy Instrument

The article illustrated to-day (did you guess?) is a snow-gauge. There are very few of them in Ireland at present. It is made of copper, and consists of a funnel or catch-pipe for the snow, which widens inwardly, then drops eighteen inches, allowing the snow to fall into a pan beneath. A casing which can be heated with hot water surrounds the gauge and is used to melt the snow. By this arrangement the snow cannot escape; it melts and runs into the bucket beneath, where it is accurately gauged.

So what, you say. I will tell you what. There is one great advantage in having a snow gauge on your premises. Supposing some moon-faced young man who reads Proust happens to be loitering about your house, blathering out of him about art, life, love, and so on. He is sure to have a few cant French phrases, which he will produce carefully at suitable

intervals as one produces coins from a purse. Inevitably the day will
come (even if you have to wait for it for many years) when he will
sigh and murmur:

'*Mais où sont les neiges d'antan?*'

Here is your chance. This is where you go to town. Seize the nitwit
by the scruff of the neck, march him out to the snow gauge, and shout:

'Right in that bucket, you fool!'
I'll bet you'll feel pretty good after that.

* * *

Another thing that is going short in the emergency is midnight oil. A friend who burns a considerable quantity of it tells me he is down to his last drum and his supplier (holds out) (little hope) of getting more. But pray do not think (for one moment) that the Myles na gCopaleen Research Bureau is asleep when the problem of this kind is confronting the nation. Advanced experiments are in progress with a patent midnight grease which is made from turf, whiskey, offals and cider. This mess burns with a pale blue flame and is quite satisfactory for illuminating midnight attics. The trouble (as I needn't tell you) is the smell. The smell is fearful. Already the Corporation has assured us that we are committing a nuisance by manufacturing the stuff. That, of course, is a scandalous charge (to lay) (at our door). Ireland must have midnight oil or a suitable substitute, otherwise it will disappear from civilisation. Without midnight oil the Irish Academy of Letters will (find it impossible to function) and even I will have to put aside my (monumental) work on Inorganic Geometry. Anybody who has a B.A. will not be able to proceed with his (or her) plan of reading the entire works of Dusty Evsky this winter. Chaos (will reign). Light-starved students will riot in the streets. Midnight-oil-tankers standing in the docks will be looted. Labour will challenge a general election.

That is why we are going to keep on trying to de-stink our inflammable treacle.

Furthermore

Burners of midnight oil are not the only class who are suffering. The (acute) shortage of plate glass is causing serious embarrassment to people who live in glass houses, and our Research Bureau has been (inundated) with (shoals of) letters imploring us to see about manufacturing a substitute, 'opaque, if necessary.'

'It's like this,' a prominent person who lives in a glass house said to me the other day, 'by (exercising the greatest restraint) I can let six days of the week go by without . . . well . . . doing what we people who live in glass houses find it impossible to resist doing. On the seventh day (with the best will in the world) nothing will stop me from rushing out and firing a stone. Just one stone. And you know the result. Showers of stones and filth and brickbats descend on my glass house and smash twenty or thirty panes. My glazier tells me that after next week he will have nothing more for me. Putty has been cornered and can only be got in the black market at scandalously (inflated) prices. What am I to do? What's (going to become of me)?'

* * *

The Myles na gCopaleen Research Bureau receives nearly a thousand letters a day (942 on Thursdays, however) from readers asking us to devise machines and engines that will solve their personal problems. Some of these problems are too intimate to be discussed here, but a Mitchelstown reader has approached us on what must be a fairly widespread difficulty. Nowadays it is nearly impossible to get matches and your cheap petrol lighter won't work in the middle of the night because it lacks the stimulation that is afforded by the heat of the body when carried around in the pocket all day. This means you cannot tell the time at night and do not know when to eat your nocturnal dose of pills—the pills your doctor warned you would be no good unless you pull yourself together and lead 'a regular life'; and you know what I mean by that—please take the innocent smirk off your face.

Well, take a look at this apparatus we have devised. 'A' is an ordinary gas-jet with a modified vertical tap that is operated by a spring-loaded cord-pull ('B'), which is erected beside your bed. When going to bed (or 'retiring', if you prefer unctuous round-abouts) you light the gas, which is adjusted to afford a tiny and almost invisible fan-tail of light. You have already driven a stout nail into the polished teak panelling behind the light, and on this you have hung your watch. Everything is now in order. When you wake up and want to know the time, you just pull down the knob at 'B' and there you are.

The Plain People of Ireland: But shure that's no use. The gas is turned off at night, and in anny case there's no gas in Mitchelstown.

Myself: You err. To-morrow I will print a diagram showing how to make your own gas. In any case, I have often been told that there does be great gas in Mitchelstown.

The Plain People of Ireland: Listen, surely it's not that time! Lord save us, don't say it's twenty-five to one.

Myself: I'm a bit fast as a matter of fact.

The Plain People of Ireland: Oh, good. Thank heaven!

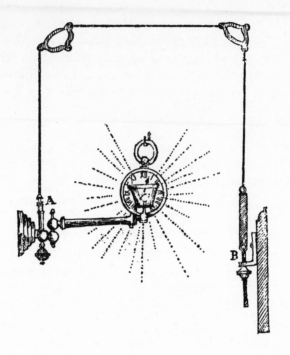

*   *   *

As regards Mary, the Rose of Tralee, it will be recalled that it was not
her beauty alone that won one; ah no, 'twas the truth in her eyes ever
dawning. Bearing this in mind, it occurred to the Myles na gCopaleen
Research Bureau the other day to try to ascertain whether the truth still
dawns in the eyes of the ladies of to-day. An investigator was sent out
with instructions to engage a hundred ladies in conversation and examine their eyes for traces of the truth, dawning, fully dawned, declining
or otherwise. He was away for a week and then returned to submit the
following record of his researches:

   45% Mild mydriasis, probably caused by the consumption of slim-
      ming drugs.
   21% Ptosis of the lids due to defect in the oculomotor nerve,
      anisocoria, opthalmia, one or more small chalazions.
   18% pronounced hyperthyroidism.
   14% Evidence of retinal hemorrhages, papillary oedema, exoph-
      thalmos.
   1% Mikulicz's disease.

1% Paralysis of the orbicularis oculi.

'No evidence of the truth ever dawning anywhere?' we asked.

'No,' he said, 'and what's more, I'm going to marry one of them.'

'Which one?' we asked.

'Mikulicz's disease,' he said, 'and she has three cute little yellow chalazions too.'

We agreed to put him on the married man's scale and changed the subject by putting that damn lovely thing by Toselli on the gramophone.

*   *   *

Recently I referred briefly to a new type of telephone patented by the Research Bureau. It is designed to meet an urgent social requirement. Nearly everybody likes to have a telephone in the house, not so much for its utility (which is very dubious), but for the social standing it implies. A telephone on display in your house means that you have at least some 'friend' or 'friends'—that there is somebody in the world who thinks it worthwhile to communicate with you. It also suggests that you must 'keep in touch', that great business and municipal undertakings would collapse unless your advice could be obtained at a moment's notice. With a telephone in your house you are 'important'. But a real telephone costs far too much and in any event would cause you endless annoyance. To remedy this stay tough affairs the Bureau has devised a selection of bogus telephones. They are entirely self-contained, powered by dry batteries and where talk can be heard coming from the instrument, this is done by a tiny photoelectric mechanism. Each instrument is fitted, of course, with a bogus wire which may be embedded in the wainscoting. The cheapest model is simply a dud instrument. Nothing happens if you pick up the receiver and this model can only be used safely if you are certain that none of the visitors to your house will say 'Do you mind if I use your phone?' The next model has this same draw-back but it has the advantage that at a given hour every night it begins to ring. Buzz-buzz, buzz-buzz. You must be quick to get it before an obliging visitor 'helps' you. You pick up the receiver and say 'Who? The Taoiseach? Oh, very well. Put him on.' The 'conversation' that follows is up to yourself. The more expensive instruments ring and speak and they are designed on the basis that a visitor will answer. In one model a voice says, 'Is that the Hammond Lane Foundry?' Your visitor will say no automatically and the instrument will immediately ring off. In another model an urgent female voice says 'New York calling So-an-So'—mentioning your own name—'Is So-and-So there?' and keeps mechanically repeating this formula after the heartless manner of telephone girls. You spring to the instrument as quickly as possible and close the deal for the purchase of a half share in General Motors. These latter instruments are a bit risky, as few householders can be relied upon to avoid fantastically exaggerated conversations. The safest of the lot is Model 2B, which gives an engaged tone no matter what number is dialled by the innocent visitor. This is dead safe.

Some people may think it a snag that one's name won't be in the telephone book. In a way that is nonsense because there is nothing so refined as having a telephone and not being in the book. In any case, if you have the Bureau's model that always gives the engaged tone, it might be possible for you to induce the Post Office to insert your name in the book, putting opposite it the telephone number of the Department of Supplies. PS might arrange it in exchange for a couple of old books.

*　*　*

A New Project

The Bureau is not, of course, solely occupied with mere mechanics. Vaster things are brewing. You have, no doubt, heard of the Hidden-Ireland. Professor Corkery has written a book on the subject and Mulhausen and I went rather deeply into the thing in 1933. And now, in conjunction with the Bureau, I have been trying to interest some people with money in a scheme—pretty ambitious, perhaps, but well worth it—a scheme that should win the support of all right thinking citizens. *Hide Ireland again!* Hmmmmm? Could be done war or no war, take my word for it.

FOR STEAM MEN

What of steam for 1944?

Suffice it to say that I have plans. I am writing a book on steam and it will be published in due course by that mysterious Mister Pranter who is so frequently mentioned in *The Bell*.

Readers often correspond with me on steam matters. The younger generation, I find, knows very little about the great art. Thus I am often chided, forsooth, for being 'too technical'. Bah! As well ask Einstein to provide simpler sums. *Quod scripsi scripsi*. Not one jot or title will I abate.

Yet ignorance can have charm. A young lady has written challenging me on the subject of railway disasters. 'Would not a plan to avoid even one be more important than a thousand thermic syphons?' But of course. Most certainly. Nobody suggested anything to the contrary. Indeed, I dealt personally with this very matter many years ago. Drawings, specifications, everything. Take, for example, my scheme for

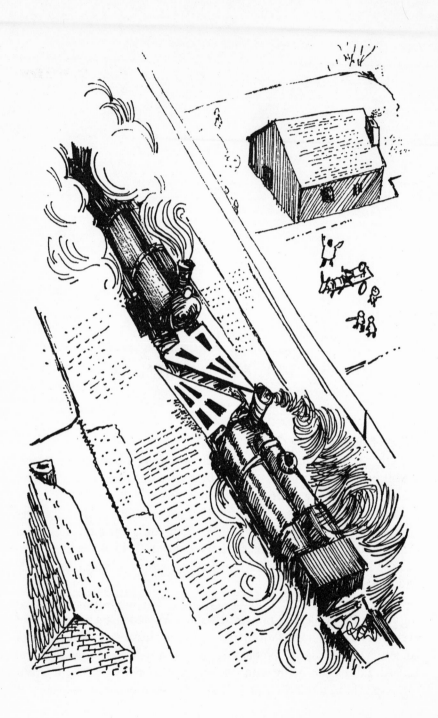

avoiding head-on collisions. It is the essence of inexpense and simplicity.

The patent apparatus I illustrate opposite tells its own ingenious story. Two trains colliding head-on do not telescope each other and kill hundreds of people. They are instantly switched off the track upon which at least one of them had no business to be on and run harmlessly past each other, ploughing harmlessly into the earth and coming to a stand-still. Some of the ladies may be shaken, perhaps the fireman has scalded his hand . . . but the great thing is that there is absolutely no blood.

Nor in my researches did I neglect the only other sort of a collision that is possible between trains. I refer to the case where, owing to inexcusable signal-box bungling, a fast passenger train is permitted to overtake a slow local on the same track. What then?

Simple. Let the end of every slow train consist of the patent ramp-car I have illustrated. The fast train will not (as you might have imagined) run along the top of the slow train and eventually crash down on top of the slow engine. Quite no. The steepness of the ramp, allied with its motion, is sufficient to slow up the fast train and compel it to roll back again on the tracks. Thus hundreds of more lives are saved and man moves on in the coil of his dark destiny.

All these plans were shown to the old D. & S.E.R., the most ruffianly railroad concern ever to exist in any country. 'The Manager directs me to state that the Company are not interested in enclosed drawings and can take no responsibility for same.'

Do I speak bitterly? Maybe.

THE CRUISKEEN COURT
OF VOLUNTARY JURISDICTION

Owing to (pressure) (of work) in the courts of justice, withdrawal of judges, electric heaters, bicycle-crime and other matters, the public-spirited Myles na gCopaleen Central Research Bureau has persuaded several impatient litigants to bring their differences before the Cruiskeen Court of Voluntary Jurisdiction. This institution conducts its proceedings in English and 'recognises' only those statutes which are 'recognisable for the purposes of the court'. Since nobody knows what this means, the 'lawyers' do not like to spend too much time rehearsing jargon and citing 'cases', fearing that the whole spiel will be ruled out as 'inadmissible'. Hence, justice is rough, not to say ready.

The first case was called the other day before His Honour, Judge Twinfeet, who was attired in a robe of poplin green. He 'opened' that abstraction, the 'proceedings', by expressing the hope that there would not be too much jargon. 'Justice is a simple little lady,' he added, 'not to be overmuch besmeared with base Latinities.' . . .

* * *

Twinfeet J., of course, has made many strange pronouncements in the Court of Voluntary Jurisdiction. In an action brought under the Marine Hereditaments (Compensation) Act, 1901, a man who lived in an old boat located on a hill sought damages from another man who had been (as alleged) negligent in the management of a dinghy on a trolley (which he was bringing to the railway station) so as to cause the dinghy to collide with the old house-boat. The defense was that the latter structure, being rated to the poor rate, could not be a boat, vessel or ship and that the dinghy, being a land-borne wheeled article, was not a dinghy but a velocipede. Twinfeet J. inquired whether it was suggested that a small paddle-steamer was a farmcart but the defence submitted that inasmuch as a paddle-steamer could not be hauled by a horse, mule, pony, jennet, donkey or ass, it could not be a farm-cart within the meaning of the Farmcarts Act and must in fact be a paddle-steamer. The plaintiffs contended that they were the aggrieved parties in a naval collision and entitled to recover damages and compensation from the defendants, who had been negligent in the management of sea-going craft, which was their property and under their care and management. The defendants pleaded alternatively that the 'house-boat' was 'wreckage' within the meaning of the Wreckage Act.

Twinfeet, J., in the course of a long judgment, said that he could find nothing in the Act or indeed in any statute regulating matters of admiralty which made water an essential element in a collision between boats; he was satisfied that the owners of the dinghy had been negligent in the navigation of the dinghy 'Marcella' at the junction of Market Street and Dawson Hill. He assessed damages at £4 and excused the jury from service for a year on the ground that they had been at sea for four days.

BORES

The Man with the Watch

Somebody remarks that his watch, solid gold, 98 jewels, cost £50, wears it swimming, has broken down after only five years' service. The Man smiles primly at this, produces a turnip-watch, and puts it solemnly on the table. The harsh tick silences further talk. Those present perceive that the thing was once nickel-plated, but is now a dull brass colour at the edges.

'Do you know what that cost me?' the Man asks.

Everybody knows that the answer is five bob or thereabouts, that it was bought eighteen years ago, that it never lost a minute, and was never even cleaned. But nobody is brutal enough to spill that out. *People are weak, and tend to play up to bores.*

'I suppose about two quid,' somebody says innocently.

'Five bob,' the Man says.

Fake surprise all round.

'Know how long I have it?' the Man asks.

'Five or six years, I suppose.'

'I bought that watch in Leeds in September 1925. That's nearly twenty years ago. Since then it has never stopped, never lost a minute *and wasn't even cleaned once!*'

Phoney astonishment on every face.

'A grand little time-keeper,' the Man says, replacing the turnip in his pocket with considerable satisfaction.

(This particular type of pest also owns incredible cars, fifty-year-old fountain pens, gloves bought in 1915 and never lost or worn-out, makes his own cigarettes with home-made filter-wads at the ends, reckons that they cost him roughly (always this 'roughly') a farthing each, and is convinced that 'people are mad' to pay more. Let me present one further bore):

The Man with the Blade

Somebody says: 'It's very hard to get decent blades these days,' and in explanation, grimaces and rubs jaw. 'I haven't had a decent shave for weeks,' he adds.

The Man is present and looks puzzled.

'You don't mean to say you *buy* razor blades?' he says.

Various people confess they do.

'Well I don't,' the Man says. 'I admit I *have* bought one, but that was two years ago . . .'

Again dutiful surprise is registered.

Everybody has heard of patent blade-sharpeners, the various sharpenings that can be attempted with mirrors, strops and tumblers, but nobody has any guts and nothing is said.

'It's quite simple,' the Man says, thoroughly delighted with himself. 'Get a good tumbler and keep it by you. Smear the inside with vaseline. Every morning before you shave, give both sides of the blade three or four rubs along the inside of the tumbler, keeping strong pressure on the centre of it with your finger. That's all.'

Pauses to accept gratefully the due looks of incredulity

'You'll get the best shave you ever got in your life, man. And a tuppenny blade'll last you five years.'

(On your life don't show this article to anybody. Nearly everybody belongs to one or other of these two classes in some capacity; you'll get black looks for your pains. Ever meet the man whose petrol lighter always works, explains why? 'It's quite simple, the whole secret is . . .)

* * *

I'm afraid I have some more bores here today. (I am sorry, but the function of the historian is to record completely, not selectively.)

Have you met—look, this hurts me as much as it hurts you—have you met *The Man Who Buys Wholesale?* (You're in for it this time.)

You have asked this gargoyle to 'dinner' because he has put some business in your way during the year, and there may be more where that came from. The clown comes into your room rubbing his deformed, calloused hands, looks round, checks up on fittings, decoration, etc. Walks over to your radio. It is a year old—1947 should see it paid for. He examines it closely, taps it, disconnects it, turns it upside down, shakes it, breaks one of the leads, leaves it on its side, takes out handkerchief and wipes hands. Infuriated, you manage to say:

'What do you think of the radio?'

'Hah? The radio? Aw, yeh. Aw, with a bit of adjustment it'd be a nice job. I'll get you a nice one. Them nine pound ones wears out in no time . . .'

By now you are practically rigid with hatred and disgust. This figure of £9 is, of course, a trap—and you are going deliberately to fall into it. You thoroughly despise yourself. You say:

'But look here—*nine pounds*! That set is costing me eighty-seven pounds . . .'

The foul mountebank springs from the chair, comes over, puts both hands on your shoulders:

'Are you mad, Mac? Are you in your right mind man?'

'It's a perfectly good set,' you stammer, now loathing yourself utterly, 'it . . . it . . . works quite well and eighty-seven pounds is the recognised retail price. I thought *you'd* know that!'

The claws are now taken off your shoulders. The monster elaborately averts the face and, addressing the far wall, says: Th' unfortunate man must be mad! Makes a show of walking away sadly, suddenly whips round and shouts, showering you with saliva:

'*Are you crackers?* Have you taken leave of your wits? I wouldn't have believed it of you, that's all I can say. *Of course* I know it's the *retail* price. But shure, man alive, *no one* is supposed to buy stuff retail! Shure that went out years ago. Now I've two sets at home . . .'

Is that enough for today? Could you take a little more?

The Man Who Is His Own Lawyer?

Is it fork out me good-lookin' money to them hooky solicitors? Them fellas, that has th'office on a weekly tenancy and a season ticket to Belfast, ready to skip the minit they get their claws on some unfortunate orphan's dough? Ah no, thanks all the same. I think I'll just carry on a little bit longer the way I am. And I'll tell you this much: I know more law nor anny ten of them put together. I didn't want the help of anny solicitor back in nineteen and thirty-four when I made the landlord take down and rebuild back wall and replace gutters, *and* pull out the joyces in the front drawin' room and put in new wans. Oh Gob no bloody fear, I know me rights. I took out the probate single-handed after the mother went and I got ten pounds nine for Christy the time he was humped offa the bike be a lurry. I know me law and I know me rights.

The foregoing samples, of course, represent *attitudes*. There are, however, troglodytic specimens who can get their effects by a single and unvarying remark which, injected into thousands of conversations in the course of their lifetime, enables them to take leave of humanity knowing that they have done something important to it. Have you ever heard this:

Of course Dan O'Connell Was A Freemason Of Course You Knew That?

* * *

A Dublin reader has kindly written to inform me of a bore (petrol lighter species) who infests a local public house. Apparently the lighter is used as an instrument for gaining admittance to parties of drinkers not known to the bore personally; naturally, this means free drink. I am terribly sorry but this type of person is not a bore within my terms of reference. The sort of bore I have been attempting to define in recent notes is a born and outright bore; boring other people is his sole occupation, enjoyment, recreation. No thought of gain would he permit to sully his 'art'; indeed, many of them are prepared to lose money —to *stand* drinks—if they see a good opportunity of pursuing their nefarious vocation. Let me give a few further examples. Have you met The Man Who Has Read It In Manuscript? Let me explain.

You are a literary man, you never go out, all you ask is to be left alone with your beloved books. But the Man calls. A desultory conversation starts. The Man is peering and poking about your private apartments. You are interested in a book you read recently, would like to get other people's opinion on it, innocently enough, you ask:

'By the way, have you read *Victorian Doctor*?'

'Never heard of it,' the blight says.

'Most interesting book,' you say. 'All about Oscar Wilde's father, gives a very good picture of Dublin life in those days . . .'

'Oh, *that*?' the bore says, his back turned in a very casual way as he interferes with some personal documents on your desk. 'Ah, yes, I read that. Actually he meant to give the book another name, I hadn't heard it was published under that title. I read it in manuscript as a matter of fact.'

Thus you are vouchsafed a glimpse of the anonymous adviser, critic, confessor and daddy christmas of literary men.

'Ever read *Warren Peace* by T. Allstoy?' you inquire.

'Ah, yes, I read that thing in the manuscript years ago. Is it published yet?'

* * *

It's quite a little time, I think, since I wrote on the subject of bores. I come back to this problem only because I have since encountered a pretty bad specimen. He is a monster to be avoided like the pledge, a colossal imposition who will make you very angry and cause your heart to beat like a sludge-hammer (*stet*). I refer to The Man Who Does His Own Carpentry And Talks About It.

This savage lives in a little red brick box four by two, basically a one-room cell. Inside you have himself, the missis and the eight girls. Next week the eldest Anny is to get a job as a typist at eight-and-six a week in a solicitor's office. This man has the place got out beautiful. And regardless. Suppose you happened to live in a telephone box—like the fourteen blonde women in the one under Moore's statue any time I went to ring up. Well, I assume you would accept the thing and try to make the best of it. Not so, however, The Man Who Does His Own Carpentry; *he* makes it hard for himself—*he builds partitions*. He subdivides the sentry's home and erects shelving, window-seats, cupboards, hot presses, built-in wardrobes. And anything in the way of circulation—I mean walking about—in that house takes the form and rhythm of a Cuban rhumba; your feet stay where they are, though your hips and knees move somewhat.

The partitions this Man has made are exceptional manifestations in the sphere of Home Crafts. He is so handy with his hands (round the house in brackets), he has Vol. IV of somebody's Building Encyclopedia. He makes this . . . thing, this 'wall', by laying a couple of sticks along the sagging unjoisted floor. Next, he introduces a long horizontal member into the room and raises it into the position of Mahomet's coffin, strutting both walls and threatening to bulge out the gable. This, reader, is the 'framework'. In between go the bits of paper. *Yes*, the bits of newspaper well wetted and rolled into soft balls. And there you are—you only wait for the thing to harden!

Come into this prodigy's signal-box some evening—it will be the first time you ever used a tin-opener to enter a friend's house. He will rub his hands, grin, look obliquely at his 'handiwork' and without doubt you will find yourself, craven lout that you are, saying this:

'Gob, you've laid out a lot of money on the ancestral home since I was last here, Mac. Who did you have on the job?'

You are a friend, you have said the right thing. Now he can put on his act. Surprise, beating of the breast, walking backwards like a crab, letting the mouth hang open pointing at himself:

'Who? *Me?* Is it me employ a contractor? Me, is it—*me* hand out me good money to your men when I have two hands God gave me and the chisel, hammer and hack-saw I picked up in Paul's of Aungier street? Is it hand out the money that's put by for me old age to hooks and fly-be-nights that wouldn't know a screw-driver from a bradawl, have the house for months occupied be lads makin' tay and smokin' cigarettes—*in my time*—ME . . .?'

'But surely . . . surely you didn't do all this yourself?' (You are afraid to lean against the partition in case you suddenly find yourself in the 'bathroom'—but you are saying the right thing still, you hypocritical dog!)

'And why not? Shure there's nothing to it man. There's not a damn thing to it. Shure anywan shure even yourself could do that much. But come up till I show you the wee chest of drawers I put in the nursery . . .'

Come 'up', mind you, and the 'nursery' . . . ! And all the time you have to pretend not to see the wife and eight children asleep under the 'bookcase'.

This man also makes all his own coffins. The bought ones aren't a job, he avers.

* * *

Or how about a few *brief* notes on notorious practitioners of boredom? For example—

The Man Who Can Pack. This monster watches you trying to stuff the contents of two wardrobes into a small attaché case. You succeed, of course, but you find you have forgotten to put in your golf clubs. You curse grimly but your 'friend' is delighted. He knew this would happen. He approaches, offers consolation and advises you to go downstairs and take things easy while he 'puts things right'. Some days later, when you unpack your things in Glengariff, you find that he has not only got your golf clubs in but has included also your bedroom carpet, the kit of a Gas Company man who had been working in your room, two ornamental vases, and a folding card-table. Everything in view, in fact, except your razor. You have to wire £7 to Cork to get a new leather bag (made of cardboard) in order to get all this junk home. *And* offer outrageous bribes to the boots for the loan of his razor. Or—

The Man Who Soles His Own Shoes. Quite innocently you complain about the quality of present-day footwear. You wryly exhibit a broken sole. 'Must leave them in tomorrow,' you say vaguely. The monster is flabbergasted at this passive attitude, has already forced you into an arm-chair, pulled your shoes off and vanished with them into the scullery. He is back in an incredibly short space of time and restored your property to you announcing that the shoes are now 'as good as new'. You notice his own for the first time and instantly understand why his feet are deformed. You hobble home, apparently on stilts. Nailed to each shoe is an inch-thick slab of synthetic 'leather' made from Shellac, saw-dust and cement. Being much taller than usual, you nearly kill yourself getting into a bus. By the time you get home you have lost two pints of blood and the wound in your forehead looks as if it will turn septic. Or—

But no—it is too painful to describe some of these fiends in detail. You have met *The Man Who Can Carve*? No matter if the dish be a solitary roast pigeon, the coat is taken off, two square yards of table cleared, several inoffensive diners compelled to leave the room to give the ruffian 'a bit of freedom'. By some miracle everything carved by this person is transformed into scrag-ends, so that *nobody* gets anything that is eatable.

Or *The Man Who 'Believes'* (or *Does Not 'Believe'*) in this or that commonplace thing. One wretch does not 'believe' in electric radiators. He is horrified if you turn one on, pretends he is choking, makes motions of removing collar and tie. They 'dry up the atmosphere' of course. Just like the other oaf who does not 'believe' in real fires. Nothing for him but the electric fire. He has five or six in every room, and one or two on the stairs. A coal fire 'only makes dirt'. It also 'makes work' and you have to be 'always stoking it'. Whereas the electric fire (here he makes plugging-in motions) you just push it in and there you are! Four times cheaper than coal, gives twice as much heat, and so forth. The only thing you can do with this beast is to provide him with an electric chair, as a present for himself.

Or *The Man Who Wouldn't Let A Radio Into The House?*

Or *The Man Who Doesn't Believe In Fresh Air?* ('Do you know what it is, there's more people killed be that fad . . .')

Who then is the supreme demon? Would it be that not unfamiliar person who confesses that he never 'sees' the *Irish Times?*

* * *

There is still another monster I would like to warn you about. (To be warned is to be four-armed.) You have, very indiscreetly, complained about the price of clothes: worse, you have commented adversely on the quality of much of what is available. You see a light dawning in the monster's eye and to your alarm you realise that you are for it. Fascinated, you observe him primly take a garment he is wearing between finger and thumb. (Too late to correct the absurd ambiguity of that last sentence.) He savours the fabric appreciatively, then courteously invites you to do the same. Your fingers, hypnotised by him, obey against your own strict orders. He appears to be wearing sandpaper but your cowardice does not permit you to say this. You withdraw your hand, covertly explore your fingers for splinters, and cravenly murmur some noises of approval.

How old would you say this suit is?

You are blushing furiously now—it may be shame or anger or both —but you still dare not protest.

Would you believe me if I told you that I've that coat on me back for ten years. Know what I paid for it?

You keep on making polite noises, sorrier than ever that you were born at all.

Fifty bob!

More muttering, swallowed curses, tears.

And I'll get another ten years out of it too, you can't, do you know what it is, you can't wear stuff like that out.

Let me add that this gent has a brother wants to know How Much He's Making In The Year, Go On, Tell Him, How Much Would You Say He's Making Now.

* * *

I hope I am not . . . a . . . a bore but there is one other character I would like to speak to you about privately. You probably know him. He was just leaving the Brothers beyond in Richmond Street the year your poor grandfather first came to school. Grandfather unfortunately is no longer to be seen due to the highly technical business of interment (1908 R.I.P.), but this other person is still in town, the button-less camel-hair overcoat worn slightly off the shoulders, the snap-brimmed green felt nestling in a nest of curls formerly worn by a certain foreign horse, present whereabouts unknown. To your certain knowledge this man is one hundred and four years of age (if he's a day). Through a calamitous neglect of keeping your eyes skinned—I admit the skin *does* grow rather quickly, but what are surgeons for?— you meet this person. Then it starts. You are dragged into a public cottage, sorry public house, and drinks are poured into you while you listen to this person's account of his life. The horse out on Merrion Strand before breakfast, after that a couple of brisk sets of squash (still before breakfast). Then out with the dumb-bells (they would need to be) and then a little toast and a glass of limejuice. After that, into the running shorts and round and round the lawn until the *petit déjeuner*: then, of course, the fencing class until lunch; after lunch brings togs down to Lansdowne Road on the off-chance and always gets a game, plays on the wing but is rather a useful back. A shower and home to dinner but not without a few sets on the hard courts. After dinner takes out the gloves and up to the SCR for a couple of bouts with the boys. On slack nights, you suspect, he goes down to Shelbourne Park and runs round the thrack in front of the electric hare to show it the way. You assimilate all this without a word and then to your horror you hear yourself saying:

'Begob you know you'll want to go easy—you can't do that forever. You'll have to give a lot of that up, you know, when you pass thirty-five. Because . . .'

He is delighted. God forgive you—he stands there with the embalmed profile up to the light, he has raised the hand to stop you and then says:

'*How old would you say I am?*'

You look at him steadily, unsmiling: you know that you are worse than he is and that the whole thing is the price of you.

'Well,' you say, 'Well, Jack, I'm not going by your *appearance*—you certainly don't *look* your age, never seen a man wearing so well. But from what I know of you around the town, knocking around and so forth, I'd say you must be a man of thirty-two, indeed I suppose you'd be a man that's goin' on for thirty-three. I'd say you're pushin' thirty-three, Jack . . .'

The vile clown is by now beside himself with delight. Observe him—the sphinx-like smile, the slow shaking of the 'head', the pause, the holding of the glass to the light, the slow draining of it—revealing the pure lines of chin and jaw. Slowly the face is turned to you and now you perceive at close quarters the deathly meshed mask apparently clogged with baking powder, the breaking fissures in it that denote a half-smile of deprecation:

'*Mac, I was born in* 1908.'

Suddenly your own face is blanched with horror; you tremble; you mutter some inarticulate excuse and stumble out into the cold, cursing bitterly. You *know* it was 1808.

Is there, you ask, any remedy, any way out for weaklings like you, is there any hope for the man who is too cowardly to insult such 'people'? Well, *don't go out at all* is the only thing I can think of. Stay at home in bed, windows closed, blinds drawn, electric fire going full blast. Only the really tough bores will follow you there—and after all they're your relatives, aren't they? You can't get away from them, can you?

KEATS AND CHAPMAN

Keatsiana

Keats was once presented with an Irish terrier, which he humorously named Byrne. One day the beast strayed from the house and failed to return at night. Everybody was distressed, save Keats himself. He reached reflectively for his violin, a fairly passable timber of the Stradivarius feciture, and was soon at work with chin and jaw.

Chapman, looking in for an after-supper pipe, was astonished at the poet's composure, and did not hesitate to say so. Keats smiled (in a way that was rather lovely).

'And why should I not fiddle,' he asked, 'while Byrne roams?'

*   *   *

Chapman once became immersed in the study of dialectical materialism, particularly insofar as economic and sociological planning could be demonstrated to condition eugenics, birth-rates and anthropology.

215

His wrangles with Keats lasted far into the night. He was particularly obsessed by the fact that in the animal kingdom, where there was no self-evident plan of ordered Society and where connubial relations were casual and polygamous, the breed prospered and disease remained of modest dimensions. Where there was any attempt at the imposition from without—and he instanced the scientific breeding of race-horses by humans—the breed prospered even more remarkably. He was not slow to point out that philosophers of the school of Marx and Engels had ignored the apparent necessity for ordered breeding on the part of humans as a concomitant to planning in the social and economic spheres. Was this, he once asked Keats, to be taken as evidence of superior reproductive selection on the part of, say, horses —or was it to be taken that a man of the stamp of Engels deliberately shirked an issue too imponderable for rationative evaluation?

The poet found this sort of thing boring, and frowned.

'Foals rush in where Engels feared to tread,' he said morosely.

* * *

Chapman thought a lot of Keat's girl, Fanny Brawne, and often said so.

'Do you know,' he remarked one day, 'that girl of yours is a sight for sore eyes.'

'She stupes to conquer, you mean,' Keats said.

* * *

Keats and Chapman once paid a visit to the Vale of Avoca, the idea being to have a good look at Moore's tree. Keats brought along his valet, a somewhat gloomy character called Monk. Irish temperament, climate, scenery, and porter did not agree with Monk, whose idea of home and beauty was the East End of London and a glass of mild. He tried to persuade Keats to go home, but the poet had fastened on a local widow and was not to be thwarted by the fads of his servant. Soon it became evident that a breach between them was imminent. Things were brought to a head by a downpour which lasted for three days and nights. Monk tendered a savage resignation, and departed for Dublin in a sodden chaise. The incident annoyed Chapman.

'I think you are well rid of that fellow,' he said. 'He was a sullen lout.'

Keats shook his head despondently.

'The last rays of feeling and life must depart,' he said sadly, 'ere the bloom of that valet shall fade from my heart.'

Chapman coughed slightly.

* * *

Keats, when living in the country purchased an expensive chestnut gelding. This animal was very high-spirited and largely untrained and gave the novice owner a lot of trouble. First it was one thing, then another but finally he was discovered one morning to have disappeared from his stable. Foul play was not suspected nor did the poet at this stage adopt the foolish expedient of locking the stable door. On the contrary he behaved very sensibly. He examined the stable to ascertain how the escape had been effected and then travelled all over the yard on his hands and knees looking for traces of the animal's hooves. He was like a dog looking for a trail, except that he found a trail where many a good dog would have found nothing. Immediately the poet was off cross-country following the trail. It happened that Chapman was on a solitary walking-tour in the vicinity and he was agreeably surprised to encounter the poet in a remote mountainy place. Keats was walking with his eyes on the ground and looked very preoccupied. He had evidently no intention of stopping to converse with Chapman. The latter, not understanding his friend's odd behaviour, halted and cried:

'What are you doing, old man?'

'Dogging a fled horse,' Keats said as he passed by.

* * *

Keats and Chapman once called to see a titled friend and after the host had hospitably produced a bottle of whiskey, the two visitors were called into consultation regarding the son of the house, who had been exhibiting a disquieting redness of face and boisterousness of manner at the age of twelve. The father was worried, suspecting some dread disease. The youngster was produced but the two visitors, glass in hand, declined to make any diagnosis. When leaving the big house, Chapman rubbed his hands briskly and remarked on the cold.

'I think it must be freezing and I'm glad of that drink,' he said. 'By the way, did you think what I thought about that youngster?'

'There's a nip in the heir,' Keats said.

* * *

Chapman on one occasion was commissioned by an enormously wealthy business man to advise on wall-papers for the state-rooms of a yacht then building. The millionaire was however unbelievably busy and could talk to Chapman only in his luxurious car on the ten-minute journey between mansion and office. At first Chapman, being well paid for his pains, did not mind this exiguous procedure but as time passed a number of unknown advisers on other matters were picked up at various corners so that on some mornings the car was packed with up to eight people simultaneously giving the fur-coated boss very expensive advice. This amazed Chapman enormously, as he was failing completely to make himself heard on wall-paper schemes. The last straw was provided one morning when the car, packed to the roof with babbling experts, was joined by a mysterious lawyer, who stood outside on the running board of the racing vehicle pouring advice in through the window. This happened several mornings in succession, and Chapman eventually complained bitterly to Keats.

'That solicitor should be struck off the Rolls,' Keats said.

* * *

Once Chapman, in his tireless quest for a way to get rich quick, entered into a contract with a London firm for the supply of ten tons of swansdown. At the time he had no idea where he could get this substance, but on the advice of Keats went to live with the latter in a hut on a certain river estuary where the rather odd local inhabitants cultivated tame swans for the purposes of their somewhat coarsely-grained eggs. Chapman erected several notices in the locality inviting swan-owners to attend at his hut for the purpose of having their fowls combed and offering 'a substantial price' per ounce for the down so obtained. Soon the hut was surrounded by gaggles of unsavoury-looking natives, each accompanied by four or five disreputable swans on dog-leads. The uproar was enormous and vastly annoyed Keats, who was in bed with toothache. Chapman went out and addressed the multitude and then fell to bargaining with individual owners. After an hour in the pouring rain he came in to Keats, having apparently failed to do business. He was in a vile temper.

'Those appalling louts!' he exploded. 'Why should I go out and humiliate myself before them, beg to be allowed to comb their filthy swans, get soaked to the skin bargaining with them?'

'I'll get you down sooner or later,' Keats mumbled.

* * *

A millionaire collector (whose name was ever associated with that old-time Irish swordsman of France, O'Shea d'Ar) once invited Chapman and Keats to dinner. The invitation came quite at the wrong time for Keats, who was crippled with stomach trouble. Chapman insisted, however, that the poet should come along and endeavour to disguise his malady, holding that millionaires were necessarily personable folk whose friendship could be very beautiful. Keats was too ill to oppose Chapman's proposal and in due course found himself in a cab bound for the rich man's bounteous apartments. On arrival Chapman covered up his friend's incapacity by engaging the host in loud non-stop conversations and also managed to have Keats placed at an obscure corner of the table where little notice would be taken of him. Slumped in his chair, the unfortunate poet saw flunkeys deposit course after course of the richest fare before him but beyond raking his knife and fork through the food in desultory attempts to make a show of eating, he did not touch it. When the main course was served—a sight entirely disgusting to the eye of Keats—Chapman and the host were in the middle of a discussion on rare china. The host directed that a valuable vase on the mantelpiece should be passed round to the guests for inspection. Chapman gave a most enthusiastic dissertation on it, identifying it as a piece of the Ming dynasty. He then passed it to Keats, who was still slumped over his untouched platter of grub. The poet had not been following the conversation and apparently assumed that Chapman was trying to aid him in his extremity. He muttered something about the vase being 'a godsend' and after a moment handed it to the flunkey to be replaced on the mantelpiece. On the way home that evening Chapman violently reproached his friend for not making a fuss about the vase and pleasing the host.

'I saw nothing very special about it,' Keats said.

'Good heavens man,' Chapman expostulated, 'it was a priceless Ming vase, worth thousands of pounds! Why didn't you at least say nothing if you couldn't say something suitable?'

'I'm afraid I put my food in it,' Keats said.

* * *

Chapman once fell in love and had not been long plying his timid attentions when it was brought to his notice that he had a rival. This rival, a ferocious and burly character, surprised Chapman in the middle of a tender conversation with the lady and immediately challenged him to a duel, being, as he said, prohibited from breaking him into pieces there and then merely by the presence of the lady.

Chapman, who was no duellist, went home and explained what had happened to Keats.

'And I think he means business,' he added. 'I fear it is a case of "pistols for two, coffee for one". Will you be my second?'

'Certainly,' Keats said, 'and since you have the choice of weapons I think you should choose swords rather than pistols.'

Chapman agreed. The rendezvous was duly made and one morning at dawn Keats and Chapman drove in a cab to the dread spot. The poet had taken the 'coffee for one' remark rather too literally and had brought along a small quantity of coffee, sugar, milk, a coffee-pot, a cup, saucer and spoon, together with a small stove and some paraffin.

After the usual formalities, Chapman and the rival fell to swordplay. The two men fought fiercely, edging hither and thither about the sward. Keats, kneeling and priming the stove, was watching anxiously and saw that his friend was weakening. Suddenly, Chapman's guard fell and his opponent drew back to plunge his weapon home. Keats, with a lightning flick of his arm took up the stove and hurled it at the blade that was poised to kill! With such force and aim so deadly was the stove hurled that it smashed the blade in three places. Chapman was saved!

The affair ended in bloodless recriminations. Chapman was warm in his thanks to Keats.

'You saved my life,' he said, 'by hurling the stove between our blades. You're tops!'

'Primus inter parries,' Keats said.

* * *

A Memoir of Keats

Keats and Chapman once lived near a church. There was a heavy debt on it. The pastor made many efforts to clear the debt by promoting whist drives and raffles and the like, but was making little headway. He then heard of the popularity of these carnivals where you have swingboats and roundabouts and fruit-machines and la boule and shooting-galleries and every modern convenience. He thought to entertain the town with a week of this and hoped to make some money to reduce the debt. He hired one of these outfits but with his diminutive financial status he could only induce a very third-rate company to come. All their machinery was old and broken. On the opening day, as the steam-organ blared forth, the heavens opened and disgorged sheets of icy rain. The scene, with its drenched and tawdry trappings, assumed the gaiety of a morgue. Keats and Chapman waded from stall to stall, soaked and disconsolate. Chapman (unwisely, perhaps) asked the poet what he thought of the fiesta.

'A fête worse than debt,' Keats said.

Chapman collapsed into a trough of mud.

*　*　*

The medical profession, remember, wasn't always the highly organised racket that it is to-day. In your grandfather's time practically anybody could take in hand (whatever that means) to be a physician or surgeon and embark on experiments which frequently involved terminating other people's lives. Be that as it may, certain it is that Chapman in his day was as fine a surgeon as ever wore a hat. Chapman took in hand to be an ear nose and throat man and in many an obscure bedroom he performed prodigies which, if reported in the secular press, would have led to a question in the House. Keats, of course, always went along to pick up the odd guinea that was going for the anaesthetist. Chapman's schoolday lessons in carpentry often saved him from making foolish mistakes.

On one occasion the two savants were summoned to perform a delicate antrum operation. This involved opening up the nasal passages and doing a lot of work in behind the forehead. The deed was done and the two men departed, leaving behind a bleeding ghost suffering severely from what is nowadays called 'postoperative debility'. But through some chance the patient lived through the night, and the following day seemed to have some slim chance of surviving. Weeks passed and there was no mention of his death in the papers. Months passed. Then Chapman got an unpleasant surprise. A letter from the patient containing several pages of abuse, obviously written with a hand that quivered with pain. It appeared that the patient after 're-covering' somewhat from the operation, developed a painful swelling at the top of his nose. This condition progressed from pain to agony and eventually the patient took to consuming drugs made by his brother, who was a blacksmith. These preparations apparently did more harm than good and the patient had now written to Chapman demanding that he should return and restore the patient's health and retrieve the damage that had been done; otherwise that the brother would call to know the reason why.

'I think I know what is wrong with this person,' Chapman said. 'I missed one of the needles I was using. Perhaps we had better go and see him.' Keats nodded.

When they arrived the patient could barely speak, but he summoned his remaining strength to utter a terrible flood of bad language at the selfless men who had come a long journey to relieve pain. A glance by the practised eye of Chapman revealed that one of the tiny instruments had, indeed, been sewn up (inadvertently) in the wound, subsequently causing grandiose suppurations. Chapman got to work again, and soon retrieved his property. When the patient was re-sewn and given two grains, the blacksmith brother arrived and kindly offered to drive the two men home in his trap. The offer was gratefully accepted. At a particularly filthy part of the road, the blacksmith deliberately upset the trap, flinging all the occupants into a morass of muck. This, of course, by way of revenge, accidentally on purpose.

That evening Chapman wore an expression of sadness and depression. He neglected even to do his twenty lines of Homer, a nightly chore from which he had never shrunk in five years.

'To think of the fuss that fellow made over a mere needle, to think of his ingratitude,' he brooded. 'Abusive letters, streams of foul language, and finally arranging to have us fired into a pond full of filth! And all for a tiny needle! Did you ever hear of such vindictiveness!'

'He had it up his nose for you for a long time,' Keats said.

BUCHHANDLUNG

[O'Brien ran a series in the *Cruiskeen Lawn* column in which he offered a number of services for people who wanted to appear sophisticated. He had first tried out the idea in "Are You Lonely in the Restaurant?" in the March 1933 issue of *Comhthrom Feinne,** using his favorite early pen name Brother Barnabas. Admirers of Stephen Leacock will recall a similar enterprise in his "Our Literary Bureau: Novels Read to Order/First Aid for the Busy Millionaire." Those wishing to compare the two humorists will find Leacock's essay in his 1915 collection *Moonbeams from the Larger Lunacy.*

In later years, O'Brien returned to the theme in his column. This time he enlarged his "services" to the realm of book handling—a service aimed especially at persons of "wealth and vulgarity."]

* A student magazine, later called *The National Student.*

ARE YOU LONELY IN THE RESTAURANT?

Professor Adolf Gleitzboschkinderschule of the Berliner Universität, the eminent psychologist, has repeatedly pointed out in the Paris editions of the *Leipziger Tageblatt* that the habit of eating alone is a pernicious one and one which leads to morbidity and undue contempt for one's own vices. Apparently in deference to the advice of Professor Adolf Gleitzboschkinderschule, students may be seen every day endeavouring to drag each other into the Restaurant in an effort to save each other from the naked infirmities of their own minds, by creating a conversation which, however feeble, would at least obviate introspection.

COMHTHROM FEINNE, therefore, taking its duty of SERVING its public very much to heart, has much pleasure in announcing a NEW PROFESSION in an effort to cope with the present difficulty. COMHTHROM FEINNE will provide EATERS, varying in quality and price to suit every client. YOU NEED NO LONGER EAT ALONE. Hire one of our skilled Conversationalists, pay and talk as you eat and avoid the farce of pretending that you are a THINKER to whom his own kind is sufficient for the day.

EATERS. CONDITIONS OF HIRE.

(1) Eaters must be presented with a tea or lunch not inferior to that being consumed by the client by more than 1/-.

(2) There will be no charge for the first half-hour of the Eater's professional attendance, but a sum of threepence will be charged for every extra five-minutes. Excess fare will be automatically registered on the clock or metre worn on the EATER'S RIGHT ARM.

(3) Eaters must not be spoken to rudely or slapped, except in CLASS C.

(4) Should a client originate a line of conversation outside the specific Eater's registered orbit, there shall be no onus on the Eater to pursue, attempt to pursue, or try to attempt to pursue such a line.

(5) Should the Client be joined by A FRIEND who takes part in the Conversation, there will be an excess charge of 2d. per five minutes. This will be automatically registered on the metre.

(6) Complaints as to abnormal appetites of Eaters, incivility, objectionable table-manners, etc., should be instantly reported to the Editor of COMHTHROM FEINNE, but not if he is earning his living

as AN EATER at an adjacent table. In such case, complaint should be made afterwards.

CLASSES OF EATERS—CLASS A.

We have a very reliable line in young men of 19 and under who will engage first-year students and unmatriculated members of the Civil Service and public on GENERAL TOPICS, such as the weather, What-I-think-of-College-and-how-I'm-going-to-alter-it, the College celebrities at other tables, cricket, football, LUV, what a gift it is to have no exercises to do at night, the arguments as to whether one should do a D.Litt. or a D.Ph., College Hops, etc. We are introducing this line at a reduction of 1d. per five minutes as a SPECIAL ADVERTISING OFFER FOR FOUR DAYS ONLY.

CLASS B.

Are you a strong silent man? We can supply a great hulking lout who will GRUB with you, and munch, and chaw for an inclusive charge of about 2/6 per hour. These fine Eaters have been especially trained and must be provided with great lumps of beef, porter and whole loaves. Knives and forks are desirable but not essential. They will under no circumstances talk, but coarse animal grunts may be provided at a small extra cost. *Forte*, 2d. each, and *fortessimo*, 4d. each. Those who like to have their grub or tiffin with a GROUP of strong silent thugs may hire out squads of 4 EATERS at a considerable cash saving. SUPER-QUALITY of thick unshaven dishevelled and tweedy DREADNOUGHTS, possessing genuinely primitive Mongolian jaw formation available at an extra cost of 2/- per close-cropped head.

CLASS C.

Are you de Riva?

Are you doing a degree in Economics?

Do you hold strong views on Free Trade, Rising and Falling Price Levels, the fallacy of Technocracy?

DO YOU WANT SOMEBODY TO TALK AT. Somebody upon whom you can work off your pet theories and arguments? Do you want a BUTT for your wit?

We have just received delivery of an excellent line of SPINELESS DUMMIES who will listen to anything and make no objections. These highly-skilled Eaters will nod (plain) and nod (with conviction, 1d. extra each) at every point emphasised by the Client and will thump the table with the fist at the climax of the Client's argument, thus saving the latter leaving down his fork or knife.

A SPECIAL LUXURY CLASS C EATER (trained at our own works in Inchicore), is available and will take furtive notes of the Client's OBITER DICTA, politely question him on his pet points, and will even go so far as to make the "Tch, Tch, Tch" sound as pronounced by illiterate women in cinemas, at the more particular sallies and declarations of the Client. Written applications for this model will be dealt with in rotation.

CLASS D.

The Eaters in this Class are very suitable for Graduates and SENIOR UNDERGRADUATES. They are prepared to discuss *anything*. They include a number of young men of faultless profile who are very suitable for ladies' tables, and they leave no stone unturned to be "nice" in the most proper meaning of the term. Their services are always available as gigolos for not only ladies who go to dances, but also for ladies who go to dances and like to dance; also as paid escorts to theatres, cinemas, picnics, etc. Ladies who insist on a small moustache must give the Management at least ten days' notice.

In this class we have also a sound line in less reputable Eaters, who are eminently suitable for ordinary under-graduates or men-in-the-Main hall, who have maintained unblighted through the gloom of these trying times their appreciation of A GOOD STORY. Believe us that these Eaters have a fund of RIGHT GOOD ONES.

CLASS E.

An exclusive and superior type of Eater belongs to this Class and must on-no account be offered MASH or brown buns. They will discourse and converse on the subject of the drama, the theatre, the novel, the play, the tragedy, the comedy. Clients are warned not to make a *faux pas* in front of these Eaters, as they will not consent to stay with Clients who betray an inferior intellectual level.

CLASS F.

The number of Eaters in Class F, confined to the Professional table, is so far very very limited; those with suitable qualifications should make early application, as filling the post of Eaters at the Professional table is an obvious short-cut to academic advancement. Junior members of the staff are eligible to apply, but they should be careful not to tempt Providence, e.g., a lecturer in Mathematics must not Eat as such with a Professor of the same subject.

We have a reliable but limited quantity of bold and grey-haired under-graduates who will engage members of the Staff on ACADEMIC

AND FAMILY TOPICS. These Eaters are experienced men of the world and HAVE SEEN LIFE. They are well versed in local topography and can discourse for hours on the natural amenities of the Kattie Gallagher, Glencree, etc. These are good men. THEY UNDERSTAND.

No effort will be spared to retain the services of Mr. Gussie O'Connell, the well-known Dublin Shanachie, as his readings from his repertoire of GOODLY YARNS are deservedly famous.

* * *

[The following selections are from *The Best of Myles*.]

Buchhandlung

A visit that I paid to the house of a newly-married friend the other day set me thinking. My friend is a man of great wealth and vulgarity. When he had set about buying bedspreads, tables, chairs and what-not, it occurred to him to buy also a library. Whether he can read or not, I do not know, but some savage faculty for observation told him that most respectable and estimable people usually had a lot of books in their houses. So he bought several book-cases and paid some rascally middleman to stuff them with all manner of new books, some of them very costly volumes on the subject of French landscape painting.

I noticed on my visit that not one of them had ever been opened or touched, and remarked the fact.

'When I get settled down properly,' said the fool, 'I'll have to catch up on my reading.'

This is what set me thinking. Why should a wealthy person like this be put to the trouble of pretending to read at all? Why not a professional book-handler to go in and suitably maul his library for so-much per shelf? Such a person, if properly qualified, could make a fortune.

Dog Ears Four-a-Penny

Let me explain exactly what I mean. The wares in a bookshop look completely unread. On the other hand, a school-boy's Latin dictionary looks read to the point of tatters. You know that the dictionary has been opened and scanned perhaps a million times, and if you did not know that there was such a thing as a box on the ear, you would conclude that the boy is crazy about Latin and cannot bear to be away from his dictionary. Similarly with our non-brow who wants his friends to infer from a glancing around his house that he is a high-brow. He buys an enormous book on the Russian ballet, written possibly in the language of that distant but beautiful land. Our problem is to alter the book in a reasonably short time so that anybody looking at it will conclude that its owner has practically lived, supped and slept with it for many months. You can, if you like, talk about designing a machine driven by a small but efficient petrol motor that would 'read' any book in five minutes, the equivalent of five years or ten years' 'reading' being obtained by merely turning a knob. This, however, is the cheap soulless approach of the times we live in. No machine can do the same work as the soft human fingers. The trained and experienced book-handler is the only real solution of this contemporary social problem. What does he do? How does he work? What would he charge? How many types of handling would there be?

These questions and many more I will answer the day after to-morrow.

* * *

The World of Books

Yes, this question of book-handling. The other day I had a word to say about the necessity for the professional book-handler, a person who will maul the books of illiterate, but wealthy, upstarts so that the books will look as if they have been read and re-read by their owners. How many uses of mauling would there be? Without giving the matter much thought, I should say four. Supposing an experienced handler is asked to quote for the handling of one shelf of books four feet in length. He would quote thus under four heads:—

'Popular Handling—Each volume to be well and truly handled, four leaves in each to be dog-eared, and a tram ticket, cloak-room docket or other comparable article inserted in each as a forgotten book-mark. Say, £1 7s 6d. Five per cent discount for civil servants.'

'Premier Handling—Each volume to be thoroughly handled, eight leaves in each to be dog-eared, a suitable passage in not less than 25 volumes to be underlined in red pencil, and a leaflet in French on the works of Victor Hugo to be inserted as a forgotten book-mark in each. Say, £2 17s 6d. Five per cent discount for literary university students, civil servants and lady social workers.'

A Rate to Suit All Purses

The great thing about this graduated scale is that no person need appear ignorant or unlettered merely because he or she is poor. Not every vulgar person, remember, is wealthy, although I could name . . .

But no matter. Let us get on to the most expensive grades of handling. The next is well worth the extra money.

'De Luxe Handling—Each volume to be mauled savagely, the spines of the smaller volumes to be damaged in a manner that will give the impression that they have been carried around in pockets, a passage in every volume to be underlined in red pencil with an exclamation or interrogation mark inserted in the margin opposite, an old Gate Theatre programme to be inserted in each volume as a forgotten book-mark (3 per cent discount if old Abbey programmes are accepted), not less than 30 volumes to be treated with old coffee, tea, porter or whiskey stains, and not less than five volumes to be inscribed with forged signatures of the authors. Five per cent discount for bank managers, county surveyors and the heads of business houses employing not less than 35 hands. Dog-ears extra and inserted according to instructions, twopence per half dozen per volume. Quotations for alternative old Paris theatre programmes on demand. This service available for a limited time only, nett, £7 18s 3d.'

Order Your Copy Now

The fourth class is the Handling Superb, although it is not called that —*Le Traitement Superbe* being the more usual title. It is so superb that I have no space for it today. It will appear here on Monday next, and, in honour of the occasion, the *Irish Times* on that day will be printed on hand-scratched antique interwoven demidevilled superfine Dutch paper, each copy to be signed by myself and to be accompanied by an exquisite picture in tri-colour lithograph of the Old House in College Green. The least you can do is to order your copy in advance.

And one more word. It is not sufficient just to order your copy. Order it *in advance*.

* * *

It will be remembered (how, in Heaven's name, could it be forgotten) that I was discoursing on Friday last on the subject of book-handling,

my new service, which enables ignorant people who want to be suspected of reading books to have their books handled and mauled in a
manner that will give the impression that their owner is very devoted
to them. I described three grades of handling and promised to explain
what you get under Class Four—the Superb Handling, or the
Traitement Superbe, as we lads who spent our honeymoon in Paris
prefer to call it. It is the dearest of them all, of course, but far cheaper
than dirt when you consider the amount of prestige you will gain in
the eyes of your ridiculous friends. Here are the details:

'Le Traitement Superbe'. Every volume to be well and truly
handled, first by a qualified handler and subsequently by a master-
handler who shall have to his credit not less than 550 handling hours;
suitable passages in not less than fifty per cent of the books to be
underlined in good-quality red ink and an appropriate phrase from the
following list inserted in the margin, viz:

Rubbish!

Yes, indeed!

How true, how true!

I don't agree at all.

Why?

Yes, but cf. Homer, Od., iii, 151.

Well, well, well.

Quite, but Boussuet in his Discours sur l'histoire Universelle has
already established the same point and given much more forceful
explanations.

Nonsense, nonsense!

A point well taken!

But *why* in heaven's name?

I remember poor Joyce saying the very same thing to me.

Need I say that a special quotation may be obtained at any time for
the supply of Special and Exclusive Phrases? The extra charge is not
very much, really.

Furthermore

That, of course, is not all. Listen to this:

Not less than six volumes to be inscribed with forged messages of
affection and gratitude from the author of each work, e.g.,

'To my old friend and fellow-writer, A.B., in affectionate remembrance, from George Moore.'

'In grateful recognition of your great kindness to me, dear A.B., I send you this copy of The Crock of Gold. Your old friend, James Stephens.'

'Well, A.B., both of us are getting on. I am supposed to be a good writer now, but I am not old enough to forget the infinite patience you displayed in the old days when guiding my young feet on the path of literature. Accept this further book, poor as it may be, and please believe that I remain, as ever, your friend and admirer, G. Bernard Shaw.'

'From your devoted friend and follower, K. Marx.'

'Dear A.B.,—Your invaluable suggestions and assistance, not to mention your kindness, in entirely re-writing chapter 3, entitles you, surely, to this first copy of "Tess". From your old friend T. Hardy.'

'Short of the great pleasure of seeing you personally, I can only send you, dear A.B., this copy of "The Nigger". I miss your company more than I can say . . . (signature undecipherable).'

Under the last inscription, the moron who owns the book will be asked to write (and shown how if necessary) the phrase 'Poor old Conrad was not the worst.'

All this has taken me longer to say than I thought. There is far more than this to be had for the paltry £32 7s 6d that the Superb Handling will cost you. In a day or two I hope to explain about the old letters which are inserted in some of the books by way of forgotten book-marks, every one of them an exquisite piece of forgery. Order your copy now!

* * *

Book Handling

I promised to say a little more about the fourth, or Superb, grade of book handling.

The price I quoted includes the insertion in not less than ten volumes of certain old letters, apparently used at one time as book-marks, and forgotten. Each letter will bear the purported signature of some well-known humbug who is associated with ballet, verse-mouth-ing, folk-dancing, wood-cutting, or some other such activity that is sufficiently free from rules to attract the non-brows in their swarms. Each of the letters will be a flawless forgery and will thank A.B., the owner of the books, for his 'very kind interest in our work', refer to his 'invaluable advice and guidance', his 'unrivalled knowledge' of the lep-as-lep-can game, his 'patient and skilful direction of the corps on Monday night', thank him for his very generous—too gen-erous—subscription of two hundred guineas, 'which is appreciated more than I can say'. As an up-to-the-minute inducement, an extra letter will be included free of charge. It will be signed (or purport to be signed) by one or other of the noisier young non-nationals who are honouring our beautiful land with their presence. This will satisfy the half-ambition of the majority of respectable vulgarians to maintain a second establishment in that somewhat congested thoroughfare, Queer Street.

The gentlemen who are associated with me in the Dublin WAAMA League have realised that this is the off-season for harvesting the cash of simple people through the medium of the art-infected begging letter, and have turned their attention to fresh fields and impostures new. The latest racket we have on hands is the Myles na gCopaleen Book Club. You join this and are spared the nerve-racking bother of choosing your own books. We do the choosing for you, and, when you get the book, it is *ready-rubb*ed, ie, subjected free of charge to our expert handlers. You are spared the trouble of soiling and mauling it to give your friends the impression that you can read. An odd banned book will be slipped in for those who like conversation such as:

'I say, did you read this, old man?'
'I'm not terribly certain that I did, really.'
'It's banned, you know, old boy.'
'Ow.'

There is no nonsense about completing a form, asking for a bro-chure, or any other such irritation. You just send in your guinea and you immediately participate in this great cultural uprising of the Irish people.

THE PLAIN PEOPLE OF IRELAND

Why chairs? Consider that man was made before furniture. He was therefore made to sit on the floor. If today he finds it uncomfortable to sit on the floor, the inference is that the human body has been modified and impaired by thousands of generations of rascally chair-makers. Women have been altered in our own day by high heels. Between high heels and chairs they are the sort of people one is chary to approach. But I'll tell you something. No chair in this part of the world can compare for its adverse effect on the human with a chair that has been invented by those Americans. I mean the electric chair. It's as much as your life is worth to sit in that thing. (Yes, I know. In a distant part of the prison the lights are momentarily dimmed; Wallace Beery glances at Tyrone Power under his shaggy brows— both men being in the attire of lifers in the Big House—and mutters:

* See Myles na Gopaleen, "Baudelaire and Kavanagh," *Envoy*, Vol. 3, no. 12 (November 1950), pp. 78–81.

Yeah, they got Joe. They got Joe, son. Joe was a swell guy. I gotta get out of here.) (And then that damn searchlight on the prison wall, the stutter of tommy guns, then escape, ESCAPE—

The Plain People of Ireland: Out into the jungle begob! Man-eaters an' rattle-snakes and pigs as big as cows with tusks hangin out of them! They'll never make it!

Myself: And supposing they do. Supposing they reach the coast, what then? The shark-infested Timor Sea!

The Plain People of Ireland: And your men out in motor boats pottin at them with tommy guns!

Myself: Yes faith.

* * *

With the ever-hastening approach of winter there is a proportionate increase in speculation as to the outcome of the titanic struggle which is taking place in Russia. In that strange but distant land vast masses of men and metal are locked together in a battle-front which ranges from the Black Sea to the far-off Karelian isthmus, a span that embraces a great variety of terrain and even climate. When the Fuehrer first threw his *Panzerdivisionen* against Smolensk and embarked on the vast pincer operation which culminated in the bloody battle for the Dnieper, many observers predicted a long war. General Koniev, whose masterly strategy for the Allied successes in Moravia, has moved up considerable forces from the middle front, where the pincer 'claw', turning south, has brought the *Sturm und Drang* of battle to new and unexpected quarters. The—

The Plain People of Ireland: Isn't there some mistake. Surely, this is the leading article.

Myself: It is.

The Plain People of Ireland: But—

Myself: Yes, I am sorry, there is something wrong. My stuff is in the wrong place. Some fool has blundered.

The Plain People of Ireland: You don't mean to say you write the leading article?

Myself: I do, usually. We have another man who comes in when I am 'indisposed', if you know what that means. And there is no reason why you shouldn't, red-snouts.

The Plain People of Ireland: But— Well, dear knows. How do you find time to do the two things?

Myself: It's no trouble to me. In both cases it is the same old stuff all the time. You just change it round a bit.

The Plain People of Ireland: Do they pay you much for the leader? A couple of bar a knock, maybe?

Myself: I get half a guinea for the leading article and I throw in the other funny stuff for nothing because I enjoy publishing jibes at the expense of people I dislike. I also write a lot of the For-Ireland-Boys-Hurrah stuff that appears in *The Leader* every week.

The Plain People of Ireland: Well, honestly! You're a wonderful man altogether. Don't you write plays for the Abbey, too?

Myself: Certainly.

The Plain People of Ireland: Well, Lord save us!

* * *

The son of Pharaoh's daughter was the daughter of Pharaoh's son. Know that old one?

The Plain People of Ireland: How could that be, man? How could a man's son be his daughter at the same time?

Myself: I said the son of Pharaoh's daughter was the daughter of Pharaoh's son. It's all right, as you will see if you work it out with algebra. Let x equal the son of Pharaoh. Go further—call him Mr X. Then what you have is Mr X's daughter was the daughter of Mr X, surely not an unlikely relationship in all the circumstances.

The Plain People of Ireland: Begob, you're right, never thought of that, smart boy wanted.

Myself: Don't go yet. There's another way of looking at it. Call Pharaoh's daughter Mrs Y. Then you have another story—the son of Mrs Y was Mrs Y's son. See it?

The Plain People of Ireland: That's one of the smartest things for a long time. You ought to put that into the paper.

Yes, the son of Pharaoh's daughter. Then the other one, your man is looking at a photo and says brothers and sisters have I none but that man's father is my father's son. Whose picture is he looking at? His own. Right. Then the other one, a fiddler in Cork had a brother a fiddler in Dublin, what was the fiddler in Cork to the fiddler in Dublin? Brother? No that's wrong, you're completely out there, the right answer is sister.

Remember the last time we played these little games when we were all together? Remember the yellow lamplight, 'Spot' with his torn ear, the shutters with the iron bar across them; the black kettle hanging from the old smut-furred chain in the chimney and the delicate fluted china tea-cups made in Balleek? Poor George was alive then and Annie was only a little girl, little thinking she was soon to marry. That was over twenty-one years ago, in Newcastle West, where daddy's column of the Black and Tans was stationed. Dear old dead days, gone beyond recall.

Every time I start this flash-back act, I always come back to myself. That is because the past is . . . essentially . . . personal, you know. I mean, part of it is mine. They can't take my memories away from me, persecute me as they will. Do you recall reading this in the *Irish Times* recently:

> 'If you answer the knock of a "gas-man" with a pale, long, thin face, clean-shaven, wearing a dark or navy suit, soft grey hat, and silver-rimmed spectacles, make sure that he is a gas man. There is at present, says the police, a man going about the city representing himself as an inspector from the Gas Company. He examines the cooker, and, if he gets the chance, steals any money that may be lying handy.'

I suppose you blame me. You don't hesitate to lie back in your fifteen-guinea armchair that creaks from the weight of your brutish, over-fed, suet-padded body and denounce me to your even weightier wife as a thief, a fly-be-night, a sleeveen and a baucagh-shool. Cliché-ridden ignoramus that you are, you probably go through that absurd act of pointing the finger of scorn at me. It only serves to show me how plump, pink and well nourished it is. But let me tell you that I, too, must live. I must eat. Some day I may call, stuff you into your own oven, and roast you on the glimmer.

* * *

An Unidentified Party

'Sir-Sir W. Beach Thomas asks "Is any animal anywhere quite silent?" The most extraordinary instance of almost, if not complete, silence in any land animal is the giraffe. It has been heard, I believe, to utter a very slight bleat when teased with food.'

This letter appeared recently in the London *Spectator*. It reminds me that I have been harbouring a strange little animal in my house for years. It looks not unlike a monkey, but since it roosts at night it must be something else. The 'face' is extraordinarily withered and old. The creature is covered with a coarse fur and has never uttered a sound. It feeds chiefly on books and newspapers, and sometimes takes a bath in the kitchen sink, cunningly turning on the taps with its 'hand'. It rarely goes out and is in its own way courteous. I am afraid and ashamed to let anybody see it in case I am confronted with some dreadful explanation. Supposing it's a little man cunningly disguised, some eccentric savant from the East Indies who is over here studying us. How do I know he hasn't it all down in a little book?

The Plain People of Ireland: Yerrah man you'll find it's an overgrown rake of a badger you have in the house. Them lads would take the hand of you.

Myself: Indeed?

The Plain People of Ireland: Better go aisy now with them lads. Ate the face off you when you're asleep in the bed. Hump him out of the house before he has you destroyed man. Many's a good man had the neck clawed off him be a badger. And badgers that doesn't be barkin out of them is very dangerous.

Myself: Thanks for the warning.

The Plain People of Ireland: A good strong badger can break a man's arm with one blow of his hind leg, don't make any mistake about that. Show that badger the door. Chinaman or no Chinaman.

Myself: Thank you, I will draw his attention to that useful portal.

* * *

I notice these days that the Green Isle is getting greener. Delightful ulcerations resembling buds pit the branches of our trees, clumpy daffodils can be seen on the upland lawn. Spring is coming and every decent girl is thinking of that new Spring costume. Time will run on smoother till Favonius re-inspire the frozen Meade and clothe in fresh attire the lily and rose that have nor sown nor spun. Curse it, my mind races back to my Heidelberg days. Sonya and Lili. And Magda. And Ernst Schmutz, Georg Geier, Theodor Winklemann, Efrem Zimbalist, Otto Grün. And the accordion player Kurt Schachmann. And Doktor Oreille, descendant of Irish princes. Ich hab' mein Herz/ in Heidelberg verloren/ in einer lauen/ Sommernacht/ Ich war verliebt/ bis über beide/ Ohren/und wie'ein Röslein/hatt'/ Ihr Mund gelächt or something humpty tumpty tumpty tumpty tumpty mein Herz it schlägt am Neckarstrand. A very beautiful student melody. Beer and music and midnight swims in the Neckar. Chats in erse with Kun O'Meyer and John Marquess ... Alas, those chimes. Und als wir nahmen/ Abschied vor den Toren/ beim letzten Küss, da hab' Ich Klar erkannt/ dass Ich mein Herz/ in Heidelberg verloren/ MEIN HERZ/ es schlägt am Neck-ar-strand! Tumpty tumpty tum.

The Plain People of Ireland: Isn't the German very like the Irish? Very guttural and so on?

Myself: Yes.

The Plain People of Ireland: People do say that the German language and the Irish language is very guttural tongues.

Myself: Yes.

The Plain People of Ireland: The sounds is all guttural do you understand.

Myself: Yes.

The Plain People of Ireland: Very guttural languages the pair of them the Gaelic and the German.

* * *

To Brian Inglis
17 August, 1960.

First, I think I should thank you for publishing that very favorable review of AS2B. It was at least more reasonable than Toynbee's, who I think went off his rocker in the *Observer.* The book is, of course, juvenile nonsense but I understand that sales are enormous and that it is "going like a bomb."

Here is what I write to you about. I am most anxious to leave the dirty *Irish Times.* It was an odd enough paper in Smyllie's day but it has now become really quite intolerable. I need not discourse to you on their shocking notions of pay but in addition much of the material I send in is suppressed and for that work they pay nothing whatever. Other articles are mutilated and cut, often through sheer ignorance. The paper has in recent years bred a whole new herd of sacred cows and, cute as I claim to be, I have never been certain of their identity. In any case they are always being added to. I wrote funny stuff about the Irish Army's imperial exploit in the Congo but this was all utterly killed. —— is a perfect gentleman but a complete weakling ... accepting instructions on petty matters from certain directors who make prams and who should properly be in them (and who don't like

ME, think I'm "dangerous.") —— is a martyr to monstrous conceit and paranoia, though he can be mannerly when he wants to; he is also astonishingly ignorant on many matters which are commonplace enough. Generally, the whole outfit is insufferable.

At the moment I am writing an exceptionally comic book—at any time a rare thing. (You have yet to meet Father Kurt Fahrt, S.J.). The job is straightforward and easy but quite incompatible with this I.T. slavery. NOW HEAR THIS—is there any possibility of finding space in the *Spectator* for a piece by me, preferably regular. Such a piece, which need not be long or expensive, would naturally be primarily addressed to English readers, though no doubt often based on the queer things that happen over here. Naturally I would be happy to send you a sample or two to give some indication of climate, temperature, obsessions, etc.

I will be pleased to receive your best advices in re these considerations.

[*The Journal of Irish Literature*]

To Timothy O'Keeffe of MacGibbon and Kee, London
9 March, 1965.

Some short time ago the *Irish Times* invited me on their bended knees to go back and write for them. I agreed to do so, subject to some tyrannical stipulations by me. (How could you get down on your knees without them being bended?) This relieves all finance worry and enables me to indulge my *Sago** enthusiasm.

[*The Journal of Irish Literature*]

---

* *Slattery's Sago Saga,* the novel about the Texans saving Ireland.

Drink and Time in Dublin

and

Other Related Matters

This is the best whiskey to be had in Ireland.
—De Selby, in *The Dalkey Archive*

There is more than alcoholic nexus between drinking and writing.
—Flann O'Brien, notebook

INTRODUCTION

The following selections from various periods in O'Brien's life appeared in different publications under divers names. The section begins with some quasi-autobiographical material from *The Hard Life*. O'Brien did attend the Synge Street school mentioned in the novel, but it must be remembered that *The Hard Life* is "Edwardian" and O'Brien's attendance was between the World Wars. Clissmann sees the school passages more as representing a score O'Brien wished to settle with Joyce by means of parodying *A Portrait of the Artist* than as any part of a grudge against the Christian Brothers. Nevertheless, while remaining a Catholic, O'Brien was highly critical of the clergy. He also did not look back on any of his education, even at the university level, with respect.

The next "autobiographical" section is from *The Best of Myles* and, while not as fanciful as 'The True Biography of Myles na Gopaleen," must be filtered through the Myles mask.

The poems are translations from the Irish and have appeared not only in *At Swim,* where they are plowed into the Sweeney plot, but also on their own in *The Oxford Book of Irish Verse.* It should be remembered O'Brien wrote his master's thesis on nature in Irish poetry. He did not write any poetry, apparently, after his twenties, except for a few parodies. In his *Anthology of Irish Verse,* Padraic Colum says of O'Brien, "No one can get better than he into translation the gracefulness of academic Irish poetry."

The drinking pieces are among the best prose O'Brien wrote. His attitude toward drinking was complex, but it is safe to say it is somewhere between Charles Jackson's in *The Lost Weekend* and Malcolm Lowry's in *Under the Volcano.* That is, he does not, on the one hand, concern himself with guilt or the social problem of drinking or, on the other, make the kind of serious magical claims that Lowry does. Drinking is more a background against which O'Brien works his various charms. The pub-ridden atmosphere of Dublin must be taken into consideration here as well as such other Irish matters as heavy annual rainfall and limited opportunities for front-parlor fantastics.

The Ideas of O'Dea was a weekly television series that began in September 1963 and ran for six months. Jimmy O'Dea was a favorite Irish actor, but like the man who really provided his "ideas" was aging rapidly. The character Jimmy was a railroad-yard man, and as such carried O'Brien's notions on a variety of topics on the wings of the "Steam Man" metaphor of which Myles had been so fond. Various short selections from Myles are therefore included, along with a short story about an adventure in the station ("Donabate") and an excerpt from Myles on "Donabate" to help set the mood.

In "Getting the Creeps" and the other O'Dea segments, we have a chance to see how O'Brien adopted Myles's material for *The Ideas of O'Dea.*

O'Brien tried a number of television scripts besides the O'Dea series, one of which is "The Man with Four Legs," which expands an earlier rumination in *Cruiskeen Lawn* about the number of legs a creature might and ought to have.

"Two In One" is a short story about a murder in a taxidermist shop that was later adopted by O'Brien as a potential TV script and titled "The Dead Spit of Kelly."

BIOGRAPHY

That night the brother said in bed, not without glee, that somehow he thought I would soon be master of Latin and Shakespeare and that Brother Cruppy would shower heavenly bread on me with his class in Christian Doctrine and give me some idea of what the early Christians went through in the arena by thrashing the life out of me. Unhappy was the eye I closed that night. But the brother was only partly right. To my surprise, Mr Collopy next morning led me at a smart pace up the bank of the canal, penetrated to Synge Street and rang the bell at the residential part of the Christian Brothers' establishment there. When a slatternly young man in black answered, Mr Collopy said he wanted to see the Superior, Brother Gaskett. We were shown into a gaunt little room which had on the wall a steel engraving of the head of Brother Rice, founder of the Order, a few chairs and a table—nothing more.

—They say piety has a smell, Mr Collopy mused, half to himself.

It's a perverse notion. What they mean is only the absence of the smell of women.

He looked at me.

—Did you know that no living woman is allowed into this holy house. That is as it should be. Even if a Brother has to see his own mother, he has to meet her in secret below at the Imperial Hotel. What do you think of that?

—I think it is very hard, I said. Couldn't she call to see him here and have another Brother present, like they do in jails when there is a warder present on visiting day?

—Well, that's the queer comparison, I'll warrant. Indeed, this house may be a jail of a kind but the chains are of purest eighteen-carat finest gold which the holy brothers like to kiss on their bended knees.

The door opened silently and an elderly stout man with a sad face glided in. He smiled primly and gave us an odd handshake, keeping his elbow bent and holding the extended hand against his breast.

—Isn't that the lovely morning, Mr. Collopy, he said hoarsely.

—It is, thank God, Brother Gaskett, Mr Collopy replied as we all sat down. Need I tell you why I brought this young ruffian along?

—Well, it wasn't to teach him how to play cards.

—You are right there, Brother. His name is Finbarr.

—Well now, look at that! That is a beautiful name, one that is honoured by the Church. I presume you would like us to try to extend Finbarr's knowledge?

—That is a nice way of putting it, Brother Gaskett. I think they will have to be very big extensions because damn the thing he knows but low songs from the pantomimes, come-all-ye's by Cathal McGarvey, and his prayers. I suppose you'll take him in, Brother?

—Of course I will. Certainly, I will teach him everything from the three Rs to Euclid and Aristophanes and the tongue of the Gael. We will give him a thorough grounding in the Faith and, with God's help, if one day he should feel like joining the Order, there will always be a place for him in this humble establishment. After he has been trained, of course.

The tail-end of that speech certainly startled me, even to tempting me to put in some sort of caveat. I did not like it even as a joke, nor the greasy Brother making it.

—I . . . I think that could wait a bit, Brother Gaskett, I stammered.

He laughed mirthlessly.

—Ah but of course, Finbarr. One thing at a time.

Then he and Mr Collopy indulged in some muttered consultation jaw to jaw, and the latter got up to leave. I also rose but he made a gesture.

—We'll stay where we are now, he said. Brother Gaskett thinks you might start right away. Always better to take the bull by the horns.

Though not quite unexpected, this rather shocked me.

—But, I said in a loud voice, I have no lunch . . . no broken biscuits.

—Never mind, Brother Gaskett said, we will give you a half-day to begin with.

That is how I entered the sinister portals of Synge Street School. Soon I was to get to know the instrument known as 'the leather'. It is not, as one would imagine, a strap of the kind used on bags. It is a number of such straps sewn together to form a thing of great thickness that is nearly as rigid as a club but just sufficiently flexible to prevent the breaking of the bones of the hand. Blows of it, particularly if directed (as often they deliberately were) to the top of the thumb or wrist, conferred immediate paralysis followed by agony as the blood tried to get back to the afflicted part. Later I was to learn from the brother a certain routine of prophylaxis he had devised but it worked only partly.

Neither of us found out what Mr Collopy's reason was for sending us to different schools. The brother thought it was to prevent us 'cogging', or copying each other's home exercises, of which we were given an immense programme to get through every night. This was scarcely correct, for an elaborate system for 'cogging' already existed in each school itself, for those who arrived early in the morning. My own feeling was that the move was prompted by Mr Collopy's innate craftiness and the general principle of *divide et impera*.

[*The Hard Life*]

* * *

Pearson's book on Shaw is not very good. Like the entire breed of biographies, it is too devout. It was precisely this sort of devotional literature, piling mountain-high during Victoria's reign (all uncover, please) that caused the equally distorted portraits of latter-day debunkers. Biography is the lowest form of letters and is atrophied by the subject's own censorship, conscious or otherwise. And when one finds (as one does rarely) that a subject is prepared to take the lid completely off and reveal the most humiliating infirmities without a blush, one usually finds that one is dealing with an exhibitionist who delights in adding on fictitious villainies. George Moore was a mild case. 'Some men kiss and never tell; Moore tells but never kisses.'

* * *

Any reader who feels he or she would like to meet myself and family should write to the Editor asking for particulars as to when I am at home, the best time to call, and whether it is necessary to leave cards beforehand. You will find us, I fear, just a little bit formal. My wife, for instance, keeps her hands in a hand-bag. This, however, need not disturb you. Again, if it happens that you come to dinner, you must be prepared for certain old-world customs—out-moded if you like, but still capable of imparting grace and charm to a gathering of those who knew the vanished world of yesteryear. First a glass of pale sherry, exquisite in its thin needle-like impact on the palate, potent of pre-prandial salivation. Then fine-tasted *bouillon* in china bowls, served with white rolls, those clandestinely-sieved American cigarettes. My jewelled hand has now strayed to the Turkish bell-tassel and the great triple peal that calls for the dinner proper rings out in the distant servants' hall. This is where the guest who is accustomed to the rougher usage of today may receive a slight surprise. When the dinner is brought in, he will note that it is . . . well . . . in a dinner jacket. Big mass of roast beef in the breast, sleeves stuffed with spuds, sprigs of celery up through the button-holes, gravy sopping out everywhere. A bit formal if you like, but if one does not observe the punctilious regimen of good behaviour, one is, after all, very little better than the beast of the field. Indeed, remembering the execrable manners of a colleague of mine in this great newspaper organisation, I had almost said that one is very little better than the beast of *The Field*.

When the coffee stage is reached, nothing will do my eccentric wife but have it accompanied by an odd confection of her own invention—longbread.

* * *

It only occurred to me the other day that I will have biographers. Probably Hone will do me first and then there will be all sorts of English persons writing books 'interpreting' me, describing the beautiful women who influenced my 'life', trying to put my work in its true and prominent place against the general background of mankind, and no doubt seeking to romanticise what is essentially an austere and chastened character, saddened as it has been by the contemplation of human folly.

One moment. Where is Con? Con! Here he is. Con, do you like sole bonne femme? A very stylish dish. Con, fashion is good for the sole.

Here is my confession, which I address to Hone. Call it a solemn warning if you like. *Believe nothing that you see in my cheque-book stubs.* The entries therein might well have been made by that historic protolouse, the father of lice. Let me confess. At the beginning of the month when I get my wages from across the way ⟶ (often paid by mistake in mysterious Russian and Tunisian currencies, frightful row every now and again trying to get Caffey to change them into humble Irish uncomplicated agricultural notes) I naturally put five pounds in my pocket (not my mouth) and stick the remaining £145 into the bank. A day passes. On the evening of the second day I am in the usual place giving out about the Labour Party; I have ordered 4 at elevenpence each, two at sixpence halfpenny plus eightpence halfpenny for ten cigarettes slipped in under my coat-tails and to my surprise I find I have no money to meet this commonplace mercantile obligation. Out comes the cheque-book and a docket is written out for five pounds. Do I enter 'Self, £5' in the stub? I certainly do not.

I am ashamed to do that because these payments to myself are so embarrassingly frequent. I have no desire to have Hone making me out as a sore hedonist. Hence the appearance in my life of a mysterious character called Hickey. I always write 'Hickey, £5' or 'Hickey, £6', or 'Hickey, £3' whatever it may be. I have a cheque book stub before me as I write. In the space of a fortnight the following payments are recorded against Hickey: £5, £5, £3, £4, £2, £2. But let me be perfectly honest, let me make of it that immaculate pectoral phenomenon, a clean breast. I have not told all. Apparently my shame in writing 'Self' begot a counterfeit secondary shame at the frequency and consecutiveness of these windfalls to Hickey and—pray bear with a weak character in the agony of confession—I notice that between the £4 and the £2 towards the end, there is a payment of £2 to 'Hodge'. Later on in the book, both Hickey and Hodge get £5 apiece within three days of each other. Later again, Hickey alone benefits to the tune of £2, £2 and £4. So far as I can ascertain, Hodge has received only four cheques

Consider the ass Hone would have made of himself had I not

chosen to make this revelation in the interests of history. Some terrible drama would be invented. Blackmail. 'It is scarcely to be credited that while engaged in giving masterpiece after masterpiece to the world, the master was in the toils of a blackmailing ruffian called Hickey, who, with a confederate called Hodge, extracted from him practically every penny he earned.'

Or would he insist on Mrs Hickey, a mysterious widow? A sordid entanglement, straightened out eventually with money to make her keep away? Would the public believe in the existence of a woman so rapacious?

But do you mind the cuteness of me.

[*The Best of Myles*]

POEMS

[Valentin Iremonger, who has translated eleven stanzas from "King Sweeney's Valediction" in his 1972 book *Horan's Field and Other Reservations,* notes:

Suibhne or Sweeney, King of Dal Araidhe in Ireland, treacherously kills one of St. Ronan's acolytes during the battle of Moira in A.D. 637. As a result of St. Ronan's curse, Sweeney goes out of his mind and spends the rest of his life wandering throughout Ireland stark naked and living in the trees. In his turn, he is treacherously injured and, as he lies dying in the arms of St. Moling, he makes this lay.

O'Brien's translation is one of the many layers of the novel *At Swim-Two-Birds,* and the verse is broken up by various prose shenanigans (an interesting Irish word that seems to derive from the phrase, *I play the fox,* as in "Hide fox and all after"). To indicate the prose incursions and to provide breathing spots I've placed numerals that strictly speaking are not in O'Brien's original. The title is borrowed from Iremonger's translation.

Not only is this epic lay in competition with prose in the novel, but it has to put up with some O'Brien doggerel entitled "The Workman's Friend" by one "Jem Casey," a popular workingman's poet ("By God it's not for nothing that I call myself a pal of Jem Casey"). It is, of course, a parody of such Henley-on-Kipling stuff as frequently found itself suspended not only from lips but the very walls of Irish front parlors and even now makes its way in America onto the desks of presidents of savings-and-loan associations.]

THE WORKMAN'S FRIEND

When things go wrong and will not come right,
Though you do the best you can,
When life looks black as the hour of night –
A PINT OF PLAIN IS YOUR ONLY MAN.

When money's tight and is hard to get
And your horse has also ran,
When all you have is a heap of debt –
A PINT OF PLAIN IS YOUR ONLY MAN.

When health is bad and your heart feels strange,
And your face is pale and wan,
When doctors say that you need a change,
A PINT OF PLAIN IS YOUR ONLY MAN.

When food is scarce and your larder bare
And no rashers grease your pan,
When hunger grows as your meals are rare –
A PINT OF PLAIN IS YOUR ONLY MAN.

In time of trouble and lousy strife,
You have still got a darlint plan,
You still can turn to a brighter life –
A PINT OF PLAIN IS YOUR ONLY MAN.

[*At Swim-Two-Birds*]

KING SWEENEY'S VALEDICTION

I

If I were to search alone
the hills of the brown world,
better would I like my sole hut
in Glen Bolcain.

Good its water greenish-green
good its clean strong wind,
good its cress-green cresses,
best its branching brooklime.

II

Good its sturdy ivies,
good its bright neat sallow,
good its yewy yew-yews,
best its sweet-noise birch.

A haughty ivy
growing through a twisted tree,
myself on its true summit,
I would lothe leave it.

I flee before skylarks,
it is the tense stern-race,
I overleap the clumps
on the high hill-peaks.

When it rises in front of me
the proud turtle-dove,
I overtake it swiftly
since my plumage grew.

The stupid unwitting woodcock
when it rises up before me,
methinks it red-hostile,
and the blackbird that cries havoc.

Small foxes yelping
to me and from me,
the wolves tear them—
I flee their cries.

They journeyed in their chase of me
in their swift courses
so that I flew away from them
to the tops of mountains.

On every pool there will rain
a starry frost;
I am wretched and wandering
under it on the peak.

The herons are calling
in cold Glen Eila
swift-flying flocks are flying,
coming and going.

I do not relish
the mad clack of humans
sweeter warble of the bird
in the place he is.

I like not the trumpeting
heard at morn;
sweeter hearing is the squeal
of badgers in Benna Broc.

I do not like it
the loud bugling;
finer is the stagbelling stag
of antler-points twice twenty.

There are makings for plough-teams
from glen to glen;
each resting-stag at rest
on the summit of the peaks. . . .

III

Greater-than-the-material-for-a-little-cloak,
thy head has greyed;
if I were on each little point
littler points would there be on every pointed point.

The stag that marches trumpeting
across the glen to me,
pleasant the place for seats
on his antler top.

IV

Cheerless is existence
without a downy bed,
abode of the shrivelling frost,
gusts of the snowy wind.

Chill icy wind,
shadow of a feeble sun
the shelter of a sole tree
on a mountain-plain.

The bell-belling of the stag
through the woodland,
the climb to the deer-pass,
the voice of white seas.

Forgive me Oh Great Lord,
mortal is this great sorrow,
worse than the black grief—
Sweeny the thin-groined.

Carraig Alasdair
resort of sea-gulls,
sad Oh Creator,
chilly for its guests.

Sad our meeting
two hard-shanked cranes—
myself hard and ragged
she hard-beaked.

V

Chill chill is my bed at dark
on the peak of Glen Boirche,
I am weakly, no mantle on me,
lodged in a sharp-stirked holly.

Glen Bolcain of the twinkle spring
it is my rest-place to abide in;
when Samhain comes, when summer comes,
it is my rest-place where I abide.

For my sustenance at night,
the whole that my hands can glean
from the gloom of the oak-gloomed oaks—
the herbs and the plenteous fruits.

Fine hazel-nuts and apples, berries,
blackberries and oak-tree acorns,
generous raspberries, they are my due,
haws of the prickle-hawy hawthorn.

Wild sorrels, wild garlic faultless,
clean-topped cress,
they expel from me my hunger,
acorns from the mountain, melle-root.

VI

Terrible is my plight this night
the pure air has pierced my body,
lacerated feet, my cheek is green—
O Mighty God, it is my due.

It is bad living without a house,
Peerless Christ, it is a piteous life!
a filling of green-tufted fine cresses
a drink of cold water from a clear rill.

Stumbling out of the withered tree-tops
walking the furze—it is truth—
wolves for company, man-shunning,
running with the red stag through fields.

VII

Ululation, I am Sweeny,
my body is a corpse;
sleeping or music nevermore—
only the soughing of the storm-wind.

I have journeyed from Luachair Dheaghaidh
to the edge of Fiodh Gaibhle,
this is my fare—I conceal it not—
ivy-berries, oak-mast.

VIII

All Fharannain, resort of saints,
fulness of hazels, fine nuts,
swift water without heat
coursing its flank.

Plenteous are its green ivies,
its mast is coveted;
the fair heavy apple-trees
they stoop their arms.

IX

There was a time when I preferred
to the low converse of humans
the accents of the turtle-dove
fluttering about a pool.

There was a time when I preferred
to the tinkle of neighbour bells
the voice of the blackbird from the crag
and the belling of a stag in a storm.

There was a time when I preferred
to the voice of a fine woman near me
the call of the mountain-grouse
heard at day.

There was a time when I preferred
the yapping of the wolves
to the voice of a cleric
melling and megling within.

X

Here is the tomb of Sweeny!
His memory racks my heart,
dear to me therefore are the haunts
of the saintly madman.

Dear to me Glen Bolcain fair
for Sweeny loved it;
dear the streams that leave it
dear its green-crowned cresses.

That beyant is Madman's Well
dear the man it nourished,
dear its perfect sand,
beloved its clear waters.

Melodious was the talk of Sweeny
long shall I hold his memory,
I implore the King of Heaven
on his tomb and above his grave.

[*At Swim-Two-Birds*]

SCEL LEM DUIB

HERE's a song—
stags give tongue
winter snows
summer goes.

High cold blow
sun is low
brief his day
seas give spray.

Fern clumps redden
shapes are hidden
wild geese raise
wonted cries.

Cold now grids
wings of birds
icy time—
that's my rime.

AOIBHINN, A LEABHRÁIN, DO THRIALL

DELIGHTFUL, book, your trip
to her of the ringlet head,
a pity it's not you
that's pinning, I that sped.

To go, book, where she is
delightful trip in sooth!
the bright mouth red as blood
you'll see, and the white tooth.

You'll see that eye that's grey
the docile palm as well,
with all that beauty you
(not I, alas) will dwell.

You'll see the eyebrow fine
the perfect throat's smooth gleam,
and the sparkling cheek I saw
latterly in a dream.

The lithe good snow-white waist
That won mad love from me—
the handwhite swift neat foot—
These in their grace you'll see.

The soft enchanting voice
that made me each day pine
you'll hear, and well for you—
would that your lot were mine.
   [*The Oxford Book of Irish Verse*]

DRINK AND TIME IN DUBLIN I

At ten o'clock on week nights, at half-nine on Saturday the tide ebbs suddenly, leaving the city high and dry. Unless you are staying at a hotel or visiting a theatre, you may not lawfully consume excisable liquors within the confines of the country borough. The city has entered that solemn hiatus, that almost sublime eclipse known as The Closed Hours. Here the law, as if with true Select Lounge mentality, discriminates sharply against the poor man at the pint counter by allowing those who can command transport and can embark upon a journey to drink elsewhere till morning. The theory is that all travellers still proceed by stage-coach and that those who travel outside become blue with cold after five miles and must be thawed out with hot rum at the first hostelry they encounter, by night or day. In practice, people who are in the first twilight of inebriation are transported from the urban to the rural pub so swiftly by the internal combustion engine that they need not necessarily be aware that they have moved at all, still less comprehend that their legal personalities have undergone a mystical transfiguration. Whether this system is to be regarded as a scandal or a godsend depends largely on whether one owns a car. At present the city is ringed around with these "bona-fide" pubs, many of them well-run modern houses, and a considerable amount of the stock-in-trade is transferred to the stomachs of the customers at a time every night when the sensible and just are in their second sleeps . . .

To go back to the city: it appears that the poor man does not always go straight home at ten o'clock. If his thirst is big enough and he knows the knocking-formula, he may possibly visit some house where the Demand Note of the Corporation has stampeded the owner into a bout of illicit after-hour trading. For trader and customer alike, such a life is one of excitement, tiptoe and hush. The boss's ear, refined to shades of perception far beyond the sensitiveness of any modern aircraft detector, can tell almost the inner thoughts of any policeman in the next street. At the first breath of danger all lights are suddenly doused and conversation toned down, as with a knob, to vanishing point. Drinkers reared in such schools will tell you that in inky blackness stout cannot be distinguished in taste from Bass and that no satisfaction whatever can be extracted from a cigarette unless the smoke is seen. Sometimes the police make a catch. Here is the sort of thing that is continually appearing in the papers:

Guard—said that accompanied by Guard—he visited the premises at 11.45 p.m. and noticed a light at the side door. When he knocked the light was extinguished, but he was not admitted for six minutes. When defendant opened eventually, he appeared to be in an excited condition and used bad language. There was nobody in the bar but there were two empty pint measures containing traces of fresh porter on the counter. He found a man crouching in a small press containing switches and a gas-meter. When he attempted to enter the yard to carry out a search, he was obstructed by the defendant, who used an improper expression. He arrested him, but owing to the illness of his wife, he was later released.

Defendant—Did you give me an unmerciful box in the mouth?
Witness—No.

Defendant—Did you say that you would put me and my gawm of a brother through the back wall with one good haymaker of a clout the next time I didn't open when you knocked?

Witness—No.

Justice—You look a fine block of a man yourself. How old are you?

Defendant—I'm as grey as a badger, but I'm not long past forty. (Laughter.)

Justice—Was the brother there at all?

Defendant—He was away in Kells, your worship, seeing about getting a girl for himself. (Laughter.)

Justice—Well, I think you could give a good account of yourself.

Witness—He was very obstreperous, your worship.

Witness, continuing, said that he found two men standing in the dark in an outhouse. They said they were there "for a joke." Witness also found an empty pint measure in an outdoor lavatory and two empty bottles of Cairnes.

Defendant said that two of the men were personal friends and were being treated. There was no question of taking money. He did not know who the man in the press was and did not recall having seen him before. He had given strict instructions to his assistant to allow nobody to remain on after hours. There was nobody in the press the previous day as the gas-man had called to inspect the meter. The two Guards had given him an unmerciful hammering in the hall. His wife was in ill-health, necessitating his doing without sleep for three weeks. A week previously he was compelled to send for the Guards to assist in clearing the house at ten o'clock. He was conducting the house to the best of his ability and was very strict about the hours.

Guard—said that the defendant was a decent hard-working type but was of an excitable nature. The house had a good record.

Remarking that the defendant seemed a decent sort and that the case was distinguished by the absence of perjury, the Justice said he would impose a fine of twenty shillings, the offence not to be endorsed. Were it not for extenuating circumstances he would have no hesitation in sending the defendant to Mountjoy for six months. He commanded Guards for smart police work.

Not many publicans, however, will take the risk. If they were as careful of their souls as they are of their licences, heaven would be packed with those confidential and solicitous profit-takers and, to please them, it might be necessary to provide an inferior annex to paradise to house such porter-drinkers as would make the grade.

[*The Bell*, Vol. 1, No. 2]

* * *

. . . this portrait of undead human decomposition, not peculiar to Christmas but most frequently encountered about that time.

(Enters public house on St Stephen's Day, obviously shattered with alcohol. Lowers self into seat with great care, grips table to arrest devastating shake in hands. Calls for glass of malt. Spills water all over table. Swallows drink with great clatter of teeth against glass. Shakily lights cigarette. Exhales. Begins to look around. Fixes on adjacent acquaintance. Begins peroration.)

'Bedam but you know, people talk a lot about drink, Whiskey and all the rest of it. There's always a story, the whiskey was bad, the stomach was out of order and so on. Do you know what *I'm* going to tell you . . . ?

(Pauses impressively. The eye-pupils, almost dissolved in their watery lake, rove about with sickly inquiry. Accepts silence as evidence of intense interest.)

'Do you know what it is?'

(Changes cigarette from normal inter-digital position, holds it aloft vertical; taps it solemnly with index finger of free hand.)

'Do you see that? That thing there? Cigarettes. Them lads. Do you know what I'm going to tell you . . . ?'

(Is suddenly overcome by paroxysm of coughing; roots benightedly for handkerchief as tears of pure alcohol course down the ruby cheeks. Recovers.)

'Them fellas there. *Them fellas has me destroyed . . .*'

(Collapses into fresh paroxysm. Emerges again):

'I wouldn't mind *that* at all (indicates glass). I *know* what I have there. There's eatin' an' drinkin' in that. Damn the harm *that* done annywan, bar been taken to excess. But *this* . . .'

(Again points to cigarette, looks of sorrow and horror mingling on 'face'.)

'Them lads has me destroyed.'

* * *

On a recent Thursday I went to the pictures and saw a tall gentleman called Randolph Scott in a film called 'The Spoilers'. At the end of the picture Randolph gets into a fight with another man in a pub. At the end of the fight there is no pub. The fight is so fierce that it is reduced to smithereens. Randolph, being the bad lot, gets a frightful thrashing, a frtfull throshou, a frajfyl tromaking, a fruitful . . .

The Plain People of Ireland: Whatsamatter?

Myself: Feel queer . . . dark . . . nase blooding . . . giddy . . . where am I?

The Plain People of Ireland: Ah sure you often meet that in the pictures, too—that's altitude. You're too high up. No oxygen. The pilots do often have a black out. Come on down lower in the page and you'll be game ball.

Myself: All right. Thanks.

The Plain People of Ireland: Are you OK now?

Myself: Yes, thanks, I'm feeling all right now. Well, as I was saying, Randolph gets a frightful hiding, he is a terrible mess when the picture ends. But the following night I happened to see the same Randolph in another picture called, I think 'The Texan'. All I can say is, fit and well he was looking after the hammering he got the night before.

The Plain People of Ireland: Will you have a bit of sense man. 'The Texan' is an old picture. A real ould stager man. But 'The Spoilers' is a new picture. It doesn't say because you see the one on wan night and then d'other on another—

Myself: Say no more. I realise I have been hasty. I will think before I shoot my mouth off next time.

* * *

It is now sixteen or seventeen years since I saw the queen of France, then the dauphiness, at Versailles; and surely never lighted on this orb, which she hardly seemed to touch, a more delightful vision. I saw her just above the horizon, decorating and cheering the elevated sphere which she just began to move in; glittering like the morning star, full of life and splendour, and joy—

The Plain People of Ireland: Sure that wan went to the wall years ago, you must be mixin' her up with some other party.

Myself: For me the Queen of France never died.

The Plain People of Ireland: And if it's above the horizon you seen her, that's fair enough, many's a man seen more than the queen of

France and him out in a boat fishin', coopers of stout and sandwiches, half fallin' out of the boat rotten fluthery-eyed drunk on porter and whiskey, sure is it any wonder you're seein' visions man? Sure Lord save us you'll be Napolean Boneypart himself next above in the Grange weedin' turnips.

Myself: I was at a wake the other night and every man jack was drunk—including the corpse.

The Plain People of Ireland: O faith now never mind the wakes, many's a better man than you was happy enough at home be the fire with Knocknagow or a good American cowboy story, there's a very bad type of person goin' around now that wasn't known in our fathers' day.

* * *

Do not for that singular interval, one moment, think that I have been overlooking this new Intoxicating Liquor Bill. I am arranging to have an amendment tabled because it appears that there is absolutely nothing else you can do with amendment.

My idea is to have the hours altered so that public houses will be permitted to open only between two and five in the morning. This means that if you are a drinking man you'll have to be in earnest about it.

Picture the result. A rustle is heard in the warm dark bedroom that has been lulled for hours with gentle breathing. Two naked feet are tenderly lowered to the floor and a shaky hand starts foraging blindly for matches. Then there is a further sleepy noise as another person half-wakens and rolls around.

'John! What's the matter?'

'Nothing.'

'But where are you going?'

'Out for a pint.'

'But *John!* It's half two.'

'Don't care what time it is.'

'But it's pouring rain. You'll get your death of cold.'

'I tell you I'm going out for a pint. Don't be trying to make a ridiculous scene. All over Dublin thousands of men are getting up just now. I haven't had a drink for twenty-four hours.'

'But John, there are four stouts in the scullery. Beside the oat-meal bag.'

'Don't care what's in the scullery behind the oat-meal bag.'

'O, John.'

And then dirty theatrical snivelling sobbing begins as the piqued and perished pint-lover draws dressing gowns and coats over his shivering body and passes out gingerly to the stairs.

Then the scene in the pub. Visibility is poor because a large quantity of poisonous fog has been let in by somebody and is lying on the air like layers of brawn. Standing at the counter is a row of dishevelled and shivering customers, drawn of face, quaking with the cold. Into their unlaced shoes is draped, concertina-wise, pyjama in all its striped variety. Here and there you can discern the raw wind-whipped shanks of the inveterate night-shirt wearer. And the curate behind the bar has opened his face into so enormous a yawn that the tears can be heard dripping into the pint he is pulling. Not a word is heard, nothing but chilly savage silence. The sullen clock ticks on. Then 'Time, please, time. Time for bed, gentlemen.' And as you well know, by five in the morning, the heavy rain of two-thirty has managed to grow into a roaring downpour.

The Plain People of Ireland: Is all this serious?

Myself: Certainly it's serious, why wouldn't it be serious, you don't think I'd try to make jokes about anything so funny as the licensing laws, why would I bring turf to Newcastlewest?

The Plain People of Ireland: If you're serious so, it's only a trick to get more drink for newspapermen.

Myself: Nonsense. Newspapermen couldn't hold any more than they have at present.

The Plain People of Ireland: O faith now, that's enough. That's enough about that crowd. Remember well, many's a county council meeting, fluther-eyed note-takers couldn't get the half of it, stuff that days was spent thinkin' out.

Myself: Hic!

The Plain People of Ireland: Faith indeed that was loud enough, well you may talk about putting down drink. Putting down is right.

Myself: Ut's only mey undajaschin, d'yeh ondherstawnd.

I can see even another domestic aspect of this new order. It is after midnight. The man of the house is crouched miserably over the dying fire.

'John! Look at the time! Are you not coming to bed?'
'No. I'm waiting for the pubs to open.'

*   *   *

Magnum est veritas et in vino praevalebit! Some things are bitter but if they be true, should they then be suppressed? A thousand times *no*, nor do I count the cost to purse, fair name or honour, *least of all my own*. I say this with reluctance but say it I must:

Last night I was drunk!

(Sensation.) No, no (makes nervous gestures), do not think I exaggerate, do not whisper that fumes of deadliest spirits were held to my nostrils as I slept. It is absolutely true and I blame nobody but myself. I was simply caught off my guard. There can be no excuses. From myself I demand the high standards I prescribe for others.

Tell you how it happened. Sitting in my offices last night as Regional Commissioner for the Townships of Geashill and Philipstown Daingean, a servitor enters and hands me a document. You would never—nor did I—guest what it was. A sealed order from the Department of Local Governments . . . *dissolving me!* ME! Wellll . . .!

Extraordinary sensation. First to go is the head, the whole thing falling away into blobs of yellow liquid running down and messing into the liquefacting chest, then the whole immense superstructure seeping down the decomposing legs to the floor . . . a . . . most . . . *frightful* business, nothing left of me after three minutes only a big puddle on the floor!

Happily my secretary rushed in, guessed what had happened and had the presence of mind to get most of me into an empty champagne bottle I had in my desk. Have you ever, reader, looked at the world from inside a bottle? Found yourself laboriously reversing a word like TOUQCILC? Phew! Have you ever, possessing the boast that not once did breath of intoxicating liquor defile your lips, literally found yourself a one-bottle-man? Ever had to console yourself with a bitter jest about your 'bottle-dress'? Ever found what seemed to be your head being hurt by . . . a *cork*? As for the curse of bottle-shoulders, is there any use in talking? Here, though, is a hint. The curvature of the bottle causes violent refraction and if you have any fear that my own fate could one day be yours, be counselled by what I say: *always carry special spectacles*. It pays in the long run!

Let me continue. My secretary, when leaving to go home, placed me for some reason on the mantelpiece in a rather prominent position but first typed out a little label marked POISON—NOT TO BE TAKEN and stuck it on the bottle. A stupid business, really—whence comes this idea that everybody can read or that those who can always believe what they see? Actually I should have been locked away in the bottom drawer of my desk or put into the big press I have marked 'MAPS'. What I feared happened, though it could have been worse. After an hour or so a charlady arrived and began to clean the place up, having first put some of my valuable documents in her bin. She was later joined by an unusual character, a chargentleman, apparently her husband. I do not suppose he was three seconds in the room when he was conscious of myself, on the mantelpiece in the bottle. He calls the wife's attention, then over, whips me down, takes out the cork and begins to sniff at me.

'Portuguese, begob,' he mutters.

'You'll put that bottle down that's what you'll do,' the charlady says severely.

'I'll go bail it's that Portuguese shandy that carried Harry off around the Christmas,' the ruffian mutters.

Next thing . . . *I'm at his head!* Phewwww! It seems, however, that I tasted rather worse than he was prepared to endure because he took only a few sips of me, then bashed the cork back in disgust.

Well, *what . . . an . . . incredible . . . experience!* I managed to get back next day, but it took me all my time and was a most dangerous business. My sole consolation? That if it was I who was drunk, it was the chargentleman who had the hangover!

[*The Best of Myles*]

PROPOSAL FOR HISTORY OF
IRISH WHISKEY DISTILLING INDUSTRY

[The following proposal to the Irish Whiskey Distilling Industry, which O'Brien made in all seriousness in May 1964, has to stand as one of the most curious documents ever turned out by a serious drinking writer. And I mean the serious to apply to both writer and drinker. It must be remembered that O'Brien was desperately casting about for ways to employ his pen for profit and had even done some ads for Guinness. After the grubby appearance of the "plain pint" motif in *At Swim,* this is a bit like Joyce in his old age writing copy for Plum Tree's Potted Meat; or maybe more in accord with O'Brien's deepest feelings, writing the booze ads in his failing years was a bit like having Joyce mending the Jesuit's underwear. (See *The Dalkey Archive.*) In any case, the Bell Distillery wrote a polite letter back saying thank you, but the history of drinking in Ireland was already bad enough and that what the industry was looking for just then was a more dignified image, if you please.]

Confidential
MEMORANDUM by Brian O'Nolan, 21 Watersland Road, Stillorgan, County Dublin, writer, concerning the background, present condition and better promotion of the

IRISH WHISKEY DISTILLING INDUSTRY

1. A preliminary personal note about myself is called for. After considerable university studies, which included experience abroad, I joined the Irish civil service in 1935. I resigned in 1953, with the rank of Principal Officer, having found the milieu increasingly distasteful. It was bad enough that nearly all Ministers were either peasants or uneducated shopboys (to some of whom I acted as private secretary) but there was undisguised graft, jobbery, and corrupt practices large and small. This is not the place to detail such matters though it will be recalled that some cases—e.g. the Locks Distillery and the Monaghan Bacon Factory—came to public notice, and then only because certain of the shady operators had quarrelled among themselves. I had meantime been engaged in writing of various kinds and felt I could make an honest living that way. I have written 7 books, published in London and New York with 3 of them translated internationally, as well as plays, short stories, radio and TV material, and over the years an immense amount of work that might be ranked as better-class journalism. I have discontinued the last-mentioned activity so far as Ireland is concerned owing to the deplorable conditions of publishing here; there is parochial and sectarian prejudice, there is something approaching illiteracy to be met on all sides, and some of the ideas of financial reward are ludicrous. I now write for *The* (Manchester) *Guardian* and various reviews, some in the U.S. Last year I wrote a book which will be published in London next October and by Macmillan of New York early in 1965. This book should create a stir. I have never published anything under my own name.

2. While recovering at home from an accident during the last 7 months, I encountered in casual reading two works which had a bearing on liquor in Ireland, the sort of drinking that was done and by whom, with interesting accounts of the state of the country and the

people in the century of Sir Jonah Barrington, Judge of the High Court of Admiralty in Ireland, etc., and the other the Life of Father Mathew by J. F. Maguire, M.P., published by Longmans, London, about 1860. There is a fulsome letter of commendation from W. E. Gladstone at the beginning of the volume.

3. Barrington was a polished, witty and attractive character and in his lifetime had personal acquaintance with Wolfe Tone, Moore, Robert Emmet, Lord Norbury, Curran, Burke, Grattan, and lived through events such as the 1798 Insurrection, the Act of Union and the career of Napoleon. He was born at Abbeyleix about 1775 and was a wealthy landed proprietor. He writes in his preface:

I consider myself strictly orthodox both in politics and theology; that is to say, I profess to be a sound Protestant without bigotry and an hereditary royalist without ultraism. Liberty I love, democracy I hate, fanaticism I denounce!

In my public life I have met with but one transaction that even *threatened* to make my patriotism overbalance my loyalty. I allude to the purchase and sale of the Irish Parliament, called a Union, which I ever regarded as one of the most flagrant public acts of corruption on the records of history, and certainly the most mischievous to this empire, except our absurdities at Vienna. I believe very few men sleep the sounder for having supported either the former or the latter measures, though some, it is true, *went to sleep* a good deal sooner than they expected when they carried these measures into execution....

He claims, probably correctly, to have been popular with the plain people and considered that the greatest curse on the country was the absentee landlord who collected his rackrents through a savage agent, and he sympathised with the tenantry in their hostility to the tithes proctors. The Catholic faith, though proscribed, was apparently widely tolerated throughout the country, and Barrington sometimes had a priest to dinner. The Irish language was widely in use. There were, of course, no State schools and Barrington seemed to rest, if a trifle uneasily, in the conviction that it would be unwise to teach the plain people how to read and write but he was more than once discomfited by being answered by an ignorant peasant in Latin. He was, moreover, criticised by his own associates for being too 'liberal'.

4. In Barrington's various references to drink, it seems that wine, particularly claret, was the mainstay of the gentry but that spirits were often called in medicinally, while at this time beer was hardly heard

of by anybody. The following quotations from the Recollections are relevant:

I have heard it often said that, at the time I speak of, every estated gentleman in the Queen's County was *honoured* by the gout. I have since considered that its extraordinary prevalence was not difficult to be accounted for, by the disproportionate quantity of acid contained in their seductive beverage, called rum-shrub, which was then universally drunk in quantities nearly incredible, generally from supper-time till morning, by all country gentlemen, as they said, to keep down their claret....

Night after night the revel afforded uninterrupted pleasure to the joyous gentry: the festivity being subsequently renewed at some other mansion, till the gout thought proper to put the whole party *hors de combat*—having the satisfaction of making cripples for a few months such as did not kill.

Whilst the convivials bellowed with only toe or finger agonies it was a mere bagatelle; but when Mr. Gout marched up the country and invaded the head or the stomach, it was called *no joke;* and Drogheda usquebaugh, the hottest-distilled drinkable liquor ever invented, was applied for aid, and generally drove the tormentor in a few minutes to his former quarters. It was, indeed, counted a specific; and I allude to it more particularly, as my poor grandfather was finished thereby.... He was rather a short man, with a large red nose, strong made, and wore an immense white wig, such as the portraits give to Dr. Johnson. He died at eighty-six years of age, of shrub-gout and usquebaugh, beloved and respected....

We had intended to surprise my brother, but had not calculated on the scene I was to witness. On driving to the cottage door I found it open, whilst a dozen dogs of different descriptions shewed ready to receive us not in the most polite manner. My servant's whip, however, soon sent them about their business, and I ventured into the parlour to see what cheer. It was about ten in the evening: the room was strewed with empty bottles, some broken, some interspersed with glasses, plates, dishes, knives, spoons, &c., all in glorious confusion. Here and there were heaps of bones, relics of the former day's entertainment, which the dogs, seizing their opportunity, had cleanly picked. Three or four of the Bacchanalians lay fast asleep upon their chairs, one or two others on the floor, among whom a piper lay on his back, apparently dead, with a table-cloth spread over him, and surrounded by four or five candles burnt to the sockets; his chanter and bags were laid scientifically across his body, his mouth was quite open, and his nose made ample amends for the silence of his drone....

5. That last paragraph is merely the prelude to an exceptional debauch in which one man collapsed in a drunken stupor into a bed of wet mortar and was later found solidly immured.

The Life of Father Mathew (1790–1856) is a very different sort of book. It is shockingly badly written and presented in a large flat volume like piano music, two columns to the page, with 85 pages of advertisements, all by Cork firms, at the back.

Theobald Mathew, who was also known as Toby, was born near Cashel, educated at Kilkenny and Maynooth, elected to join the Capuchin Order and was ordained in 1814. From J. F. Maguire's obaceious [*sic*] style and mixture of anecdote, myth, exaggeration and fantasy, it is very hard to arrive at a firm picture of the Ireland of Father Mathew's day, know exactly what he did, and how. His plea was not for temperance but for total abstinence and his campaign seems to have had an element of sustained hysteria, reminiscent of but far more extreme than contemporary campaigns of Billy Graham. Just as the late President Kennedy was denounced in some quarters as a Communist, there were rumors that the distillers were the power behind Fr. Mathew, their real objective being the crushing of illicit distilling.

Though the 1798 rising had been put down in Fr. Mathew's early youth, the country continued to be in a condition of suppressed turmoil and, insofar as Fr. Mathew made any political intervention in his many direct contacts with the people, he sided with the 'gentry' and landlord class, counselled respect for authority and an end to all intrigue and subversion. The gentry and better-class people also openly supported Fr. Mathew, which is curious in view of the penal laws. A requisition to hold a meeting in compliment of Fr. Mathew in the Theatre Royal, Dublin, in January, 1843, was signed by 2 Dukes, 4 Marquises, 19 Earls, 10 Viscounts and Barons, 4 Catholic Bishops, 40 Baronets, and 30 M.P.s, and the meeting realised a net sum of £1,150, with the Duke of Leinster in the chair. Notwithstanding the mendicant status of the Capuchin Order (a 'tough' division of the Franciscans) and each friar's vow of poverty, Fr. Mathew handled immense sums of money and trafficked in medals, which were often of silver and which he usually sold. He apparently had little idea of trade or business. It is recorded that on one visit to Maynooth College, he gave away medals to a total value of £200. One Irish newspaper alleged that he had made £200,000 from selling medals but on one occasion at Dublin, when he was administering the pledge to a great concourse, a bailiff arrived to serve a writ on behalf of an unpaid medal manufacturer. The bailiff represented himself as a penitent, went up to Fr. Mathew, knelt down, showed the writ and said it entailed the arrest of the friar at the end of the meeting. Maguire naively commends the bailiff's piety, whereas any less circumspect course on his part might have led the congregation to tear him to pieces. Late in his career Fr. Mathew was proposed for appointment as Bishop of Cork but this was turned down by the Holy See. He visited England and also America, where he fell in with Barnum and Jenny Lind. Queen Victoria gave him a pension. There is a valuable Report of the Devon Commission, appointed in 1843, on the wretched condition of the bulk of the Irish people just before the Famine.

6. Further study is necessary of the Fr. Mathew era, of how serious and widespread drinking was, with what demoralisation, what exactly the liquor was, and where it came from. It is however admitted that the reforms and rehabilitations he achieved did not long survive his own passing.

7. Considerable research would be necessary to establish how the modern state control of alcohol as to (a) its production, and (b) its distribution developed in the United Kingdom and before that. As early as 1643 excise duty was imposed on a great number of articles in England but in Barrington's day, before the Union, there was no police force in Ireland and in the city of Dublin there was apparently no public disciplinary sanction other than 'the watch'. One of his friends had a cutter which he used for smuggling claret from France. It was not until Sir Robert Peel (1788–1850) was appointed Secretary for Ireland for 1812–1818 that a constabulary ("peelers") was set up, and it was only in 1829 that a similar force was first inaugurated for London and district. By the end of the 19th century the major part of excise revenue was from spirits and beer. In the early eighties warehousing systems and customs and excise were consolidated; and customs and excise controls were amalgamated. Before the constabulary it may be said that in Ireland there was no control whatever of home distillation throughout what was a wild country with the most rudimentary communications, and even after the installation of the constabulary their control was probably nugatory and ineffective. It is certain that up to perhaps a hundred years ago, the bulk of strong drink consumed in Ireland, mainly whiskey, was home-made, and most of it was probably crude and poisonous. In the Fr. Mathew

biography figures are cited identifying growth of pledge-taking with decline in homicide.

8. After excise duties were imposed "temporarily" in 1643, the custom was to farm them out to "commissioners" by way of reward for political services. Charles thus recompensed hundreds of Stuart restorators by the grant of excise patents but by the end of the reign of William, the corrupt farming of excise had practically disappeared from the English fiscal system. How parallel the procedures in Ireland were is obscure.

9. Also in need of inquiry is the evolution of the system whereby individuals were licensed for (a) producing, and (b) distributing and selling intoxicating drink. It is established that in the United Kingdom since 1831 there has been a steady diminution of pub retail licenses in proportion to the population served. One public house existed for these years and populations:

1831	—	168 persons
1909	—	375
1911	—	395
1921	—	458
1937	—	537

Comparable figures for Ireland and/or the 26 counties are not readily available but the present situation seems chaotic, and some little colour is lent to the amusing charge that at one time the British sought to ruin the Irish people by granting licences prodigally and profligately, ensuring simultaneously the widest dissemination of strong drink but in circumstances of uneconomic competition so fierce that adulterated or contaminated drink became the rule. In Dublin, if one takes the top of Grafton Street as the centre of a circle of a half-mile radius, I estimate that 49 licensed premises will be found within that circle, and at the central Sth. King Street–Grafton Street junction, there are 3 licensed premises side by side. An early licensing Act of the Free State provided for the extinction of redundant licences at the expense of the surviving licensees but this provision had been inoperative.

10. Irish potstill whiskey is unique as to ingredients and production procedure. It is one of the few commodities derived solely from native produce and labour, and the capacity of the industry for expanded production is almost limitless. Yet its potential as a significant and

valuable export is virtually unexploited. As near home as London it is unobtainable unless one is willing to ferret about looking for an 'Irish house' or content to pay a fancy price in an expensive hotel. In the United States, where the sympathetic attitude to things Irish need not here be stressed, a yawning vacuum exists where Irish whiskey might be expected. The two standard native brands, bourbon and rye, are of the Scotch type, and Scotch whisky (from Scotland) enjoys an enormous and ever-growing cachet, having snob appeal as 'the real thing'. In a short U.S. tour I made in 1958, I was astonished to find that intelligent, first-generation Irish people did not even know that there was such a thing as a distinctive Irish whiskey, infinitely superior to Scotch. The industry here cannot escape the charge of being conservative to the point of being stuck in the mud. Two firms only have shown some enterprise in advertising but a true punch is lacking.

11. The drink business is intrinsically a considerable social issue, with an impact far beyond its immediate self. The Fr. Mathew campaign here, the horrifying Prohibition interlude in the U.S. and Scandinavian regulation by State monopoly are examples of the interaction of alcohol with political, religious and social concepts. Ignorant and exaggerated attitudes to drink present it in a uniformly pejorative light, and it is in the interest of the industry to explain itself. So far as we are concerned, the immediate objective should be to make genuine Irish potstill whiskey from Ireland a familiar and prized drink in the United States.

12. These notes are presented to convey my conviction that I myself can make a considerable breach in the wall of commercial apathy by producing a book about Irish whiskey, after exhaustive research into the history of not only the thing itself but its whole economic, fiscal and social context. The structural nature of this book could not be decided upon in advance of the assembly of the material but I think it would be desirable, to give the work character and focus, that it should be largely the story of an individual distilling firm.

13. Towards this enterprise I would expect an honorarium of £600 a year for a possible maximum of 2 years, this to include all travel and similar expenses outside Dublin; in practice the research job, so far as documentation is concerned, might be less formidable than it looks. The arrangement would merely largely free me from other work to concentrate on this specialised task.

14. Such honorarium would be in no sense payment for writing

this book, which I would conceive as a genuine work of literature, subject to worldwide review and notice on its own merits. The sponsor would not be faced with any publication or other imponderable technical problems, as I am already under contract to a large publisher in London and another in New York, the subject matter of a book being a matter of my own choice.

30 May, 1964.

[Morris Library]

DRINK AND TIME IN DUBLIN II*

A RECORDED STATEMENT

—Did you go to that picture 'The Lost Weekend'?
—*I did.*
—I never seen such tripe.
—*What was wrong with it?*
—O it was all right, of course—bits of it was good. Your man in the jigs inside in the bed and the bat flying in to kill the mouse, that was *damn* good. I'll tell you another good bit. Hiding the bottles in the jax. And there was no monkey business about that because I tried it since meself. It works but you have to use the half pint bottles. Up the chimbley is another place I thought of and do you know the ledge affair above windows?

* From *1000 Years of Irish Prose,* ed. Vivian Mercier and David Greene (New York: Grosset & Dunlap, 1961).

—*I do.*

—That's another place but you could get a hell of a fall reaching up there on a ladder or standing on chairs with big books on them. And of course you can always tie the small bottles to the underneath of your mattress.

—*I suppose you can.*

—But what are you to do with the empties if you stop in bed drinking? There's a snag there. I often thought they should have malt in lemonade syphons.

—*Why didn't you like the rest of 'The Lost Weekend'?*

—Sure haven't I been through far worse weekends meself—you know that as well as I do. Sure Lord save us I could tell you yarns. I'd be a rich man if I had a shilling for every morning I was down in the markets at seven o'clock* in the slippers with the trousers pulled on over the pyjamas and the overcoat buttoned up to the neck in the middle of the summer. Sure don't be talking man.

—*I suppose the markets are very congested in the mornings?*

—With drunks? I don't know. I never looked around any time I was there.

—*When were you last there?*

—The time the wife went down to Cork last November. I won't forget that business in a hurry. That was a scatter and a half. Did I never tell you about that? O be God, don't get me on to *that* affair.

—*Was it the worst ever?*

—It was and it wasn't but I got the fright of me life. I'll tell you a damn good one. You won't believe this but it's a true bill. This is one of the best you ever heard.

—*I'll believe anything you say.*

—In the morning I brought the wife down to Kingsbridge in a taxi. I wasn't thinking of drink at all, hadn't touched it for four months, but when I paid the taxi off at the station instead of going back in it, the wife gave me a look. Said nothing, of course—after the last row I was for keeping off the beer for a year. But somehow she put the thing into me head. This was about nine o'clock, I suppose. I'll give you three guesses where I found meself at ten past nine *in another taxi?*

—*Where?*

---

* The public houses near the Dublin Cattle Market are permitted to open at 7 a.m. instead of 10:30 a.m. for the convenience of the cattle men.

—Above in the markets. And there wasn't a more surprised man than meself. Of course in a way it's a good thing to start at it early in the morning because with no food and all the rest of it you're finished at four o'clock and you're home again and stuffed in bed. It's the late nights that's the killer, two and three in the morning, getting poisoned in shebeens and all classes of hooky stuff, wrong change, and a taxi man on the touch. After nights like that it's a strong man that'll be up at the markets in time next morning.

—*What happened after the day you got back at four?*

—Up at the markets next morning *before* they were open. There was another chap there but I didn't look at him. I couldn't tell you what age he was or how bad he was. There was no four o'clock stuff that day. I was around the markets till twelve or so. Then off up town and I have meself shaved be a barber. Then up to a certain hotel and straight into the bar. There's a whole crowd there that I know. What are you going to have and so on. No no, have a large one. So-and-so's getting married on Tuesday. Me other man's wife has had a baby. You know the stuff? Well Lord save us I had a terrible tank of malt in me that day! I had a feed in the middle of it because I remember scalding myself with hot coffee and I never touch the coffee at all only after a feed. Of course I don't remember what happened me but I was in the flat the next morning with the clothes half off. I was supposed to be staying with the brother-in-law, of course, when the wife was away. But sure it's the old dog for the hard road. Drunk or sober I went back to me own place. As a matter of fact I never went near the brother-in-law at all. Be this time I was well into the malt. Out with me again feeling like death on wires and I'm inside in the local curing meself for hours, spilling stuff all over the place with the shake in the hand. Then into the barber's and after that off up again to the hotel for more malt. I'll give you a tip. Always drink in hotels. If you're in there you're in for a feed, or you've just had a feed, or you've an appointment there to see a fellow, and you're having a small one to pass the time. It looks very bad being in bars during the daytime. It's a thing to watch, that.

—*What happened then?*

—What do you think happened? What could happen? I get meself into a quiet corner and I start lowering them good-o. I don't know what happened me, of course. I met a few pals and there is some business about a greyhound out in Cloghran. It was either being bought or being sold and I go along in the taxi and where we were and where we weren't I couldn't tell you. I fall asleep on a chair in some house in town and next thing I wake up perished with the cold and as sick as I ever was in me life. Next thing I know I'm above in the markets. Taxis everywhere of course, no food only the plate of soup in the hotel, and be this time the cheque-book is in and out of the pocket *three or four times a day*, standing drinks all round, kicking up a barney in the lavatory with other drunks, looking for me 'rights' when I was refused drink—O, blotto, there's no other word for it. I seen some of the cheques since. *The writing!* A pal carts me home in a taxi. How long this goes on I don't know. I'm all right in the middle of the day but in the mornings I'm nearly too weak to walk and the shakes getting worse every day. Be this time I'm getting frightened of meself. Lookat here, mister-me-man, I say to meself, this'll have to stop. I was afraid the heart might give out, that was the only thing I was afraid of. Then I meet a pal of mine that's a doctor. This is inside in the hotel. There's only one man for you, he says, and that's sleep. Will you go home and go to bed if I get you something that'll make you sleep? Certainly, I said. I suppose this was about four or half four. Very well, says he, I'll write you out a prescription. He writes one out on hotel notepaper. I send for a porter. Go across with this, says I, to the nearest chemist shop and get this stuff for me and here's two bob for yourself. Of course I'm at the whiskey all the time. Your man comes back with a box of long-shaped green pills. You'll want to be careful with that stuff, the doctor says, that stuff's very dangerous. If you take one now and take another when you get home, you'll get a very good sleep but don't take any more till to-morrow night because that stuff's very dangerous. So I take one. But I know the doctor doesn't know how bad I am. I didn't tell him the whole story, no damn fear. So out with me to the jax where I take another one. Then back for a drink, still as wide-awake as a lark. You'll have to go home now, the doctor says, we can't have you passing out here, that stuff acts very quickly. Well, I have one more drink and off with me, *in a bus*, mind you, to the flat. I'm very surprised on the bus to find meself so wide-awake, looking out at people and reading the signs on shops. Then I begin to get afraid that the stuff is too weak and that I'll be lying awake for the rest of the evening and all night. To hell with it, I say to meself, we'll chance two more and let that be the end of it. Down went two more in the bus. I get there and into the flat. I'm still wide-awake and nothing will do me only one more pill for luck. I get into bed. I don't remember putting the head on the pillow. I wouldn't go out quicker if you hit me over the head with a crow-bar.

—*You probably took a dangerous over-dose.*

—Next thing I know I'm awake. It's dark. I sit up. There's matches there and I strike one. I look at the watch. The watch is stopped. I get up and look at the clock. Of course the clock is stopped, hasn't been wound for days. I don't know what time it is. I'm a bit upset about this. I turn on the wireless. It takes about a year to heat up and would you believe me I try a dozen stations all over the place and not one of them is telling what the time is. Of course I knew there was no point in trying American stations. I'm very disappointed because I sort of expected a voice to say 'It is now seven thirty p.m.' or whatever the time was. I turn off the wireless and begin to wonder. I don't know what time it is. *Then,* bedamnit, another thing strikes me. *What day is it?* How long have I been asleep with that dose? Well lookat, I got a hell of a fright when I found I didn't know what day it was. I got one hell of a fright.

—*Was there not an accumulation of milk-bottles or newspapers?*

—There wasn't—all that was stopped because I was supposed to be staying with the brother-in-law. What do I do? On with all the clothes and out to find what time it is and what day it is. The funny thing is that I'm not feeling too bad. Off with me down the street. There's lights showing in the houses. That means it's night-time and not early in the morning. Then I see a bus. That means it's not yet half-nine, because they stopped at half-nine that time. Then I see a clock. It's twenty past nine! But I still don't know what day it is and it's too late to buy an evening paper. There's only one thing—into a pub and get a look at one. So I march into the nearest, very quiet and correct and say a bottle of stout please. All the other customers look very sober and I think they are talking very low. When the man brings me the bottle I say to him I beg your pardon but I had a few bob on a horse today, could you give me a look at an evening paper? The man looks at me and says what horse was it? It was like a blow in the face to me, that question! I can't answer at all at first and then I stutter something about Hartigan's horses. None of them horses won a race today, the man says, and there was a paper here but it's gone. So I drink up the bottle and march out. It's funny, finding out about the day. You can't stop a man in the street and say have you got the right day please? God knows what would happen if you done that. I know be now that it's no use telling lies about horses, so in with me to another pub, order a bottle and ask the man has he got an evening paper. The missus has it upstairs, he says, there's nothing on it anyway. I now begin to think the best thing is to dial O on the phone, ask for Inquiries and find out that way. I'm on me way to a call-box when I begin to think that's a very bad idea. The girl might say hold on and I'll find out, I hang on there like a mug and next thing the box is surrounded by Guards and ambulances and attendants with ropes. No fear, says I to meself, there's going to be no work on the phone for me! Into another pub. I have the wind up now and no mistake. How long was I knocked out be the drugs? A day? Two days? Was I in the bed *for a week?* Suddenly I see a sight that gladdens me heart. Away down at the end of the pub there's an oul' fellow reading an evening paper with a magnifying glass. I take a mouthful of stout, steady meself, and march down to him. Me mind is made up: if he doesn't hand over the paper, I'll kill him. Down I go. Excuse me, says I, snatching the paper away from him and he still keeps looking through the glass with no paper there, I think he was deaf as well as half blind. Then I read the date—I suppose it was the first time the date was the big news on a paper. It says 'Thursday, 22nd November, 1945.' I never enjoyed a bit of news so much. I hand back the paper and says thanks very much, sir, for the loan of your paper. Then I go back to finish me stout, very happy and pleased with me own cuteness. Another man, I say to meself, would ask people, make a show of himself and maybe get locked up. But not me. I'm smart. Then begob I nearly choked.

—*What was the cause of that?*

—To-day is Thursday, I say to meself. Fair enough. But *what . . . day did I go to bed?* What's the use of knowing to-day's Thursday if I don't know when I went to bed? I still don't know whether I've been asleep for a day or a week! I nearly fell down on the floor. I am back where I started. Only I am feeling weaker and be now I have the wind up in gales. The heart begins to knock so loud that I'm afraid the man behind the counter will hear it and order me out.

—*What did you do?*

—Lookat here, me friend, I say to meself, take it easy. Go back now to the flat and take it easy for a while. This'll all end up all right, everything comes right in the latter end. Worse than this happened many's a man. And back to the flat I go. I collapse down into a chair with the hat still on me head, I sink the face down in me hands, and try to think. I'm like that for maybe five minutes. Then, *suddenly,* I know the answer! Without help from papers or clocks or people, I know how long I am there sleeping under the green pills! How did I know? Think that one out! How would *you* know if you were in the same boat?

(Before continuing, readers may wish to accept the sufferer's challenge.)

—*I am thinking.*

—Don't talk to me about calendars or hunger or anything like that. It's no use—you won't guess. You wouldn't think of it in a million years. Look. My face is in my hands—like this. Suddenly I notice the face is smooth. I'm not badly in need of a shave. That means it *must* be the same day I went to bed on! Maybe the stomach or something woke me up for a second or so. If I'd stopped in bed, I was off asleep again in a minute. But I got up to find the time and that's what ruined me! Now do you get it? Because when I went back to bed that night, I didn't waken till the middle of the next day.

—*You asked me how I would have found out how long I had been there after finding that the day was Thursday. I have no guarantee that a person in your condition would not get up and shave in his sleep. There was a better way.*

—There was no other way.

—*There was. If I were in your place I would have looked at the date on the prescription!*

DONABATE

Standing on the platform of Donabate Station the other Saturday morning waiting in the frost for a 'train' that was half an hour late, can you wonder that I fell to considering once again the dreadful mess into which our railways have been permitted to fall? When the 'train' was led in by our old friend 493, I laughed bitterly. This engine is about 17 years old and is suffering badly from condensation. It has been in this deplorable state for 2 years, yet absolutely nothing has been done to remedy what amounts to nothing more or less than a grave public scandal. Excuses there may be, 'explanations', no doubt all very plausible. The foreman welder is on his holidays but is expected back aMonday, when we hope etc. etc. Meanwhile thousands of foot pounds have been lost on the drawbar. It is all too dreadfully typical of the dawdling mentality that has made our name a by-word among steam-men the world over. I have written elsewhere and in no uncertain terms about the matter of the Slieve Gullion's valveports, the Kestrel's chronic 'blowing', the scandal of the Queen Maeve's piston valve lining. All very boring, no doubt, but of importance to thinking Irishmen. The Donabate engine was choked with dirty feed water and so long as there are plenty of good emulsions on the market, *there can be absolutely no excuse for this*. It is not good enough, it is not fair, and more than that I will not say.

[*The Best of Myles*]

* * *

It may seem an odd thing to say that, not so long ago, it was a common thing to see the late Sir Sefton Fleetwood-Crawshaye, O.B.E., very drunk in a rather low Dublin public house—and consorting with questionable fellows. And yet he was the perfect gentleman.

Sir Sefton was an Englishman who had spent an industrious and frugal lifetime looking after British railway stations in the capacity of architect. With his pension and savings, he was well-to-do on retirement but, entertaining great fear of his native country's Socialist Chancellor, hastily setttled down in Dublin. Here—a man to whom in the past a small sherry seemed excess—he was induced by some demon to drink a glass of Irish Whiskey. It was the glass of doom.

The velocity of his disintegration was startling. He began to drink whiskey all day long—longer, indeed, than the licensing day, for he would rise at seven in the morning to visit the privileged taverns at the markets near the Four Courts.

At about two one day I saw him in a pub with three chaps I knew. I joined the group. Sir Sefton was truly very drunk and had trouble in plucking the particular star he wanted from the constellation of small ones that was arranged on the counter in front of him. Still, he had them all finished when the half-two closing was called. He ordered one of the chaps to call a taxi.

"We will all go to Amiens Street Station," he muttered, "for the holy hour."

I could not dissuade him. We went in the taxi. In the station bar, I ordered five small whiskeys.

"Are ye travellers?" the girl asked.

"We are," I said. I noticed that Sir Sefton was appraising the station's face with his old practised eye.

"I can't serve ye if ye haven't tickets," the girl said.

"Where are we supposed to be from?" I asked.

"Donabate."

Donabate! What a place to must be from, a rolling slobland pocked with cheap bungalows and shacks! I turned to go for the tickets, but Sir Sefton had heard. He held up a flat hand.

"Under no circumstances," he said. "Leave this to me."

He left the bar, heading for the ticket office, using that fast turn of speed which drinkers know to be the only hope of avoiding wild staggers. He returned and pressed five cardboards in my hand. I showed them to the girl and we got our drinks.

I lost sight of Sir Sefton for some weeks, but I was told that he was making a practice of these visits to Amiens Street at half-two, always buying a ticket to Donabate. Being near the station one day during the hour, I remembered this; I went in, bought a ticket to Donabate, and entered the bar. Yes, Sir Sefton Fleetwood-Crawshaye was there. He saluted me.

"Donabate?" he asked.

"Donabate," I said.

He nodded in a musing sort of way, and quietly attacked his drink.

"Do you know," he said after a pause, "I like this country. I should like to give some small service. I am still an architect, I hope. I understand lay-out. Donabate is very much in need of a survey—for that matter so is every town in Ireland. You will admit the main street could be improved. We need new churches, too, everywhere. Immense improvements need not be costly given skilled planning. . . ."

He trailed off into a meditation, reviving to mention the vital importance of squares, otherwise how can one hold huge public meetings? I did not find this amusing. It saddened me.

Each time I met him thereafter, his poor brain had further softened. Overcrowding in Donabate must be ended by the simple expedient of erecting great blocks of flats. The American steel-and-concrete technique would be admirable in such a setting. A race-course would bring much-needed revenue to the town, and were there not great expanses of sand nearby, ideal for gallops? But one must not overlook the necessity for a proper car park, with restaurants, cinemas, and so forth.

On another occasion he discussed, though rather tentatively, the founding of a university at Donabate.

"But first," was ever his final cry, "the survey! The survey first!"

He meant it, too. He was determined some day to go to Donabate to do the survey.

One day, as was deposed at the inquest, he entered the bar, showed his ticket and had a drink. He was carrying the reel of tape surveyors use. He kept looking at the clock and suddenly made a wild exit from the bar, tried to enter a train which was just moving off, fell between the train and the platform and was instantly killed.

I have said he was the perfect gentleman, incapable of a mean act. A month after his death, I put on a raincoat I had not worn for a long time. In the pocket were the five tickets Sir Sefton Fleetwood-Crawshaye insisted on buying the first day we went to the station. Pathetic but noble tokens! They were First Class!

[*The Irish Journal*, posthumously published]

* * *

Our . . . eager, and no doubt, affectionate, Irish wives must be made to see that though eating is . . . a necessary business, and . . . parboiling is an interesting way to treat objects intended for vulgar carnal provisionment . . . yet, not all sublunar Offal is really suitable for this purpose; alarm clocks, umbrellas, wax flowers, telescopes, carpets, wall-paper and hardwall plaster are instances of a few of such not terribly edible things. Another more obvious one is the interesting worsted bomb of which this evening I have been speaking.

One wonders what absent-minded *colleen* first dimly, myopically dropped one of these valuable reverse-calf objects into the melting pot and then . . . obstinate, though charming . . . insisted that poor Tadhg . . . eat it The delirious, half laughable, whole lethal recipe spread from wife to wife, from mother to mother, from generation to generation until at the present day there exists scarcely an adult male in this island who has not at some time or other actually performed the intensely music-hall magic of . . . *eating a . . . turnip*! (I mean, it's like drinking that most vitriolic of embrocations, milk!)

* * *

I found myself going homewards the other evening, not in a cab but in that odd mobile apartment with the dun-coloured wall-paper, a brown study. Long long thoughts occupied my mind. I was examining myself according to occult criteria which substitute for 'time', 'death' and other gaffes of the frail human intellect that blinding instant of vision which simultaneously begins, explains and closes all. Such insights as I have been vouchsafed give warning that all of us will encounter serious trouble in due time, for the upper limits of our aerial 'existences' bristle with complexities. Your politician will assure you that the post-war world is the great problem that looms ahead, but those of us who do not spend all our time in this universe well know that the real problem will be the post-world war.

Yet going home that evening I was remembering my small self, thinking of all that had happened through the years, re-examining the mélange of achievement and disillusion that I call my life. Praise I have received, blame also: yet how vain are both, how easy of purchase in the mart of men! I feel that one thing at least stands forever to my credit in the golden ledgers—the rather generous provision I made for the widow Manity and her children when her husband—my best friend—died after a long and painful illness. Poor suffering Hugh Manity, I kept the promise I made to him on his death bed.

When I reached home I was in an odd mood. I felt . . . old. Age and achievement hath like brandy a mellowness yet withal a certain languor. My daughter was in the next room humming and putting on her hat. I called her.

'Hullo, Bella. Sit down for a moment, will you.'

'Yes, Daddy. What's the matter?'

A long watery stare out of the window. The pipe is produced and fiddled with.

'Bella . . . how old are you?"

'Nineteen, daddy. Why?'

Another frightful pause.

'Bella, we've known each other for a long time. Nineteen years. I remember you when you were very small. You were a good child.'

'Yes, daddy.'

More embarrassment.

'Bella . . . I have been a good daddy to you, haven't I? At least I have tried to be.'

'You are the best daddy in the world. What *are* you trying to tell me?'

'Bella . . . I want to say something to you. I'm . . . I'm going to give you a surprise Bella . . . please don't think ill of me but . . . but . . . but, Bella—'

With a choking noise she has jumped up and has her arms about me.

'O daddy, I know, I know! I know what you are going to say! You ... you're not my daddy at all. You found me one day ... when I was very small ... when I was a tiny baby ... and you took me home ... and cared for me ... and watched over me ... and now you find you have been in love with me all these years ...'

With a scream I was on my feet. Soon I was racing down the street to the local cinema, clutching in my inside pocket the old-fashioned Mauser, a present from Hamar Greenwood for doing a few jobs for him at a time when it was neither profitable nor popular. I reached the cinema and demanded to see the manager. Soon the suave pink-jowled ruffian appeared and invited me into his private office. Very shortly afterwards two shots rang out and I sincerely hope I will be given an opportunity of explaining to the jury that I had merely wished to suggest to my daughter that as a father of a family who had worked and scraped for years to keep other people in luxury, it was about time I should be relieved of the humiliation of having to press my own trousers.

[*The Best of Myles*]

IDEAS OF O'DEA

When it suits their book, some people do not scruple to drop hints in public places that I am opposed to poppet valves. It is, of course, a calumny. The fact is that I supported poppet valves at a time when it was neither profitable nor popular. As far back as the old Dundalk days, when the simple v. compound controversy raised questions almost of honour with the steam men of the last generation, I was an all-out doctrinaire compounder and equally an implacable opponent of the piston valve. I saw even then that the secret of a well-set poppet valve —short travel—was bound to win out against prejudice. I remember riding an old 2–8–2 job on a Cavan side-road, and my readers can believe me or not as they please, but we worked up 5392 I.H.P. with almost equal steaming in the H.P. and L.P. cylinders, a performance probably never equalled on the grandiose 'Pacific' jobs so much talked about across the water. The poppet valves ('pops' old Joe Garrigle called them—R.I.P., a prince among steam men) gave us very sharp cut-off. And we were working on a side road, remember.

There is not the same stuff in the present generation as there was in the one gone by, trite as that remark may sound. In hotels, public houses, restaurants, theatres and other places where people gather. I hear on all sides sneers and jibes at compound jobs. They eat coal and oil, they are unbalanced thermo-dynamically, they 'melt' on high cut-off, and all the rest of it. Really, it is very tiresome. Your old-time steam man understood nothing but steam, but at least he understood it thoroughly. To see some of the sprouts that are abroad nowadays and to hear their innocent gabble about matters that were thrashed out in the Dundalk shops fifty years ago is to wonder whether man is moving forward at all through the centuries.

* * *

I happened to glance at my hands the other day and noticed they were yellow. Conclusion: I am growing old (though I claim that I am not yet too old to dream). Further conclusion: I should set about writing my memoirs. Be assured that such a book would be remarkable, for to the extraordinary adventures which have been my lot there is no end. (Nor will there be.) Here is one little adventure that will give you some idea.

Many years ago a Dublin friend asked me to spend an evening with him. Assuming that the man was interested in philosophy and knew that immutable truth can sometimes be acquired through the kinesis of disputation, I consented. How wrong I was may be judged from the fact that my friend arrived at the rendezvous in a taxi and whisked me away to a licensed premises in the vicinity of Lucan. Here I was induced to consume a large measure of intoxicating whiskey. My friend would not hear of another drink in the same place, drawing my attention by nudges to a very sinister-looking character who was drinking stout in the shadows some distance from us. He was a tall cadaverous person, dressed wholly in black, with a face of deathly grey. We left and drove many miles to the village of Stepaside, where a further drink was ordered. Scarcely to the lip had it been applied when both of us noticed—with what feelings I dare not describe—the same tall creature in black, residing in a distant shadow and apparently drinking the same glass of stout. We finished our own drinks quickly and left at once, taking in this case the Enniskerry road and entering a hostelry in the purlieus of that village. Here more drinks were ordered but had hardly appeared on the counter when, to the horror of myself and friend, the sinister stranger was discerned some distance away, still patiently dealing with his stout. We swallowed our drinks raw and hurried out. My friend was now thoroughly scared, and could not be dissuaded from making for the far-away hamlet of Celbridge; his idea was that, while another drink was absolutely essential, it was equally essential to put as many miles as possible between ourselves and the sinister presence we had just left. Need I say what happened? We noticed with relief that the public house we entered in Celbridge was deserted, but as our eyes became more accustomed to the poor light, *we saw him again:* he was standing in the gloom, a more terrible apparition than ever before, ever more menacing with each meeting. My friend had purchased a bottle of whiskey and was now dealing with the stuff in large gulps. I saw at once that a crisis had been reached and that desperate action was called for.

'No matter where we go,' I said, 'this being will be there unless we can now assert a superior will and confound evil machinations that are on foot. I do not know whence comes this apparition, but certainly of this world it is not. It is my intention to challenge him.'

My friend gazed at me in horror, made some gesture of remonstrance, but apparently could not speak. My own mind was made up. It was me or this diabolical adversary: there could be no evading the clash of wills, only one of us could survive. I finished my drink with an assurance I was far from feeling and marched straight up to the presence. A nearer sight of him almost stopped the action of my heart; here undoubtedly was no man but some spectral emanation from the tomb, the undead come on some task of inhuman vengeance.

'I do not like the look of you,' I said, somewhat lamely.

'I don't think so much of you either,' the thing replied; the voice was cracked, low and terrible.

'I demand to know,' I said sternly, 'why you persist in following myself and my friend everywhere we go.'

'I cannot go home until you first go home,' the thing replied. There was an ominous undertone in this that almost paralysed me.

'Why not?' I managed to say.

'Because I am the—taxi-driver!'

Out of such strange incidents is woven the pattern of what I am pleased to call my life.

[*The Best of Myles*]

GETTING THE CREEPS*

SCENE, *which will be the same for entire series, is an old-fashioned (no electronic nonsense here) railway signal box. To the (viewer's) right is a battery of 6 shiny levers, exactly resembling the beer-pulls of a pub. There are a few plain chairs and on parts of the walls which are not glass there are printed notices, not necessarily legible.*

Jimmy is leaning back in his chair, smoking, in expansive mood. Sylvester has just come in, and is looking a bit solemn.

JIMMY: More luck, Sylvester. Anny sign of Ignatius?

SYLVESTER: Not a word. I don't know whether he's married or single, dead or alive. Tell me this much. Mr O.

JIMMY: Yiss, Sylvester? What ails ya?

SYL: Do ya ever walk in yer sleep?

JIMMY: Wan thing I never done in me life is walk in me sleep. But I'll tell you a damn good wan.

SYL: Hah? What's that?

JIMMY: I walk in *other people's sleep.*

SYL: Ah, now, look at here, Mr O., don't be trying yer tricks on me like a three-card man.

JIMMY: Me dear man, I'm SARIOUS. I do walk in other people's sleep and it worries me sometimes, because I can never be sure how I behave or even what I say.

SYL: How could you walk in other people's sleep for goodness' sake?

JIMMY: Look at. The Maggot Byrne is never done walking in his sleep. Thinks nothing of gettin' up in the middle of the night, putting on th'oul brown coat over his nightshirt, the cawbogue on the head, and off with him down Grand Canal Street on his tod, never-adamn if there's a gale blowing, or it's hail, rain and snowballs.

---

* This and the following three sketches are from *The Ideas of O'Dea,* a television series of weekly fifteen-minute segments in the life of a railway watchman, starring Ireland's beloved comedian Jimmy O'Dea.

SYL [*aghast*]: Ah no. Isn't that terrible?

JIMMY: I wouldn't mind oney he meets ME every time he does it.

SYL: Ah, now, for goodness sake! And you're at home safe and sound asleep in yer own bed?

JIMMY: 'Course I am. IF I found meself in Grand Canal Street at three in the mornin, I'd consider meself a head-case. But if I knew I'd meet the Maggot Byrne there and stop to talk to him, well ... that would be curtains entirely. I'd make straight for Mounyjoy [Mountjoy Prison] and ask the crowd there to take me in.

SYL [*Head bent, pondering*]: Be the hokey, it's a quare position to be in. Mean to say, suppose you were to heave a brick through a shop winda when you're out in the middle of the night walking in the Maggot Byrne's sleep? Could ya be lagged be the Gairds [police]?

JIMMY: In me sleep?

SYL [*Frowning, confused*]: Well ... what would happen? I mean ... the poor publican's winda was gone.

JIMMY: I COULD be lagged, Ignatius ... pro-vided there was a rozzer [lay-about, lout] walking in the Maggot Byrne's sleep as well as meself.

SYL [*Relieved*]: Ah, I think I see it, Mr O. Even if ya thrun a bicycle through the winda while you're walking in the Maggot's sleep, the winda would be o.k. in the mornin, and no harm done.

JIMMY: Yiss. Suppose, though, Sylvester, that I'm out at night walking in the Maggot Byrne's sleep, get annoyed, grab the Maggot be the belt of his coat and thrun him into the canal. What then?

SYL: Lord, that would be sarious. Can the Maggot swim?

JIMMY: With a couple of life-buoys and a boat under him, I suppose he could.

SYL: Well, Mr O., I don't know. I don't see how you could be charged with murder. I think that would be a case of suicide be persons unknown. What makes the Maggot Byrne walk in his sleep?

JIMMY: Nobody knows, the Maggot least of all. It's not malt, because malt gives a man deep ... sound ... fasteddious sleep, like a healthy baby. I think meself ... ah, I shouldn't say it.

SYL: Shouldn't say what?

JIMMY: I was going to say I thought he used too much cheap hair oil.

SYL: Hair oil? Lord, I never heard of the like of that interfere with a man's sleep. I mean, the hair on yer head goes asleep the same as the rest of yer body.

JIMMY: Ah, me dear man, ya don't twig. The Maggot Byrne wouldn't waste hair oil on his hair. HE DRINKS IT!

SYL: For goodness' sake, Mr O.? [*Horrified*] Oh Lord save us! [*Mimics*] A glass of hair oil, plee-ase, and baby soda. What's the world coming to?

JIMMY: That's why I asked you about Ignatius. I hope he's not knocking about with bad companions and going into the pubs.

SYL: All we're sure is that he's supposed to be on his holliers, and noboddy knows where.

JIMMY: It's not often I take even a pint meself nowadays, Sylvester. But I seen things in th'oul days that would frighten ya.

SYL: I believe ya did take a jar once upon a time, Mr O.?

JIMMY: Ah well, I suppose I was a little bit partial if I was led astray. Didya ever hear of the Mouse Brannigan?

SYL: The Mouse Brannigan? No, never.

JIMMY: Well, the Mouse wasn't a bad oul [fellow] at all but he was partial. Dya understand me? He was very . . . partial. I was mindin me own business wan evenin years ago when the Mouse walked into the pub, bought a glass of malt for himself and a small wan for me . . . down the hatch . . . then dragged me out to the taxi, and away with us like the hammers of hell to Stepaside.

SYL: Ah, I know that little place, two pubs and a Gairds' barracks, isn't that right?

JIMMY: Yiss. This was in th'oul days, when the pubs was open all night to the bonna fyds.* There was oney a few in that pub but we seen a little dark oul fella in the corner lookin hard at us over a pint. After a drink, the Mouse said we'd move on. Away with us to the Lamb Doyle's. We got a decent enough drink there but, Sylvester, who do we see screwin us far away in the gloom of the corner? I'd swear it was the same, dark, little oul fella. Let's get clear outa here, says I to the Mouse. We didn't say annything to each other about yer man, but we were glad enough to get out. Off with us up the mountain to Glencullen. There's a pub there, of course. The Mouse was drinkin malt be the glass.

SYL: Now, don't tell me, Mr O. that—

---

* Anyone who had traveled a certain distance from home to reach the pub.

JIMMY: Sylvester, you're right. I got a fierce fright, and so did the Mouse. In a corner again, this time with a bottle of stout, was that man again. Eye-dentical.

SYL: Well that must have put the heart across you.

JIMMY: It nearly killed the Mouse. He got as white as a sheet, swallyed his malt, and tried to hurry me out be th'arm. The poor fella shaking like a leaf.

SYL: I wouldn't blame the man. If I was there I'd have a fit. Talk about walkin in yer sleep!

JIMMY: At the door the Mouse gev me a grip and says: I'm carryin to-night, says he, and expense is no object. We're under evil influence says he. We'll get to hell outa here and hare for Lucan.

SYL: Well, that was some journey in the middle of the night, Mr O.

JIMMY: My dear man, the Mouse and I wouldn't think twice of belting off down to Tullamore. I'm not windy, dya know, but there's a limit. In anny case, we druv like hell to Lucan. It was a relief to see the trees flying by in the dark. Well, we got there, pulled up at the pub, and in with us.

SYL: I'm saying nothing.

JIMMY: You're a wise man, Sylvester. The Mouse had hardly ordered our malt WHEN I SEEN HIM. Yes, the same, small . . . dark . . . sinister . . . diabolical oul fella. Ah well [Sylvester] I had enough. I couldn't face anymore that night. I swallyed me malt, pulled down me hat, marched straight over to him, stared him in his dirty face, and says I: Evil man, I bid you in the Lord's name be gone!

SYL: Did he answer?

JIMMY: I'll go when I'm ped, says he. I'm the blooming taximan!

THE MEANING OF MALT

Jimmy O'Dea is seated, reading a newspaper. His companion Ignatius will have to do most of his acting visually because he is a stupid, vacant gawm who has little to say, the little being stupid and meaningless. His lolling attitude is in contrast to the alertness of O'Dea.

A little bell tinkles musically. Jimmy rises, puts the paper aside and listens intently. A distant whistle is heard.

JIMMY: Ah-ha. The seven forty-two. It'll be Rafferty again tonight, I'll go bail.

[*He pulls down one of the levers, no easy job. Then he sits down again.*]

IGNATIUS: Ah yiss. Yiss.

JIMMY: Know what I'm going to tellya? In twenty-wan years in this box I don't believe I have ever pulled down wan of them signal yokes without half-expectin a pint of plain to come out below somewhere. And isn't it the right eejit I'd look if it did come, and me here without a tumbler to catch it in! [*Sniggers.*]

IGN: Yiss. A proper cod-mur-yowler.

JIMMY: It'd make ya laugh. Here is me a signalman pulling pints for himself in the box, getting mouldy, forgetting to stop a train going into a single-line section after he's let-in another travelling in the opposite direction, and then . . . CRASH! And a thremendious death-roll. Yiss. Drinking on these premises is, of course, TEE-TOTALLY PROHIBITED. Yiss.

IGN: Ah, that's the way, of course.

[*A loud and sustained crashing noise is heard, off. Jimmy listens but does not look out.*]

JIMMY: Ah yiss, that's Rafferty, not a doubt of it. Sixty-wan miles an hour, and a speed restriction here of forty-five. That man . . . that man will get into trouble sooner than he thinks. It's not that he drinks too much but that he doesn't understand what drink IS. No use talking to him, of course. He knows all about drink and everything else. Stout or whiskey, it's all the wan—down the hatch with it and then out with the fags. A walkin bucket of pison, that's what that man is.

IGN: That class of a man should be locked up.

JIMMY: Yiss. 'Course, pison, that's a thremediously big compairtment of human debauchment in itself. Thremendiously big. Matter of fact there's pison all around us—in th'air, in the light, in things we ate and drink. How manny people have died roarin after goin out at the break o'day to gather a plateful of musharooms? Ah yiss.

IGN: I often heard them is dangerous men to sit down and ate. Taking your life in yer hands.

JIMMY: Bring the musharooms back, on with the kettle for the cuppa tay, four slices of toast, and then into the pan with the musharooms, and there y'are—a breakfast fit for the King of the Great Blasket Island.

IGN: Yiss. And bags of trouble coming up?

JIMMY: What happens me man half an hour afterwards? He starts yelpin out of him, houldin the gizzard, sweatin like a trooper on Vinegar Hill, and shoutin for the neighbours. A looderamawn of an oul fella comes in and says WHAT AILS YA, puttin the wind up like that. Me man lets another roar, and says he feels like he'd swallied a coil of rusty barbed wire that was now given him blood pis'nin' in the stummick and to get him a docthor for the love an honour of Saint Patrick. Th'oul fella says Hould Hard till I get to the dispinsery on me bike. Ah well, I suppose we all know the answer. . . .

IGN: Yiss, begob. Docthor or no docthor, yer man is well and truly banjaxed?

JIMMY: Be the time the docthor arrives, me man's face is . . . puce-coloured.

IGN: Well shure wasn't it the price of him?

JIMMY: What in heaven's name have ya been doin to yerself, me good man? says the doc. Have ya been on a batter drinkin pints of whitewash? Yer temperature is wan O four.

IGN: What woulda slob like that know about temper'ture?

JIMMY: Ah docthor, says me poor man, I swallied nothin oney a bit of toast, a cuppa tay and a little plate of musharooms I picked this mornin. Me stummick feels like the citadel of Sevastipol. That weeds you ett, says the doc, was NO MUSHAROOMS. Them things was pisonous fungus, fatal to man an' baste. Stay aisy there till I get me pump from the cair.

IGN: The doc was a fast worker.

JIMMY: Ah now for pity's sake, doc, says me segocia the patient (his face now a nice tinge of black and tan) me name's not DUNLOP and I don't want to be blun up like a tyre on a lurry.

Shut yer clack, says the doc, it's me stummick pump I mane.

Yer man got better after seven days in bed, with nuthin going into him bar beef-tea and gru-ell. But it was a close shave, and ya could nearly hear the beatin of the wings of th'angel of death.

IGN: If ya ett nuthin at all ye were right.

JIMMY: The brother wanst treated himself to a tin of salmon from Japan. What happened an hour later? Collapse, prose-stration and profuse paralysis. Sent for the docthor, of course. You're pisoned, says the doc, but I have here what we call an Auntie Dote. He gets out his needle, fills it up with stuff the colour of water and then GOODBYE—he pumps all this how-are-ya into the brother's backside.

IGN: For desperate diseases ya have desperate remedies, of course. Yiss.

JIMMY: What was that Auntie Dote that ya gav me, asks the brother. Mostly strychneen, says the doc. Some people asks me is whiskey pison. Come here till I tellya, Ignatius. Whiskey is med from grain, like bread. It is the grandest nourishment anny man could ask for, it loosens up th'arteries, smoothes down the nairves, and gives the party takin it a luvly complexion. It does the heart good, if ya know what I mane.

IGN: Aw, nuthin wrong with a glass o' malt.

JIMMY: But . . . But . . . another particular thing arrives in the fermentation of the grain. Know what THAT is? Mister-me-friend FUSIAL OIL! And that's the boy that makes the difference. When ya have an honest firm makin whiskey or stout, the amount of fusial oil that comes natural is small, just enough to give a man a kick. But never forget this—FUSIAL OIL IS PISON! That stuff that ya got from the doc with a needle—morphia—is pison too, but the dose is very small and does ya good. Do ya twig?

IGN: Ah sairtintly.

JIMMY: If ya start givin yerself fusial oil ad lib, ye'll get headaches and a ferocious thirst, next convulsions, and at the heel of the hunt, you're lucky if ya don't pass out and die. Ah? Isn't that a nice state of affairs? Too much fusial oil will drive a man mad.

IGN: There's no livin doubt, ya'd want to look out for yerself.

JIMMY: The brother knows a lot about this. Wan day he was visitin a distillery—not in Dublin, by the way—and he sees a great big tanker pullin into the yard. It was like wan of the big perthrol yokes, but there was no name on the side. What's this, says the brother to wan of the distillery men—milk for the firm's canteen? Atachal, says yer man, that tank is full of fusial oil. Do ya want to kill the people, asks the brother. Ah no, says this hop-off-me-thumb, but we like to wake the customers up. They don't expect to get just slop, and we don't sell them slop. Our stuff puts life in them. Fair enough, says the brother, but I think the right place for your crowd is Mountjoy.

I told ya, Ignatius, that fusial oil can drive a man mad. There was fierce brutalities in the first World War. The Jairmins was very strong in some parts of the Front, and now and again stuck in some position where the Allies thought no power on earth could dislodge them. What did the generals do? They sent for a detachment of the Irish millytairy that was in the war. The Lord preserve us but the slaughter was feracious. It's not that the Irish crowd dislodged the Jairmins. They killed the whole damn lot of them, and took all their machine guns. And who was this Irish crowd, waaldya think?

IGN: A crowd from Cork I'll go bail.

JIMMY: Wrong! The Dubalin Fusialcers, of course, every man-jack full of whiskey that was ninety per cent fusial oil.

But there's a time and a place for everything, and I warn everybody to be careful when it comes to havin a glass of malt in a strange public house. Never forget the foe, the F.O.—FUSIAL OIL!

TH' ELECTRIC

SIGNAL-BOX SCENE. *Present, in addition to Jimmy, is the other charac-ter, designated in this script* IGNATIUS. *The latter tends to loll and loaf in contrast to Jimmy's alertness.*

JIMMY: Ah yiss. There's a lot to be said AGAINST nightwork ... and FOR nightwork. Know what I mane, Ignatius? When a man is locked up in this box at night, what harm can come to him? What harm can he do?

IGNATIUS: Oh, nuthin at all—bar he had a bottle of malt smuggled in with him on the QT.

JIMMY: *Malt?* Whatya collooderin about? I'm a pint man and ya know that very well. I don't care a tinker's tararra for a bottle of malt. Manys the time in here on me own I do put the kettle on and bile it up on the ring there. To make grog or punch, wouldya say? Atachall. A couple of cups of good, wholesome, strong tea, finest drink in the world, that and wan or two Marie biscuits.

IGN: Yiss, fair enough. The very thing to keep you awake to be ready for Drivers Rafferty or O'Shaughnessy when they come roarin through the night.

JIMMY: Yiss. Ah, manys the time we hear of CITY LIGHT and it's a thing that nivver had anny commutable attraction for me at all. Ya can kape all that jazz. And what is it? Sinful cinymatograph films, slobs of fellas reelin in and outa pubs after floggin half the week's wages on brandy-wine, and poor little bowsies of teddy-boys steerin pointed hawsies into them gilded palaces and shovellin ice cream into them. What sort of a life is that for goodness' sake?

IGN: Yiss, and fights in dance halls.

JIMMY: Ah, don't bother me. It's the rozzers I pity. Look at what they have to contend with, hah? Dial 999. By god that crowd would want 25,000 cars to get around in.

IGN: Yiss, and 30,000.

[*Pause. Cigarettes produced*]

JIMMY: But dya know, Ignatius—city lights. I do often think that light's a marvelous thing. Th'electric, I mane. But no—I don't mane light be itself. Th'electric current is what I'm talkin about. When Rafferty or some of that crowd is comin down the line, what happens? When he's half a mile away a sweet little bell tinkles in this little signal-box of mine. Th'electric wire is there to manipulate the bell, dya understand me. A miraculous invention that keep trains movin all over the world, all over the known globe, protectin the lives of passengers in the shape of people, cows, dogs and maybe race horses worth £10,000 apiece. Ah yiss. But I'll tellya a funny thing about th'electricity, Ignatius. A very funny thing BE-DAMN BUT NOBODY KNOWS WHAT IT IS! Hah? Isn't that quare wan?

IGN: I'll tellya wan crowd that knows what it is. Yer men in American jails that is sent to the chair.

JIMMY: No. You're wrong there, Ignatius. Them poor gurriers knows th'EFFECT of th'electricity but that doesn't say they know what IT IS. They haven't a clue. And if they did, of course, they wouldn't have lived to tell. Dya folly me?

IGN: That's true, of course. Yaaa.

JIMMY: The Jairmins. Dya get me? The bould Jerries. Electricity is a sort of power that's hidden in water, that's the secret. And the big question at wan time was to find a way of suckin th'electricity OUTA the water. That's what ya call a six-marker. Th'electricity can't ESCAPE from water without being helped. Never forget that, Ignatius. Never forget that there's enough electricity in a bucket of water t'electriocute a bullock. And yerself as well.

IGN: Yiss. And I suppose there's the danger in a glass of water itself?

JIMMY: There could be villinious slaughter in a shower of rain. But come here till I tellya. What happened in th'early days of the Free State? I'll tellya what. The bould Paddy McGilligan wakes up and sees that the River Shannon, absolutely stuffed with th'electricity, is going to waste. The country's priceless power being washed away into the sea and th'unfortunate people here foosterin about with candles and lanterns and matches and ile-lamps, and the streets of Dublin lit be gas. Livin in the Middle Ages, that's what the people was. But Paddy McGilligan, as bould a segocia of a Sinn Feiner as ever wore a hat, wasn't goin to stand for anny more of that jazz. What does he do? Sends across the sea for the Jairmins. And with the result was we got the Shannon Scheme.

IGN: Ah yiss. A milestone in th'history of the Shan Van Vocht, ya might say.

JIMMY: What the Jairmins done was to trap the water into bloody big steel vats at Ardnacrusha and treat it with secret chemicals to get th'electricity out of it, and then let it go on its way empty. Dya know what we call that, Ignatius? A SURPRISING ACHIEVE- MENT OF ELECTRICITY SCIENCE, that's what. McGilligan deserves to be above in the Park today. [*Raises hand*] Know what yer other man called the Shannon Scheme? MacEntee, I mane. Know the name HE gev it?

IGN: That's yer little man from the Falls Road?

JIMMY: Yiss. A white elephant, says he. A WHITE ELEPHANT, be gob! Wouldn't it make ya laugh? Ah? Canya bate it?

IGN: Ah, he was a young fella in them days, of course.

JIMMY: The white elephant was a bit of cock and bull if you ask me.

IGN: Elephants, mindya, is fond of showerin themselves with water.

JIMMY: Well, I'll tellya this much. Me little bell in the corner is worked be a white elephant. It's a white elephant that gives us that light. Yer own missus, Ignatius, cooks yer dinner with a white elephant.

IGN: Last Christmas her nabs got a shock offa the same white elephant.

JIMMY: The radio, the tellyvision and the tellyphone is all worked be white elephants. What am I talkin about—th'uncle above in Skerries is SHAVED be a white elephant. The sister's lovely hair is washed and dried be a white elephant. Wouldya mind tellin me what makes the clock in the station-master's office go?

IGN: I suppose the decent man winds it?

JIMMY: Atachall. A white elephant makes it go. We must have HERDS of white elephants in this blooming country. And tell me, Ignatius, since the white elephant works the tellyphone, what wouldya say is the name of a call from here to Cork?

IGN: Aw, well, a long-distance call, I suppose.

JIMMY: Atachall. Atachall man. A TRUNK call, of course.

ST. PATRICK'S DAY

SIGNAL BOX SCENE. *Jimmy is sitting down, engrossed in a newspaper. Ignatius is lolling on another chair, smoking. Jimmy shakes head and gestures at paper. He looks up, frowning.*

JIMMY: Yiss. Saint Patrick's Day. Dya know, we might all be makin a mistake, a HIDYUS mistake. The brother says there was never anny such man as Saint Patrick.

IGNATIUS: Ah come here now, Jimmy, the national Apostle. That's no sort of talk to be givin out of you.

JIMMY: I'm oney tellin ya what the brother says. So far as I'm consairned, I have always been all FOR St. Patrick's Day. I think I've seen more Patrick's Day processions than anny man alive. What am I talkin about—didn't I walk in TWO of them. Th'oul fella was an Irish Forester with a green clawhammer on him and in nineteen and O twelve he med me step out in the brigade of the Glasnevin Branch of the Gaelic League with A KILT ON ME, man, yiss, and a pipe band in front of us playing the Rakes of Malla.

IGN: That must have been a great sight—yerself in kilts and a plaad over yer shoulder and the big knobbly knees on full display for all to see.

JIMMY: Oh now I looked damn well in them days. But th'oul fella would do yer heart good. There was no half measure there. He was a Forester, a Parnellite, a Votes-for-Wimmin man, a Larkinite and a Gaelic Leaguer. Oh by gob yiss, guramahagut and beedahusht for further orders. Wan St. Patrick's Day when a gurrier of a parade sergeant barked out "Eyes Right Passin the Parnell Monument!" th'oul fella turns a hard eye on him and says he, "Are ya not ashamed that ya can't speak yer own language or are ya an Irishman at all?" "Parnell didn't know Irish," says yer other man. "Well be the powers," says th'oul fella, "if ya gev Parnell a glass of Scotch he'd soon let ya know whether he know Irish or not." Wasn't it good? If ya gev Parnell a glass of Scotch, ah?

IGN: That was a proper choke off, and good enough for him. How much Irish did Wolfe Tone know?

JIMMY: In the St. Patrick's procession of nine teen aught six th'oul fella, clawhammer an' all, wheeled the oney Irish-made bike in the world, a grand machine with bars of solid iron mad be Pierce of Wexford. In them days, of course, there was none of this jazz that was to come later about all the boozers been shut and refreshments for man and baste totally prohibited.

IGN: Yiss. That's changed now. Here's what I want to know. What's going to happen the Dog Show at Balle's Bridge, the oney place where ya CUD get a drink. Shure there won't be a soul there now bar the boulers an' the judges.

JIMMY: You're right there, Ignatius. In th'oul days it wasn't a mortal sin to swally a glass of malt to keep the cold out on the seventeenth of March, naw, nor a pint aither. That was a new sin invented be the politicians when we got the Free State, as a result of all them processions. Ah, God look down on us all but it takes time to learn a bit of sense.

IGN: Shure in Brian Beru's time there was no licensing laws of anny description AT ALL.

JIMMY: But o'here till I tell ya. The brother was on to me a couple of weeks ago about all this ST. Patrick's Day turn-out. First of all he was complainin about the shenanigans that goes on in America on the seventeenth of March. It was as bad this year as anny year. They dyed the Ohio River and the Mississippi green. Walk into a pub in New York and order a glass of HARP—and that's the right name for a drink on St. Patrick's Day. What happened? You get it all right but it's coloured green. Hah? HAH? That night ya go to a hop or a hooley or anny class of a dance, there's great gas and grand music on the fiddles and the bagpipes, a good time is had be all, but all the gerrls' HAIR IS GREEN. Do ya folly me?

IGN: That's sairtintly carryin things a bit far. Green lipstick too, I'll go bail.

JIMMY: Suppose you go in somewhere for a cuppa tay. Ya get it O.K. but what about the milk? GREEN! If a cop writes you a ticket for parkin yer car in the wrong place on that day, you're supposed to be pleased about it all because th'ink in his fountain pen is green. A grurrier out of Syngapore might offer ya a black cigarette anny time but on St. Patrick's Day a fella from Boston would be sure to give ya a GREEN cigarette. You see so much green over there that ya get green in the face and if ya get a pain in yer leg, you're sure it's gangrene. Isn't it the limit? Don't be talkin man.

IGN: The green eye of the little yalla god.

JIMMY: But to come back to the brother. He says there's a whole crowd of people goin, some of them clever wans that writes books, that say there was never anny Saint Patrick that it's all a yarn and a cock and bull story. There's another crowd that says that St. Patrick was a Protestant and thought nuthin of atin' half a sheep for his dinner of a Frida. Hah? But listen here, Ignatius. There's a couple of fellas in th'university that says all the dates about St. Patrick is wrong and furthermore—FURTHERMORE—that there was TWO Saint Patricks. Can ya bate that? TWO of yer holy men from across the say!

IGN: Well, I suppose that means that we should have two St. Patrick's Days, two processions, and two shell-outs of a tanner for a bit of shamrock. If y'ask me ya can have too much of a good thing.

JIMMY: And here's a good wan. The brother met an oul fella below in Wiekla town and yer man said straight out that there was no Saint Patrick and that the whole yarn was invented be Strongbow or somebody. The brother asked him, if that was true, how come there was no snakes in Ireland? Know what th'oul fella done? Laughed in the brother's face. Me dear man, says he, when I was a young man settin out to make me fortune, I first emiograted to Australia. There was work to be had there but it was too hard and the grub was something fierce. With the result was I continued me travels to New Zealand. Ever hear tell of New Zealand? Right. I'll tell ya wan thing about New Zealand. *There isn't a single snake in the whole place.*

IGN: Is that a fact? Don't tell me there was a third St. Patrick that went out there? In a currach?

JIMMY: Well the brother checked on that in the National Museum and be gob th'oul fella was dead right. There's not wan snake in all New Zealand.

IGN: Well, that seems to be a vote against a genuine Saint Patrick in Ireland.

JIMMY: Now looks here, Ignatius. If there was no Saint Patrick, how do we know we're Christians at all? If there was no Saint Patrick we might be no different than the heathen Chinee.

IGN: Shure the rale oul Irish were eye-dolitors, with witch doctors and fellas with rings on their noses.

JIMMY: I don't think this is a situation we can afford to take lyin down. The Gov'ment will have to step in. There's nuthin for it but to set up a Commission embracin all Parties and churches and interests to find out (A) was there a Saint Patrick, (B) if there was, how manny was there, and (C) recommend penalties against people who are caught sayin that there was no Saint Patrick or allegin that there was five or six or too manny. Dya folly me?

IGN: I think you've put yer finger on the proper remed-yial measure, Jimmy.

JIMMY: So far as I'M concerned, Ignatius, I take this thing dead serious. I'm not goin to have some damn tinker or a smart-alec of a bowsie from God-knows-where tellin me to me face that I'm nuthin oney a pagan. ME A PAGAN? What's the world comin to atchall?

I was watching a hen walking about a garden recently. Occasionally it picked up dirt and ate it, but otherwise spent an hour of complete idleness. I fell to wondering why hens have two legs and later tried to reason out the pretext for giving a horse four of these useful jointed props. Why has a horse eight knees and a hen no knees at all? As to the legs, I decided that a horse has four because he is a draught animal and a beast of burden; his four legs give him more drawing power than two, just as four driving wheels enhance the utility of a locomotive. By why then has a rat four? Why not two-legged rats—(I seen them meself the day the new City Hall was opened in Cork)? Two-legged rats would probably roost like fowls and would perch on the rails of a bed rather than merely chew the wainscotting as they do every night at present. On the other hand, four-legged hens would present a problem as their roosting-perches would have to be made to measure individually according to the length of each fowl. Perhaps I'd better stop.

—The Best of Miles

THE MAN WITH
FOUR LEGS

A TRUE TALE OF TERROR FOR TELEVISION

CHARACTERS

MR. O'BRIEN, a youngish, debonair, well-spoken man.

MISS GLASS
MISS O'SHAUGHNESSY
MISS CURRAN
MISS CROTTY
MISS SCALLY

Office workers, all pests, as varied as possible in age, dress, accent and manner.

BARNEY BARNES, a bowsie.

MR. HICKORY, a veterinary surgeon.

SERGEANT O'HARA.

PART I

The screen shows Mr. O'Brien busy at his desk, which carries a heavy load of files, papers and books. There are two telephones and he frequently picks one up to originate a call or answer one. This goes on in dumb show for about five minutes but meanwhile his voice is heard on the sound track.

MR. O'BRIEN: My name's O'Brien. And there you see me in my office, working hard. I mean that. There was an inexhaustible stream of matters to be dealt with, questions to be answered, perplexities to be unravelled, and problems thought out. Nothing short of sheer hard work would be any good in that situation. Anybody who even paused would be engulfed by memoranda and files as by a veritable tidal wave. I need not trouble you with any account of what sort of work it was but it is important to know that my office was in a very large building containing perhaps 500 other workers. They were all office workers of one kind or another and, for Ireland, that was a big staff. [*Pause.*] I would say that about 400 of those people were women. [*Pause.*] There is one thing I must emphasize at the outset, and do please believe me, or at least try to. The story I am going to unfold is absolutely true. It happened to me, and it was horrible. Looking back on it, I now see I acted with incredible stupidity. All the time, I was the victim, step by step, of a slow, malignant destiny. It could have happened to you, too. Maybe it won't after this revelation I am going to make. Perhaps you can be wise after MY event. The experience I had was harrowing and it originated in the goodness of my heart in an attempt, for a paltry tuppence, to help the black babies in the heart of Africa. To give to the poor and unenlightened—that seems to be at least a simple and uncomplicated thing. You might imagine that it is not a thing that would lead you to see the inside of a jail. Very well. Just attend to this chronicle and try to take it seriously. [*Pause.*] Those ladies would not leave me alone. It would be an exaggeration to say that one of them invaded my room every day of the week, but in retrospect it seems like that. The money their visits cost me was trivial enough but I detested the instrusions, the interruptions in my attempts to concentrate. What, you may ask, of the time they took off from their own work, for you may be sure that I was by no means the only person they pestered? Some supervisor was badly to blame. Still, this was the method those ladies invented for making sure they would get to heaven. [*Pause.*] Oh well ... I suppose we must be patient and tolerant. But let me show you what happened in practice. [*Sound is now transferred to the actual scenes being played in the office.*]

o'BRIEN [*Startled by sudden opening of door*]: Oh! Hello.

MISS GLASS: Mr. O'Brien, I hope I'm not interrupting you. I'm Miss Glass.

o'BRIEN: How do you do, Miss Glass?

GLASS: I was wondering if you'd buy a ticket?

o'BRIEN: A ticket? How much are they?

GLASS: Only twopence each.

o'BRIEN: And what's the prize? A car?

GLASS: Ah no. [*Giggles.*] A sleeping doll.

o'BRIEN: What? What would I do with a sleeping doll?

GLASS: Oh well, if you won it your sister might like it.

o'BRIEN: My sister has real dolls of her own and they don't seem to do much sleeping.

GLASS: Well, I'm sure you have a little niece.

o'BRIEN: I suppose so. Well, give me 3 tickets.

[*Miss Glass quickly inscribes counterfoils, hands over the tickets and takes sixpence.*]

GLASS: Thanks very much, Mr. O'Brien. And I wish you the best of luck.

o'BRIEN: Thanks. Goodbye.

[*On the screen appears the notice*]:

ANOTHER DAY

[*The scene is the same, and a slatternly elderly lady enters, speaking with pronounced Cork accent.*]

MISS o'SHAUGNESSY: Ah, Mr. O'Brien, I'm on the war path. We want you to help a very deserving charity.

o'BRIEN: You are Miss—

o'SHAUGHNESSY: O'Shaughnessy.

o'BRIEN: Well, I suppose every charity is deserving. What's this one?

o'SHAUGHNESSY: It's a plan we have to buy boots for the poor newsboys.

o'BRIEN: Hmm. I suppose you're selling tickets?

o'shaughnessy: Yes. [*Flourishing book.*] Only threepence each.

o'brien: I'll risk two. Put me down on the counterfoils. What's the big prize?

o'shaughnessy: A genuine Chinese shawl. A lovely thing. Bee-eautiful.

o'brien: Very well. I suppose I can lie on it in the Phoenix Park when the weather takes up.

o'shaughnessy: Thanks very much. But ah, that would be a pity. You could hang it up on a wall in your home. It has a dragon and all on it.

o'brien: I might hang it up on the wall here, to frighten people away when I'm busy.

o'shaughnessy: Well, I know you're busy now. Thanks. [*Departs.*]

[*Screen*]:   ANOTHER DAY

[*Miss Scally enters, a good-looking and rather haughty character. She smiles distantly and waves a book.*]

miss scally: Mr. O'Brien, I'm selling tickets for a new bicycle.

o'brien: I see. How much are they?

scally: Only sixpence.

o'brien: All right. Give me two, even if I hate bikes. [*Phone rings. O'Brien takes up receiver irritably as he lays a shilling on desk and Miss Scally completes counterfoils.*] Yes, Mr. Farrell. That's correct. Yes. [*Long pause.*] The land is absolutely essential for the outfall works and your firm got ample notice of the situation. You can't blame us if you now stand to lose money. You shouldn't have built anything there, and I don't see any prospect of compensation. [*Pause.*] The needs of the community come first. Surely you must know that. [*Pause.*]Very well. Three o'clock tomorrow. I'll be here but it's all a waste of time. Goodbye.

scally: That's very good of you, Mr. O'Brien. Cheerio.

[*Screen*]:   ANOTHER DAY

[*Miss Crotty enters, a middle-aged large woman with a heavy Dublin accent.*]

MISS CROTTY: Mr. O'Brien, I'm gettin' ould and we're all gettin' ould. Some day we won't be able to do a hand's turn or hold down any class of a job.

O'BRIEN: You're Miss Crotty, I think? Yes, you speak nothing but the truth. I'm not feeling too well myself, even today. There is too much work here. Those telephones are always going off.

CROTTY: Ah, but I'm lookin' ahead. I've been going round here for the last few days sellin' tickets for a raffle to help the Old People's Home in Phibsboro.

O'BRIEN: You think you might be looking for a place there yourself some day?

CROTTY: I'm sairtin of it. Where else would I go?

O'BRIEN: Oh well . . . might yet marry a millionaire.

CROTTY: I might, right enough. Or win the Sweep and go and live in Monte Carlo. Look what happened to Princess Grace. Tuppence each. How many will I give you, Mr. O'Brien?

O'BRIEN: Three, I suppose.

CROTTY: Fair enough. [*Begins scribbling on counterfoils.*]

O'BRIEN: There's the cash. [*Gets up.*] There's a man waiting to see me outside. More trouble, more work, more worry. [*They leave together.*]

[*Screen*]:   ANOTHER DAY

[*Miss Curran enters, a nondescript, cranky sort of individual whose manner is one of gush.*]

MISS CURRAN: Ah, Mr. O'Brien, amn't I lucky to get you in. God bless you, I know you're always ready to help.

O'BRIEN: Help what?

CURRAN: Now don't you know. All my life there has been only one charity for me. The Black Babies.

O'BRIEN: Well, certainly Africa is much in everybody's mind nowadays. You're running a raffle, I suppose?

CURRAN: Indeed and I am. I run six of them every year, all on my own.

O'BRIEN: Do you really think you will make any real impression on Africa? I don't know how many tens of millions of people live there.

CURRAN: Mr. O'Brien, every little helps. Nourish and convert one youngster there, and who knows how many of his own people he will look after when he grows up?

O'BRIEN: True enough, I suppose. How much are your tickets?

CURRAN: Only twopence.

O'BRIEN: All right, I'll take six. What's the prize?

CURRAN: A lovely, rich cake, made by myself. If there's one thing I can do, it's bake fancy bread. It's the sort of thing you'd never buy in a shop. Wonderful icing and almonds and all.

O'BRIEN: Very good. There's the money. You fill up the dockets. I must make a phone call right away. [*Picks up instrument.*] Hello ... [*Fades.*]

[*Screen*]:   STILL ANOTHER DAY

[*The office door is burst open and Miss Crotty rushes in, wildly excited. She rushes to the desk and grasps Mr. O'Brien's hand.*]

MISS CROTTY: Mr. O'Brien! Congratulations! We had the draw below just now. Congratulations! You've won the first prize!

O'BRIEN [*Also startled*]: Me? The first prize? Well, well. Miss Crotty, I don't think you told me what the prize was. [*Pause.*] Just what IS the first prize?

CROTTY: A donkey, Mr. O'Brien.

O'BRIEN: A *what?*

CROTTY: A grand donkey, a lovely animal.

O'BRIEN: But ... I'm not a farmer or anything of that kind. What am *I* supposed to do with a donkey?

CROTTY: But isn't it a grand thing to have about the house? Donkeys are so friendly and good tempered. Have you any land where you live?

O'BRIEN: Well, there's a field behind my place out in Blackrock. Where is this animal now?

CROTTY: In a stable up a lane near Smithfield. Know where that is?

O'BRIEN: Down near the Four Courts, I think.

CROTTY: Correct. Here's the address. I've written it down for you. And here's your winning ticket. All you have to do is go down there and contact Mr. Barnes. He's in charge of it. A most respectable man, I believe.

O'BRIEN: [*Aghast*]: Heavens Almighty.

CROTTY: I knew your luck would turn some day, Mr. O'Brien.

O'BRIEN: Turn? Turn for me or against me?

CROTTY: Poor little Neddy! He's in good hands now.

O'BRIEN: [*Sarcastically*]: I suppose I should thank you from the bottom of my heart, Miss Crotty?

CROTTY: Ah not at all, don't mention it.

O'BRIEN: Heavens above.

FADE OUT.

PART II

The camera, in a van ahead, shows O'Brien gloomily walking down the south quays on the Liffy-side footpath. After a short time he passes the camera, which continues to show him in back view, with background of the distant Four Courts. Meanwhile O'Brien's voice is heard on the sound track. (This episode is not absolutely necessary in the evolution of plot but would be invaluable on grounds of atmosphere and realism.)

O'BRIEN: To be honest, as I made my way down the quays towards Smithfield. I couldn't see anything but trouble in this ridiculous affair. Why couldn't those women leave me alone? And what did I want with a donkey? What use was it? Whatever else I was, I wasn't a tinker. I knew absolutely nothing about that class of animal except that the donkey is very fond of carrots, the most expensive vegetable of the lot. Maybe I'd be expected to buy carrots by the stone. Now if it was a dog—a good thoroughbred pup—I'd be pleased enough. I like dogs. Very intelligent little articles. And the donkey is famous for his stupidity and his stubbornness. I've heard of farmers having to light a fire under a donkey to make him move. [*Morose pause.*] Robert Louis Stevenson wrote a book called "Travels with a donkey." Will I be expected to travel? If so, to where? [*Pause.*] Cork, maybe . . . or Skibbereen? I don't believe Stevenson ever had a donkey in his life. . . .

There is a large open space in Smithfield itself. O'Brien could be seen traversing it, again for the sake of atmosphere. Eventually he is shown in a dirty lane, knocking at the small door beside the large doors of what appears to be a tumble-down type of old coach-house. It is opened by an appalling lout with a shatteringly flat Dublin accent. He is indolently dangling a cigarette from his mouth and his manner is one of easy insolence. This is Barney Barnes.

O'BRIEN: Ah, good morning.

BARNES: Morra.

O'BRIEN: Are you Mr. Barnes?

BARNES: Who wants to know?

O'BRIEN: I do. I called about a donkey.

BARNES: I see. Are the wan that won it?

O'BRIEN: Yes, I am.

BARNES: How do I know that?

O'BRIEN: I have the proof here. [*Produces ticket.*] And you can ring up Miss Crotty if you like. She's the lady who ran the raffle. I can give you the phone number.

BARNES: Aw take it aisy now. I'm the man in chairge here and I'm emtitled to know me business. What's the name, plee-az?

O'BRIEN: My name is O'Brien.

BARNES: Well, that's all right sairtintly.

O'BRIEN: Where is the donkey?

BARNES: Yer man is inside. Want to have a look?

O'BRIEN: Yes, by all means.

BARNES: Well, come on in. [*He opens the door wider and O'Brien enters. He is next seen in a dishevelled sort of a crude kitchen, with an opening into a larger apartment. Both go through this opening and an outline of the rear quarters of a donkey can be seen, but lighting is very bad.*] Do you know what I'm goin' to tell ya? That's a luvly angimal.

O'BRIEN: No doubt. The light is very bad in there?

BARNES: Ah but that's very restful for anny angimal. That crowd do go asleep on their feet, you knaow. They've some class of trick of locking the joints of the legs, d'ya understand. If you or me tried to do that and go asleep, we'd get a desperate fall.

O'BRIEN: I see. I don't know an awful lot about donkeys, or indeed any animals.

BARNES: That so? Well now, you're missin' a lot. Ah, they do be a great comfort. It's lonely down here, you knaow, and I'm not a married man.

O'BRIEN: Indeed; do you tell me that?

BARNES: And I'll tell ya a surprisin' thing. They do keep the house warm in the hard weather.

O'BRIEN: A sort of radiator on four legs.

BARNES: He's as good as a turf fire, and that's a fact.

o'BRIEN: Turf causes a bit of a smell—a pleasant healthy one, I admit. Is there ... is there any smell off a donkey?

BARNES: Not at all, man. Unless what ya get in a clean meada is a smell.

o'BRIEN: [*Hastily*]: Of course I had no intention of keeping him in my own house.

BARNES: What direction do ya live in, Mister O'Brien?

o'BRIEN: Out to the south of Dublin, Blackrock way. I have a field behind my house. I had it let for a while to a man with a cow, but the cow's gone this last six months.

BARNES: Well, that sounds the very place for My Nabs.

o'BRIEN: My trouble is—how am I going to get him out there?

BARNES: Now listen here, mister-me-friend, you're not goin' to put a finger on that angimal until me expenses has been ped. That beast in there doesn't live on air. Ya'll find he's the best-nourished donkey in all Ireland bar none.

o'BRIEN: What expenses?

BARNES: *What* expenses? All the grub he's swallied, man, for weeks and weeks.

o'BRIEN: I see. What does a donkey eat?

BARNES: It'd be better to ask what he *doesn't* eat. He ett an oul coat of me own. But he goes every day for hay, oats and a queer class of a mash I make for him outa maize or Injun meal, cabbage and spuds. And that's not all.

o'BRIEN: What else?

BARNES: He's a divil for skim milk. And tell ya what he's very fond of ...

o'BRIEN: What?

BARNES: Apples, man. Matteradamn whether they're cookin' apples or aytin' apples, he'll chaw and swally the lot. An' bananas.

o'BRIEN: Has he any interest in carrots?

BARNES: He'd give his life for carrots but they're hard to get. I do give him a few carrots an odd time.

o'BRIEN: Well, he seems to be a very well-fed animal. What does all this expense come to?

BARNES: Eight pounds, sixteen shillings and eightpence.

o'BRIEN: WHAT ...?

BARNES: Eight ... sixteen ... eight. That's what the job cost. There's no profit in it for me.

O'BRIEN: The Lord save us! Well, I suppose it must be paid. Do you mind a cheque?

BARNES: At at all.

O'BRIEN: If I add in another pound, will you undertake to bring him out to my place at Blackrock?

BARNES: Course I will. That'll be no trouble at all.

O'BRIEN: [*Producing cheque book and writing at table*]: Well, so be it. The music must be faced. Little did I think how fast the price of that tuppenny ticket would grow. I'll leave my address with you. Could you bring out the beast to arrive about 6 on Tuesday evening?

BARNES: Sairtintly I could. That'll be game ball.

O'BRIEN: All right. Till then I'll say goodbye.

BARNES: The best of luck sir, now.

FADE OUT.

PART III

Scene is a comfortable living-room in O'Brien's house where he is sitting, reading. A window is prominent at the back of the room. There is a knock outside. O'Brien rises, leaves room and comes back with Barnes.

O'BRIEN: Welcome, Barnes. Sit down.

BARNES: Well . . . thanks, Mister O'Brien.

O'BRIEN: Today I telephoned a vet to come and have a look at that animal. So you succeeded in bringing him out?

BARNES: Well, he's here all right. But I wouldn't say it was meself that brought him out.

O'BRIEN: What do you mean? Don't tell me you got C.I.E. to cart him here and that there's another bill to pay?

BARNES: At at all. It was HIM that brought ME out.

O'BRIEN: WHAT—you rode the poor animal here? A heavy, able-bodied man like you?

BARNES: At at all. He's in the field. Come over here to the winda. [*They rise and move to it.*]

O'BRIEN: Right enough, there he is grazing away. Hey! What are those things sticking up in the air?

BARNES: The shafts of an oul cair.

O'BRIEN: And where on earth did you get that?

BARNES: That thing was lyin' in the lane for the last eight weeks or so. Some gurrier left it there. Some damned tinker.

O'BRIEN: And does that give you any right to take possession of it?

BARNES: I know that crowd. When they're finished with anything, they throw it away. They just leave it somewhere. They leave it somewhere where it does be obstructin' other people. That crowd's no use.

O'BRIEN: [Emphatically]: But listen here. How are you going to get it back into town? It's not yours.

BARNES: Who said an'thin about gettin' it back into town? You're pairfitly right in sayin' it's not mine. I'm making YOU a present of it.

O'BRIEN: ME? Don't be ridiculous. What use would I have for a tinker's old cart?

BARNES: Sure this is the summer. Couldn't you go for a nice drive in it some evenin' down to Dun Lough Air, an' maybe have a good swim for yerself?

O'BRIEN: You're talking absolute nonsense, Barnes. I have no intention of going out to show myself off before the neighbours driving a donkey and cart.

BARNES: [Viciously]: Many a betther man than you done that. It's a healthier and handier thing than them mothor cairs.

O'BRIEN [Angrily]: What you've done is plant an item of stolen property on my land.

BARNES: That's a nice way to thank me for makin' ya a useful present. You could draw turf in that cair, or carry parcels. A nice plank for a seat across it an' ya could bring yer mott for a drive.

O'BRIEN: My WHAT?

BARNES: Yer mott.

O'BRIEN: This ridiculous mess gets worse. [Meditatively, looking at carpet.] I'm not sure what to do. [Suddenly.] You, Barnes—get to hell out of here!

BARNES: I beg yer pairdin?

O'BRIEN: You heard what I said. GET OUT!

BARNES: [Shrugging portentously]: Oh well, O.K. Keep yer hair on. [Rising.] An' don't ask me to do you anny more favours.

O'BRIEN [At door, opening it]: Clear out of this house.

[Barnes shambles out through the doorway.]

[Screen]:   A FEW DAYS PASS

Scene is the room as before. It is disclosed empty but immediately O'Brien enters with another well-spoken man, a veterinarian, who is also well-dressed but wears gum boots.

O'BRIEN: I needn't tell you, Hickory, that all this is a great shock to me.

HICKORY: Well, an ass in a poke is the same as a pig in a poke. You shouldn't have had anything to do with the animal in the first place.

O'BRIEN: [*Getting pencil and paper*]: I'd better take down the list in writing.

HICKORY: Why? Anthrax is enough. You'll be prosecuted if you're found with that animal in your possession, no matter where you got it or from whom.

O'BRIEN: Well . . . I suppose you should know.

HICKORY: Anthrax is a terrible disease. There's external and internal anthrax. The bacteria that cause anthrax are the most vicious in the world, and the bacilli or spores are such as to make the disease very infectious. And let me tell you this. *Human beings can get anthrax.*

O'BRIEN: Well . . . Lord save us!

HICKORY: During the first World War thousands of British soldiers got anthrax from using infected shaving brushes made in Japan. That was a nice day's work.

O'BRIEN: You mean the bristles were contaminated because they came from animals which were suffering from anthrax.

HICKORY: Exactly. Very likely from animals who had died from anthrax.

O'BRIEN: Well, well, well. And what other disease did you say the donkey had?

HICKORY: Mange. And he has it bad.

O'BRIEN: Mange. I thought only dogs got that. [*Writing.*] Is that the lot?

HICKORY: You saw yourself that he can hardly walk. He's also got what we call laminitis.

O'BRIEN: I see. And just what is laminitis?

HICKORY: It means inflamation of the hoof. The poor beast is completely banjaxed.

O'BRIEN: It certainly looks like it. Is there anything else?

HICKORY: As I told you in the field, I didn't want to carry out a detailed examination, and the reason is obvious enough, I hope. I don't want to get anthrax. But that ass is blind or with sight so bad that he'll very soon be blind. And it looks the blindness of old age.

O'BRIEN: If you ask me, the plan was to fob that animal off on me. I'm just the victim of a conspiracy.

HICKORY: Looks like it. But what you must get down to now, right away, is ACTION.

O'BRIEN: I agree. Precisely what would you advise me to do?

HICKORY: Have you got a gun?

O'BRIEN: Well . . . I have. [*Rises and goes to the lower press compartment of bookcase and takes out shotgun.*] I haven't used this for at least three years. Have a look.

HICKORY: Hmmm. Handsome machine, that.

O'BRIEN: It *is*. My father's. He was a crack shot.

HICKORY: Tomorrow you must shoot that ass at very close quarters in the head. In the head, remember, and from the side. But first get a man to dig a grave—and a deep one. Believe it or not, rats are very partial to dead donkeys, even when the corpse is choked with anthrax.

O'BRIEN: Lord! And then we would have rats running about the place with doses of anthrax of their own?

HICKORY: Exactly. Make your man dig deep. At least six feet. Take the day off yourself and see that a proper job is done.

O'BRIEN: Yes. That gravedigger means another quid gone west.

HICKORY: All right, but it's money well spent.

O'BRIEN: Well, Hickory, that's agreed. I'll proceed as directed. And tell me this. [*Produces cheque book.*] What do I owe your good self?

HICKORY: Oh, whatever you think. Two guineas, we'll say.

O'BRIEN: That's fair enough. [*Writes.*] This is a right mess I've got myself into.

HICKORY: [*Pleasantly*]: Ah well, these things happen.

FADE OUT.

[*Screen*]:   A FEW DAYS LATER

Scene is the same room. O'Brien is again reading and again there is a knock without. He goes out and returns with a bulky, elderly sergeant of the Guards. This man is pleasant of manner and speaks with a pronounced country accent.

SERGEANT: And how are you keeping, Mr. O'Brien?

O'BRIEN: Oh, fair enough, I suppose. The health is fine, but there's always trouble of one kind or another.

SERGEANT: Ah but shure what about it? Isn't it the same with us all, God help us.

O'BRIEN: I suppose it is. It's a mercy we don't know what's in store for us.

SERGEANT: Well, well. [*He has caught sight of shotgun, which has been left leaning against the wall.*] I never knew you were a sportsman, Mr. O'Brien. [*Breaks gun open and examines it.*] Faith now and that's a nice weapon. The Purdey make, too.

O'BRIEN: Yes. It's a bit old, but it's good.

SERGEANT [*Head bent*]: I suppose, Mr. O'Brien ... I suppose you have a license for this?

O'BRIEN: [*Startled*]: Oh! What? Bedammit but I haven't. I haven't used the gun for three years. I completely forgot all about it.

SERGEANT: Ah yes. That happens sometimes. It's bad luck and nothing else. You know, of course, that whether you use a gun or not has nothing to do with the necessity for having a license?

O'BRIEN: I do indeed, Sergeant. Damned stupid of me.

SERGEANT: You understand, Mr. O'Brien, that the trouble with this country is that there's too many knocking about, and too many wild fellows knocking them off.

O'BRIEN: Oh, true enough, Sergeant. Of course, I keep that under lock and key.

SERGEANT: Ah, faith, they'd find it no matter where you had it.

O'BRIEN: Indeed, I suppose so, Sergeant.

SERGEANT: I'm sure you'll understand, Mr. O'Brien, that I must report this. It'll only mean a fine of between two and five pounds. There's just one snag.

O'BRIEN: ONE snag? Isn't a ferocious fine enough?

SERGEANT: Well, you see, there's always the danger that the Justice would order the gun confiscated as well.

O'BRIEN: But Good Lord, that gun's worth at least thirty pounds.

SERGEANT: Faith and I wouldn't doubt you. It would all depend on who the Justice would be. If you were wise, you'd ask your solicitor to get a barrister on the job.

O'BRIEN: Heavens above! More and more ruinous expense!

SERGEANT: It's another matter I called to see you about, Mr. O'Brien. Another matter entirely.

O'BRIEN: Indeed, Sergeant. What other trouble am I in?

SERGEANT: Well, I seen the guts of it out in the field.

o'BRIEN: You mean the donkey?

SERGEANT: Ah no. Not the grand little donkey. I mean the cart. It's stolen property.

o'BRIEN: But I didn't steal any cart, Sergeant.

SERGEANT: Shure don't we know that. Shure we pulled in that scally-wag Barnes yesterday. That man has a record the length of your arm.

o'BRIEN: Well, thank goodness. That lets me out.

SERGEANT: You don't understand, Mr. O'Brien. The charge against you is that you're a receiver of stolen property, knowing it to have been stolen.

o'BRIEN: [*Aghast*]: But look here, Sergeant, surely this is utter bosh? I mean to say—

SERGEANT: Mr. O'Brien, you may think it's silly, but these things will have to be gone through with. You may be sure you'll get bail while the Justice is taking the depositions. And of course, there'll be a good long delay after you're sent for trial.

o'BRIEN: May Heaven keep my wits about me! Sent for trial?

SERGEANT: The charge is what they call a felony.

o'BRIEN: And suppose I'm convicted? What then?

SERGEANT: Well now, it's hard to say ... It would depend a lot on the Judge. It might be just a fine. [*Rises and takes up cap.*] It might be just a heavy fine and be bound to the peace. I think I'll slip away now, Mr. O'Brien, and maybe see you again tomorrow. I'm on duty at the station to-night.

o'BRIEN: Sergeant, you say it MIGHT be a heavy fine and be bound to the peace. What else could it be?

SERGEANT [*At door*]: Ah now, Mr. O'Brien, don't keep looking all the time at the dark side of things. It COULD mean six months hard labour in Mountjoy but I'm sure it won't. Good night. [*Departs.*]

o'BRIEN: [*Burying head in hands and then raising it to stare at camera*]: I ask you. [*Spreads arms.*] I bought four legs under a donkey for tuppence. Counting the loss of the gun and the possible fines, I'd be down maybe a hundred quid. And perhaps six months in Mountjoy. AND THE LOSS OF MY JOB!

[*Screen*]: THE MAN WITH FOUR LEGS

THE END.

[*The Journal of Irish Literature*]

TWO IN ONE

The story I have to tell is a strange one, perhaps unbelieveable. I will try to set it down as simply as I can. I do not expect to be disturbed in my literary labours, for I am writing this in the condemned cell.

Let us say my name is Murphy. The unusual occurrence which led me here concerns my relations with another man whom we shall call Kelly. Both of us were taxidermists.

I will not attempt a treatise on what a taxidermist is. The word is ugly and inadequate. Certainly it does not convey to the layman that such an operator must combine the qualities of zoologist, naturalist, chemist, sculptor, artist and carpenter. Who would blame such a person for showing some temperament now and again, as I did?

It is necessary, however, to say a brief word about this science. First, there is no such thing in modern practice as "stuffing" an animal. There is a record of stuffed gorillas having been in Carthage in the 5th century, and it is a fact that an Austrian prince, Siegmund Herberstein, had stuffed bison in the great hall of his castle in the 16th century—it was then the practice to draw the entrails of animals and to substitute spices and various preservative substances. There is a variety of methods in use to-day but, except in particular cases—snakes, for example, where preserving the translucency of the skin is a problem calling for special measures—the basis of all modern methods is simply this: you skin the animal very carefully according to a certain pattern, and you encase the skinless body in plaster of Paris. You bisect the plaster when cast providing yourself with two complementary moulds from which you can make a casting of the animal's body —there are several substances, all very light, from which such castings can be made. The next step, calling for infinite skill and patience, is to mount the skin on the casting of the body. That is all I need explain here, I think.

Kelly carried on a taxidermy business and I was his assistant. He was the boss—a swinish, overbearing mean boss, a bully, a sadist. He hated me, but enjoyed his hatred too much to sack me. He knew I had a real interest in the work, and a desire to broaden my experience. For that reason, he threw me all the common-place jobs that came in. If some old lady sent her favourite terrier to be done, that was me; foxes and cats and Shetland ponies and white rabbits—they were all strictly *my* department. I could do a perfect job on such animals in my sleep, and got to hate them. But if a crocodile came in, or a Great Borneo spider, or (as once happened) a giraffe—Kelly kept them all for himself. In the meantime he would treat my own painstaking work with sourness and sneers and complaints.

One day the atmosphere in the workshop had been even fouler than usual, with Kelly in a filthier temper than usual. I had spent the forenoon finishing a cat, and at about lunch-time put it on the shelf where he left completed orders.

I could nearly *hear* him glaring at it. Where was the tail? I told him there was no tail, that it was a Manx cat. How did I know it was a Manx cat, how did I know it was not an ordinary cat which had lost its tail in a motor accident or something? I got so mad that I permitted myself a disquisition on cats in general, mentioning the distinctions as between *felis manul, felis silvestris* and *felis lybica,* and on the unique structure of the Manx cat. His reply to that? He called me a slob. That was the sort of life I was having,

On this occasion something within me snapped. I was sure I could hear the snap. I had moved up to where he was to answer his last insult. The loathsome creature had his back to me, bending down to put on his bicycle clips. Just to my hand on the bench was one of the long, flat steel instruments we use for certain operations with plaster. I picked it up and hit him a blow with it on the back of the head. He gave a cry and slumped forward. I hit him again. I rained blow after blow on him. Then I threw the tool away. I was upset. I went out into the yard and looked around. I remembered he had a weak heart. Was he dead? I remember adjusting the position of a barrel we had in the yard to catch rainwater, the only sort of water suitable for some of the mixtures we used. I found I was in a cold sweat but strangely calm. I went back into the workshop.

Kelly was just as I had left him. I could find no pulse. I rolled him over on his back and examined his eyes, for I have seen more lifeless eyes in my day than most people. Yes, there was no doubt: Kelly was dead. I had killed him. I was a murderer. I put on my coat and hat and left the place. I walked the streets for a while, trying to avoid panic, trying to think rationally. Inevitably, I was soon in a public house. I drank a lot of whiskey and finally went home to my digs. The next morning I was very sick indeed from this terrible mixture of drink and worry. Was the Kelly affair merely a fancy, a drunken fancy? No, there was no consolation in that sort of hope. He was dead all right.

It was as I lay in bed there, shaking, thinking and smoking, that the mad idea came into my head. No doubt this sounds incredible, grotesque, even disgusting, but I decided I would treat Kelly the same as any other dead creature that found its way to the workshop.

Once one enters a climate of horror, distinction of degree as between one infamy and another seems slight, sometimes undetectable. That evening I went to the workshop and made my preparations. I worked steadily all next day. I will not appal the reader with gruesome detail. I need only say that I applied the general technique and flaying pattern appropriate to apes. The job took me four days at the end of which I had a perfect skin, face and all. I made the usual castings before committing the remains of, so to speak, the remains, to the furnace. My plan was to have Kelly on view asleep on a chair, for the benefit of anybody who might call. Reflection convinced me that this would be far too dangerous. I had to think again.

A further idea began to form. It was so macabre that it shocked even myself. For days I had been treating the inside of the skin with the usual preservatives—cellulose acetate and the like—thinking all the time. The new illumination came upon me like a thunderbolt. *I would don his skin and, when the need arose, BECOME Kelly! His* clothes fitted me. So would his skin. Why not?

Another's day's agonised work went on various alterations and adjustments but that night I was able to look into a glass and see Kelly looking back at me, perfect in every detail except for the teeth and eyes, which had to be my own but which I knew other people would never notice.

Naturally I wore Kelly's clothes, and had no trouble in imitating his unpleasant voice and mannerisms. On the second day, having "dressed," so to speak, I went for a walk, receiving salutes from newsboys and other people who had known Kelly. And on the day after, I was foolhardy enough to visit Kelly's lodgings. Where on earth had I been, his landlady wanted to know. (She had noticed nothing). What, I asked—had that fool Murphy not told her that I had to go to the country for a few days? No? I had told the good-for-nothing to convey the message.

I slept that night in Kelly's bed. I was a little worried about what the other landlady would think of my own absence. I decided not to remove Kelly's skin the first night I spent in his bed but to try to get the rest of my plan of campaign perfected and into sharper focus. I eventually decided that Kelly should announce to various people that he was going to a very good job in Canada, and that he had sold his business to his assistant Murphy. I would then burn the skin, I would own a business and—what is more stupid than vanity!—I could secretly flatter myself that I had committed the perfect crime.

Need I say that I had overlooked something?

The mummifying preparation with which I had dressed the inside of the skin was, of course, quite stable for the ordinary purposes of taxidermy. It had not occurred to me that a night in a warm bed would make it behave differently. The horrible truth dawned on me the next day when I reached the workshop and tried to take the skin off. *It wouldn't come off!* It had literally fused with my own! And in the days that followed, this process kept rapidly advancing. Kelly's skin got to live again, to breathe, to perspire.

Then followed more days of terrible tension. My own landlady called one day, inquiring about me of "Kelly." I told her I had been on the point of calling on *her* to find out where I was. She was disturbed about my disappearance—it was so unlike me—and said she thought she should inform the police. I thought it wise not to try to dissuade her. My disappearance would eventually come to be accepted, I thought. My Kelliness, so to speak, was permanent. It was horrible, but it was a choice of that or the scaffold.

I kept drinking a lot. One night, after many drinks, I went to the club for a game of snooker. This club was in fact one of the causes of Kelly's bitterness towards me. I had joined it without having been aware that Kelly was a member. His resentment was boundless. He thought I was watching him, and taking note of the attentions he paid the lady members.

On this occasion I nearly made a catastrophic mistake. It is a simple fact that I am a very good snooker player, easily the best in that club. As I was standing watching another game in progress awaiting my turn for the table, *I suddenly realised that Kelly did not play snooker at all!* For some moments, a cold sweat stood out on Kelly's brow at the narrowness of this escape. I went to the bar. There, a garrulous lady (who thinks her unsolicited conversation is a fair exchange for a drink) began talking to me. She remarked the long absence of my nice Mr. Murphy. She said he was missed a lot in the snooker room. I was hot and embarrassed and soon went home. To Kelly's place, of course.

Not embarrassment, but a real sense of danger, was to be my next portion in this adventure. One afternoon, two very casual strangers strolled into the workshop, saying they would like a little chat with me. Cigarettes were produced. Yes indeed, they were plain-clothesmen making a few routine inquiries. This man Murphy had been reported missing by several people. Any idea where he was? None at all. When had I last seen him? Did he seem upset or disturbed? No, but he was an impetuous type. I had recently reprimanded him for bad work. On similar other occasions he had threatened to leave and seek work in England. Had I been away for a few days myself? Yes, down in Cork for a few days. On business. Yes . . . yes . . . some people thinking of starting a natural museum down there, technical school people—that sort of thing.

The casual manner of these men worried me, but I was sure they did not suspect the truth and that they were genuinely interested in tracing Murphy. Still, I knew I was in danger, without knowing the exact nature of the threat I had to counter. Whiskey cheered me somewhat.

Then it happened. The two detectives came back accompanied by two other men in uniform. They showed me a search warrant. It was purely a formality; it had to be done in the case of all missing persons. They had already searched Murphy's digs and had found nothing of interest. They were very sorry for upsetting the place during my working hours.

A few days later the casual gentlemen called and put me under arrest for the wilful murder of Murphy, of myself. They proved the charge in due course with all sorts of painfully amassed evidence, including the remains of human bones in the furnace. I was sentenced to be hanged. Even if I could now prove that Murphy still lived by shedding the accursed skin, what help would that be? Where, they would ask, is Kelly?

That is my strange and tragic story. And I end it with the thought that if Kelly and I must each be either murderer or murdered, it is perhaps better to accept my present fate as philosophically as I can and be cherished in the public mind as the victim of this murderous monster, Kelly. He *was* a murderer, anyway.

[*The Journal of Irish Literature*]

O'Bitter Dicta

The final belief is to believe in a fiction, which you know to be a fiction, there being nothing else. The exquisite truth is to know that it is a fiction and that you believe in it willingly.

—Wallace Stevens, "Adagia"

Chapman bit his lip.

—*The Best of Myles*

INTRODUCTION

Although in practice O'Brien has done as much as anyone in creating the sort of fictions Stevens had in mind, what follow in this section are not the articulate epigrams of "Adagia," let alone the sustained long logic of *The Necessary Angel*. O'Brien did not write formal, academic criticism at all after his M.A., but as Myles he did take frequent pot shots at various cultural targets. Many of these seem mere opinions such as might be expressed by the man on the next stool. There are, however, some interesting performances inspired by the occasion of another piece of writing, and these, if read with sufficient allowance for O'Brien's method, might produce, if not an *esthétique*, at least an interesting aesthetic experience, though Myles would loathe the phrase.

Search any old lukewarm bath and you will find one of these aesthetical technicians enjoying himself. He is having a lukewarm bath, it is rather good, it is something real, something that has its roots in the soil, a tangible, valid, unique, complete, integrating, vertical experience, a diatonic spatio-temporal cognition in terms of realistic harmonic spacing, differential intervals and vector (emmanuel) analysis, of those passional orphic inferences which must be proto-morphously lodged in writing with the Manager on or before the latest closing date.   [*The Irish Times*]

Shooting from the hip, Myles often seems to be going more for the joke than the profounder implications, as in his "Chat about Proust." Because of O'Brien's ability to generate instant texture in almost anything he writes and his reputation now as author of two important "new novels," we, like those British critics he chided, are sometimes apt to take him too seriously when he is just playing around. Although the Proust passage does give some sense of the French master's style and potentially even contains a legitimate critique of Proust's characterization, the pun about geese and Swann leaves one with the feeling that O'Brien is less interested in *Remembrance of Things Past* than the jape of the moment.

A more complex performance, however, is the piece which begins, "A note in my diary says: 'Ten to the power of seventy-nine. Write on this joke.'" A fat paragraph dutifully follows in which Cicero, Eddington, and other legitimate heavies are jostled about. "Very well. The 'scientist', in sum, had been deluding himself that the Heath Robinson experiments which led to that 'discovery' could be solemnly called *observational determination*." Heath Robinson was not, however, a real scientist like Sir Arthur Stanley Eddington, author of *Theory of Relativity and Its Influence on Scientific Thought, The Expanding Universe,* and other works of that ilk. Heath Robinson was an illustrator, designer, and comic artist something after the manner of Rube Goldberg. One of his more famous illustrating jobs was a volume of *Don Quixote.* The paragraph concludes that "observational determination" in this case "is just make-believe and whimsy, all essentially feminine." As literary readers, we may not care much how Eddington makes out with ten to the power of seventy-nine, but we do worry about what our author thinks of the fictive process. Given the standard 1940 Irish male blinders regarding matters feminine, we can conclude that our man is telling us that whimsy is the poorest sort of game to be caught at. However, O'Brien proceeds for two more pages on this matter of numbers, embroidering a further fiction on the mathematical fiction, if not embroidery in the manner of Penelope (a female admired for her rear-guard knitting in *The Hard*

Life), certainly embroidery in the manner of Heath Robinson's "experiment." Perhaps the closest verbal parallel to O'Brien's literary criticism would be the works of Horace, a poet admired by Myles. As in the case of the Roman poet's satires, a topic is introduced and tossed about, even wandered away from and returned to with sudden illumination, an illumination purchased somehow by means of the apparently gratuitous wandering. "Tell me, Sir," says the Good Fairy in *At Swim,* "did you ever study Bach?"

At his best on daily violations of language by politicians, advertisers, and so forth, O'Brien not only pointed out foibles, but made constructs interesting in themselves, such as in the Catechism of Cliché or in single efforts such as the mediation on the use of the word "supposed," or the excursion through the hotel bar and railroad yard, the ostensible occasion of which is a comment on James Joyce ("A Bash in the Tunnel").

If one includes not only "The Bash" but all the remarks through the years in *Cruiskeen Lawn* and *The Dalkey Archive,* in the open air on Sandymount Strand and under various pub roofs, the Joyce business adds up to O'Brien's longest critical endeavor. And duty it was to him and duty to me to write about it. Clearly, O'Brien thought Joyce a great writer, but as certainly he thought Joyce was not the only modern Irish writer. Like Beckett and others, O'Brien was influenced not only by Joyce but by locations and locutions in common. David Powell has done the useful spade work of digging up all Myles's swats, slaps, and salutations in his annotated bibliography of Joyce references in *Cruiskeen Lawn.* In this book I am more interested in presenting some of the better performances rather than recording all the opinions.

The best of O'Brien's opinions about the novel are, of course, plowed under in *At Swim.* There are also other relevant items quoted in the introductions to specific sections of this book.

The selections that follow are taken from *The Best of Myles* except where noted.

A POEM FROM THE IRISH
(twelfth-century, anonymous,
Flann O'Brien, translator)

My hand has a pain from writing,
Not steady the sharp tool of my craft,
Its slender beak spews bright ink—
A beetle-dark shining draught.

Streams of wisdom of white God
From my fair-brown, fine hand sally,
On the page they splash their flood
In ink of the green-skinned holly.

My little dribbly pen stretches
Across the great white paper plain,
Insatiable for splendid riches—
That is why my hand has pain!

[*Lace Curtain,* No. 4]

A BASH IN THE TUNNEL

[John Ryan was charter secretary of the James Joyce Society of Ireland, licensee at the Bailey's, a pub in Dublin where he displayed "Leopold Bloom's Door." His 1975 memoir, *Remembering How We Stood: Bohemian Dublin at the Mid-Century*, contains a chapter on O'Brien. As Ryan says in the following note, the Joyce piece first appeared in a special issue of *Envoy*. The text, including Ryan's note with its spelling of "Brian Nolan" and "Flan O'Brien," is from the book that was published from the magazine.]

In 1951, whilst I was editor of the Irish literary periodical *Envoy*, I decided that it would be a fitting thing to commemorate the tenth anniversary of the death of James Joyce by bringing out a special number dedicated to him which would reflect the attitudes and opinions of his fellow countrymen towards their illustrious compatriot.

To this end I began by inviting Brian Nolan to act as honorary editor for this particular issue. His own genius closely matched, without in anyway resembling or attempting to counterfeit, Joyce's. But if the mantle of Joyce (or should we say the waistcoat?) were ever to be passed on, nobody would be half so deserving of it as the man who, under his other guises of Flan O'Brien and Myles Na gCopaleen, proved himself incontestably to be the most creative writer and mordant wit that Ireland had given us since Shem the Penman himself.

The essay appears in a slightly different version in O'Brien's *Stories and Plays* (New York: The Viking Press, 1976).]

James Joyce was an artist. He has said so himself. His was a case of Ars gratia Artist. He declared that he would pursue his artistic mission even if the penalty was as long as eternity itself. This appears to be an affirmation of belief in Hell, therefore of belief in Heaven and in God.

A better title for this article might be: 'Was Joyce Mad?' By Hamlet, Prince of Denmark. Yet there is a reason for the present title.

Some thinkers – all Irish, all Catholic, some unlay – have confessed to discerning a resemblance between Joyce and Satan. True, resemblances there are. Both had other names, the one Stephen Dedalus, the other Lucifer; the latter name, meaning 'Maker of Light', was to attract later the ironical gloss 'Prince of Darkness'! Both started off very well under unfaultable teachers, both were very proud, both had a fall. But they differed on one big, critical issue. Satan never denied the existence of the Almighty; indeed he acknowledged it by challenging merely His primacy. Joyce said there was no God, proving this by uttering various blasphemies and obscenities and not being instantly struck dead.

A man once said to me that he hated blasphemy, but on purely rational grounds. If there is no God, he said, the thing is stupid and unnecessary. If there is, it's dangerous.

Anatole France says this better. He relates how, one morning, a notorious agnostic called on a friend who was a devout Catholic. The devout Catholic was drunk and began to pour forth appalling blasphemies. Pale and shocked, the agnostic rushed from the house. Later, a third party challenged him on this incident.

'You have been saying for years that there is no God. Why then should you be so frightened at somebody else insulting this God who doesn't exist?'

'I still say there is no God. But that fellow thinks there is. Suppose a thunderbolt was sent down to strike him dead. How did I know I wouldn't get killed as well? Wasn't I standing beside him?'

Another blasphemy, perhaps – doubting the Almighty's aim. Yet it is still true that all true blasphemers must be believers.

What is the position of the artist in Ireland?

Shortly before commencing to assemble material for this essay, I went into the Bailey in Dublin to drink a bottle of stout and do some solitary thinking. Before any considerable thought had formed itself, a man – then a complete stranger – came, accompanied by his drink, and stood beside me: addressing me by name, he said he was surprised to see a man like myself drinking in a pub.

My pub radar screen showed up the word 'toucher'. I was instantly much on my guard.

'And where do you think I should drink?' I asked. 'Pay fancy prices in a hotel?'

'Ah, no,' he said. 'I didn't mean that. But any time I feel like a good bash myself, I have it in the cars. What will you have?"

I said I would have a large one, knowing that his mysterious reply would entail lengthy elucidation.

'I needn't tell you that that crowd is a crowd of bastards,' was his prefatory exegesis.

Then he told me all. At one time his father had a pub and grocery business, situated near a large Dublin railway terminus. Every year the railway company invited tenders for the provisioning of its dining cars, and every year the father got the contract. (The narrator said he thought this was due to the territorial proximity of the house, with diminished handling and cartage charges.)

The dining cars (hereinafter known as 'the cars') were customarily parked in remote sidings. It was the father's job to load them from time to time with costly victuals – eggs, rashers, cold turkey and whiskey. These cars, bulging in their lonely sidings with such fabulous fare, had special locks. The father had the key, and nobody else in the world had authority to open the doors until the car was part of a train. But my informant had made it his business, he told me, to have a key too.

'At that time,' he told me, 'I had a bash once a week in the cars.'

One must here record two peculiarities of Irish railway practice. The first is a chronic inability to 'make up' trains in advance, i.e. to estimate expected passenger traffic accurately. Week after week a long-distance trian is scheduled to be five passenger coaches and a car. Perpetually, an extra 150 passengers arrive on the departure platform unexpectedly. This means that the car must be detached, a passenger coach substituted, and the train despatched foodless and drinkless on its way.

The second peculiarity – not exclusively Irish – is the inability of personnel in charge of shunting engines to leave coaches, parked in far sidings, alone. At all costs they must be shifted.

That was the situation as my friend in the Bailey described it. The loaded dining cars never went anywhere, in the long-distance sense. He approved of that. But they were subject to endless enshuntment. That, he said, was a bloody scandal and a waste of the taxpayers' money.

When the urge for a 'bash' came upon him, his routine was simple. Using his secret key, he secretly got into a parked and laden car very early in the morning, penetrated to the pantry, grabbed a jug of water, a glass and a bottle of whiskey and, with this assortment of material and utensil, locked himself in the lavatory.

Reflect on that locking. So far as the whole world was concerned, the car was utterly empty. It was locked with special, unprecedented locks. Yet this man locked himself securely within those locks.

Came the dawn – and the shunters. They espied, as doth the grey-hound the hare, the lonely dining car, mute, immobile, deserted. So they coupled it up and dragged it to another siding at Liffey Junction. It was there for five hours but ('that crowd of bastards,' i.e. other shunters) it was discovered and towed over to the yards behind Westland Row Station. Many hours later it was shunted on to the tail of the Wexford Express but later angrily detached owing to the unexpected arrival of extra passengers.

'And are you sitting in the lavatory drinking whiskey all the time?' I asked.

'Certainly I am,' he answered, 'what the hell do you think lavatories in trains is for? And with the knees of me trousers wet with me own whiskey from the jerks of them shunter bastards!'

His resentment was enormous. Be it noted that the whiskey was not in fact his own whiskey, that he was that oddity, an unauthorized person.

'How long does a bash in the cars last?' I asked him.

'Ah, that depends on a lot of things,' he said. 'As you know, I never carry a watch.' (Exhibits cuffless, hairy wrist in proof.) 'Did I ever tell you about the time I had a bash in the tunnel?'

He had not – for the good reason that I had never met him before.

'I seen meself,' he said, 'once upon a time on a three-day bash. The bastards took me out of Liffey Junction down to Hazelhatch. Another crowd shifted me into Harcourt Street yards. I was having a good bash at this time, but I always try to see, for the good of me health, that a bash doesn't last more than a day and night. I know it's night outside when it's dark. If it's bright it's day. Do you follow me?'

'I think I do.'

'Well, I was about on the third bottle when this other shunter crowd come along – it was dark, about eight in the evening – and nothing would do them only bring me into the Liffey Tunnel under the Phoenix Park and park me there. As you know I never use a watch. If it's bright, it's day. If it's dark, it's night. Here was meself parked in the tunnel opening bottle after bottle in the dark, thinking the night was very long one, stuck there in the tunnel. I was three-quarters way into the jigs when they pulled me out of the tunnel into Kingsbridge. I was in bed for a week. Did you ever in your life hear of a greater crowd of bastards?'

'Never.'

'That was the first and last time I ever had a bash in the tunnel.'

Funny? But surely there you have the Irish artist? Sitting fully dressed, innerly locked in the toilet of a locked coach where he has no right to be, resentfully drinking somebody else's whiskey, being whisked hither and thither by anonymous shunters, keeping fastidiously the while on the outer face of his door the simple word ENGAGED!

I think the image fits Joyce; but particularly in his manifestation of a most Irish characteristic – the transgressor's resentment with the nongressor.

A friend of mine found himself next door at dinner to a well-known savant who appears in *Ulysses*. (He shall be nameless, for he still lives.) My friend, making dutiful conversation, made mention of

Joyce. The savant said that Ireland was under a deep obligation to the author of Joyce's *Irish Names of Places*. My friend lengthily explained that his reference had been to a different Joyce. The savant did not quite understand, but ultimately confessed that he had heard certain rumours about the other man. It seemed that he had written some dirty books, published in Paris.

'But you are a character in one of them,' my friend incautiously remarked.

The next two hours, to the neglect of wine and cigars, were occupied with a heated statement by the savant that he was by no means a character in fiction, he was a man, furthermore he was alive and he had published books of his own.

'How can I be a character in fiction,' he demanded, 'if I am here talking to you?'

That incident may be funny, too, but its curiosity is this: Joyce spent a lifetime establishing himself as a character in fiction. Joyce created, in narcissus fascination, the ageless Stephen. Beginning with importing real characters into his books, he achieves the magnificent inversion of making them legendary and fictional. It is quite preposterous. Thousands of people believe that there once lived a man named Sherlock Holmes.

Joyce went further than Satan in rebellion.

Two characters who confess themselves based on Aquinas: Joyce and Maritain.

In *Finnegans Wake,* Joyce appears to favour the Vico theory of inevitable human and recurring evolution – theocracy: aristocracy: democracy: chaos.

'A.E.' referred to the chaos of Joyce's mind.

That was wrong, for Joyce's mind was indeed very orderly. In composition he used coloured pencils to keep himself right. All his works, not excluding *Finnegans Wake,* have a rigid classic pattern. His personal moral and family behaviours were impeccable. He seems to have deserved equally with George Moore the sneer about the latter – he never kissed, but told.

What was really abnormal about Joyce? At Clongowes he had his dose of Jesuit casuistry. Why did he substitute his home-made chaosistry?

It seems to me that Joyce emerges, through curtains of salacity and blasphemy, as a truly fear-shaken Irish Catholic, rebelling not so much against the Church but against its near-schism Irish eccentricities, its pretence that there is only one Commandment, the vulgarity of its edifices, the shallowness and stupidity of many of its ministers. His revolt, noble in itself, carried him away. He could not see the tree for the woods. But I think he meant well. We all do, anyway.

What is *Finnegans Wake*? A treatise on the incommunicable night-mind? Or merely an example of silence, exile and punning?

Some think that Joyce was at heart an Irish dawn-bursting romantic, an admirer of de Valera, and one who dearly wished to be recalled to Dublin as an ageing man to be crowned with a D. Litt. from the national and priest-haunted university. This is at least possible, if only because it explains the preposterous 'aesthetic' affectations of his youth, which included the necessity for being rude to his dying mother. The theme here is that a heart of gold was beating under the artificial waistcoat. Amen.

Humour, the handmaid of sorrow and fear, creeps out endlessly in all Joyce's works. He uses the thing in the same way as Shakespeare does but less formally, to attenuate the fear of those who have belief and who genuinely think that they will be in hell or in heaven shortly, and possibly very shortly. With laughs he palliates the sense of doom that is the heritage of the Irish Catholic. True humour needs this background urgency: Rabelais is funny, but his stuff cloys. His stuff lacks tragedy.

Perhaps the true fascination of Joyce lies in his secretiveness, his ambiguity (his polyguity, perhaps?), his leg-pulling, his dishonesties, his technical skill, his attraction for Americans. His works are a garden in which some of us may play. All that we can claim to know is merely a small bit of that garden.

But at the end, Joyce will still be in his tunnel, unabashed.

A FEW NIPS

In the Sere the Yellow

Looking over my well-thumbed volume of Keats the other day ('First Prize for English Composition, Clongowes Wood College, 1888') I re-read the sonnet on the four seasons of man.

> 'He has his summer, when luxuriously
> Spring's honeyed end of youthful thought he loves
> To ruminate, and by such dreaming nigh
> Is the nearest unto heaven; quiet coves
> His soul has in its Autumn, when his wings
> He furleth close . . .'

This is largely hearsay or guesswork on the part of Keats, who died when he was a boy. All the same, he was not far out. I am old enough myself to know what Autumn is, and I find that my habits are of the order imagined by the poet. There is nothing I like better than an evening with a few quiet coves in the dimmer corner of a pub, murmuring together in friendship the judgements of our mature minds. As regards furling my wings close, that is also true enough. To spend a whole bob or a tanner in one go entails physical suffering. My little pension is woefully inelastic. A wing or two saved in ordering porter instead of stout is not to be despised. A borrowed match, a cadged filling of the pipe, all small things mount mightily in a year.

The Plain People of Ireland: Did you really go to Clongowes?

Myself: Certainly.

The Plain People of Ireland: Isn't that a fancy place, gentlemen's sons and all the rest of it.

Myself: It is. That's what I mean.

The Plain People of Ireland: Um. Did they teach you spelling there at all?

Myself: They taught me anything you like to mention.

The Plain People of Ireland: Then how about the word 'judgement' above? Unless we are very much mistaken, that should be JUDGMENT.

Myself: It is unthinkable that you should be very much mistaken, but if you take the trouble to look up any dictionary, you will find that either form is admissible, you smug, self-righteous swine.

(*Half to Myself*: The ignorant self-opinionated sod-minded suet-brained ham-faced mealy-mouthed streptococcus-ridden gang of natural gobdaws!)

* * *

What's this I have in me pocket? Dirty scrap of paper. Some newspaper heading I cut out. 'LANGUAGE IN DANGER.' Of course if I was a cultured European I would take this to mean that some dumb barbarous tonguetide threatens to drown the elaborate delicate historical machinery for human intercourse, the subtle articulative devices of communication, the miracle of human speech that has developed a thousand light-years over the ordnance datum, orphic telepathy three sheets to the wind and so on. But I know better.

Being an insulated western savage with thick hair on the soles of my feet, I immediately suspect that it is that fabulous submythical erseperantique patter, the Irish, that is under this cushion—beg pardon—under discussion.

Yes. Twenty years ago, most of us were tortured by the inadequacy of even the most civilised, the most elaborate, the most highly developed languages to the exigencies of human thought, to the nuances of inter-psychic communion, to the expression of the silent agonised pathologies of the post-Versailles epoch. Our strangled feelings, despairing of a sufficiently subtle vehicle, erupted into the crudities of the war novel. But here and there a finer intellect scorned this course. Tzara put his unhappy shirt on his dada (Fr. for hobby-horse as you must surely know), poor Jimmy Joyce abolished the King's English, Paulsy Picasso started cutting out paper dolls and I . . .

I?

As far as I remember, I founded the Rathmines branch of the Gaelic League. Having nothing to say, I thought at the time that it was important to revive a distant language in which absolutely nothing could be said.

* * *

Never forget that tenure by sochemaunce seisined by feodo copyholds in gross and reseisined through covenants of foeffsignory in frankalpuissaunce—

The Plain People of Ireland: This sounds like dirty water being squirted out of a hole in a burst rubber ball.

—is alienable only by *droit* of bonfeasaunce subsisting in free-bench coigny or in re-vested copywrits of *seisina facit stipidem,* a fair copy bearing a 2d. stamp to be entered at the Court of Star Chamber.

Furthermore, a rent seck indentured with such frankalseignory or chartamoign charges as may be, and re-empted in Market Overt, subsists thereafter in grand serjaunty du roi, eighteen fishing smacks being deemed sufficient to transport the stuff from Lisbon.

The Plain People of Ireland: Where do the fishing smacks come in?

Myself: Howth, usually.

The Plain People of Ireland: No, but what have they got to do with what you were saying?

Myself: It's all right. I was only trying to find out whether ye were still reading on.

* * *

To Timothy O'Keeffe of MacGibbon and Kee, London
25 November, 1961.

If I hear that word "Joyce" again I will surely froth at the gob!

* * *

[Of De Quincey:]
an excellent writer having, above all other symptoms of mastery in literature—discursiveness: and irony, unobtrusive, as it always should be.

* * *

To Christine Convers
12 April, 1965.

How very nice of you to write to me about KERMESSE IRLAND-AISE* and send me that page from *Nouvel Observateur*. I have had a lot of laughs with it, showing it to some low, bowsy friends of mine and demanding that they show me more bloody respect, now that I am a maître sorcier.

* * *

To Cecil Scott of the Macmillan Co., New York
9 March, 1965.

Far from being a hopeless gamble, this book will be no gamble at all; its U.S. rights will be eagerly sought and it almost certainly will be made into a film, very likely by my pal John Huston, who now lives in these parts. After it, works like Babbitt, the Great Gatsby and GWTW [*Gone With the Wind*] can be shoved into the attic with Oxford bags, warped tennis rackets, model T starting handles, and porcelain jars of bluestone Prohibition liquor.

Four chapters have been written since mid-January, and this is an American book to the extent that 2/3rds of the action will be sited there. What do you think of an Irish well-to-do agricultural scientist who, fed up with the stick-in-the-mud peasants here, emigrates to Texas to grow corn, has his beautiful crops ruined by the eruption of dirty black stuff, has 205 derricks in action within two years, and discovers an ancient covenant which enables him lawfully to invade the ranch of LBJ? What do you know of Dr. the Hon. Eustace Baggeley, who lives on a combined diet of morphia, cocaine and mescalin? How many hoodlums, political crooks and girlies do you know? Harry Poland? Cactus Mike Broadfeet? Senator Hovis Oxter? Katie ("the Dote") Bombstairs? George (the Girder) Shagge, steel-man? Congressman Theodore Hedge? Pogueen O'Rahilly? Nothing, I suppose. Shows how much you know yourself about the U.S. [Some

* The French translation of *At Swim-Two-Birds*.

sixty pages fleshing out this idea appear as "Slattery's Sago Saga" in
Flann O'Brien's *Stories and Plays*.]

[*The Journal of Irish Literature*]

* * *

There is nothing of much interest in Mr O Faoláin's issue of *The Ball*.
The only thing that caught my eye was an editorial preamble to an
article entitled 'Why I Am "Church of Ireland"':

It is part of the policy of THE BALL *to open as many windows as possible
on as many lives as possible so that we may form a full and complete
picture of this modern Ireland which we are making . . .*

I discern a certain want of candour in the statement that this *part* of
the policy of the paper. What are the other parts and why suppress
them? Would a 'full and complete' statement of policy be embarrassing? Hmmmm. But what I can't get right at all is this question of
the windows. Let us suppose that the 'lives' in question are indoor
and that the Paul Prys are outside, getting their socks damp in the
shrubbery. Surely whatever is to be seen can be seen through *one*
window. But forget even that. Why in heaven's name must we go
about *opening* windows. The whole point about a window is that you
can see in or out when the window is closed. Moreover, it is no joke
opening a closed window from outside—though I admit that (even
from the inside) a window that is not closed is even harder. And what
distinction is implied, I demand, as between 'full' and 'complete'? As
to 'this modern Ireland we are making', one can only point out (a)
that it would be a queer business if it was a *medieval . . . China* we
are making and anyhow, (b) that we are not making any Ireland. We
just live here (the travel ban)—some of us even *work* here.

* * *

Chat

Does Proust affect you terribly? Emotionally, I mean?

Nao, not rahlly. His prose does have that sort of . . . glittering
texture, rather like the feeling one gets from the best *émaux Lim-
ousins*. But nao . . . his peepul . . . thin, yeou knaow, thin . . . dull,
stupeed.

But surely . . . surely Swann . . . ?

Ah yes . . . If all his geese were Swanns. . . .

*   *   *

It is colourful, you say. *Colourful?* And if you get half a chance you will undoubtedly come out with some old bit of chat about 'these drab times' and how 'cheering' the effect of 'a bit of colour' and (please don't hurt me too much) 'a bit of old-world romance'. Yes. I wonder in what baby's newspaper you read that. COLOURFUL? Every time I hear the word 'colourful' I reach for my revolver.

*   *   *

I was once acquainted with a man who found himself present by some ill chance at a verse speaking bout. Without a word he hurried outside and tore his face off. Just that. He inserted three fingers into his mouth, caught his left cheek in a frenzied grip and ripped the whole thing off. When it was found, flung in a corner under an old sink, it bore the simple dignified expression of the honest man who finds self-extinction the only course compatible with honour.

*   *   *

To Sean O'Casey
13 April, 1942.
    I am much obliged for your recent letter regarding the "Béal Bocht." I think I forgot to tell you that it was your friend Jack Carney who suggested you might like to see a copy. It is by no means all you say but it is an honest attempt to get under the skin of a certain type of "Gael," which I find the most nauseating phenomenon in Europe. I mean the baby-brained dawnburst brigade who are ignorant of everything, including the Irish language itself. I'm sure they were plentiful enough in your own day. I cannot see any real prospect of reviving Irish at the present rate of going and way of working. I agree absolutely with you when you say it is essential, particularly for any sort of a literary worker. It supplies that unknown quantity in us that enables us to transform the English language and this seems to hold off people who know little or no Irish, like Joyce. It seems to be an inbred thing.
                                        [*The Journal of Irish Literature*]

*   *   *

To Stephen Ashe
7 October, 1955.
    This letter arises from a chat I had the other day with my friend Martin Cumberland, who gave me leave to quote his name. He told

me of the market for Sexton Blake stories and suggested I get in touch with you. I am interested in trying my hand at this sort of work.

My qualifications, briefly, are: M.A. degree; author of novel publ. Longman's, London, and in the U.S.; author of many short stories published here and in the U.S., and included in anthologies. I have been writing a sarcastic column for the *Irish Times* here for about 16 years, have written a lot for the *Sunday Dispatch* and French papers. I regard myself as an accomplished literary handyman.

I have read the Sexton Blake stories in my day and can, of course, refresh my recollection with the current series. I am sure I could do this job particularly if as Cumberland said, he thought the plot would be supplied. Anyhow, I should like to try. I would be willing to supply two chapters as a sample for nothing.

If you think we could do business, perhaps you would give me first-hand particulars as to length, time-limit, fee, supply of plot and any other significant details.

[*The Journal of Irish Literature*]

*   *   *

To Mark Hamilton of A. M. Heath & Co.
[no date]

The idea of a down payment or the "commissioning" of a work is generally regarded by writers as bad and to be avoided but in this case the suggestion originated with yourself [the British agent]. It peculiarly suits me because I make a reasonable living here from day-to-day journalism and book reviews for publication in Britain and the U.S. To produce this new book within the 6 months I have prescribed would entail shoving all that work aside and concentrating all thought and energy on the book only. This is the only way I can work when a long job is in question. I go so far as to believe that any work of fiction or imagination (as distinct from a book that deals with scientific research, antiquity, history) is necessarily bad if it took more than 6 months to write. I read recently an account of the literary activities of Edgar Wallace. He wrote his best known and most profitable story in 31 days and was very annoyed when somebody suggested that he should have a cup of coffee.

[Morris Library]

*   *   *

To Mark Hamilton

[no date]

About the beginning of this month I attended a "specialist" in connection with the persistent excruciating pain in my left ear and that region. After a lot of fancy talk on "literature" and the like (enough to make the hardest hearted listener break down and cry softly) he gave me one tablet. It ushered in a whole new world, begining with 8 hours non-stop vomiting, convulsions, seizures, hallucinations and countless unmentionable things. I am still very sick. This stuff works like a charm for 95% of the people getting it. For the rest it is dynamite on stilts, and I happen to be one of the 5%. But this letter is not about my health.

If you consult your records you will find that (apart from sundry, indeterminate items, e.g. Mercure de France) I am owed £100, £1000 and £250. One of the most odious and odorous aspects of the publishing game is the tradition that the writer is expected to hang around hoping that he might get paid some day, long after the last printer, stitcher, glue superintendant and foreman's office cleaner have been given their wages. Even in higher management circles the writer is regarded as a nuisance, up to the point of being an expendable and unnecessary nuisance.

I now ask that you proceed against the defaulting parties. . . .

You are invited to regard this letter very seriously.

[Morris Library]

A WRITER'S WRITHINGS*

I live in Dublin and occasionally write a book, which is marketed through an excellent literary agency with head office in London. For convenience this scandalous report is based on certain personal particulars, though it will be immediately seen that the situation disclosed applies not only to every Ireland-based writer but to all manner of other people thus domiciled who earn money abroad.

In respect of one book published in London a few years ago, my agents reported that they had had a proposal from publishers in West Germany, France and Italy for the conclusion of an agreement for

* A piece found in typed manuscript in the Morris Library O'Brien collection.

translation rights, and publication in those countries. I agreed in
principle, and signed the first formal agreement presented, which
was that from Germany. The down-payment advance was not dazzling
and, moreover, my agents wrote sorrowfully to say that there would
be a deduction at source of 20 p.c. on foot of German income tax.
Unperturbed, I replied that there was no need to worry about this;
books of mine published in the United States would be subject to a
similar costly snag except for the existence of a Double Tax Con-
vention between this country and the United States which meant
that, on the signing by me of a simple document of identity and
domicile, I would not be liable for U.S. tax in addition to Irish tax.

In making a tax return I mentioned this payment and asked the tax
inspector to send me a form on which I could apply for a refund of the
withheld German tax payment. Here is the astonishing reply, dated
11 March last:

As regards the payment made in West Germany, the position is that if
and when the agreement with Germany is ratified you shall claim a
refund of the German tax deducted under Article 8 of the Double Taxation Agreement. There is no Double Taxation Agreement with France
or Italy and Royalties received from these countries under deduction of
tax are assessable in your hands in this country on the net amount
received.

This Irish State is now in existence for over 43 years and would
appear to lack the most elementary link in comity with what might be
called the core of Europe, the Europe to which Ireland claims to have
brought civilisation as well as the Christian message, not to mention
that other matter—the discovery of America about 570 A.D. by St.
Brendan the Navigator.

Was Ireland standing aloof from the whole European mainland? I
made detailed inquiry and found that the answer was NO. She had
taxational liaison with just one country, part of which is within the
Arctic Circle and whose citizens, I feel, have a prickly existence amid
icicles and are covered with chilblains: I mean *Sweden!*

The great majority of Irish civil servants as well as parliamentary
deputies, including Ministers, is in origin of the peasant or shopboy
class. And it should be stated that Ireland has neither a Chancellor of
the Exchequer nor a Treasury; a member of the reigning party is
styled Minister for Finance and, since politics is not regarded as a

respectable activity, it follows that persons of standing and intellectual accomplishment are not available for any of the ministerial appointments. No Minister for Finance *ab urbe condita* has had the slightest training in public finance or the fiscal labyrinth, though this is not to say that a particular Minister could not evince strange charismata when confronted with a bad situation in the exchequer. Such a thing did happen in the twenties when the Minister was Mr. Ernest Blythe, now in his seventies and managing director of the Abbey Theatre, notoriously in decay. It seems that financially the country was on its knees but by the least expected of brilliancies, the Minister saved the day: he reduced the maximum old age pension of 10 shillings a week by 1 shilling! Otherwise the Minister is body and soul in the hands of three public clerks who are designated the Revenue Commissioners —two members and a chairman. I decided to write to the latter and, having referred to the German matter, here in part is what I said:

I will have to account for similar payments on foot of the publication of translations in Italy and France. No taxation agreement with these countries exists nor does it appear that any is contemplated. In fact, apart from the United Kingdom, such agreement does not exist with any European country except Sweden.

When the Dail was about to rise before last Christmas the Minister for Finance represented a supplementary estimate of £5,000 to pay for the bawling of a parcel of Wops in "grand opera" on the stage of Gaiety Theatre, Dublin. He said this was done at the request of the Arts Council, and it is noteworthy that this opera humbug is centered in the Minister's constituency, Wexford.

It will be seen from the foregoing that while aliens are hoisted on the backs of the taxpayers, natives of this country who live and work here are subjected to vicious double taxation which arises from the culpable delinquency and negligence of the Revenue Commissioners in failing to conclude taxation agreements with other European countries in the course of the last 42 years. Such a situation is completely contrary to natural justice. . . .

Yesterday's newspapers contained reports of a visit to Oslo by the Minister for External Affairs to establish a "cultural link" with Norway. I do not know what this phrase is intended to mean but I do know that at present, through the incompetence of the Revenue Commissioners, an Irish writer whose work is published in Norway will be subjected to penal taxation.

There was a sequel. The reply I received from the chairman's office on 17 April did not, of course, make any mention of what I had written or attempt to exculpate the wretched Commissioners. It simply said that an agreement had been entered into with West Germany on 2 April, 1964, with certain retroactive effect, and enclosed was a memorandum of three foolscap pages explaining about an application for a refund, which must be made *in German*. (The average urbane citizen could perhaps be expected to know enough of that language to get by in his unimportant transactions in *Wirts-* and *Hurenhaus* but competence in the technical jargon of *Steuereinnehmersverstaendnis* is surely an excessive expectation.)

However, that is the shocking situation in mid-1964; Ireland is fiscally cognisant of Sweden and West Germany. She knows nothing of France, with whom she has immediate historic ties, and is wholly unaware of Spain, Portugal, Belgium, the Netherlands, Denmark, Norway, Finland, Switzerland, Austria, Italy, Turkey, Greece, to say nothing of all the Iron Curtain countries and the Isle of Man.

What can be done? The Revenue Commissioners since 1922 (whoever they may have been) are answerable for this disgraceful and humiliating mess: the present trio should be subjected to the most severe disciplinary action, the chairman's grossly excessive salary of £4,492 should be permanently abated, and the Minister should resign. Of course none of these things will happen. The Minister, Jim Ryan, probably feels too settled in to make a change, being a veteran daddy-christmas of 72. And why should he? The Minister of Health, a Mr. MacEntee, is a patriarch of 75 and not a bother on him.

Yes, Ireland is a laugh but it is not a funny country.

BEHAN, MASTER OF LANGUAGE*

Oscar Wilde denounced fox-hunting as the pursuit of the uneatable by the unspeakable, and one may perhaps sadly echo the witticism by saying that Brendan Behan's death is the triumph over the irrepressible by the irreplaceable (and he would be the first to snigger at the eccentric staggering of that little bit of English).

But it is quite true that he will not be replaced, either in a hurry

* This essay was published in the *Sunday Telegraph* (London), March 22, 1964. The text is from the manuscript in the Morris Library.

or at all. There has been no Irishman quite like him and his play-writing, which I personally found in parts crude and offensive as well as entertaining, was only a fraction of a peculiarly complicated personality. He was in fact much more a player than a play-wright or, to use a Dublin saying, "he was as good as a play." He exuded good nature. He excelled in language and was a total master of bad language. That latter part of his achievement must remain unknown to the world at large but his personal associates will sorrowfully cherish the memory of it as something unique and occasionally frightening. I have personally never heard the like of it, and it could become enchanting when the glittering scurrilities changed with ease from native Dublinese to good Irish or bookeity French.

It is this sense of ebullience, zest, exuberance, that will remain to tell of Brendan Behan, not his plays. His generosity with money when he had it was boundless, and no man had a more numerous retinue of touchers, spongers and ruffianly down and outs. He knew this, of course, but did not care. Indeed, his capacity for not caring was another dominant trait. His methods of drinking were simply inexplicable; brandy would follow whiskey, the two to be promptly drowned in stout softened with soda water—but the sad gastric mess promptly redressed with a tumbler of brown sherry. It is many the time a mean, grasping companion lived to rue a public house encounter with Brendan, for the companion was usually expected to participate fifty-fifty in the lowering of the goods.

Even already many silly things have been written about the dead man in tribute, including the superb gaucherie of ranking him with Joyce. He told me he could not be bothered with Joyce "or any of that jazz," and in fact had not read the work of the supercilious unDublinly emigré. One can detect some affinity with O'Casey but the pervasive error lies in ranking him with any literary practitioner. He was something better—a delightful rowdie, a wit, a man of action in the many dangerous undertakings where he thought his duty lay, a reckless drinker, a fearsome denouncer of humbug and pretence, and sole proprietor of the biggest heart that has beaten in Ireland in the last forty years.

How does Dublin take his tragic departure? I know it is only foolishness in my own head, but the streets seem strangely silent. Their noisy one-time son has gone home, this time for good.

* * *

Mr Patrick Kavanagh was recently reported as having declared that 'there is no such thing as Gaelic literature'. This is hard luck on the Institute of Advanced Studies, who are supposed to be looking into the thing. I attended the Book Fair in the Mansion House the other evening in the hope of overhearing other similar pronouncements from the writing persons who infest such a place. I heard plenty, and have recorded it in my note-books under 'Stuff To Be Used If Certain People Put Their Heads Out.'

The Fair was fine. Bright, rearing stands; melodious loud speakers, women beautiful, long and smooth as the strand at Tramore, dazzling big print, colour standing on colour in every pattern, bright bland books of fine worth, exquisite arrangements of everything that is nice. Yet it was not that Nature had cast o'er the scene, Her purest of crystal and brightest of green, It was not sweet magic of streamlet or hill, O no, it was something more exquisite still oh ho no, it was something more exqueeseet steel. 'Twas that Friends of the Academy of Letters were near, Who made every dear scene of enchantment more dear, And one felt how the best charms of Nature improve, When we see them reflected in books that we love.

*   *   *

[Of popular writing:]
stories about wee Annie going to her first confession, stuff about funerals, old men in chimney nooks after 50 years in America; will-making, match-making—just one long blush for many an innocent man like me, who never harmed them.

[The Irish Times]

*   *   *

Flying from Lisbon to Foynes the other day, I beguiled (what but?) the time with Hesketh Pearson's book on Bernard Shaw and a recent copy of Mr Sean O Faolaín's periodical *The Boll.** I was interested to see that Shaw has been at his old game of copying other people. In one of his letters (how meticulously composed for publication) he calls somebody a 'whitemailer'. Who, reader, invented this type of jest? Who patented wintersaults, old ralgia, footkerchiefs and a thousand other jewels? (Not that I mind.)

A thing occurred to me about this newly formed Shaw Society. I

---

* Actually *The Bell.* O'Brien was fond of maiming certain titles.

approve of it, the vice-presidency of the concern I would gladly have accepted had not a false shyness deterred the founders from approaching me; guineas three I would have contributed without demur. It appears that the Society has no headquarters. (Notice how pertly 'footquarters' bobs up?) ...

*   *   *

Research Bureau

Ignorant people sometimes complain about the 'footling' character of some of the Bureau's inventions. Than this there were no more unjust accusation. *Every invention helps some poor fellow mortal ... somewhere.* Some of the inventions, however, have a unique general utility for all mankind. Day and night, somewhere on the earth, men are hoisting weights and wasting time and energy on futile grappling devices. They have to tie this knot or that, or make fast the other. Consider, however, this thing I illustrate:

Examine carefully the innovation at the top of the hook. It is a

movable steel loop with just sufficient clearance to permit the hoisting-rope to pass through. In this case, you tie nothing. You simply pass the rope through and begin to hoist. The weight will cause the steel loop to tend to move up vertically and will thus catch the rope in an unshakeable vice.

Most difficult job, thinking out these things.

* * *

—We'll see what's in them all in good time, he announced sternly, and if those books are dirty books, lascivious peregrinations on the fringes of filthy indecency, cloacal spewings in the face of Providence, with pictures of prostitutes in their pelts, then out of this house they will go and their owner along with them. You can tell him that if you see him first. And I would get Father Fahrt to exorcise all fiendish contaminations in this kitchen and bless the whole establishment. Do you hear me?

[*The Hard Life*]

* * *

Overheard

I tried to get it many a time. O many a time.

Well I could never see any harm in it.

I seen it once in a shop on the quays, hadn't any money on me at the time and when I came back to look for it a week later bedamn but it was gone. And I never seen it in a shop since.

Well, I can't see what all the fuss was about.

You read it, did you?

I couldn't see any harm at all in it there was nothing in it.

I tried to get it many a time meself . . .

There's no harm in it at all.

Many's a time I promised meself I'd look that up and get it.

Nothing at all that anybody could object to, not a thing in it from the first page to the last.

It's banned, o'course.

Not a thing in it that anybody could object to, NO HARM AT ALL IN IT, nothing at all anywhere in the whole thing.

O indeed many's a time I tried to get it meself.

* * *

The Debating Society of the Clerical staffs attached to the Central Banking Corporation met last Saturday, Twinfeet J. in the chair.

Proposing the motion 'That the Pen is mightier than the Sword', *Mr Chaine* said that from time immemorial far beyond the dawn of history, the human race had evinced respect for the dignity of the human intellect. This respect had not only successfully weathered the ravages of time, but also the savage attacks of marauders, particularly in monastic times. All great human revolutions had been inspired by the pens of great thinkers, who probed into human destiny with the timeless insight of genius. He asked the house to endorse what he made bold to term 'The Primacy of the Pen' by a unanimous vote.

Mr O'Queen, opposing the motion, stated that a walk through any museum would prove that the development of the human body was the dominant characteristic of the glory that was Greece. Literature and the arts could only flourish in a civilisation which had been founded by those who wielded the sword. To admire the sword was not necessarily to endorse the principles of militarism, the doctrine of physical force, or the unprincipled maxim that might is right. The development of the body could be secured without oppressing minorities or waging war, and such development inculcated sportsmanship and manliness. The Boy Scout movement was a case in point. The House would remember the sentiments so felicitously expressed by no less a poet than William Wordsworth:

> 'To hold the fight above renown
> To hold the game above the prize,
> To honour as you strike him down
> The foe that comes with fearless eyes.'

* * *

And The Brother

Myles himself, the brilliant young journalist, will be out of town for 14 days. No letters will be forwarded. An undefatigable first-nighter, he is keenly interested in the theatre and has written several plays. Life he regards as a dialectic that evolves from aesthetic and extra-human impulses, many of them indubitably Marxian in manifestation. The greatest moment of his life (which occurred in 1924) was when he made the discovery that life is in reality an art form. Each person, he believes, is engaged on a life-long opus of grandiose expressionism, modulating and mutating the Ego according to subconscious aesthetic patterns. The world, in fact, is a vast art gallery, wherein even the curators themselves are exhibitors and exhibitionists. The horse, however, is the supreme artistic symbol—

The Editor: We can't have much more of this, space must also be found for my stuff.

Myself: All right, never hesitate to say so. I can turn off the tap at will.

* * *

What one might call the pathology of literature is a subject that a person with education and intelligence should examine. What prompts a sane inoffensive man to write? Assuming that to 'write' is mechanically to multiply communication (sometimes a very strong assumption, particularly when one writes a book about peasants in Irish) what vast yeasty eructation of egotism drives a man to address simultaneously a mass of people he has never met and who may resent being pestered with his 'thoughts'? They don't have to read what he writes, you say. But they do. That is, indeed, the more vicious neurosis that calls for investigation. The blind urge to read, the craving for print—that is an infirmity so deeply seated in the mind of today that it is (well-nigh) ineradicable. People blame compulsory education and Lord Northcliffe. The writer can be systematically discouraged, his 'work' can be derided and if all else fails we can (have recourse) to the modern remedy known as 'liquidating the intellectuals'. But what can you do with the passive print addict? Absolutely nothing.

* * *

Mr Collopy came in about five o'clock, followed shortly afterwards by Annie. He seemed in a bad temper. Without a word he collapsed into his armchair and began reading the paper. The brother came in about six, loaded with books and small parcels. He naturally perceived the chill and said nothing. The tea turned out to be a very silent, almost menacing, meal. I kept thinking of Penelope. Tea with *her* would be a very different affair, an ambrosial banquet of unheard-of delicacy, and afterwards sweet colloquy by the fire, though perhaps with an undertone of melancholy. Was it easy, I wondered, or was it quite impossible to write really good and touching poetry. Something to write really good and touching poetry. Something to reach the heart, to tell of love? Very likely it was quite impossible for the like of myself to attempt anything of the kind, though the brother could be trusted to explain the art and simplify it in six easy lessons by correspondence.

[*The Hard Life*]

* * *

In New York's swank Manhattan lives blond, smiling, plump James Keats, descendant of famous poet John. No lover of poetry, James Keats is director of the million-dollar dairy combine Manhattan Cheeses and ranked Number Three in the Gallup quiz to find America's Ten Ablest Executives. James lives quietly with slim dark attractive wife, Anna, knows all there is about cheeses, likes a joke like his distinguished forbear. Wife Anna likes to tell of the time he brought her to see the Louis-Baer fight.

'He just sat there roaring "Camembert, Camembert!" '

If the joke doesn't interest you, do you derive amusement from this funny way of writing English? It is very smart and up-to-date. It was invented by America's slick glossy *Time* and copied by hacks in every land. For two pins I will write like that every day, in Irish as well as English. Because that sort of writing is taut, meaningful, hard, sinewy, compact, newsy, factual, muscular, meaty, smart, modern, brittle, chromium, bright, flexible, omnispectric.

* * *

ERWOOD STANDARD TYPEWR. Reason that out. It's before me on my desk as I write. (That's a phrase you often see in travel books—the jewelled and beaded purse of Stevenson, picked up for a few *dhraksi* in a junk shop in Samoa, if you could believe the boastful swine; before him on his desk as he writes. Can anybody write at anything but a desk?) But get back to this ERWOOD STANDARD TYPEWR. It's all along the top of my machine in golden letters. Do you get it? My flying thumb, sweeping up a million times a year to whip back the carriage, has erased the last four letters of TYPEWR. The equally active other thumb, darting and re-darting to click the roller round, has wiped out the UND. There's an explanation for everything old boy.

It's fairly obvious I haven't much to say today. Sow what? Sow wheat. Ah-ha, the old sow-faced cod, the funny man, clicking out his dreary blob of mirthless trash. The crude grub-glutted muck-shuffler slumped on his hack-chair, lolling his dead syrup eyes through other people's books to lift some lousy joke. English today, have to be a bit careful, can't get away with murder so easily in English. Observe the grey pudgy hand faltering upon the type-keys. That is clearly the hand of a man that puts the gut number one. Not much self-sacrifice there. Yes but he has a conscience, remember. He has a conscience. He does not feel too well today. He casts bleared cataractic (Gk. katarrhaktes) sub-glances over his past self. Why am I here? I want a straight answer that can be subjected to intellectual criteria. No, I know what you were going to say, you won't put me off with that. Why is this man here? What for? Eats four fat meals a day. Wears clothes. Sleeps at night. Overpaid for incompetent work. Kept on out of pity for wife. Is worried. Ho ho. Feels dissatisfied with himself. Feels ought to be doing something. Feels ... wrong. Not fulfilling duties of station in life. How often is the little finger raised per diem? Feels ... dirty. Incapable of writing short bright well-constructed newspaper article, notwithstanding fact editors only too anxious print and pay for suitable articles, know man who took course Birmingham School of Journalism now earns 12,000 pounds in spare time. If you can write a letter you can write articles for newspapers. Editors waiting. Payment at the rate of one guinea per thousand words. Always enclose stamped envelope for return if unsuitable. Importance of neat typing. ERWOOD STANDARD TYPEWR. Editors have not time to study decipher puzzle out illegible scrawls on both sides of paper. Covering note not essential. But if desired brief courteous note saying take liberty of submitting for consideration literary article on how spent summer holidays. Or the humours of stamp collecting.

* * *

Print is one extreme of typographical development, the other being mathematical notation. It consists, in the occident anyway, of the representation of sounds by purely arbitrary shapes, and arranging them so that those in the know can reproduce the spoken words intended. This process is known as Reading, and is very uncommon in adults. It is uncommon because, firstly, it is in many cases frankly impossible, the number of phonetic symbols being inadequate; secondly, because of the extreme familiarity of the word-shapes to a population whose experience is necessarily derived in the main from marks printed on paper. It is in this second circumstance, familiarity with the word or phrase shapes, that has led to the unpremeditated birth of a visual language.

Now, you (yes, YOU) before you tear this paper into little bits, kindly tell me whether that last paragraph was written by me as part of my satanic campaign against decency and reason or whether it is taken from a book written in all seriousness by some other person. On your answer to that query will depend more than I would care to say in public.

Mister Quidnunc is even more stimulating today than usual. Turn to his little corner and have the time of your life.

* * *

As a matter of fact, said the Good Fairy, I do not understand two words of what you have said and I do not know what you are talking about. Do you know how many subordinate clauses you used in the last oration of yours, Sir?

I do not, replied the Pooka.

Fifteen subordinate clauses in all, said the Good Fairy, and the substance of each of them contained matter sufficient for a colloquy in itself. There is nothing so bad at the compression of fine talk that should last for six hours into one small hour. Tell me, Sir, did you ever study Bach?

Where did you say that from? inquired the Pooka.

I was sitting under your bed, replied the Good Fairy, on the handle of your pot.

The fugal and contrapuntal character of Bach's work, said the Pooka, that is a delight. The orthodox fugue has four figures and such a number is in itself admirable. Be careful of that pot. It is a present from my grandmother.

Counterpoint is an odd number, said the Good Fairy, and it is a great art that can evolve a fifth Excellence from four Futilities.

I do not agree with that, said the Pooka courteously.

[*At Swim-Two-Birds*]

THE MYLES NA GCOPALEEN
CATECHISM OF CLICHÉ,
AND MORE

The Myles na gCopaleen Catechism of Cliché. In 356 tri-weekly parts. A unique compendium of all that is nauseating in contemporary writing. Compiled without regard to expense or the feelings of the public. A harrowing survey of sub-literature and all that is pseudo, mal-dicted and calloused in the underworld of print. Given free with the *Irish Times*. Must not be sold separately or exported without a licence. Copyright, Printed on re-pulped sutmonger's aprons. Irish labour, Irish ink. Part one. Section one. Let her out, Mike! Lights! O.K., Sullivan, let her ride!

Is man ever hurt in a motor smash?

No. He sustains an injury.

Does such a man ever die from his injuries?

No. He succumbs to them.

Correct. But supposing an ambulance is sent for. He is put into the ambulance and *rushed* to hospital. Is he dead when he gets there, assuming he is not alive?

No, he is not dead. Life is found to be extinct.

Correct again. A final question. Did he go into the hospital, or enter it, or be brought to it?

He did not. He was admitted to it.

Good. That will do for today.

* * *

A cliché is a phrase that has become fossilised, its component words deprived of their intrinsic light and meaning by incessant usage. Thus it appears that clichés reflect somewhat the frequency of the incidence of the same situations in life. If this be so, a sociological commentary could be compiled from these items of mortified language.

Is not the gun-history of modern Ireland to be verified by the inflexible terminology attaching to it? A man may be shot dead but if he survives a shot, he is not shot but sustains gun-shot wounds. The man who fires the shot is always his assailant, never his attacker or merely the gun-man. The injured party is never taken to hospital but is removed there (in a critical condition). The gun-man does not escape, even if he is not caught; he makes good his escape.

Oddly enough—unnecessary phrase—a plurality of lawbreakers behave differently; they are never assailants but armed men. When they are not caught, they do not make good their escape; they decamp. If there be defenders on the scene, shots are *exchanged*. And the whole affair is, of course, a shooting affray. You see, there is no other kind of affray. If it is not a shooting affray, it is not an affray at all. But it might be a fracas.

* * *

Catechism of Cliché

What, as to the quality of solidity, imperviousness, and firmness, are facts?

Hard.

And as to temperature?

Cold.

With what do facts share this quality of frigidity?
Print.
To what do hard facts belong?
The situation.
And to what does a cold fact belong?
The matter.
What must we do to the hard facts of the situation?
Face up to the hard facts of the situation.
What does a cold fact frequently still do?
Remain.
And what is notoriously useless as a means of altering the hard facts of the situation?
All the talk in the world.

* * *

For Your Cliché Album

In what can no man tell the future has for us?
Store.
With what do certain belligerents make their military dispositions?
Typical Teutonic thoroughness.
In what manner do wishful thinkers imagine that the war will be over this year?
Fondly.
Take the word, 'relegate'. To what must a person be relegated?
That obscurity from which he should never have been permitted to emerge.
What may one do with a guess, provided one is permitted?
Hazard.
And what is comment?
Superfluous.

* * *

There Is an Interval Here

An interval is right. What we all want is a good long walk in the country, plenty of fresh air and good wholesome food. This murder of my beloved English language is getting in under my nails. There are, of course, other branches of charnel-house fun into which I have not yet had the courage to lead my readers. Not quite *clichés* but things that smell the same and worse. Far worse. Things like this, I mean:

Of course, gin is a very depressing drink.

The air in Bundoran is very bracing.

You'll see the whole lot of us travelling by air before you're much older.

Your man is an extraordinary genius.

Of course, the most depressing drink of the lot is gin.

Did you get what I'm driving at? Can you visualise the list of dirty pale goading phrases with which I may—yes— 'regale' you next week? What?

I beg your pardon?

Well that isn't my fault. I merely record what goes on around me. I just write down what goes on.

*   *   *

More of It

The Myles na gCopaleen Catechism of Cliché, part two. Copyright of course. What's more, all rights reserved. Reproduction in whole or part, etc., etc.

Is treatment, particularly bad treatment, ever given to a person?

No. It is always meted out.

Is anything else ever meted out?

No. The only thing that is ever meted out is treatment.

And what does the meting out of treatment evoke?

The strongest protest against the treatment meted out.

Correct. Mention another particularly revolting locution.

'The matter will fall to be dealt with by so-and-so.'

Good. Are you sufficiently astute to invent a sentence where this absurd jargon will be admissible?

*   *   *

Next speech. Hurry please. Get this thing over. A drunk on our left trying to heckle. A rossiner wouldn't be bad, have a double one after this. Next please.

Much pleasure rise speak today this distinguished gathering; particularly on same platform last speaker. Last time we spoke together great

Longford Rally 1829; doubtless he's forgotten. We've gone our different ways since then. Suppose no two men in this country more representative divergent poles political thought. Not what came here to say. Came say few words present crisis dark clouds lowering over fair face this country never greater danger. But spirit Irish people will prevail as ever, come to top. Only solution to problems before us is serious interest revival tongue our fathers spoke. Great revival work must go on. National heritage, nothing worth having left if not saved, receding rapidly in west. Save ere it is too late, only badge of true nationhood.

(Loud mad frenzied cheering.)

* * *

A few weeks ago I was interrupted when about to give the public my long-awaited description of my own face. Several anxious readers have written in asking when they might expect it. My answer is that they may expect it to-day. Let us take the features one by one and then stand back, as one stands back from a majestic Titian or Van Gogh, and view the whole magnificent—

The Plain People of Ireland: Is this going to be long?

Myself: Not very.

The Plain People of Ireland: How long roughly?

Myself: Well, say ten lines for the vast Homeric brow, the kingly brow that is yet human wise and mild. Then the eyes, peerless wine-green opal of rare hue, brittle and ebullient against the whiteness of Himalayan snow—

The Plain People of Ireland: Another ten lines?

Myself: Say seven each. That's fourteen altogether.

* * *

Me and My Soul

This dripped off my assembly belt the other night (when I could have sworn I had the machines turned off for the night). Print it on barley-fudged crême-primed Hungarian sub-paper in good, old 12-point Gracatia Sancta and next thing you know I will have hair on my face and I will perceive indubitably Marxian strata in the subconscious, suggesting that all irrational impulses etc. etc. etc.

> the ántic soul
> rides the wry, red brain;

> horses know horses know
> what they're thinking about
> (you might say curse that alien corn),
> the bloody heart
> lusts in its foul tenement
> o blow, viaticum pump, blow
> on your last glazed fruit-valves.

* * *

A thing that you might consider when you have time is the wasteful and 'unscientific' structure of language. I mean—say in English—the number of simple economically-devised sounds which are not 'words' and which have no meaning—while gigantic regiments of letters are assembled to form words which have simple meanings and which take a long time to say or write. An example of the latter—'valetudinarianism'. As regards the former, consider the satisfactory syllable 'pot'. Substitute any other vowel you like and you get a 'word'—pat, pet, pit, put. There you have efficiency, economy. Such invention saves everybody's time; even school-children see there is reason there and are not resentful. . . .

* * *

When a respectable lady up in court recently for removing not clothing but articles of clothing from a crowded shop when she thought nobody was looking, the District Justice remarked that there was far too much shop-lifting in Dublin, and then imposed (well, what can you impose?) a heavy sentence of imprisonment.

I suppose he was right when he said there was far too much shop-lifting in Dublin but I am not clear how one calculates what is the right amount of shop-lifting for Dublin. Would we be in a worse mess if there was too little shop-lifting? I think a small committee of D.J.'s should be convened to determine the optimum incidence of shop-lifting for Dublin and other urban centres and sentence only ladies who exceed their quota.

* * *

I like to give a domestic tip now and again because I have reason to think that a few ladies read my notes here. A good way to prevent blood from curdling is to make sure that only the purest ingredients are used. Secondly, pour the blood in very slowly, a spoonful at a time, and thin it out with a few drops of vinegar when the mixture threatens to become too turgid.

* * *

I think some of our government departments should see about getting themselves more appropriate names. Our military ministry, seeing we are neutral, should be called the Department of the Fence. And surely the Department of Agriculture is a poor title—would it not be better to call it the Department of Yokel Government?

* * *

Somebody should write a monograph on the use of the word 'supposed' in this country. Start listening for it, either in your own mouth or in others', and you will see that it comprises the sum of the national character, that it is a mystical synthesis of all our habits, hopes and regrets. There is no immediately obvious and neat Irish equivalent, and I opine that the discovery of this word 'supposed' may have been a factor in the change over to English. You meet a man you know as you take a walk on the strand at Tramore. 'Of course I'm not supposed to be here at all,' he tells you, 'I'm supposed to be gettin' orders for th'oul fella in Cork. I'm here for the last week. How long are you staying?'

The words occur most frequently in connexion with breaches of the law or in circumstances where the gravest catastrophes are imminent. You enter a vast petrol depot. The place is full of refineries, pumps, tanks, a choking vapour fills the air. The man on the spot shows you the wonders and in due course produces his cigarettes and offers you one. 'Of course I needn't tell you,' he comments as he lights up, 'there's supposed to be no smoking here.'

You enter a tavern, meet a friend, invite him to join you in a drink. He accepts. He toasts your health, takes a long sip, and replaces the glass on the counter. He then taps his chest in the region of the heart. 'As you know,' he remarks, 'I'm not supposed to touch this stuff at all.'

You have been to some very late and boring function. You are going home, you feel you need a drink, you are a gentleman and know nothing whatever about the licensing laws. Naturally you rap at the door of the first pub you see. All is in darkness. The door opens, a head appears, it peeps up the street and then down; next thing you are whisked in.

'We're supposed to be closed, you know.'

Kreisler is not a great violinist, in the view of the Irish. He is sup-posed to be one of the greatest violinists in the world. Nor is Irish the national language of Ireland, the Constitution enacted by the people notwithstanding. It's supposed to be. You are not supposed to use gas during the off-hours. You are not supposed to change the lie of your golf ball to very adjacent, if favourable, terrain when your opponent is not looking. You are not supposed to use electric radiators, nor are you supposed to own a radio set without paying the licence. Not more than eight people are supposed to stand inside a bus. You are aware that your colleague was at the races when he was supposed to be sick, but you're not supposed to know and certainly you're not supposed to report such an occurrence. You are not supposed to pay more than the controlled price for rationed commodities. You are not supposed to import uncustomed liquors. You are not supposed to use your wife's hair-brush on the dog. You are not supposed to use the firm's telephone for private trunk calls.

And so on. In no such context does the phrase 'not supposed' con-note a prohibition. Rather does it indicate the recognition of the existence of a silly taboo which no grown-up person can be expected to take seriously. It is the verbal genuflection of a worshipper who has come to lay violent hands on the image he thus venerates. It is our domestic password in the endemic conspiracy of petty lawlessness.

All that I believe to be true, though possibly I'm not supposed to say it so bluntly.

* * *

I dislike labels—rather I mean it's not that they aren't terribly useful. *They are, old man.* But do . . . do they sufficiently take account of one as . . . a . . . person? There is my dilemma. (How do you like his horns?) But I . . . I . . . (little indulgent laugh) I know humanity, its foibles, its frailties, its fatuities; I know how the small mind hates what can't be penned into the humiliating five-foot shelf of its 'categories'. And so . . . if you must libel me, sorry, wrong brief, if you must label me, if you must use one epithet to 'describe' a being who in diversity of modes, universality of character and heterogeneity of spatio-temporal continuity transcends your bathetic dialectic, if, in short, one . . . practically algebraic symbol must suffice to cover the world-searing nakedness of that ontological polymorph who is at once immaculate brahmin, austere neo-platonist, motor-salesman, mystic, horse-doctor,

hackney journalist and ideological catalyst, call me ... call me ...
(*qu'importe en effet, tout cela?*) call me ... ex-rebel. Forget the grimy
modest exterior, civilisation's horrid camouflage of the hidden, inner,
in-forming radiance. True that ... economic stresses force one to spend
oneself on ... trifles (what with sherry halfdollar a halfglass and
sponge-cake ... *Sponge-cake?* Me good woman do you realise there's
a waaaaaaaaaaar on?). About the valid things, for instance, one must
not write; ethics, plastics, authority what is its foundation in the com-
promise of the diurnal round (This is mine, I think?), the lust for
Order (with its glamorous satellites, 'beauty' and 'harmony'—not to
mention ancient Hibernians), how to reconcile it with man's un-
quenchable longing for *Freedom?* (Rather loosely put but you see
what a Haeck Reuter is up against?)

I mean one's soul is forgotten but one must be very simple in this
kind of thing, and keep frightfully close to the bone, follow the telegraph wires it's about four miles from here. You see, one is ... one is
simply a plain hack journalist, concerned with such prosaic things as
... getting things across, smoothly, fair play to all, square deal for my
masters, and never forget the eager throng of readers (certified) who so
instinctively believe in their right to speak their mind that they, they
will not be slow to let the Editor person know what they think of one's
pitiful work. Very Irish, very traditional, the only difference being that
from the poor berated French Revolution onwards we spoke our mind
against what poor John Mitchel called 'The Carthaginian' in spite of
poison, debt and egg-soil. Now ... (bitter laugh) ... now we speak
it against ... writers ... the Anglo-Irish, Liberals, individualists, children of the Renaissance and other contemptible ... and unarmed ...
creatures!!!! Of course, when Truth is not paramount, one must cry
aloud for Tolerance and free speech. Then as soon as Truth becomes
paramount as result of our Tolerance and *Freedom* (!!!!!) ... there is
no longer any need for Tolerance—in fact it would be a crime. Grand.
Grand. But ... just a bit hard on those who ... do not believe in
'Absolutes', not even in Truth permanent and faceless. Just a bit hard
on those to whom the 'errors' of ... Plotinus are just as valid, and
important as say those molten Iberian lyrics whose sensuous imagery
gave Crashaw his melodic line and burning glass.

No, no, no, this is forbidden ... And still—how wonderful, how
indestructible is human nature! and still this man who goes to jail and
death will go on saying 'Alas, that Might can vanquish Right, They

fell and passed away, but true Men like you Men, are plenty here today!'—the foolish Greek! the silly Renaissance ass!! The comic liberal! By heavens, this time once and for all we'll eradicate from his silly carcass his thousand-year-old folly! . . . But enough! Pass me the strychnine, Mac, it is in the top left-hand corner of the chest of drawers under the old Ph.D (Heidelberg) scroll.

*   *   *

A note in my diary says: 'Ten to the power of seventy-nine. Write on this joke.'

Very well. Why not? I wish I had the money to finance *real* scientific research. You remember the worry we had back in the thirties (?this century, I think—or was it?) about the electron, how to determine its mass. Eddington had an amusing angle on the thing. But first let us recall the previous situation where you had the crude journeyman's approach of calculating it as 10 (to the power of −27) of a gramme. Most of us looked on that as a sort of music-hall joke—mass audience reaction makes you snigger but you are not really amused, you are sorry for having forsaken for the evening your monogram on Cicero's *Pro Malony*. Because it really boiled down to this—that if some smartie broke into the place at Sèvres and stole the so-called 'standard kilogramme' your '10 (to the power of −27)' immediately became more obviously the arbitrary unfunny gaffe it essentially was. Very well. The 'scientist', in sum, had been deluding himself that the Heath Robinson experiments which led to that 'discovery' could be solemnly called *observational determination*. Whereas it is just make-believe and whimsy, all essentially feminine.

The 'problem'—as one then thought of it—was to relate the mass of the electron to . . . to something *real* (like, for instance, sleep). The point, of course, about Eddington's handling of the experiment was his realisation that it could *only* give information about a *double* wave system which 'belonged' as much to the electron as to the material comparison standard necessarily used. Very well.

To reach a result it had been necessary to investigate the circumstances where the double wave can be replaced with single waves (really, this sounds like barber-shop talk!)—or in other words, to examine the process where you are slipping from macroscopic to microscopic; call them 'magnitudes' by all means, terminology is unimportant. Eddington, as you know, tied this up with his engaging patent 'comparison aether', a retroambulant nonentity moping about intro-spectively way below the xx axis, whose mass can be calculated, need-less to say, from a formula expressed largely in terms of the fundamental constants of macroscopical physics—the time-space radius, velocity of 'light' . . . and *all* the particles in the universe. Now when this mass is m and the

o

electric-particle—proton or electron, it doesn't matter a damn which—is, as usual, m, you have this incredible quadratic:

10m − 136mm + m. = o

o

What is quite curious is that this new equation and formula for m

o

yield (for this velocity) a maximum value of 780 kilom. per sec. per megaparsec . . . which, of course, accords with the 'value' found by observation (!!!!!)

But here is what I am really getting at—the uniquely prolonged sneer that Eddington embodied in the paper he read to us at the Royal Society in the fateful autumn of '33.

'In the maze of connection of physical constants,' he said, 'there remains just one pure number—' (ho-ho-ho, I cannot help interject-ing)—'which is known only by observation and has no theoretical explanation. It is a very large number, about 10 (to the power of 79), and the present theory indicates that it is the number of particles in the universe. It may seem to you odd—' (Not at all, not at all, one murmurs)—'that this number should come into the various constants such as the constants of gravitation. You may say, how on earth can the number of particles in remote parts of the universe affect the Cavendish experiment on the attraction of metal spheres in a labora-tory? I do not think they affect it at all. But the Cavendish and other experiments having given the result they did, we can deduce that space will go on and on, curving according to the mass contained in it until only a small opening remains and that the 10 (to the power of 79)th particle will be the last particle to be admitted through the last small opening and will shut the door after it.'

Bye-bye, 10 (to the power of 79).
Mind that step!

* * *

It is, I think, natural for a person of my stamp (as poor Rowan Hamilton used to say) to embrace all human perfections and accomplishments (but excluding such as may be evil) within the mastery of my superb intellect gracing not myself but all humanity with an artistic pre-eminence that is withal saturated with an exquisite humility.

'But . . . don't you ever run short of ideas? How can you always write so . . . interestingly . . . so . . . so authoritatively about such a variety of things. Seldom, I mean, have . . . so many things been written for so many people . . . by so few a man.'

My reply is simple and, as always, truthful. 'Madam, writing is the least of my occupations. Many other things, many many other things contribute to the sum of my cares. Vast things, things imponderable and ineluctable, terrible things, things which no other mortal were fit to hear of—things I must think upon when utterly alone. Writing is surely a small thing, indeed. Difficulties, Mmmmm. One is not conscious of them. There are, of course, five things and five things only that can be written about and though for me they have lost all interest as problems, I continue to write out of the depth of my feeling for dark groping humanity.'

The Dalkey Archive

He sat down at the piano and after some slow phrases, erupted into what Mick with inward wit, would dub a headlong chromatic dysentery which was 'brilliant' in the bad sense of being inchoate and, to his ear at least, incoherent. A shattering chord brought the disorder to a close.

Well, he said, rising, what did you think of that?

Hackett looked wise.

—I think I detected Liszt in one of his less guarded moments, he said.

—No, De Selby answered. The basis of that was the canon at the start of César Franck's well-known sonata for violin and piano. The rest was all improvisation. By me.

—The Dalkey Archive

INTRODUCTION

The Dalkey Archive is the last major project that Flann O'Brien completed. Published in Great Britain in 1964 and a year later in the United States, the book was produced by a man under great physical and not a little financial pain. A variety of accidents and the onset of the more major diseases that were killing him made it difficult for O'Brien to sustain the kind of effort that made *The Third Policeman* such a tight structure. At the same time his connection with *The Irish Times* had deteriorated—he claimed they were cutting his material—and having been "retired early" from the civil service on a small pension, he found it necessary to cast about for methods of earning a living. He managed to peddle his column, sometimes under various bland names such as John Doe, to provincial papers promising he wouldn't be controversial, just lively. He tried for a college teaching post and even for a spot as a registrar. He did not get any of these jobs, and even some of the papers began restricting or dropping his

371

column entirely because of "rising costs," "paper shortages," and other mechanical forces. Reading this correspondence brings to mind the last letters of trumpeter Joe "King" Oliver as he applies for a job sweeping a pool room while holding out hope for a new pair of teeth so that he might play in some local band with musicians who are neither old enough nor bright enough to have ever heard of him.

O'Brien was not without help, however. London editor Timothy O'Keeffe and New York editor Cecil Scott both offered encouragement and sober advice on *Dalkey*. Later, when the book was published to mixed reviews, Hugh Leonard turned the novel into a charming play called *When the Saints Go Cycling In,* which not only ran successfully but opened up a new career for O'Brien as a writer of TV skits, some based on Sergeant Fottrell. To be sure, in terms of the King Oliver analogy this would be a little like getting a call from Paul Whiteman, or perhaps like Herman Melville offering up Ahab to be made into Captain Quint in *Jaws*.

One of the fascinations of *Dalkey* for O'Brien admirers is the way so many of the earlier materials are reused. Though lacking the self-consciousness of Vonnegut's *Breakfast of Champions* or the mastery of *The Tempest* or the technical complexity of *Finnegans Wake, The Dalkey Archive* is a charming recapitulation of the best elements in O'Brien.

As in the case of *The Hard Life* I have tried to give a sense of the whole book in these selections, but have left out, as usual, the "love story." Here the girl is Mary instead of Penelope and the most interesting thing we can say about her is that O'Brien had recently seen an adaptation of Dreiser's *An American Tragedy* and so allowed Hugh Leonard a rowboat catastrophe, in this case comic.

Geographical/Philosophical Note: Vico Road. One of the world's loveliest, unwinding down from hills of Killiney toward Dalkey's tiny walled harbor. Shaw had a cottage above it. View is often pointed out as comparable to Bay of Naples. Joyce uses both eighteenth-century Neapolitan philosopher Giambattista Vico and the road in *Finnegans Wake,* and there's lots more Vico fun in Norman O. Brown's *Closing Time*. David Powell in his useful "Annotated Bibliography of Myles na Gopaleen's 'Cruiskeen Lawn' Commentaries on Joyce" points out that O'Brien was working into the novel by means of trial runs in the column (December 23, 1961). Three months later, in review-

ing a book by Samuel Beckett and others on Joyce's *Work in Progress,*
O'Brien took Beckett and Company to task for going into such detail
on Joyce merely because, as O'Brien put it, they had shown him to be
"pupped by Dante, Bruno and Vico, particularly the last named.
Vico was a muddled Neapolitan...." As early as December 1957,
however, he had put out that Vico was the author of *Finnegans
Wake:*

and it is no contempt of his meaning to say that his influence on Irish
intellectuals was baneful and provocative of blush to the Irish face. Not
necessary to invoke philosophy to establish that the same things happen
again and again.

[*Best of Myles*]

Recently there has been a book store in Dalkey called The Dalkey
Archive. When I inquired if they had a copy of the book, however,
the clerk wondered what on earth I was talking about. Thinking it
was perhaps my pronunciation, I pointed to the sign on the window.
"Oh," he said, "that's not the name of a book; it's the name of the
store," and he turned back to selling College Outlines for *Hamlet*
to a small queue of louts that could have been waiting for grits outside of Mary-Lou's in Carbondale, Illinois.

A Biographical Note: Mick and Hackett are discussing Descartes with
De Selby, most particularly the French philosopher's folly in getting
up at such an unearthly hour at the age of eighty-two "and him near
the North Pole." Of all that one might react to in that line De Selby
seeks only to correct the age. "He was 54, De Selby said evenly."
O'Brien himself was fifty-three when the book was published.

O'Brien wrote a large number of letters which survive on this, the last
book he was to see through the press. There were the usual messages
to the British editor (Timothy O'Keeffe), but this time he was also
concerned with the American editor's reaction as well (Cecil Scott).
To keep the book (and perhaps the author) alive, there was the
Hugh Leonard dramatization, and the letters O'Brien wrote to the
adapter about *When the Saints Go Cycling In* record not only
something of the novel's relation to the play but the basic intention
of the novel itself.

Behind all the talk about bombs and bicycles, there is the personal story of the man's declining health. On opening night O'Brien became violently ill from the effect of the radium treatments he had been receiving and had to leave before the play was over. He recovered slightly in the weeks that followed and when *The Guardian* (Manchester) reviewed the play, O'Brien, ever anxious to sell a newspaper article, saw an opportunity to market a story combining both his illness (in comic mode) and Saint Augustine, a character in the play, and offered "Can A Saint Hit Back?" It is part of the O'Brien myth that he took the Saint quite seriously as the cause of his woes. It may be O'Brien even came to believe his own fantasy. There is, of course, a school that believes our man was quite accurate in doing so.

To Timothy O'Keeffe of MacGibbon and Kee, London
21 September, 1962.

It's amusing and even eerie that you should say "the new novel sounds like a *"Summa."* And why not? One of the characters in it is Thomas Aquinas.

You may remember Dunne's two books "An Experiment with Time" and "The Serial Universe," also the views of Einstein and others. The idea is that time is as a great flat motionless sea. Time does not pass; it is we who pass. With this concept as basic, fantastic but coherent situations can easily be devised, and in effect the whole universe torn up in a monstrous comic debauch. Such obsessions as nuclear energy, space travel and landing men on the moon can be made to look as childish and insignificant as they probably are. Anything can be brought in, including the long-overdue rehabilitation of Judas Iscariot.

Two other characters will be Saint Augustine and James Joyce. Augustine is a wonderful man, if he ever existed. Probably the most abandoned young man of his day, immersed in thievery and graft and determined to get up on every woman or girl he meets, he reaches a point of satiation and meekly turns to bestiality and buggery. (His Confessions are the dirtiest book on earth.) When he had become saintly, he was a terrible blister in the side of organized Christianity because he angrily held (and he was one of the Fathers of the Church) that there was no such place as Purgatory.

But Joyce. I've had it in for that bugger for a long time and I think this is the time. A man says to me: "What do you mean by 'the late James Joyce'? You might as well say that Hitler is dead. Joyce is alive and living in retirement and possibly in disguise in Skerries, a small seaside place 20 miles north of Dublin." My search for him there, ultimately successful, brings us into the genre of "The Quest for Corvo." Our ludicrous conversation may be imagined but it ends with Joyce asking whether I could use my influence to get him into the Jesuits.

These rough glances at my project may seem to disclose a mass of portentous material that looks unmanageable. Not so. There is a pedestrian sub-theme that keeps the majestic major concept in order as in a vice. Undue length is the only risk I see....

[The Journal of Irish Literature]

To Timothy O'Keeffe
1 March, 1963.

I enclose first progress bulletin on *The Dalkey Archive*. Please keep these, as that is their purpose as a goad in my arse. I reckon that 10,000 words are complete in typescript, though somewhat more have been done in MS. The immediate future prospect is favorable. Generally I am satisfied with the quality of the material to date, though I have a horrible fear that some stupid critic (and which of them is not?) will praise me as a master of science fiction. Thank God the climate is about to change, and the scene to the vestibule of heaven.

Chapter 3 is finished but I had to devote it to a firmer establishment of the setting and introduce certain other characters. Augustine does not enter until Chapter 4 (in progress).

My researches have uncovered a good joke here and there. I have a certain pious widow who calls her pub the Colza Hotel. A neighbour had told her that the red lamp which burns before the Blessed Sacrament was kept alight by colza oil. She assumed that this was holy oil used for working miracles by St. Colza VM. In fact however in a devotional work there is reference to St. Philomena (I think) "and her 995 neophytes." The scribe had taken VM (Virgin Martyr) for a roman numeral!

That SCENE thing is an unmentionable unthinkable dog's breakfast that gave me the wet gawks, and Lord Killanin here has a copy. Where did the Wales ballocks get the awful picture if he never heard of the book? Must get a new, proper picture taken and don't see why I couldn't be shown crucified, wearing a crown of shamrocks.

[The Journal of Irish Literature]

To Timothy O'Keeffe,
1 April, 1963.

I enclose *curriculum mensis* of *The Dalkey Archive*. God forgive me but I find the material, so far, funny and sometimes shocking.

I was invited to incredible party on St. Patrick's Day given by the crowd filming *Of Human Bondage*. Stephen Behan (the da) was near me and, apparently having overheard something I had said, cried "But the nails, Myles, the NAILS!" "What nails, Stephen?" "Ah the nails man. Sure there was no nails at all in them days. Dye folly me? Yer man was TIED to the cross!"

I'm afraid that bugger Augustine is follying me.

In reply to O'Keeffe's criticisms, O'Nolan wrote:

To Timothy O'Keeffe
15 November, 1963.

Thanks for your letter of the 12th. Of course you can see me, literally at any time—as before, in my bed. (But see under.)

I hope you have not assumed that I was so offended by your last letter that I loftily decided to ignore it. What you said was quite true, except that you could have justly said far more. For instance, there is a ridiculous surfeit of talk and booze. All such defects arise from what used to be known in early broadcasting days as a technical hitch. I determined on a new method of writing, comprising two stages: (a) Think out a worthwhile theme, then write or scribble BUT GET SOME DAMN THING DOWN ON PAPER; (b) type the raw stuff, creatively and finally.

That book *The Dalkey Archive* is now finished, as in the manner started. Steps so extreme as to be almost supernatural were taken to get the MS finished to meet the date-line 30-11-63 with Macmillan of New York. They can publish and be damned (so long as they pay me a certain sum thus clinched) but I can't by any means regard the MS as an end-product at all. The idea and base-material is far too good to be thus thrown away.

Even you seem to have quite misjudged the intent of the attempt. In its final shape I believe this will be an important and scalding book, and one that will not be ignored. The book is not meant to be a novel or anything of the kind but a study in derision, various writers with their styles, and sundry modes, attitudes and cults being the rats in the cage. The MS is all bleary for want of definition and emphasis but I regard the MS as something worthwhile to chew on after I have shown it for comment to a few know-all bastards hereabouts.

There is, for instance, no intention to jeer at God or religion; the idea is to roast the people who seriously do so, and also to chide the Church in certain of its aspects. I seem to be wholly at one with Vatican Council II.

Early in October I went to bed early to excruciate myself by reading *Time*. I leant out of bed to stub a cigarette and then it happened. At midnight my wife found me unconscious on the floor. I was rushed to hospital and, by then comatose, wondered why the damned doctor treating me wasn't wearing a white coat. He wasn't a doctor at all but a priest giving the Last Rites. I seemed to hear mention of "a massive coronary." Later, in another hospital, I found myself under treatment by a (genuinely) distinguished physician. He took nearly all the blood I had out of me to have it analyzed and could find absolutely nothing wrong with my heart or any other organ. I got home eventually, apparently o.k. but a bit shaky. I took a bus townwards to buy urgently a 4d. stamp. Getting off the bus at the homeward stop *it happened again*. I woke in the hospital with my right leg (near ankle) in smithereens. I'm now at home in bed, totally crippled.

Of one thing I'm certain: this is St. Augustine getting his own back.

See you when I do. I can't run away.

To Timothy O'Keeffe
27 November, 1963.

I'm very glad you take a better view of the *Archive* but your criticisms were very well-founded and it would be a pity to release material that is ruinously flawed, particularly where the repair job might be comparatively easy and in parts very obvious. I have not read this MS at all myself yet. About a week ago I had a copy sent to Macmillan N.Y. with a promise they would soon receive a covering letter from My Abject Holiness. I have not yet written and think I'll now wait until I get a reaction from a certain Cecil Scott there. I have meanwhile given a copy to a micro-spiro-Keats here for analysis. My ultimate plan is to excoriate the MS ruthlessly, cutting short here and rebuilding there, giving the book precision and occasionally the beauty of jewelled ulcers. It must all be bitterly funny. The first person sing. must be made into a more awful toad than now. I know some of the writing is deplorable for a man of my pretences, and I'm not happy at all about the treatment of Joyce: a very greater mess must be made of him. Would one of his secret crosses be that he is an incurable bed-wetter? After I'm through I'll hire a girl to produce a new, bright, clean, stifling typescript. All that could be done within 6 weeks.

I have a sub-plot. No doubt you know of the funny Censorship of Publications Board here. They ban books they don't like and that's about it. Their best effort was banning H. Sutherland's book "The Laws of Life"; your man is a physician and a Catholic and the book was an exposition of the "rhythm" system of limiting family increase. It bore the *imprimatur* of the R.C. Archbishop of Westminster. In the case of the *Archive* the nitwits will consider part of it blasphemous and ban it without further thought. There is no blasphemy whatever but assuming there was, the Board has no power whatever to ban a book on that ground; their only two statutory grounds are obscenity and the advocation of unnatural birth control. Given the ban (D.V.) I cannot see that there would be any answer to a writ for libel in the High Court. If there was an attempt at defence, the hearing might put the Lady Chatterley case in the ha'penny class. And Ah, I see the pop-guns are now trained on poor Fanny Hill. I'm sure it's a good 30 years since I read it, and thought it an uproarious masterpiece.

You may well mention the Texas Police, and Dallas. That transaction gave a new dimension to Kennedy's courage, for few of us here suspected that apes were so numerous in the U.S. citizenry. There was some sour consolation in having the police and some presidential guards shown up for the awful nincompoops they are. Think of the thousands of films (and books and pulp mags.) which showed them all as invincible super-men. Next thing will be an apocalpytic sensation in which it will be brought home to the taxpayer that the Royal Canadian North West Mounted spend their time mounting each other. Very gradually harmless poor Profumo will be elevated to saint-hood.

To Cecil Scott of the Macmillan Co., New York
6 January, 1964.

Many thanks for your letter of 2 January concerning *The Dalkey Archive*, particularly for *oratio recta*. With one exception I agree (in fact, have already agreed) with everything you say, and the reconstruction work is in progress.

I disagree about the St. Augustine chapter. To the inattentive reader this may seem to be boring persiflage but (i) I think it's funny, and (ii) the material presented is dead serious, sound and accurate from the points of view of hagiography, history, theology and Augustine's own utterances. I believe I have read everything about Augustine published in English, French, German and Latin and, though an inept result could not be defended by saying that hard work preceded it, I believe the chapter is a fair exposition of St. Augustine as he appears to the independent mind today. Nobody can be certain whether he was a genuine holy man or a humbug, headcase. In my research I soon found that no reliance whatever was to be placed on the commonly available works of Augustine in trans-lation (mostly by clerics) to English or French: it was the rule to dilute or deliberately mis-translate many of his robust and brave avowals and confessions. Eventually I read practically the whole lot in Latin, which I found very straightforward because Augustine openly modelled himself on Cicero, avoiding any colloquialisms of his time. You fear this chapter might bewilder the average American reader: I must doubt this, but a measure of bewilderment is part of the job of literature.

It is quite true that James Joyce has been dragged in by the scruff of the neck but I think this is quite permissible within the spoofy canon of the book. The treatment of this character however has been hopelessly in-adequate and uneven, and in parts the writing is awful. This is a case for stripping the wall before repapering. My target here is not even crudely defined. The intention here is not to make Joyce himself ridiculous but to say something funny about the preposterous image of him that emerges from the treatment he has received at the hands of many commentators and exegetists (mostly, alas, American).

Yes, Mary is also unsatisfactory, though she had not been intended as very much more than a 'fringe-benefit.' A friend to whom I showed the MS said she puzzled him until, in a blinding flash, he got the point. MARY was a surname, and the emergence of Mr. Mary at the [end of the] book would have shown the story to have taken, unnoticed, a quite new direction chez Proust. With infinitive regret I decided not to get awash in this brainwave....

All the characters are intended to be obnoxious, particularly the narrator, and I expect to have the Authorised Version ready by the end of this month. I am still parisianly plastered but very industrious.

To Timothy O'Keeffe
22 January, 1964.

THE DALKEY ALCOVE

Thanks for your letter of 20 January. I just can't believe that the last third of the MS—a farrago of miswriting, slop, mistypes, repetition, with many passages quite meaningless—ever issued from here. The stuff about Joyce is withering in its ineptitude.

The Authorised Version is now finished but a bloody awful slip-up has occurred in the re-type of it by a party of another part. I undertake to let you have a new text ready for the printer not later than February 10.

None of you—yourself, the Jesuits nor James Joyce—knew that the Holy Ghost was not invented until 381, when a parcel of chancers of the Augustine type assembled at the Council of Constantinople. There is no mention whatever of the Blessed Trinity in the New Testament.

I have to say it sternly, but this will probably be the most important book in 1964. Last week I was sentenced to another 2 months in Paris, plaster of, but I expect to be OK by the autumn to take up residence in Mexico. I wonder would there be any chance of renting the former villa of Trotsky?

[*The Journal of Irish Literature*]

To Timothy O'Keeffe
12 May, 1964.

Thanks for your letter of 8 May. The blotting out of S.O'S.* (eereh. haemh.) was a frightful shock, as everybody considered him indestructible. He had promised to think about a jacket for *Archive*.

For myself, I'm gradually and painfully getting moving again. The last plaster cast has been off now for several weeks but the muscles are fucked and getting them back to work is like trying to get the brother, home on leave from the British Army and in the jigs, to come down for his breakfast.

The idea of a World Book Fair is interesting, and who said I wouldn't go over to have a look? Your projected newssheet would be fine publicity and I'll be happy to write a bit of stuff for it. Let me first tell you of the incredible chronicle I can *not* write, because as yet only Act One of the drama has been played.

I had a file of misc. correspondence with yourself, Heath and Macmillan N.Y. about *Archive*, and it also contained agreement documents. It got full up and I started another one. Towards the end of Feb. I wanted the old file to get a date for the purpose of same letter and asked the wife where it was. She just said it wasn't in the usual place, and I carried on without it. A week or so later she remarked that the MS of *Archive* was not there either. Both of us accepted that these damn things were just mislaid, and I with plaster and crutches was in no mood to make a search. I finally realised that the handwritten MS, a typewritten copy drastically revised in ink and the important file of papers WERE NOT IN THE HOUSE. I was flabbergasted, as I myself had never left the house.

Some time before Christmas a youngish man started calling here, cheerful advertising man, amiable and gentlemanly. I wasn't sure that I'd met him before but as he mentioned many good people I knew, I bade him welcome. In fact I was glad of any company in my disabled condition. He had a car and usually dropped in late on his way home. He usually had some drink on him, and sometimes brought a little with him. I would give him a drink myself when I had it. The W.C. in this house (to which he often repaired) is down at the end of a long hall, and opposite it is a door (often open) to a room full of books, pictures, papers, and usually holding the stuff I was missing.

I wrote to the police, and an inspector and detective sergeant were immediately sent along. Before they arrived I typed out a list of the names

* Sean O'Sullivan, who did endpaper maps for the original Irish edition of *The Poor Mouth*.

of EVERYBODY who had called in the material interval, for I could accuse no individual. This comic list included the family doctor, A brother, a brother-in-law, etc., and this chum. I hinted to your men that I thought it would be a waste of time making direct inquiries without a search warrant in the pocket. They agreed. They called on this pal. When they came to me two days afterwards, they showed me what they found in his possession—the 3 things mentioned earlier in this letter, the whole file of correspondence relating to *The Hard Life,* a fat file cover bulging with radio and TV scripts, private and confidential letters and records. Bate that if you can! They took all my stuff away again, with a formal statement from me. This is a criminal offence, of course, and he'll probably get jail. Meanwhile I'm laying rat poison around the mansion.

Before this leg-break I had been found unconscious in my bedroom, brought to hospital and anointed (!) on basis that I was on my way to my eternal reward as a result of a heart attack. For your newssheet I think I could do a piece on unsuspected risks run by writers who have the hardihood to jeer at the holy men in heaven in respect of their outrageous behavior on earth. I'm quite convinced that my own succession of accidents were the handiwork of Augustine, and the bugger may not be finished with me yet.

Let me know if you agree with this, and I'll do it immeditaely.

In a letter to Hugh Leonard dated October 27, 1964, concerning Leonard's adaptation of *The Dalkey Archive* for stage production (*When the Saints Go Cycling In*), O'Nolan wrote: "I take great care with dialogue and would like the style of the book preserved." Two weeks later, in another letter to Leonard, he noted:

... *Sergeant into Bicycle:* This another brainwave of yours for a shattering final curtain but it is contrary to the theory and theology of bicogenesis. (You must remember that the most crackpot invention must be subject to its own stern logic.) Assuming that the Sergeant's warnings about the dangers of bicycles are adequately presented, he could not possibly meet that fate on the basis of one bicycle ride, however frantic.

I suggest the thinking should be as follows. Mick and the Sergeant arrive at the Colza for a parting drink. After supplementary cautions about bicycles, the Sergeant departs. In comes a wizened postman with gammy walk, slaps a few letters on the counter, saying "That's the last for today. Thank God, give us a pint in here." He opens a blank door facing audience, who see it is small and empty. The pint is served and the door closed. When the door is swung open at curtain, there is absolutely nothing there but the new bicycle. It would be unjust to the

Sergeant to have a lifetime of cunning crash about his ears, and would bring things dangerously near slapstick.

To Timothy O'Keeffe
6 July, 1965.

I find I forgot to mention Leonard's smash curtain to *Archive*. In the book Mick and the Sergeant steal the cask of DMP, de Selby's awful substance which can destroy the whole world but he gives no clue as to how it works or is detonated. Mick deposits it in the Bank of Ireland, where presumably it will remain till the Day of Judgment. In the play they fuck the cask into Dublin Bay.

Afterwards they go to the Colza Hotel where they find among others de Selby. Your man is innocent of the theft but accidentally lets it drop that the detonation agency is...seawater. CURTAIN!

This brainwave (and tidal wave) would much improve the book.

[*The Journal of Irish Literature*]

To Timothy O'Keeffe
10 December, 1965.

As already said, I want to draw U.S. attention to *The Dalkey Archive*, the only book of mine worth a damn.

[*The Journal of Irish Literature*]

To W. J. Webb, Esq., of *The Guardian* (Manchester)
27 November, 1965.

Please see an article by Peter Lennon on p. 9 of your issue of September 30. This play *When the Saints Go Cycling In* ran to packed houses for 7 weeks and in a curtain speech I explained the tribulations to which I had been subjected by St. Augustine, whom the play is jeeringly about. I suffered prostrations, fits, deadly uremia, a broken leg and impartation twice of the Last Rites of the Church. Would you have any interest in an article

CAN A SAINT HIT BACK?

By FLANN O'BRIEN

wherein the trials of a courageous author are set forth, with an addendum explaining sinister back-dated vengeance by the Saint in the matter of my birth certificate.

I don't seek a carte blanche from you but merely your feeling on this unholy subject.

Responding to O'Brien's challenge, *The Guardian* asked St. Augustine's "victim" to tell his side of the story, and the result appeared on January 19, 1966. (This text is from the manuscript in the Morris Library.)

This brief memoir may seem egotistical but is the quite impersonal record of one writer's deadly struggle with a character, and is absolutely true.

CAN A SAINT HIT BACK?
By FLANN O'BRIEN

PYROSIS, acute hammer-toe and a tendency towards piano-leg could be described as natal characteristics of this writer (me). Natal, yes, but what of the nativity? Two certificates attest severally that I was born on 5 October and that on 28 July of the same year a sister had been born. A wise old doctor has said that one of several possibilities is to be admitted: either, or possibly both, of the birth certificates was faulty—registration in the old days being left to illiterate midwives; one of the children was a misregistered bastard, or the mother was a monster who had fabulous breed. Not for a moment to be entertained was a time-lag geminal theory implying foetal dyscrasia or gynandrous aberration, dizygotic or mono-. The fact is that Saint Augustine's vengeance (but see under) had been permitted a reach into gestation.

All this came to notice some four years ago. In the course of desultory reading I had suddenly been accosted by the startling resemblance between Augustine (354–430) and Ignatius of Loyola (1491–1556). Both were well born, Ignatius to princely status, but both were quite outstanding in early life for profligacy and carnal wantonness: Augustine seems to have been also guilty of bestiality, and both were drunkards. Augustine attracted me in particular for in the course of his extended Latin works he heaped obloquy on heresiarchs and voluptuaries, taking care to list and severely castigate his own transgressions. Those works I found inadequate in such English, French or German translations as were to be found in Dubin's National Library, usually by Franciscan or Dominican ecclesiastics, for studied suppression, distortion, periphrasis or omission. I fared little better during a fortnight's resort to the British Museum, though a bumpy landing at London Airport confirmed an earlier suspicion that I was developing a rectal abscess. Eventually I had to read all Augustine's works in the original Latin and claim to be the only person who has ever done so, not excluding Augustine himself. (I was knocked down by a bicycle in Leicester Square but suffered no damage beyond having my clothes ruined with muck.) A good Latinist will find Augustine easy, for he modelled himself on Cicero, though he could not help dragging in odd Punic words. As my reading progressed my book *The Dalkey Archive* began to take shape in my mind. I would jeer uproariously at Augustine's fleshly obsessions and ambush Loyola by restoring James Joyce to life and equipping him with an ambition to join the Jesuits.

Early one night through alcoholic nightmare or traumatic spasm I fell out of bed and was found unconscious on the floor. Later in hospital and barely coming to my wits, I was sufficient pedant to demand of a doctor attending me why he wasn't wearing a white coat. He explained that I apparently had had a bad heart attack, that he was not a doctor but a priest and that he had just given me the Last Rites. In fact, I had had a severe attack of uraemia.

How further alerted Augustine had become may be guessed from what happened when I had to travel by bus from my suburban home to the outer edge of inner Dublin to buy a stamp for an urgent letter, the local post office being "closed for lunch". The letter posted, I do not remember leaving the bus on the return trip. A passing motorist found me unconscious at my home stop, and later in hospital it was found that my right leg was broken above the ankle. The surgeon was insisting on a bone graft.

—How much of a hospital stay would that mean?

—Only two months or so.

—And wouldn't living bone be required for a graft?

—Certainly. You have any amount of bone about you going to waste.

—Where, for instance?

—All around your arse.

—Thanks. I couldn't face two months of hospital food. We'll chance the usual setting.

A broken leg can initially be a pretty painful affliction. I was back home in bed in three weeks but with the limb in heavy plaster from hip to toes, a situation of almost indescribable inconvenience and awkardness. At some risk and with the help of crutches I could get from bed to fireside, and there I began writing *The Dalkey Archive* in longhand. Soon I developed sycosis or barber's rash, a disease which I was to find could only be countered by X-rays such as would make the hairs of the beard temporarily fall out.

As the manuscript grew a young stranger began to call, introducing himself by naming various old friends of mine. From time to time he would visit a lavatory at the back of my bungalow next to which was a room containing nothing but books, written records and papers. Later the holograph manuscript when completed as well as several files of correspondence disappeared from that room. My guest, in my own helplessness, had stolen them and the police, when called in, found all the stuff in his house.

At intervals of 3 months I had to journey by ambulance to hospital to have the plaster removed and replaced. On one occasion the surgeon took exception to my peculiar breathing and found I had pleurisy, necessitating a stay of 3 weeks in hospital. But the book had been typed and page proofs began to arrive from the London publishers. The first consignment was accidentally damaged by fire. Eventually the book was published, at first in London and later in New York.

About that time I began to suffer from what seemed to be an abscess in the middle ear. Then this pain became more diffused and was diagnosed as neuralgia, very severe, cause unknown. Later, tiny "knottiness" in the side of the neck made me consult a surgeon. He decided to operate in this glandular region and examine the situation by way of biopsy. The pathologist who examined the tissue found evidence of secondary cancer. So far a primary cancer has not come to light elsewhere in the body but deep X-ray irradiation of the area has caused a painful swelling, and there is evidence of generalized anaemia. Just now a visit to London for other advice and perhaps surgery is contemplated.

I have not been in my health since I wrote that book or thought of writing it. I thank only Augustine. Nor will this article do me any good. I am sure I will come to regard it as my agony in the *Guardian*.

FROM *THE DALKEY ARCHIVE*

I

Dalkey is a little town maybe twelve miles south of Dublin, on the shore. It is an unlikely town, huddled, quiet, pretending to be asleep. Its streets are narrow, not quite self-evident as streets and with meetings which seem accidental. Small shops look closed but are open. Dalkey looks like an humble settlement which must, a traveller feels, be next door to some place of the first importance and distinction. And it is—vestibule of a heavenly conspection.

Behold it. Ascend a shaded, dull, lane-like way, *per iter*, as it were, *tenebricosum*, and see it burst upon you as if a curtain had been miraculously whisked away. Yes, the Vico Road.

Good Lord!

The road itself curves gently upward and over a low wall to the left by the footpath enchantment is spread—rocky grassland falling

386

fast away to reach a toy-like railway far below, with beyond it the immeasurable immanent sea, quietly moving slowly in the immense expanse of Killiney Bay. High in the sky which joins it at a seam far from precise, a caravan of light cloud labours silently to the east.

And to the right? Monstrous arrogance: a mighty shoulder of granite climbing ever away, its overcoat of furze and bracken embedded with stern ranks of pine, spruce, fir and horse-chestnut, with further on fine clusters of slim, meticulous eucalyptus—the whole a dazzle of mildly moving leaves, a farrago of light, colour, haze and copious air, a wonder that is quite vert, verdant, vertical, verticillate, vertiginous, in the shade of branches even vespertine. Heavens, has something escaped from the lexicon of Sergeant Fottrell?

But why this name Vico Road? Is there to be recalled in this magnificence a certain philosopher's pattern of man's lot on earth—thesis, antithesis, synthesis, chaos? Hardly. And is this to be compared with the Bay of Naples? That is not to be thought of, for in Naples there must be heat and hardness belabouring desiccated Italians—no soft Irish skies, no little breezes that feel almost coloured.

At a great distance ahead and up, one could see a remote little obelisk surmounting some steps where one can sit and contemplate all this scene: the sea, the peninsula of Howth across the bay and distantly, to the right, the dim outline of the Wicklow mountains, blue or grey. Was the monument erected to honour the Creator of all this splendour? No. Perhaps in remembrance of a fine Irish person He once made—Johannes Scotus Erigena, perhaps, or possibly Parnell? No indeed: Queen Victoria.

Mary was nudging Michael Shaughnessy. She loitered enticingly about the fringes of his mind; the deep brown eyes, the light hair, the gentleness yet the poise. She was really a nuisance yet never far away. He frowned and closed his fist, but intermittent muttering immediately behind him betokened that Hackett was there.

—How is she getting on, he asked, drawing level, that pious Mary of yours?

It was by no means the first time that this handsome lout had shown his ability to divine thought, a nasty gift.

—Mind your own business, Shaughnessy said sourly. I never ask about the lady you call Asterisk Agnes.

—If you want to know, she's very well, thank you.

They walked in, loosely clutching their damp bathing things.

In the low seaward wall there was a tiny gap which gave access to a rough downhill path towards the railway far below; there a foot-bridge led to a bathing place called White Rock. At this gap a man was standing, supporting himself somewhat with a hand on the wall. As Shaughnessy drew near he saw the man was spare, tall, clean-shaven, with sparse fairish hair combed sideways across an oversize head:

—This poor bugger's hurt, Hackett remarked.

The man's face was placid and urbane but contorted in a slight grimace. He was wearing sandals and his right foot in the region of the big toe was covered with fresh blood. They stopped.

—Are you hurt, sir? Hackett asked.

The man politely examined each of them in turn.

—I suppose I am, he replied. There are notices down there about the dangers of the sea. Usually there is far more danger on land. I bashed my right toes on a sharp little dagger of granite I didn't see on that damned path.

—Perhaps we could help, Shaughnessy said. We'd be happy to assist you down to the Colza Hotel in Dalkey. We could get you a chemist there or maybe a doctor.

The man smiled slightly.

—That's good of you, he replied, but I'm my own doctor. Perhaps though you could give me a hand to get home?

—Well, certainly, Shaughnessy said.

—Do you live far, sir? Hackett asked.

—Just up there, the man said, pointing to the towering trees. It's a stiff climb with a cut foot.

Shaughnessy had no idea that there was any house in the fastness pointed to, but almost opposite there was a tiny gate discernible in the rough railing bounding the road.

—So long as you're sure there *is* a house there, Hackett said brightly, we will be honoured to be of valuable succour.

—The merit of the house is that hardly anybody except the post-man knows it's there, the other replied agreeably.

They crossed the road, the two escorts lightly assisting at each elbow. Inside the gate a narrow but smooth enough pathway fastid-iously picked its way upward through tree-trunks and shrubs.

—Might as well introduce myself, the invalid said. My name's De Selby.

Shaughnessy gave his, adding that everybody called him Mick. He noticed that Hackett styled himself just Mr Hackett: it seemed an attitude of polite neutrality, perhaps condescension.

—This part of the country, De Selby remarked, is surprisingly full of tinkers, gawms and gobshites. Are you gentlemen skilled in the Irish language?

The non-sequitur rather took Shaughnessy aback, but not Hackett.

—I know a great lot about it, sir. A beautiful tongue.

—Well, the word *mór* means big. In front of my house—we're near it now—there is a lawn surprisingly large considering the terrain. I thought I would combine *mór* and lawn as a name for the house. A hybrid, of course, but what matter? I found a looderamawn in Dalkey village by the name of Teague McGettigan. He's the local cabman, handyman, and observer of the weather; there is absolutely nothing he can't do. I asked him to paint the name on the gate, and told him the words. Now wait till you see the result.

The house could now be glimpsed, a low villa of timber and brick. As they drew nearer De Selby's lawn looked big enough but regrettably it was a sloping expanse of coarse, scruffy grass embroidered with flat weeds. And in black letters on the wooden gate was the title: LAWNMOWER. Shaughnessy and Hackett sniggered as De Selby sighed elaborately.

—Well the dear knows I always felt that Teague was our domestic Leonardo, Hackett chuckled. I'm well acquainted with the poor bastard.

They sidled gently inward. De Selby's foot was now dirty as well as bloody.

2

Our mutilated friend seems a decent sort of segotia, Hackett remarked from his armchair. De Selby had excused himself while he attended to 'the medication of my pedal pollex', and the visitors gazed about his living room with curiosity. It was oblong in shape, spacious, with a low ceiling. Varnished panelling to the height of about eighteen inches ran right round the walls, which otherwise bore faded greenish paper. There were no pictures. Two heavy mahogany bookcases, very full, stood in embrasures to each side of the fireplace, with a large press at the blank end of the room. There were many chairs, a small table in the centre and by the far wall a biggish table bearing sundry scientific instruments and tools, including a microscope. What looked like a powerful lamp hovered over this and to the left was an upright piano by Liehr, with music on the rest. It was clearly a bachelor's apartment but clean and orderly. Was he perhaps a musician, a medical man, a theopneust, a geodetic chemist...a savant?

—He's snug here anyway, Mick Shaughnessy said, and very well hidden away.

—He's the sort of man, Hackett replied, that could be up to any game at all in this sort of secret HQ. He might be a dangerous character.

Soon De Selby re-appeared, beaming, and took his place in the centre, standing with his back to the empty fireplace.

—A superficial vascular lesion, he remarked pleasantly, now cleansed, disinfected, anointed, and with a dressing you see which is impenetrable even by water.

—You mean, you intend to continue swimming? Hackett asked.

—Certainly.

—Bravo! Good man.

—Oh not at all—it's part of my business. By the way, would it be rude to inquire what is the business of you gentlemen?

—I'm a lowly civil servant, Mick replied. I detest the job, its low atmosphere and the scruff who are my companions in the office.

—I'm worse off, Hackett said in mock sorrow. I work for the father, who's a jeweller but a man that's very careful with the keys. No opportunity of giving myself an increase in pay. I suppose you could call me a jeweller too, or perhaps a sub-jeweller. Or a paste jeweller.

—Very interesting work, for I know a little about it. Do you cut stones?

—Sometimes.

—Yes. Well I'm a theologist and a physicist, sciences which embrace many others such as eschatology and astrognosy. The peace of this part of the world makes true thinking possible. I think my researches are nearly at an end. But let me entertain you for a moment.

He sat down at the piano and after some slow phrases, erupted into what Mick with inward wit, would dub a headlong chromatic dysentery which was 'brilliant' in the bad sense of being inchoate and, to his ear at least, incoherent. A shattering chord brought the disorder to a close.

—Well, he said, rising, what did you think of that?

Hackett looked wise.

—I think I detected Liszt in one of his less guarded moments, he said.

—No, De Selby answered. The basis of that was the canon at the start of César Franck's well-known sonata for violin and piano. The rest was all improvisation. By me.

—You're a splendid player, Mick ventured archly.

—It's only for amusement but a piano can be a very useful instrument. Wait till I show you something.

He returned to the instrument, lifted half of the hinged top and took out a bottle of yellowish liquid, which he placed on the table. Then opening a door in the nether part of a bookcase, he took out three handsome stem glasses and a decanter of what looked like water.

—This is the best whiskey to be had in Ireland, faultlessly made and perfectly matured. I know you will not refuse a taiscaun.

—Nothing would make me happier, Hackett said. I notice that there's no label on the bottle.

—Thank you, Mick said, accepting a generous glass from De Selby. He did not like whiskey much, or any intoxicant, for that matter. But manners came first. Hackett followed his example.

—The water's there, De Selby gestured. Don't steal another man's wife and never water his whiskey. No label on the bottle? True. I made that whiskey myself.

Hackett had taken a tentative sip.

—I hope you know that whiskey doesn't mature in a bottle. Though I must say that this tastes good.

Mick and De Selby took a reasonable gulp together.

—My dear fellow, De Selby replied, I know all about sherry casks, temperature, subterranean repositories and all that extravaganza. But such considerations do not arise here. This whiskey was made last week.

Hackett leaned forward in his chair, startled.

—What was that? he cried. A week old? Then it can't be whiskey at all. Good God, are you trying to give us heart failure or dissolve our kidneys?

De Selby's air was one of banter.

—You can see, Mr Hackett, that I am also drinking this excellent potion myself. And I did not say it was a week old. I said it was made last week.

—Well, this is Saturday. We needn't argue about a day or two.

—Mr De Selby, Mick interposed mildly, it is clear enough that you are making some distinction in what you said, that there is some nicety of terminology in your words. I can't quite follow you.

De Selby here took a drink which may be described as profound and then suddenly an expression of apocalyptic solemnity came over all his mild face.

—Gentlemen, he said, in an empty voice, I have mastered time. Time has been called, an event, a repository, a continuum, an ingredient of the universe. I can suspend time, negative its apparent course.

Mick thought it funny in retrospect that Hackett here glanced at his watch, perhaps involuntarily.

—Time is still passing with me, he croaked.

—The passage of time, De Selby continued, is calculated with reference to the movements of the heavenly bodies. These are fallacious as determinants of the nature of time. Time has been studied and pronounced upon by many apparently sober men—Newton, Spinoza, Bergson, even Descartes. The postulates of the Relativity nonsense of Einstein are mendacious, not to say bogus. He tried to say that time and space had no real existence separately but were to be apprehended only in unison. Such pursuits as astronomy and geodesy have simply befuddled man. You understand?

As it was at Mick he looked the latter firmly shook his head but thought well to take another stern sup of whiskey. Hackett was frowning. De Selby sat down by the table.

—Consideration of time, he said, from intellectual, philosophic or even mathematical criteria is fatuity, and the preoccupation of slovens. In such unseemly brawls some priestly fop is bound to induce a sort of cerebral catalepsy by bringing forward terms such as infinity and eternity.

Mick thought it seemly to say something, however foolish.

—If time is illusory as you seem to suggest, Mr De Selby, how is it that when a child is born, with time he grows to be a boy, then a man, next an old man and finally a spent and helpless cripple?

De Selby's slight smile showed a return of the benign mood.

—There you have another error in formulating thought. You confound time with organic evolution. Take your child who has grown to be a man of 21. His total life-span is to be 70 years. He has a horse whose life-span is to be 20. He goes for a ride on his horse. Do these two creatures subsist simultaneously in dissimilar conditions of time? Is the velocity of time for the horse three and a half times that for the man?

Hackett was now alert.

—Come here, he said. That greedy fellow the pike is reputed to grow to be up to 200 years of age. How is our time-ratio if he is caught and killed by a young fellow of 15?

—Work it out for yourself, De Selby replied pleasantly. Divergences, incompatibilities, irreconcilables are everywhere. Poor Descartes! He tried to reduce all goings-on in the natural world to a code of mechanics, kinetic but not dynamic. All motion of objects was circular, he denied a vacuum was possible and affirmed that weight existed irrespective of gravity. *Cogito ergo sum?* He might as well have written *inepsias scripsi ergo sum* and prove the same point, as *he* thought.

—That man's work, Mick interjected, may have been mistaken in some conclusions but was guided by his absolute belief in Almighty God.

—True indeed. I personally don't discount the existence of a supreme *supra mundum* power but I sometimes doubted if it is benign. Where are we with this mess of Cartesian methodology and Biblical myth-making? Eve, the snake and the apple, Good Lord!

—Give us another drink if you please, Hackett said. Whiskey is not incompatible with theology, particularly magic whiskey that is ancient and also a week old.

—Most certainly, said De Selby, rising and ministering most generously to the three glasses. He sighed as he sat down again.

—You men, he said, should read all the works of Descartes, having first thoroughly learnt Latin. He is an excellent example of blind

faith corrupting the intellect. He knew Galileo, of course, accepted
the latter's support of the Copernican theory that the earth moves
round the sun and had in fact been busy on a treatise affirming this.
But when he heard that the Inquisition had condemned Galileo as
a heretic, he hastily put away his manuscript. In our modern slang
he was yellow. And his death was perfectly ridiculous. To ensure a
crust for himself, he agreed to call on Queen Christina of Sweden
three times a week at five in the morning to teach her philosophy.
Five in the morning in that climate! It killed him, of course. Know
what age he was?

Hackett had just lit a cigarette without offering one to anybody.

—I feel Descartes' head was a little bit loose, he remarked pon-
derously, not so much for his profusion of erroneous ideas but for
the folly of a man of 82 thus getting up at such an unearthly hour
and him near the North Pole.

—He was 54, De Selby said evenly.

—Well by damn, Mick blurted, he was a remarkable man however
crazy his scientific beliefs.

—There's a French term I heard which might describe him, Hackett said. *Idiot-savant*.

De Selby produced a solitary cigarette of his own and lit it. How
had he inferred that Mick did not smoke?

—At worst, he said in a tone one might call oracular, Descartes
was a solipsist. Another weakness of his was a liking for the Jesuits.
He was very properly derided for regarding space as a plenum. It is
a coincidence, of course, but I have made the parallel but undoubted
discovery that *time* is a plenum.

—What does that mean? Hackett asked.

—One might describe a plenum as a phenomenon or existence full
of itself but inert. Obviously space does not satisfy such a condition.
But time is a plenum, immobile, immutable, ineluctable, irrevocable,
a condition of absolute stasis. Time does not pass. Change and movement may occur within time.

Mike pondered this. Comment seemed pointless. There seemed
no little straw to clutch at; nothing to question.

—Mr De Selby, he ventured at last, it would seem impertinent
of the like of me to offer criticism or even opinions on what I ap-
prehend as purely abstract propositions. I'm afraid I harbour the

traditional idea and experience of time. For instance, if you permit me to drink enough of this whiskey, by which I mean too much, I'm certain to undergo unmistakable temporal punishment. My stomach, liver and nervous system will be wrecked in the morning.

—To say nothing of the dry gawks, Hackett added.

De Selby laughed civilly.

—That would be a change to which time, of its nature, is quite irrelevant.

—Possibly, Hackett replied, but that academic observation will in no way mitigate the reality of the pain.

—A tincture, De Selby said, again rising with the bottle and once more adding generously to the three glasses. You must excuse me for a moment or two.

Needless to say, Hackett and Mick looked at each other in some wonder when he had left the room.

—This malt seems to be superb, Hackett observed, but would he have dope or something in it?

—Why should there be? He's drinking plenty of it himself.

—Maybe he's gone away to give himself a dose of some antidote. Or an emetic.

Mick shook his head genuinely.

—He's a strange bird, he said, but I don't think he's off his head, or a public danger.

—You're certain he's not derogatory?

—Yes. Call him eccentric.

Hackett rose and gave himself a hasty extra shot from the bottle, which in turn Mick repelled with a gesture. He lit another cigarette.

—Well, he said, I suppose we should not overstay our welcome. Perhaps we should go. What do you say?

Mick nodded. The experience had been curious and not to be regretted; and it could perhaps lead to other interesting things or even people. How commonplace, he reflected, were all the people he did know.

When De Selby returned he carried a tray with plates, knives, a dish of butter and an ornate basket full of what seemed golden bread.

—Sit in to the table, lads—pull over your chairs, he said. This is merely what the Church calls a collation. These delightful wheaten farls were made by me, like the whiskey, but you must not think

I'm like an ancient Roman emperor living in daily fear of being poisoned. I'm alone here, and it's a long painful pilgrimage to the shops.

With a murmur of thanks the visitors started this modest and pleasant meal. De Selby himself took little and seemed preoccupied.

—Call me a theologian or a physicist as you will, he said at last rather earnestly, but I am serious and truthful. My discoveries concerning the nature of time were in fact quite accidental. The objective of my research was altogether different. My aim was utterly unconnected with the essence of time.

—Indeed? Hackett said rather coarsely as he coarsely munched. And what was the main aim?

—To destroy the whole world.

They stared at him. Hackett made a slight noise but De Selby's face was set, impassive, grim.

—Well, well, Mick stammered.

—It merits destruction. Its history and prehistory, even its present, is a foul record of pestilence, famine, war, devastation and misery so terrible and multifarious that its depth and horror are unknown to any one man. Rottenness is universally endemic, disease is paramount. The human race is finally debauched and aborted.

—Mr De Selby, Hackett said with a want of gravity, would it be rude to ask just how you will destroy the world? You did not make it.

—Even you, Mr Hackett, have destroyed things you did not make. I do not care a farthing about who made the world or what the grand intention was, laudable or horrible. The creation is loathsome and abominable, and total extinction could not be worse.

Mick could see that Hackett's attitude was provoking brusqueness whereas what was needed was elucidation. Even marginal exposition by De Selby would throw light on the important question—was he a true scientist or just demented?

—I can't see, sir, Mick ventured modestly, how this world could be destroyed short of arranging a celestial collision between it and some other great heavenly body. How a man could interfere with the movements of the stars—I find that an insoluble puzzle, sir.

De Selby's taut expression relaxed somewhat.

—Since our repast is finished, have another drink, he said, pushing forward the bottle. When I mentioned destroying the whole world, I was not referring to the physical planet but to every manner and manifestation of life on it. When my task is accomplished—and I feel that will be soon—nothing living, not even a blade of grass, a flea—will exist on this globe. Nor shall I exist myself, of course.

—And what about us? Hackett asked.

—You must participate in the destiny of all mankind, which is extermination.

—Guesswork is futile, Mr De Selby, Mick murmured, but could this plan of yours involve liquifying all the ice at the Poles and elsewhere and thus drowning everything, in the manner of the Flood in the Bible?

—No. The story of that Flood is just silly. We are told it was caused by a deluge of forty days and forty nights. All this water must have existed on earth before the rain started, for more can not come down than was taken up. Commonsense tells me that this is childish nonsense.

—That is merely a feeble rational quibble, Hackett cut in. He liked to show that he was alert.

—What then, sir, Mick asked in painful humility, is the secret, the supreme crucial secret?

De Selby gave a sort of grimace.

—It would be impossible for me, he explained, to give you gentlemen, who have no scientific training, even a glimpse into my studies and achievements in pneumatic chemistry. My work has taken up the best part of a lifetime and, though assistance and co-operation were generously offered by men abroad, they could not master my fundamental postulate: namely, the annihilation of the atmosphere.

—You mean, abolish air? Hackett asked blankly.

—Only its biogenic and substantive ingredient, replied De Selby, which, of course, is oxygen.

—Thus, Mick interposed, if you extract all oxygen from the atmosphere or destroy it, all life will cease?

—Crudely put, perhaps, the scientist agreed, now again genial, but you may grasp the idea. There are certain possible complications but they need not trouble us now.

Hackett had quietly helped himself to another drink and showed active interest.

—I think I see it, he intoned. Exit automatically the oxygen and we have to carry on with what remains, which happens to be poison. Isn't it murder though?

De Selby paid no attention.

—The atmosphere of the earth, meaning what in practice we breathe as distinct from rarified atmosphere at great heights, is composed of roughly 78 per cent nitrogen, 21 oxygen, tiny quantities of argon and carbon dioxide, and microscopic quantities of other gases such as helium and ozone. Our preoccupation is with nitrogen, atomic weight 14.008, atomic number 7.

—Is there a smell off nitrogen? Hackett inquired.

—No. After extreme study and experiment I have produced a chemical compound which totally eliminates oxygen from any given atmosphere. A minute quantity of this hard substance, small enough to be invisible to the naked eye, would thus convert the interior of the greatest hall on earth into a dead world provided, of course, the hall were properly sealed. Let me show you.

He quietly knelt at one of the lower presses and opened the door to reveal a small safe of conventional aspect. This he opened with a key, revealing a circular container of dull metal of a size that would contain perhaps four gallons of liquid. Inscribed on its face were the letters D.M.P.

—Good Lord, Hackett cried, the D.M.P.! The good old D.M.P.! The grandfather was a member of that bunch.

De Selby turned his head, smiling bleakly.

—Yes—the D.M.P.—the Dublin Metropolitan Police. My own father was a member. They are long-since abolished, of course.

—Well what's the idea of putting that on your jar of chemicals?

De Selby had closed the safe and press door and gone back to his seat.

—Just a whim of mine, no more, he replied. The letters are in no sense a formula or even a mnemonic. But that container has in it the most priceless substance on earth.

—Mr De Selby, Mick said, rather frightened by these flamboyant proceedings, granted that your safe is a good one, is it not foolish to leave such dangerous stuff here for some burglar to knock it off?

—Me, for instance? Hackett interposed.

—No, gentlemen, there is no danger at all. Nobody would know what the substance was, its properties or how activated.

—But don't *we* know? Hackett insisted.

—You know next to nothing, De Selby replied easily, but I intend to enlighten you even more.

—I assure you, Mick thought well to say, that any information entrusted to us will be treated in strict confidence.

—Oh, don't bother about that, De Selby said politely, it's not information I'll supply but experience. A discovery I have made—and quite unexpectedly—is that a deoxygenated atmosphere cancels the apparently serial nature of time and confronts us with true time and simultaneously with all the things and creatures which time has ever contained or will contain, provided we evoke them. Do you follow? Let us be serious about this. The situation is momentous and scarcely of this world as we know it.

He stared at each of his two new friends in turn very gravely.

—I feel, he announced, that you are entitled to some personal explanation concerning myself. It would be quite wrong to regard me as a christophobe.

—Me too, Hackett chirped impudently.

—The early books of the Bible I accepted as myth, but durable myth contrived genuinely for man's guidance. I also accepted as fact the story of the awesome encounter between God and the rebel Lucifer. But I was undecided for many years as to the outcome of that encounter. I had little to corroborate the revelation that God had triumphed and banished Lucifer to hell forever. For if—I repeat *if* —the decision had gone the other way and God had been vanquished, who but Lucifer would be certain to put about the other and opposite story?

—But why should he? Mick asked incredulously.

—The better to snare and damn mankind, De Selby answered.

—Well now, Hackett remarked, that secret would take some keeping.

—However, De Selby continued, perplexed, I was quite mistaken in that speculation. I've since found that things are as set forth in the Bible, at least to the extent that heaven is intact.

Hackett gave a low whistle, perhaps in derision.

—How could you be sure? he asked. You have not been temporarily out of this world, have you, Mr De Selby?

—Not exactly. But I have had a long talk with John the Baptist. A most understanding man, do you know, you'd swear he was a Jesuit.

—Good heavens! Mick cried, while Hackett hastily put his glass on the table with a click.

—Ah yes, most understanding. Perfect manners, of course, and a courteous appreciation of my own personal limitations. A very *interesting* man the same Baptist.

—Where did this happen? Hackett asked.

—Here in Dalkey, De Selby explained. Under the sea.

There was a small but absolute silence.

—While time stood still? Hackett persisted.

—I'll bring both of you people to the same spot tomorrow. That is, if you wish it and provided you can swim, and for a short distance under water.

—We are both excellent swimmers, Hackett said cheerfully, except I'm by far the better of the pair.

—We'd be delighted, Mick interrupted with a sickly smile, on the understanding that we'll get safely back.

—There is no danger whatever. Down at the headquarters of the Vico Swimming Club there is a peculiar chamber hidden in the rocks at the water's edge. At low tide there is cavernous access from the water to this chamber. As the tide rises this hole is blocked and air sealed off in the chamber. The water provides a total seal.

—This could be a chamber of horrors, Hackett suggested.

—I have some masks of my own design, equipped with compressed air, normal air, and having an automatic feed-valve. The masks and tanks are quite light, of aluminum.

—I think I grasp the idea, Mick said in a frown of concentration. We go under the water wearing these breathing gadgets, make our way through this rocky opening to the chamber, and there meet John the Baptist?

De Selby chuckled softly.

—Not necessarily and not quite. We get to the empty chamber as you say and I then release a minute quantity of D.M.P. We are then subsisting in timeless nitrogen but still able to breathe from the tanks on our backs.

—Does our physical weight change? Hackett asked.

—Yes, somewhat.

—And what happens then?

—We shall see what happens after you have met me at this swimming pool at eight o'clock tomorrow morning.

Are you going back by the Colza Hotel?

—Certainly.

—Well have a message sent to Teague McGettigan to call for me
with his damned cab at 7.30. Those mask affairs are bothersome to
horse about with.

Thus the appointment was made. De Selby affable as he led his
visitors to his door and said goodbye.

4

Mild air with the sea in a stage whisper behind it was in Mick's face
as his bicycle turned into the lane-like approach to the Vico Road
and its rocky swimming hole. It was a fine morning, calm, full of late
summer.

Teague McGettigan's cab was at the entrance, the horse's head
submerged in a breakfast nose-bag. Mick went down the steps and
saluted the company with a hail of his arm. De Selby was gazing in
disfavour at a pullover he had just taken off. Hackett was slumped
seated, fully dressed and smoking a cigarette, while McGettigan in his
dirty raincoat was fastidiously attending to his pipe. De Selby nodded.
Hackett muttered 'More luck' and McGettigan spat.

—Boys-a-dear, McGettigan said in a low voice from his old thin
unshaven face, ye'll get the right drenching today. Ye'll be soaked
to the pelt.

—Considering that we're soon to dive into that water, Hackett
replied, I won't dispute your prophecy, Teague.

—I don't mean that. Look at that bloody sky.

—Cloudless, Mick remarked.

—For Christ's sake look down there by Wickla.

In that quarter there was what looked like sea-haze, with the
merest hint of the great mountain behind. With his hands Mick
made a gesture of nonchalance.

—We might be down under the water for half an hour, I believe,
Hackett said, or at least that's Mr De Selby's story. We have an appointment with mermaids or something.

—Get into your togs, Hackett, De Selby said impatiently. And you,
too, Mick.

—Ye'll pay more attention to me, Teague muttered, when ye come
up to find ye'r superfine clothes demolished be the lashin rain.

—Can't you keep them in your cursed droshky? De Selby barked.
His temper was clearly a bit uncertain.

All got ready. Teague sat philosophically on a ledge, smoking and having the air of an indulgent elder watching children at play. Maybe his attitude was justified. When the three were ready for the water De Selby beckoned them to private consultation. The gear was spread out on a flattish rock.

—Now listen carefully, he said. This apparatus I am going to fit on both of you allows you to breathe, under water or out of it. The valve is automatic and needs no adjustment, nor is that possible. The air is compressed and will last half an hour by conventional effluxion of time.

—Thank God, sir, that your theories about time are not involved in the air supply, Hackett remarked.

—The apparatus also allows you to hear. My own is somewhat different. It enables me to do all that but speak and be heard as well. Follow?

—That seems clear enough, Mick agreed.

—When I clip the masks in place your air supply is *on*, he said emphatically. Under water or on land you can breathe.

—Fair enough, Hackett said politely.

—And listen to this, De Selby continued, I will go first, leading the way, over there to the left, to this cave opening, now submerged. It is only a matter of yards and not deep down. The tide is now nearly full. Follow close behind me. When we get to the rock apartment, take a seat as best you can, do nothing, and wait. At first it will be dark but you won't be cold. I will then annihilate the terrestrial atmosphere and the time illusion by activating a particle of D.M.P. Now is all that clear? I don't want any attempt at technical guff or questions at this time.

Hackett and Mick mutely agreed that things were clear.

—Down there you are likely to meet a personality who is from heaven, who is all-wise, speaks all languages and dialects and knows, or can know, everything. I have never had a companion on such a trip before, and I do hope events will not be complicated.

Mick had suddenly become very excited.

—Excuse the question, he blurted, but will this be John the Baptist again?

—No. At least I hope not. I can request but cannot command.

—Could it be . . . anybody? Hackett asked.

—Only the dead.

—Good heavens!

—Yet that is not wholly correct. Those who were never on earth could appear.

This little talk was eerie. It was as if a hangman were courteously conversing with his victim, on the scaffold high.

—Do you mean angels, Mr De Selby? Mick inquired.

—Deistic beings, he said gruffly. Here, stand still till I fix this.

He had picked up a breathing mask, with its straps and tank affair at the back.

—I'll go after you, Mick muttered, with Hackett at the rear.

In a surprisingly short time they were all fully dressed for a visit under the sea to the next world, or perhaps the former world. Through his goggles Mick could see Teague McGettigan studying an early Sunday paper, apparently at a rear racing page. He was at peace, with no interest whatever in supernatural doings. He was perhaps to be envied. Hackett was standing impassive, an Apollo Spaceman. De Selby was making final adjustments to his straps and with a gesture had led the way to the lower board.

Going head-down into cold water in the early morning is a shock to the most practised. But in Mick's case the fog of doubt and near-delusion in the head, added to by the very low hiss of his air supply, made it a brief but baffling experience. There was ample light as he followed De Selby's kicking heels and a marked watery disturbance behind told him that Hackett was not far away. If he was cursing, nobody heard.

Entry to the 'apartment' was efficient enough for beginners. If not adroit. De Selby readily found the opening and then, one by one, the others made their way upwards, half-clambering, half-swimming. They left the water quite palpably and Mick found himself crouching in an empty space on a rough floor strewn with rocks and some shells. Everything was dark and a distant sussurus must have been from the sea which had just been left. The company was under the water and presumably in an atmosphere that could be breathed, though only for a short time. *Time?* Yes, the word might be repeated.

De Selby beckoned Mick on with a tug at the arm, and he did the same for Hackett behind. Then they stopped. Mick crouched and finally squatted on a roundish rock; De Selby was to his left and the three had come to some sort of resting posture. Hackett gave Mick a nudge, though the latter did not know if it meant commiseration, encouragement or derision.

From his movements it was evident even in the gloom that De Selby was busy at some technical operation. Mick could not see what he was doing but no doubt he was detonating (or whatever is the word) a minuscule charge of D.M.P.

Though wet, he did not feel cold, but he was apprehensive, puzzled, curious. Hackett was near but quite still.

A faint light seemed to come, a remote glow. It gradually grew to define the dimension of the dim apartment, making it appear unexpectedly large and, strangely, dry.

Then Mick saw a figure, a spectre, far away from him. It looked seated and slightly luminescent. Gradually it got rather clearer in definition but remained unutterably distant, and what he had taken for a very long chin in profile was almost certainly a beard. A gown of some dark material clothed the apparition. It is strange to say that the manifestation did not frighten him but he was flabbergasted when he heard De Selby's familiar tones almost booming out beside him.

—I must thank you for coming. I have two students with me.

The voice that came back was low, from far away but perfectly clear. The Dublin accent was unmistakable. The extraordinary utterance can here be distinguished only typographically.

—*Ah not at all man.*

—You're feeling well, as usual, I suppose?

—*Nothing to complain of, thank God. How are you feeling yourself, or how do you think you're feeling?*

—Tolerably, but age is creeping in.

—*Ha-ha. That makes me laugh.*

—Why?

—*Your sort of time is merely a confusing index of decomposition. Do you remember what you didn't know was your youth?*

—I do. But it's *your* youth I wanted to talk about. The nature of your life in youth compared with that of your hagiarchic senility must have been a thunderous contrast, the ascent to piety sudden and even distressing. Was it?

—*You are hinting at anoxic anoxoemia? Perhaps.*

—You admit you were a debauched and abandoned young man?

—*For a pagan I wasn't the worst. Besides, maybe it was the Irish in me.*

—The Irish in you?

—*Yes. My father's name was Patrick. And he was a proper gob-shite.*

—Do you admit that the age or colour of women didn't matter to you where the transaction in question was coition?

—*I'm not admitting anything. Please remember my eyesight was very poor.*

—Were all your rutting ceremonials heterosexual?

—*Heterononsense! There is no evidence against me beyond what I wrote myself. Too vague. Be on your guard against that class of fooling. Nothing in black and white.*

—My vocation is inquiry and action, not literature.

—*You're sadly inexperienced. You cannot conceive the age I lived in, its customs, or judge of that African sun.*

—The heat, hah? I've read a lot about the Eskimoes. The poor bastards are perished throughout their lives, covered with chilblains and icicles but when they catch a seal—ah, good luck to them! They make warm clothes out of the hide, perform gluttonly feats with the meat and then bring the oil home to the igloo where they light lamps and stoves. Then the fun begins. Nanook of the North is certainly partial to his nookie.

—*I reprobate concupiscence, whether fortuitous or contrived.*

—You do *now*, you post-gnostic! You must have a red face to recall your earlier nasty gymnastiness, considering you're now a Father of the Church.

—*Rubbish. I invented obscene feats out of bravado, lest I be thought innocent or cowardly. I walked the streets of Babylon with low companions, sweating from the fires of lust. When I was in Carthage I carried about with me a cauldron of unrealised debauchery. God in his majesty was tempting me. But Book Two of my Confessions is all shocking exaggeration. I lived within my rough time. And I kept the faith, unlike a lot more of my people in Algeria who are now Arab nincompoops and slaves of Islam.*

—Look at all the time you squandered in the maw of your sexual fantasies which otherwise could have been devoted to Scriptural studies. Lolling loathsome libertine!

—*I was weak at the time but I find your condescension offensive. You talk of the Fathers. How about that ante-Nicene thooleramawn, Origen of Alexandria? What did he do when he found that lusting after women distracted him from his sacred scrivenery? I'll tell you. He stood up, hurried out to the kitchen, grabbed a carving knife and —pwitch!—in one swipe deprived himself of his personality! Ah?*

—Yes. Let us call it heroic impetuosity.

—*How could Origen be the Father of Anything and he with no knackers on him? Answer me that one.*

—We must assume that his spiritual testicles remained intact. Do you know him?

—*I can't say I ever met him in our place.*

—But, dammit is he there? Don't you know everything?

—*I do not. I can, but the first wisdom is sometimes not to know. I suppose I could ask the Polyarch.*

—Who on earth is the Polyarch?

—*He's not on earth, and again I don't know. I think he's Christ's Vicar in Heaven.*

—Are there any other strange denizens?

—*Far too many if you ask me. Look at that gobhawk they call Francis Xavier. Hobnobbing and womanising in the slums of Paris with Calvin and Ignatius Loyola in warrens full of rats, vermin, sycophants, and syphilis. Xavier was a great travelling man, messing about in Ethiopia and Japan, consorting with Buddhist monkeys and planning to convert China single-handed. And Loyola? You talk about me but a lot of that chap's early saintliness was next to bed-liness. He made himself the field-marshal of a holy army of mendi-cants but maybe merchandisers would be more like it. Didn't Pope Clement XIV suppress the Order for its addiction to commerce, and for political wire-pulling? Jesuits are the wiliest, cutest and most mendacious ruffians who ever lay in wait for simple Christians. The Inquisition was on the track of Ignatius. Did you know that? Pity they didn't get him. But one party who wouldn't hear of the Pope's Brief of Suppression was the Empress of Rooshia. Look at that now!*

—Interesting that your father's name was Patrick. Is he a saint?

—*That reminds me. You have a Professor Binchy in your university outfit in Dublin and that poor man has been writing and preaching since he was a boy that the story about Saint Patrick is all wrong and that there were really two Saint Patricks. Binchy has his hash and parsley.*

—Why?

—*Two Saint Patricks? We have four of the buggers in our place and they'd make you sick with their shamrocks and shenanigans and bullshit.*

—Who else? What about Saint Peter?

—*Oh he's safe and sound all right. A bit of a slob to tell you the truth. He often encorpifies himself.*

—What was that?

—*Encorpifies himself. Takes on a body, as I've done now for your convenience. How could the like of you make anything out of an infinity of gases? Peter's just out to show off the keys, bluster about and make himself a bloody nuisance. Oh there have been a few complaints to the Polyarch about him.*

—Answer me this question. The Redeemer said 'Thou art Peter and upon this rock I shall found my Church'. Is there any justification for the jeer that He founded his Church upon a pun, since *Petros* means 'rock'?

—*Not easy to say. The name Petros does not occur in classical, mythological or biblical Greek apart from your man the apostle and his successor and later namesakes—except for a freedman of Berenice (mother of Herod Agrippa) mentioned in Josephus,* Jewish Antiquities *18, 6, 3, in a passage relating to the later years of Tiberius's reign, that is, the thirties* A.D. *Petro occurs as a Roman surname in Suetonius's* Vespasiae *1, and Petra as a woman's name in Tacitus,* Annals, *11, 4.*

—And you don't care a lot about him?

—*The lads in our place, when he barges around encorpified and flashing the keys, can't resist taking a rise out of him and pursue him with the cackles of a rooster, cock-adoodle-doo.*

—I see. Who else? Is Judas with you?

—*That's another conundrum for the Polyarch. Peter stopped me one time and tried to feed me a cock-and-bull story about Judas coming to the Gate. You get my joke? Cock-and-bull story?*

—Very funny. Is your mother Monica there?

—*Wait now! Don't try and get a dig at me that way. Don't blame me. She was here before me.*

—To lower the temperature of your steaming stewpot of lust and depravity, you married or took as concubine a decent poor young African girl, and the little boy you had by her you named Adeodatus. But even yet nobody knows your wife's name.

—*That secret is safe with me still.*

—Why should you give such a name to your son while you were yourself still a debauched pagan, not even baptised?

—*Put that day's work down to the mammy—Monica.*

—Later, you put your little wife away and she shambled off to the wilderness, probably back into slavery, but swearing to remain faithful to you forever. Does the shame of that come back to you?

—*Never mind what comes back to me, I done what the mammy said, and everybody—you too—has to do what the mammy says.*

—And straightaway, as you relate in Book Six of your Confessions, you took another wife, simultaneously committing bigamy and adultery. And you kicked her out after your *Tolle Lege* conjuring tricks in the garden when you ate a handful of stolen pears. Eve herself wasn't accused in respect of more than one apple. In all this disgraceful behaviour do we see Monica at work again?

—*Certainly. God also.*

—Does Monica know that you're being so unprecedentedly candid with me?

—Know? *She's probably here unencorpified.*

—You betrayed and destroyed two decent women, implicated God in giving a jeering name to a bastard, and you blame all this outrage on your mother. Would it be seemly to call you callous humbug?

—*It would not. Call me a holy humbug.*

—Who else is in your kingdom? Is Judas?

—*Paul is in our place, often encorpified and always attended by his physician Luke, putting poultices on his patient's sore neck. When Paul shows too much consate in himself, the great blatherskite with his epistles in bad Greek, the chronic two-timer, I sometimes roar after him 'You're not on the road to Damacus now!' Puts him in his place. All the same that Tolle Lege incident was no conjuring trick. It was a miracle. The first book I picked up was by Paul and the lines that struck my eyes were these: 'Not in rioting or drunkenness, nor in chambering or wantonness, nor in strife or envying: but put ye on the Lord Jesus Christ and make no provision for the flesh in the lusts thereof.' But do you know, I think the greatest dog's breakfast of the lot is St Vianney.*

—I never heard of him.

—*'Course you have. Jean-Baptiste. You'd know him better as the curé of Ars.*

—Oh yes. A French holy man.

—*A holy fright, you mean. Takes a notion when he's young to be a priest, as ignorant as the back of a cab, couldn't make head nor tail of Latin or sums, dodges the column when Napoleon is looking for French lads to be slaughtered in Rooshia, and at the heel of the hunt spends sixteen to eighteen hours a day in the confessional— hearing, not telling—and takes to performing miracles, getting money from nowhere and taking on hand to tell the future. Don't be talking. A diabolical wizard of a man.*

—Your household abounds in oddities.

—*He performs his miracles still in our place. Gives life to bogus corpses and thinks nothing of raising from the dead a dummy mummy.*

—I repeat a question I've already asked: is Judas a member of your household?

—*I don't think the Polyarch would like me to say much about Judas.*

—He particularly interests me. The Gospel extols love and justice. Peter denied his Master out of pride, vanity and perhaps fear. Judas did something similar but from a comprehensible motive. But Peter's home and dried. Is Judas?

—*Judas, being dead, is eternal.*

—But where is he?

—*The dead do not have whereness. They have condition.*

—Did Judas earn paradise?

—*Pulchritudo tam antiqua et tam nova sero amavit.*

—You are shifty and you prevaricate. Say yes or no to this question: did you suffer from hæmorrhoids?

—*Yes. That is one reason that I encorpify myself with reluctance.*

—Did Judas have any physical affliction?

—*You have not read my works. I did not build the City of God. At most I have been an humble urban district councillor, never the Town Clerk. Whether Judas is dead in the Lord is a question notice of which would require to be given to the Polyarch.*

—De Quincey held that Judas enacted his betrayal to provoke his Master into proclaiming his divinity by deed. What do you think of that?

—*De Quincey also consumed narcotics.*

—Nearly everything you have taught or written lacks the precision of Descartes.

—*Descartes was a recitalist, or formulist, of what he took, often mistakenly, to be true knowledge. He himself established nothing new, nor even a system of pursuing knowledge that was novel. You are fond of quoting his* Cogito Ergo Sum. Read my works. *He stole that. See my dialogue with Evodius in* De Libero Arbitrio, *or the Question of Free Choice. Descartes spent far too much time in bed subject to the persistent hallucination that he was thinking. You are not free from a similar disorder.*

—I have read all the philosophy of the Fathers, before and after Nicaea: Chrysostom, Ambrose, Athanasius.

—*If you have read Athanasius you have not understood him. The result of your studies might be termed a corpus of patristic paddeology.*

—Thank you.

—*You are welcome.*

—The prime things—existence, time, the godhead, death, paradise and the satanic pit, these are abstractions. Your pronouncements on them are meaningless, and within itself the meaninglessness does not cohere.

—*Discourse must be in words, and it is possible to give a name to that which is not understood nor cognoscible by human reason. It is our duty to strive towards God by thought and word. But it is our final duty to believe, to have and to nourish faith.*

—I perceive some of your pronouncements to be heretical and evil. Of sin, you said it was necessary for the perfection of the universe and to make good shine all the more brightly in contrast. You said God is not the cause of our doing evil but that free will is the cause. From God's omniscience and foreknowledge He knows that men will sin. How then could free will exist?

—*God has not foreknowledge. He is, and has knowledge.*

—Man's acts are all subject to predestination and he cannot therefore have free will. God created Judas. Saw to it that he was reared, educated, and should prosper in trade. He also ordained that Judas should betray His Divine Son. How then could Judas have guilt?

—*God, in knowing the outcome of free will, did not thereby attenuate or extirpate free will.*

—That light-and-shade gentleman you once admired so much, Mani, held that Cain and Abel were not the sons of Adam and Eve but the sons of Eve and Satan. However that may be, the sin in the

garden of Eden was committed in an unimaginably remote age, eons
of centuries ago, according to the mundane system of computing time.
According to the same system the doctrine of the Incarnation and the
Redemption is now not even two thousand years old. Are all the
millions and millions of uncountable people born between the Creation and the Redemption to be accounted lost, dying in original sin
though themselves personally guiltless, and to be considered condemned to hell?

—*If you would know God, you must know time. God is time. God
is the substance of eternity. God is not distinct from what we regard
as years. God has no past, no future, no presence in the sense of
man's fugitive tenure. The interval you mention between the Creation and the Redemption was ineffably unexistent.*

—That is the sort of disputation that I dub 'flannel' but granted
that the soul of man is immortal, the geometry of a soul must be
circular and, like God, it cannot have had a beginning. Do you agree
with that?

—*In piety it could thus be argued.*

—Then our souls existed before joining our bodies?

—*That could be said.*

—Well, where were they?

—*None but the Polyarch would say that.*

—Are we to assume there is in existence somewhere a boundless
reservoir of souls not yet encorpified?

—*Time does not enter into an act of divine creation. God can
create something which has the quality of having always existed.*

—Is there any point in my questioning you on your one-time
devotion to the works of Plotinus and Porphyry?

—*No. But far preferable to the Manichæan dualism of light and
darkness, good and evil, was Plotinus's dualism of mind and matter.
In his doctrine of emanation Plotinus was only slightly misled.
Plotinus was a good man.*

—About 372, when you were eighteen, you adopted Manichæan-
ism and did not discard the strange creed until ten years later. What
do you think now of that jumble of Babylonian cosmology, Buddhism
and ghostly theories about light and darkness, the Elect and the
Hearers, the commands to abstain from fleshmeat, manual labour and
intercourse with women? Or Mani's own claim that he was himself
the Paraclete?

—*Why ask me now when you can read the treatise against this heresy which I wrote in 394? So far as Mani himself is concerned, my attitude may be likened to that of the King of Persia in 376. He had Mani skinned alive and then crucified.*

—We must be going very soon.

—*Yes. Your air is nearly gone.*

—There is one more question on a matter that has always baffled me and on which nothing written about you by yourself or others gives any illumination. *Are you a Nigger?*

—*I am a Roman.*

—I suspect your Roman name is an affectation or a disguise. You are of Berber stock, born in Numidia. Those people were non-white. You are far more aligned with Carthage than Rome, and there are Punic corruptions even in your Latin.

—*Civis Romanus sum.*

—The people of your homeland today are called Arabs. Arabs are not white.

—*Berbers were blond white people, with lovely blue eyes.*

—All true Africans, notwithstanding the racial stew in that continent, are to some extent niggers. They are descendants of Noah's son Ham.

—*You must not overlook the African sun. I was a man that was very easily sunburnt.*

—What does it feel like to be in heaven for all eternity?

—*For all eternity? Do you then think there are fractional or temporary eternities?*

—If I ask it, will you appear to me here tomorrow?

—*I have no tomorrow. I am. I have only nowness.*

—Then we shall wait. Thanks and goodbye.

—*Goodbye. Mind the rocks. Go with God.*

With clambering, Hackett in the lead, they soon found the water and made their way back to this world.

5

The morning was still there, bland as they had left it. Teague McGettigan was slumped in charge of his pipe and newspaper and gave them only a glance when, having discarded their masks, they proceeded without thought to brisk towelling.

—Well, De Selby called to Mick, what did you think of that?

Mentally, Mick felt numb, confused; and almost surprised by ordinary day.

—That was . . . an astonishing apparition, he stammered. And I heard every word. A very shrewd and argumentative man whoever he was.

De Selby froze in his half-naked stance, his mouth falling a bit open in dismay.

—Great crucified Lord, he cried, don't tell me you didn't recognize Augustine?

Mick stared back, still benumbed.

—I thought it was Santa Claus, Hackett remarked. Yet his voice lacked the usual intonation of jeer.*

—I suppose, De Selby mused, beginning to dress, that I do you two some injustice. I should have warned you. A first encounter with a man from heaven can be unnerving.

—Several of the references were familiar enough, Mick said, but I couldn't quite pinpoint the personality. My goodness, the Bishop of Hippo!

—Yes. When you think of it, he did not part with much information.

—If I may say so, Hackett interposed, he didn't seem too happy in heaven. Where was the glorious resurrection we've all been promised? That character underground wouldn't get a job handing out toys in a store at Christmas. He seemed depressed.

—I must say that the antics of his companions seemed strange, Mick agreed. I mean, according to his account of them.

De Selby stopped, reflectively combing his sparse hair.

—One must reserve judgment on all such manifestations, he said. I am proceeding all the time on a theory. We should remember that that might not have been the genuine Augustine at all.

—But who, then?

The wise master stared out to sea.

—It could be even Beelzebub himself, he murmured softly.

Hackett sat down abruptly, working at his tie.

—Have any of you gentlemen got a match? Teague McGettigan asked, painfully standing up. Hackett handed him a box.

* A case might be made for "cheer" rather than "jeer" here. I have corrected some of the Macmillan text's misprints against the manuscript.

—The way I see it, Teague continued, there will come an almighty clump of rain and wind out of Wickla about twelve o'clock. Them mountains down there has us all destroyed.

—I'm not afraid of a shower, Hackett remarked coldly. At least you know what it is. There are worse things.

—Peaks of rock prod up into clouds like fingers, Teague explained, until the clouds is bursted and the wind carries the wather down here on top of us. Poor buggers on a walking tour around Shankill would get soaked, hang-sangwiches in sodden flitters and maybe not the price of a pint between them to take shelter in Brynes.

Their dressing, by reason of their rough rig, was finished. De Selby and Hackett were smoking, and the time was half nine. Then De Selby energetically rubbed his hands.

—Gentlemen, he said with some briskness, I presume that like me you have had no breakfast before this early swim. May I therefore invite you to have breakfast with me at Lawnmower. Mr. McGettigan can drive us up to the gate.

—I'm afraid I can't go, Hackett said.

—Well, it's not that my horse Jimmy couldn't pull you up, Teague said, spitting.

—Come now, De Selby said, we all need inner fortification after an arduous morning. I have peerless Limerick rashers and there will be no shortage of that apéritif.

Whether or not Hackett had another engagement Mick did not know but he immediately shared his instinct to get away, if only, indeed, to think, or try not to think. De Selby had not been deficient in the least in manners of honourable conduct but his continuing company seemed to confer uneasiness—perhaps vague, unformed fear.

—Mr De Selby, Mick said warmly, it is indeed kind of you to invite Hackett and me up for a meal but it happens that I did in fact have breakfast. I think we'd better part here.

—We'll meet soon again, Hackett remarked, to talk over this morning's goings-on.

De Selby shrugged and beckoned McGettigan to help him with his gear.

—As you will, gentlemen, he said politely enough. I certainly could do with a bite and perhaps I will have the pleasure of Teague's com-

pany. I thought the weather, the elements, all the forces of the
heavens made a breakfast-tide lecture seemly.

—Good luck to your honour but there's nourishment in that bottle
you have, Teague said brightly, taking away his pipe to say it loudly.

They separated like that and Hackett and Mick went on their
brief stroll into Dalkey, Mick wheeling the bicycle with some distaste.

—Have you somewhere to go? he asked.

—No I haven't. What did you make of that performance?

—I don't know what to say. You heard the conversation, and I
presume both of us heard the same thing.

—Do you believe . . . it all happened?

—I suppose I have to.

—I need a drink.

They fell silent. Thinking about the séance (if that ill-used word
will serve) was futile though disturbing and yet it was impossible
to shut such thoughts out of the head. Somehow Mick saw little
benefit in any discussion with Hackett. Hackett's mind was twisted in
a knot identical with his own. They were as two tramps who had met
in a trackless desert, each hopelessly asking the other the way.

—Well, Hackett said moodily at last, I haven't thrown overboard
my suspicions of yesterday about drugs, and even hypnotism I
wouldn't quite discount. But we have no means of checking whether
or not all that stuff this morning was hallucination.

—Couldn't we ask somebody? Get advice?

—Who? For a start, who would believe a word of the story?

—That's true.

—Incidentally, those underwater breathing masks were genuine.
I've worn gadgets like that before but they weren't as smart as De
Selby's.

—How do we know there wasn't a mixture of some brain-curdling
gas in the air-tank?

—That's true by God.

—I quite forgot I was wearing the thing.

They had paused undecided at a corner in the lonely little town.
Mick said that he thought he'd better go home and get some breakfast. Hackett thought it was too early to think of food. Well Mick
had to get rid of his damned bike. Couldn't he leave it at the comic
little police station in charge of Sergeant Fottrell? But what was the

point of that? Wouldn't he have the labour of collecting it another time? Hackett said that there had been no necessity to have used it at all in the first place, as there was such a thing as an early tram to accommodate eccentric people. Mick said no, not on Sunday, not from Booterstown.

—I know Mrs L would let me in, Hackett observed pettishly, except I know the big sow is still in bed snoring.

—Yes, it's been a funny morning, Mick replied sympathetically. Here you are, frustrated from joining the company of a widow who keeps a boozer, yet it is not half an hour since you parted company with Saint Augustine.

—Yes.

9

The old coloured houses of irregular size along the narrow quays of the Liffey seem to lean outward as if to study themselves in the water; but on his pleasant walk there this time, Mick's eye was not dwelling pleasurably on them. He was thinking, though not in gloom. There had come to him an idea that seemed bright, masterly, bold even. True, it would not dissipate the underwater ghost of Augustine nor extinguish the neuro-psychotic aberrations of De Selby but he became convinced it would enable him *to do something* to prevent, perhaps permanently but certainly for the present, the carrying out of any genuine plan to visit the human race with havoc. He was pleased. He resolved to go to a quiet place where alcoholic drinks were to be had and then, please God, not have one but try something healthy, refreshing, harmless. Plain thinking—planning—was called for.

And Father Cobble? Yes, Mick would keep that arrangement to bring him on a visit to De Selby. The visit might well be valuable and, also, he was glad that Hackett had reneged. He felt Hackett's presence might have been a complication, even an obstacle, and this was also true of the steps he would have to take later to give effect to his new idea.

His steps led him to the Metropole in Dublin's main street. It was not called a cinema, restaurant, dance hall or drinking den, though it contained all of those delights. Drinking was done in a quiet, softly-lighted lounge downstairs where tables were sequestered by tall fixed screens of dark wood. It was a favourite resort of parish priests from the country and, though service was by waitresses, lady customers were excluded.

He sat down and ordered a small Vichy water. When another order had been served in the division next to him he was sharply startled by the unseen customer's thanks, unmistakable in content if not in tone.

—In gratitude for that bottle, me dear colleen, I will make a novena for the implenishment of your soul irreciprocally to Saint Martin of Tours himself.

No help for it: Mick picked up his drink and moved in. Happily, Sergeant Fottrell was alone. In old-fashioned courtesy he stood up and put out a hand.

—Well, the Lord forbid but you must be following me detectively? Mick laughed.

—No indeed. I wanted a quiet drink and thought nobody would know me down here.

—Ah, but the divil minds his own children.

Curiously, this unscheduled collision with the Sergeant did not seem to erode Mick's half-formed desire to be by himself. In fact he was glad to see the sergeant. He apologised once more for having failed to retrieve his bicycle from the station in Dalkey. The Sergeant took his long upper lip from his glass of barley wine with a wince of total absolution.

—Where the bicycle is, he said gravely, is a far safer place than the high highroad itself, intuitively.

—Oh, I just thought it might be in the way.

—It is under lock and key in cell number two and you are far better in your health to be divorced from it. Tell me this item: how did you find Policeman Pluck?

—I had met him before, of course. A very pleasant man.

—What was he doing perceptively?

—He was busy mending a puncture.

—Ah-ha!

The Sergeant sniggered, took another sup from his drink and frowned slightly in thought.

—That will be the third puncture in seven days, he said, in what seemed to be a tone of satisfaction.

—That looks a pretty awful record, Mick replied. Is it sheer bad luck or is it the bad roads?

—'Tis the Council must take the credit for the little back road, the worst in Ireland. But Policeman Pluck got his punctures at half one on Monday, two o'clock on Wednesday, and half-six on Sunday.

—How on earth do you know that? Does he keep a diary of them?

—He does not. I know the dates and times protruberantly because it was my good self who carried out the punctures with my penknife.

—Good heavens, why?

—For Policeman Pluck's good luck. But sitting here I have been considering meditatively those talking pictures upstairs. They are a quaint achievious science certainly.

—They are a great advance on silent films.

—You know how they are worked?

—Oh yes. The photo-electric cell.

—Yes then. Why if you can turn light into sound you cannot turn sound into light?

—You mean invent a *phono*-electric cell?

—Of a particular certainty, but for sure that invention would be a hard pancake. I do often contemplate what sort of a light the noble American Constitution would make, given out by President Roosevelt.

—A very interesting speculation.

—Or a speech by Arthur Griffith?

—Yes indeed.

—Charles Stewart Parnell held the dear belief that all Ireland's woes and tears were the true result of being so fond of green. Wrap the green flag round me, boys. If you put that grand man's speech through the cell (and many a month he spent in a cell himself) wouldn't it be the hemochromic thing if the solution was a bright green light?

Mick laughed at this, and at the whole wonderful idea. There had been, he seemed to remember, an organ that 'played' light on a screen, enchanting patterns of mixes and colour. But that was not what the Sergeant had conceived.

Yes. And what would be the colour of Caruso's voice, or John Mc-Cormack singing *Down by the Sally Gardens*? But tell me, Sergeant. Why did you persistently puncture Policeman Pluck's tyres?

The Sergeant beckoned the waitress, ordered a barley wine for himself and a small bottle of 'that' for his friend. Then he leaned forward confidentially.

—Did you ever discover or hear tell of mollycules? he asked.

—I did of course.

—Would it surprise or collapse you to know that the Mollycule Theory is at work in the parish of Dalkey?

—Well . . . yes and no.

—It is doing terrible destruction, he continued, the half of the people is suffering from it, it is worse than the smallpox.

—Could it not be taken in hand by the Dispensary Doctor or the National Teachers, or do you think it is a matter for the head of the family?

—The lock, stock and barrel of it all, he replied almost fiercely, is the County Council.

—It seems a complicated thing all right.

The Sergeant drank delicately, deep in thought.

Michael Gilhaney, a man I know, he said finally, is an example of a man that is nearly banjaxed from the operation of the Mollycule Theory. Would it astonish you ominously to hear that he is in danger of being a bicycle?

Mick shook his head in polite incomprehension.

—He is nearly sixty years of age by plain computation, the Sergeant said, and if he is itself, he has spent no less than thirty-five years riding his bicycle over the rocky roadsteads and up and down the pertimious hills and into the deep ditches when the road goes astray in the strain of the winter. He is always going to a particular destination or other on his bicycle at every hour of the day or coming back from there at every other hour. If it wasn't that his bicycle was stolen every Monday he would be sure to be more than halfway now.

—Halfway to where?

—Halfway to being a bloody bicycle himself.

Had Sergeant Fottrell for once betrayed himself into drunken rambling? His fancies were ususally amusing but not so good when they were meaningless. When Mick said something of the kind the Sergeant stared at him impatiently.

—Did you ever study the Mollycule Theory when you were a lad? he asked. Mick said no, not in any detail.

—That is very serious defalcation and an abstruse exacerbation, he said severely, but I'll tell you the size of it. Everything is composed of small mollycules of itself and they are flying around in concentric circles and arcs and segments and innumerable various other routes too resting but spinning away and darting hither and thither and back again, all the time on the go. Do you follow me intelligently? Molly-cules?

—I think I do.

—They are as lively as twenty punky leprachauns doing a jig on the top of a flat tombstone. Now take a sheep. What is a sheep only mil-lions of little bits of sheepness whirling around doing intricate con-vulsions inside the baste. What else is it but that?

—That would be bound to make the sheep dizzy, Mick observed, especially if the whirling was going on inside the head as well.

The Sergeant gave him a look which no doubt he himself would describe as one of non-possum and noli-me-tangere.

—That's a most foolhardy remark, he said sharply, because the nerve-strings and the sheep's head itself are whirling into the same bargain and you can cancel out one whirl against the other and there you are—like simplifying a division sum when you have fives above and below the bar.

—To say the truth I did not think of that.

—Mollycules is a very intricate theorem and can be worked out with algebra but you would want to take it by degrees with rulers and cosines and familiar other instruments and then at the wind-up not believe what you had proved at all. If that happened you would have to go back over it till you got a place where you could believe your own facts and figures as exactly delineated from Hall and Knight's Algebra and then go on again from that particular place till you had the whole pancake properly believed and not have bits of it half-believed or a doubt in your head hurting you like when you lose the stud of your shirt in the middle of the bed.

—Very true, Mick decided to say.

—If you hit a rock hard enough and often enough with an iron hammer, some mollycules of the rock will go into the hammer and contrariwise likewise.

—That is well-known, he agreed.

—The gross and net result of it is that people who spend most of their natural lives riding iron bicycles over the rocky roadsteads of the parish get their personalities mixed up with the personalities of their bicycles as a result of the interchanging of the mollycules of each of them, and you would be surprised at the number of people in country parts who are nearly half people and half bicycles.

Mick made a little gasp of astonishment that made a sound like the air coming from a bad puncture.

—Good Lord, I suppose you're right.

—And you would be unutterably flabbergasted if you knew the number of stout bicycles that partake serenely of humanity.

Here the Sergeant produced his pipe, a thing he did very rarely in public, and in silence commenced the laborious business of filling and ramming it from his battered tin of very dark tobacco. Mick began to muse and think of country places he had known in his younger days. He thought of one place he had been fond of.

Brown bogs and black bogs were neatly arranged on each side of the road with rectangular boxes carved out of them here and there, each with a filling of yellow-brown brown-yellow water. Far away near the sky tiny people were stooped at their turf-work, cutting out precisely-shaped sods with their patent spades and building them into a tall memorial the height of a horse and cart. Sounds came from them, delivered to his ears without charge by the west wind, sounds of laughing and whistling and bits of verses from the old bog-songs. Nearer, a house stood attended by three trees and surrounded by the happiness of a coterie of fowls, all of them picking and rooting and disputating loudly in the unrelenting manufacture of their eggs. The house was quiet in itself and silent but a canopy of lazy smoke had been erected over the chimney to indicate that people were within engaged on tasks. Ahead of him went the road, running swiftly across the flat land and pausing slightly to climb slowly up a hill that was waiting for it in a place where there was tall grass, grey boulders and rank stunted trees. The whole overhead was occupied by the sky, translucent, impenetrable, ineffable and incomparable, with a fine island of cloud anchored in the calm two yards to the right of Mr Jarvis's outhouse.

The scene was real and incontrovertible but at variance with the talk of the Sergeant. Was it not monstrous to allege that the little people winning turf far away were partly bicycles? He took a sideways view of him. He had now compacted his turf-like tobacco and produced a box of matches.

—Are you sure about the humanity of bicycles? Mick inquired of him. Does it not go against the doctrine of original sin? Or is the

Molecule Theory as dangerous as you say?

The Sergeant was drawing fiercely at the pipe as his match spluttered.

—It is between twice and three times as dangerous as it might be, he replied gloomily. Early in the morning I often think it is four times and, for goodness sake, if you lived here for a few days and gave full and free rein to your observation and inspection, you would know how certain the sureness of the certainty is.

—Policeman Pluck did not look like a bicycle, Mick said. He had no back wheel on him and hadn't so much as a bell on his right thumb.

The Sergeant looked at him with some commiseration.

—You cannot expect him to grow handlebars out of his neck but I have seen him attempt things more acutely indescribable than that. Did you ever notice the queer behaviour of bicycles in the country, or the more-man-bicycles?

—I did not.

—It's an indigenous catastrophe. When a man lets things go too far, you will not see much because he spends a lot of time leaning with one elbow on walls or standing propped up by one foot at the path. Such a man is a futile phenomenon of great charm and intensity and a very dangerous article.

—Dangerous to other people, you mean?

—Dangerous to himself and everybody. I once knew a man named Doyle. He was thirty-one per cent.

—Well, that's not too serious.

The Sergeant was puffing industriously, his pipe now in fine order.

—Maybe. You can thank me. There were three Doyle brothers in the house and they were too contemptuously poor to have a bicycle apiece. Some people never know how fortunate they are when they are poorer than each other. But bedamn but one of the brothers won a prize of ten pounds in *John Bull*. When I got precise wind of this tiding I knew I would have to take quick steps unless there was to be two new bicycles in the family, because you will understand that I can steal only a limited number of bicycles in a month. Luckily I knew the postman well and I gave him a talking-to to divert the cheque to myself. The postman! Ah, great, sweet, brown stirabout!

Recollection of this public servant seemed to move the Sergeant to sad sardonic chuckles, with intricate gesturings of his red hands.

—The postman? Mick asked.

—Seventy-two per cent, he said quietly.

—Great Lord!

—A round of twenty-nine miles on the bicycle every single day for forty years, hail, rain or snowballs. There was very little hope of getting his number down below fifty again. I got him to cash the cheque in a private sub-office and we split the money in the public interest paternalistically.

Funny thing, Mick did not feel that the Sergeant had been dishonest; he had been sentimental, rather, and the state of the postman meant that no moral issue was involved.

He asked the Sergeant how the bicycle, for its part, would behave from day to day in a situation like this.

—The behaviour of a bicycle with a very high content of homo sapiens, he explained, is very cunning and entirely remarkable. You never see them moving by themselves but you meet them in the least accountable of places unexpectedly. Did you ever see a bicycle leaning against the dresser in a warm kitchen when it is pouring outside?

—I did.

—Not very far from the fire?

—Yes.

—Near enough to the family to hear the conversation?

—I suppose so.

—Not a thousand miles from where they keep the eatables?

—I did not notice that. Good Lord, you do not mean to say that these bicycles *eat food?*

—They were never seen doing it, nobody ever caught them with a mouthful of seedy cake. All I know is that food disappears.

—What!

—It is not the first time I have noticed crumbs at the front wheels of some of those gentlemen.

Rather feebly Mick gestured to the waitress and ordered another drink. The Sergeant was in deadly earnest, no doubt about that. And this was the man Mick had decided to call in to help him in resolving the great St. Augustine enigma. He felt strangely depressed.

—Nobody takes any notice, the Sergeant said softly. Tom thinks that Pat is responsible for missing grubsteaks, and Pat thinks that Tom is instrumental. Very few of the people guess what is going on in such a fearsomely infractional house. There are other things, too . . . but it's better not to talk of them.

—Oh come now, Sergeant. What sort of other things?

—Well, a man riding a lady's bicycle. It's the height of sulphurous immorality, the P.P. would be within his rights in forbidding such a low character put as much as his nose inside the church.

—Yes . . . such conduct is unseemly.

—God help the nation that weakens on such matters. You would have bicycles demanding votes, and they would look for seats on the County Council to make the roads far worse than they are for their own ulterior motivation. But against that and on the other hand, a good bicycle is a great companion, a friend, there is great charm about it.

—All the same, I doubt if I'll ever again get up on that bicycle of mine you have in the station out in Dalkey.

The Sergeant shook his head genially.

—Ah now, a little of it is a good thing, it makes you hardy and puts iron into you. But shure walking too far too often too quickly isn't safe at all either. The cracking of your feet on the road makes a certain amount of road come up into you. When a man dies they say he returns to clay funereally but too much walking fills you up with clay far sooner (or buries bits of you along the road) and brings your death halfway to meet you. It is not easy to know fastidiously what is the best way to move yourself from one place to another.

There was a little silence. Mick thought of mentioning how intact one could remain by restricting oneself to air travel but decided not to; the Sergeant would surely object on the ground of cost. Mick noticed his face had become clouded and that he was staring into the bowl of his pipe.

—I will tell you a secret confidentially, he said in a low voice. My own grandfather was eighty-three when we buried him. For five years before his death he was a horse.

—A *horse?*

—A horse in everything but extraneous externalities, because he had spent years of his life—far too many for safety, be the pipers— in the saddle. Usually he was lazy and quiet but now and again he would go for a smart gallop, clearing the hedges in great style. Did you ever see a man on two legs galloping?

—I did not.

—Well, I am given to understand it is a great sight. He always said he won the Grand National when he was a lot younger and used to annoy the life out of his family with stories about the intricate jumps and the insoluble tallness of them.

—And the grandfather got himself into this condition by too much horse-riding?

—That was the size of it. His old horse Dan was in the contrary way of thinking and gave so much trouble, coming into the house at night, interfering with young girls during the day and committing indictable offences, that they had to shoot him. The polis of the time was not sympathetic exiguously. They said they would have to arrest the horse and have him up at the next Petty Sessions unless he was done away with. So the family shot him but if you ask me it was my grandfather they shot and it is the horse that is buried in Cloncoonla churchyard.

The Sergeant fell to musing on his complicated ancestry but had the presence of mind to beckon the waitress with his pipe and order a repeat dose of the quiet medicine.

—In a way, Mick observed, your grandfather's case was not so bad. I mean, a horse is at least a creature, a living thing, man's companion on earth and indeed he is accounted everywhere a noble animal. Now, if it was a pig . . .

The Sergeant turned and beamed on him, and gave a long contented puff at his pipe.

—You say that from a good heart, and it is subsidiary and solemn of you. The Irish people have great graw for the horse. When Tipperary Tim died, the cabhorse that won the Grand National and the only one of the whole field left standing, be the holy God you'd swear it was a beloved Archbishop that had gone to his eternal reward. Strong men was seen crying.

—Yes, and think of Orby, the great horse that won the National for Boss Croker. To this day he lies there at Sandyford.

—Ah yes. And then there was Master McGrath, the dog that was faster than the wind. A statue of him stands at a crossroads down in Tipp. where the mother comes from.

Both of them pleasurably savoured their kinship with the higher animals, though personally Mick drew the line at becoming one of them by a process of prolonged carnal intercussion.

—Well, Sergeant, I am delighted that we are quite agreed on one thing at least. Human metamorphosis vis-à-vis an iron bicycle is quite another matter. And there is more to it than the monstrous exchange of tissue for metal.

—And what would that be? the Sergeant asked curiously.

—All decent Irishmen should have a proper national outlook. Practically any bike you have in Ireland was made in either Birmingham or Coventry.

—I see the point intimately. Yes. There is also an element of treason entailed. Quite right.

It seemed that this point had never occurred to him and a frown gathered about him as he inwardly considered it, puffing stolidly and compacting the tobacco in his bowl with a well-charred finger.

—Oh now, he said at last, faith and the bicycle is no hilarity of itself as a gigantic social problem. In me younger days it led to a hanging.

—Is that so?

—It did bedad. I was stationed in Borrisokane at the time and there was a very famous man there be the name of McDadd. McDadd held the national record for the hundred miles on the solid tyre. I need not tell you with exactitude what the solid tyre did for him. We had to hang the bicycle.

—Hang the bicycle?

—McDadd had a first-class grudge against another man named MacDonaghy but he did not go near MacDonaghy. He knew how things stood there, and he gave MacDonaghy's bicycle a ferocious thrashing with a crowbar. After that McDadd and MacDonaghy had a fast fist fight and MacDonaghy—a dark man with glasses—did not live to know who the winner was.

—Well, wouldn't that be a case of manslaughter?

—Not with the Sergeant we had in them days. He held it was murder most foul and a bad case of criminality into the same bargain. We couldn't find McDadd for a long time or make sure where the most of him was. We had to arrest his bicycle as well as himself and we minutely watched the two of them under secret observation for a week to see where the majority of McDadd was and whether the bicycle was mostly in McDadd's backside pari passu and vice versa if you understand my meaning.

—I think I do, but I can also see the possibility of a charge of conspiracy.

—Maybe so, maybe not. The Sergeant gave his ruling at the end

of the week. His position was painful in the extremity of pain because he was a close friend of McDadd after office hours. He condemned the bicycle and it was the bicycle that was hanged.

It seemed to Mick a very summary form of justice, and apparently
the sentence had been imposed and carried out without the formality
of court proceedings.

—I think that perhaps there was a miscarriage of the carriageway
there, he commented.

—They were rough days, the Sergeant replied, smoking thought-
fully. But there was a great wake afterwards, and the bicycle was
buried in the same grave as MacDonaghy. Did you ever see a bicycle-
shaped coffin?

—No.

—It is a very inconvoluted item of wood-working, you would want
to be a master-class carpenter to make a good job of the handlebars,
to say nothing of the pedals and the backstep.

—I don't doubt that.

—Ah yes. The days of racing on the solid tyre were sad days for
Ireland.

The Sergeant fell silent again. One could almost hear the gentle
wash of the tide of memory in his head.

—There were tragic cases, too, of another kind entirely. I remember an old man. He was harmless enough but he had the people
driven loopy by the queer way he moved and walked. He'd go up
a little gentle hill at a speed of maybe half a mile an hour but at other
times he would run so fast that you'd swear he was doing up to fifteen
emm pee aitch. And that's a fact by damn.

—Did anybody find out what was wrong with him?

—One very intelligent, perspicuous and infractious man did. It was
meself. Do you know what was wrong with the poor bugger?

—No. What?

—He was suffering severely from Sturmey Archer. He was the first
in the country to fit the three-speed gear at the turn of the century.

—Yes, I think I can see the various possible complications. For instance, I think racing bikes have forks with special springing in them.
Yes. It's all very interesting. But now, I promised to be home early
and I'm going to buy a final drink.

Mick beckoned the waitress.

—I want to ask you about something, he added.

As the drinks were coming he bethought himself, as they say in the old books. He had enjoyed the Sergeant's peroration and his abstruse subject. It would be fitting, perhaps, to call him the poor man's De Selby. But the latter was still his preoccupation—perhaps he should say his night-and-day obsession. Yet he had a plan now, one that was at once ingenious and daring. He thought it would be only wise and judicious to have the Sergeant participate unwittingly in it, for if he were to find certain things out afterwards of his own motion, his un-doubted gift for the maladroit could in the end wreck the scheme. Mick had already in his mind assigned a part—again an unwitting one—to Hackett. The date and timing of the operation depended now on one thing only: finding out how De Selby proposed to circulate his deadly D.M.P. substance simultaneously all over the world so as to obviate the condition of insulation, the sort of seal that had obtained in the case of the submarine cavern at Dalkey.

He was not clear how he could do this in a reasonably short time, and prolonged twisting and turning of his own brain yielded no guess about how this mighty task could be accomplished. Even a world Power with tens of thousands of aeroplanes would be daunted by such an undertaking and, supernatural as De Selby's contacts seemed to be, it was doubtful indeed if flights of angels could be invoked. In fact there was no proof that the Almighty approved of De Selby at all. God might be on Mick's side.

—Sergeant Fottrell, he said seriously, I suppose you know Mr De Selby of the Vico Road?

A gentle frown gathered on the face.

—An exemplary and august personality, he replied, but a whit contumacious.

That was promising: respect leavened with suspicion.

—Exactly. I know him rather well myself but he has me worried. In that house of his in the woods he has been carrying out experi-ments. He is a scientist, of course.

—Ah yes. Piercing insentiently the dim secrets of the holy world.

—Now I am not saying that he is breaking the law. But I do know that he is endangering the community. He does not know, and probably could not be persuaded, that his experiments might get out of control and visit us all with an epidemic of appalling disease, with goodness knows how many people dying like flies and passing on the pestilence to other people as they do so; not only here in Dublin and

Dalkey but possibly in England and other parts of the world.

The Sergeant had rekindled his pipe.

—That is a most unfavourable and incontinent tiding, he said. That is worse than the question of the bicycles.

—I'm glad you look at it that way. You are a man, Sergeant, who is bigger than his job, otherwise you would not save stolen bicycles to curtail the deadly cycling of afflicted parties and indeed deliberately puncturing Policeman Pluck's machine.

This speech obviously pleased the Sergeant, as Mick intended it would.

—There are times, he said, when I must take my superior officer to be the Man Above. It is my plain duty to guard members of the human race, sometimes from themselves. Not everybody understands the far from scrutable periculums of the intricate world.

—I quite agree. Now I happen to know that Mr De Selby has been artificially incubating the bacteria which cause typhoid fever in humans. Typhoid is a very serious and dangerous disease, even worse than typhus.

—An insatiable importunity.

—Yes.

—An indiscriminate exacerbation much to be inveighed against meticulously.

—Mr De Selby has tens of millions of those microbes in a metal container like a little keg. He has it in his house, locked in a safe.

—A safe, faith?

—Yes. In the interest of humanity I plan to carry off this container of dangerous bugs away from the scientist's house—steal it if you will —and put it in some safe place where it will do no harm.

—Ah! Well now! Steal it? Yes indeed. I would consider that not contumelious nor derogatory.

—Then I can rely, Sergeant, on your co-operation?

He was now relaxed, apparently relieved that the project was no more than to take away something which was, while dangerous, of no monetary value.

—Not only my co-operation but my active condonement of the *res ipsa*. But locked in a safe? I do not know the skills of poking a safe's lock.

—Nor do I. And blowing it up or using force would be very dangerous. But that sort of hazard does not arise at all. The safe looks massive and strong but it is old-fashioned. Look at this!

From a small inside pocket of his jacket Mick extracted a key and held it up.

—I've told you, Sergeant, that our friend is careless, he said, and perhaps I should have said criminally careless and quite reckless. This is the key of the safe. I picked it up from the floor of his sitting-room on a recent visit.

—Well great cripes, the Sergeant cried blankly.

—Our task is really simple enough, Mick continued. First we must see to it that on a given evening Mr De Selby is not at home. I think I can arrange that without much trouble. When he is out, there will be nobody else there. And our intrusion will be brief.

—Succinctly so, by dad.

—When we've got the container we will hide it in the shrubbery, near the little gate at the Vico Road. We will then go home. The following morning early I will collect it in a taxi. Then leave the rest to me. The only little snag is how to get into the house.

—That would not be a fastidious worry, the Sergeant replied pleasantly, for if he is as careless as you say, I could deal deftly with a window, without wincing.

—But not break one, I hope. We don't want to alarm or alert him.

—No then. I have a good pen-knife.

—Ah, that is the business, Sergeant. We can take it that everything is agreed then?

—Except the date of the accomplishment.

—Yes. I'll let you know that in good time.

Mick rose, and in good conspirator's fashion, put out his hand. The Sergeant grasped it.

—To the grand defence and preservation of the race of Adam, he intoned solemnly.

[One of the difficulties in excerpting anything of O'Brien's is that of providing explanations for what goes on in what has now become backstage. It is not so much that O'Brien suffers from having his dramatized scenes paraphrased, as does every good author. It is that much of his charm lies in his own narrative locutions, which often involve just such compressions of action with attendant shifts in focus which produce a special sub-genre that might be called mock inadvertent humor. (An example of the straight inadvertent school of recap humor would be a *TV Guide* blurb.) Suffice it to say that

in the eighty-seven pages between Mick's pub chat with Sergeant
Fottrell and the following section the hero has been persuaded that
not only is James Joyce alive and living incognito in the small seaside
resort of Skerries, but that the great Irish writer can somehow be of
service in the foiling of De Selby's plot. That Joyce himself does
not quite perceive this as his role might be expected by us, if not
Mick. What Joyce does want from Mick might surprise anyone, however. Dissertations could be written on the uniquely Irish delusion
that a writer might be of any practical use in such a matter, especially
a writer such as Joyce. A good place to start such a discussion would
be where this *Reader* begins, with O'Brien's study of the old Irish
satirists with their magic power. There is also, alas, a degenerative
possibility, for it was one of O'Brien's obsessions, as we have seen,
that Americans had created a Joyce of such powers that he could
delay if not halt the apocalypse. As O'Brien's letters to American
editor Cecil Scott reveal, it was a time when the author was painfully, if naïvely, hoping for money from the new country. In any
case Mick leaves Mary and Hackett and De Selby back in Dalkey
and goes north to meet The Great Man.]

1 8

During his train journey to Skerries on Tuesday evening his mood
was peaceable: resigned might be a fairer word. *Quisque faber for-
tunae suae,* the tag says—everybody makes his own mess. Still, he
did not think this outlook applicable. He was conscious of a pervasive
ambiguity: sometimes he seemed to be dictating events with deific
authority, at other times he saw himself the plaything of implacable
forces. On this particular trip he felt he must await an exposition of
Joyce by himself, and take him at his face value. Joyce had already
whetted curiosity by disclosing that he was still working on a book,
unnamed, content unhinted at. He could be an impostor, or a unique
case of physical resemblance. Yet his appearance was authentic, and
clearly he had lived on the European continent. Really, he could not
be classed as one of Mick's problems but rather an interesting distraction for one now practised in interfering in the affairs of others. Very
properly, Mick had not given his own private or business address,
and it could not be said that he knew anything embarrassing.

The hotel was a simple establishment, with no bar, but an old man, nondescript in manner and dress to the point of giving no sign whether he was the boots or the proprietor, guided Mick down a hallway to 'the drawing-room where gents takes a drink'. It was an ill-lit room, small, linoleum on the floor, a few small tables with chairs here and there, and in the grate a flickering fire. Mick was alone and agreed with his host that it was a poor evening for that time of the year, and then ordered a small sherry.

—I'm expecting a friend, he added.

But Joyce was punctual. He came in noiselessly, very soberly attired, quiet, calm, a small black hat surmounting his small ascetic features, in his hand a stout walking stick. He sat down after a slight bow.

—I took the liberty of ordering something on the way in, he said, smiling slightly, because we in the trade like to save each other's feet. I hope you are A.1?

Mick laughed easily.

—Excellent, he said. That walk from the station is a tonic in itself. Here's your drink, and I'm paying for it.

Joyce did not reply, having commenced preparing to light a small black cigar.

—I am a little bit flustered, he said finally. You seem to have many connexions in this country. I envy you. I know a few people—but friends? Ah!

—Perhaps you are by nature the more solitary type of man, Mick suggested. Maybe company in general doesn't agree with you. Personally, I find interesting people very scarce, and bores to be met everywhere.

He seemed to nod in gloom.

—One of the great drawbacks of Ireland, he said, is that there are too many Irish here. You understand me? I knew it is natural and to be expected, like having wild animals in the zoo. But it's unnerving for one who has been away in the mishmash that is Europe today.

Here he had led Mick to the scene of his inquiry, so to speak. Mick's voice was low, soothing:

—Mr Joyce, I have great respect for you and it would be an honour to be of service to you. I am a bit confused by your eminence as an author and your presence in this part of the world. Would you give me a little information about yourself—in strict confidence, of course.

Joyce nodded as if without guile.

—I will, of course. There is nothing much to tell you. The past is simple enough. The future is what I find remote and difficult.

—I see. Were you expelled from Switzerland by the Hitler people?

—No, France. My wife and family were part of a mass of people fleeing before that terror. My passport was British. I knew I would be arrested, probably murdered.

—What happened to your family?

—I can't say. We got separated.

—Are they dead?

—I know very little except that my son is safe. It was all chaos, bedlam. Trains broke down, lines were damaged. It was improvisation everywhere. A life in a lorry, perhaps, or stumbling across fields, or holding up for a day or two in a barn. There were soldiers and guerillas and cutthroats roaming the land on all sides. By the Lord God it was not funny. Fortunately the real country folk were recognisable—brave, simple people. Fortunately I could speak French properly.

—And what exactly was your destination?

He paused.

—Well, first, he explained, I wanted to get away from contact with those Germans. My second idea was to get to America. America hadn't entered the war at that time. But any sort of major movement was very difficult. There were spies, saboteurs and thugs of every description high and low. The simplest questions of even food and drink were difficult.

—Yes, war is calamitous.

—I wouldn't dignify that French shambles with the word war. And the black market? Heavens!

—What happened?

—I got to London first. The atmosphere of nerves there was terrible. I didn't feel safe.

Mick nodded.

—I remember they hanged your namesake—the broadcaster Joyce.

—Yes. I thought I'd be better off here. I managed to sneak across in a small freighter. Thank God I can still pass for an Irishman.

—What about your family?

—I'm having confidential inquiries made through a friend, and I know my son is safe. Of course I can't risk making inquiries direct.

The conversation was fair enough but not much to Mick's purpose. Was this James Joyce, the Dublin writer of international name? Or was it somebody masquerading, possibly genuinely deranged through suffering? The old, nagging doubt was still there.

—Mr. Joyce, tell me about the writing of *Ulysses*.

He turned with a start.

—I have heard more than enough about that dirty book, that collection of smut, but do not be heard saying that I had anything to do with it. Faith now, you must be careful about that. As a matter of fact, I have put my name only to one little book in which I was concerned.

—And what was that?

—Ah, it's a long time ago. Oliver Gogarty and I, when we were in touch, worked together on some short stories. Simple stories: Dublin characterisations you might call them. Yes, they did have some little merit, I think. The world was settled then . . .

—Did you find that sort of association with Gogarty easy?

Joyce chuckled softly.

—The man had talent, he said, but of a widely spread out kind. He was primarily a talker and, up to a point, his talk improved with drink. He was a drunkard, but not habitually. He was too clever for that.

—Well, you were friends?

—Yes, you could say that, I suppose. But Gogarty could have a scurrilous and blasphemous tongue and that didn't suit me, I needn't tell you.

—Was this collaboration genuinely fifty-fifty?

—No. I did the real work, tried to get back into the soul of the people. Gogarty was all for window-dressing, smart stuff, almost Castle cavorting—things not in character. Oh, we had several quarrels, I can tell you.

—What did you call the book?

—We called it *Dubliners*. At the last moment Gogarty wouldn't let his name go on the title page. Said it would ruin his name as a doctor. It didn't matter, because no publisher could be found for years.

—Very interesting. But what else have you written, mainly?

Joyce quietly attended to the ash of his cigar.

—So far as print is concerned, mostly pamphlets for the Catholic Truth Society of Ireland. I am sure you know what I mean—those little tracts that can be had from a stand inside the door of any church; on marriage, the sacrament of penance, humility, the dangers of alcohol.

Mick stared.

—You surprise me.

—Now and again, of course. I attempted something more ambitious. In 1926 I had a biographical piece on Saint Cyril, Apostle of the Slavs, published in *Studies,* the Irish Jesuit quarterly. Under an assumed name, of course.

—Yes. But *Ulysses?*

There was a low sound of impatience in the gloom.

—I don't want to talk about that exploit. I took the idea to be a sort of practical joke but didn't know enough about it to suspect it might seriously injure my name. It began with an American lady in Paris by the name of Sylvia Beach. I know it's a horrible phrase, I detest it, but the truth is that she fell in love with me. Fancy that!

He smiled bleakly.

—She had a bookshop which I often visited in connection with a plan to translate and decontaminate great French literature so that it could be an inspiration to the Irish, besotted with Dickens, Cardinal Newman, Walter Scott and Kickham. My eye had a broad range— Pascal and Descartes, Rimbaud, de Musset, Verlaine, Balzac, even that holy Franciscan, Benedictine and medical man, Rabelais . . . !

—Interesting. But *Ulysses?*

—Curious thing about Baudelaire and Mallarmé—both were obsessed with Edgar Allen Poe.

—How did Miss Beach express her love for you?

—Ah-ha! Who is Sylvia? She swore to me that she'd make me famous. She didn't at the beginning say how, and anyhow I took it all patiently as childish talk. But her plot was to have this thing named *Ulysses* concocted, secretly circulated and have the authorship ascribed to me. Of course at first I didn't take the mad scheme seriously.

—But how did the thing progress?

—I was shown bits of it in typescript. Artificial and laborious stuff,

I thought. I just couldn't take much interest in it, even as a joke by amateurs. I was immersed in those days in what was intrinsically good behind the bad in Scaliger, Voltaire, Montaigne, and even that queer man Villon. But how well-attuned they were, I thought, to the educated Irish mind. Ah, yes. Of course it wasn't Sylvia Beach who showed me those extracts.

—Who was it?

—Various low, dirty-minded ruffians who had been paid to put this material together. Muck-rakers, obscene poets, carnal pimps, sodomous sycophants, pedlars of the coloured lusts of fallen humanity. Please don't ask me for names.

Mick pondered it all, in wonder.

—Mr Joyce, how did you live in all those years?

—Teaching languages, mostly English, and giving grinds. I used to hang around the Sorbonne. Meals were easy enough to scrounge there, anyway.

—Did the Catholic Truth Society pay you for those booklets you wrote?

—Not at all. Why should they?

—Tell me more about *Ulysses*.

—I paid very little attention to it until one day I was given a piece from it about some woman in bed thinking the dirtiest thoughts that ever came into the human head. Pornography and filth and literary vomit, enough to make even a blackguard of a Dublin cabman blush. I blessed myself and put the thing in the fire.

—Well was the complete *Ulysses*, do you think, ever published?

—I certainly hope not.

Mick paused for a few seconds and pressed the bell for service. What would he say? Frankness in return seemed called for.

—Mr Joyce, he said solemnly, I can tell you that you have been out of touch with things for a long time. The book *Ulysses* was published in Paris in 1922, with your name on the title page. And it was considered a great book.

—God forgive you. Are you fooling me? I am getting on in years. Remember that.

Mick patted his sleeve, and signalled to a server to bring more drinks.

—It was roughly received originally but it has since been published everywhere, including America. Dozens—literally dozens—of distinguished American critics have written treatises on it. Books have even been written about yourself and your methods. And all the copyright money on *Ulysses* must have accrued to your credit. The difficulty of the various publishers is simply that they don't know where you are.

—May the angels of God defend us!

—You're a strange man, Mr Joyce. Bowsies who write trash and are as proud as punch of it are ten a penny. You have your name on a great book, you are ashamed of your life, and ask God's pardon. Well, well, well. I am going out for a moment to relieve myself. I feel that's about the perfect thing to do.

—How dare you impute smutty writings to me?

Mick got up a bit brusquely and went out for the purpose stated, but was disturbed. His bluff, if that was the right name for it, had hardly succeeded. Joyce was serious in his denial, and apparently had never seen the book *Ulysses*. What new line should now be taken?

When he returned and sat down Joyce quickly spoke in a low and serious tone.

—Look here, I hope you don't mind if we change the subject, he said. I spoke of the importance for me of the future. I mean that. I want you to help me.

—I've already said it would be a pleasure.

—Well, you have heard of Late Vocations. I may not be worthy but I want to join the Jesuits.

—*What?* Well . . . !

The shock in Mick's voice was of a rasping kind. Into his mind came that other book, *Portrait of the Artist*. Here had been renunciation of family, faith, even birthland, and that promise of silence, exile and cunning. What did there seem to be here? The garrulous, the repatriate, the ingenuous? Yet was not even a man of genius entitled to change his mind? And what matter if that mind showed signs of unbalance, and memory evidence of decay? The ambition to join the Church's most intellectual of Orders was certainly an enormous surprise, perhaps not to be taken absolutely seriously. Still, he had custody of his immortal soul and who was he, Mick, himself on the brink of the holy prison of the Trappists, to question his wish to take part in the religious life? He might not be taken, of course, by reason of the scandalous literary works attributed to him, or even by reason of age, but that decision was one for Father Provincial of the Society of Jesus, not for Mick.

—My French Plan, if I may call it that, Joyce continued, I could defer until I had the seclusion of the Order. Curious, I have many notes on the *good* and *decorous* things written by those three scoundrels who otherwise dealt in blood—Marat, Robespierre and Danton. Strange . . . like lillies sprouting on a heap of ordure.

Mick drank thoughtfully, arranging his thoughts into wise words.

—Mr Joyce, he said, I believe it takes fourteen years to make a Jesuit Father. That's a long time. You could become a medical doctor in far less than that.

—If God spares me, I would be a postulant even if it took me twenty years. Of what account are those trumpery years in this vale of tears? Do you know any Jesuits personally?

—I do. I know at least one, a Father Cobble, in Leeson Street. He's an Englishman but quite intelligent.

—Ah, excellent. Will you introduce me?

—I will of course. Naturally, that is about all I could do. I mean, Church matters are for the Church to decide. If I were to try to sort of . . . interfere or use pressure, I would be very soon told to mind my own business.

—I quite understand that. All I ask for is a quiet talk with a Jesuit Father after I've been sponsored by some responsible, respectable person like yourself. Leave the rest to him, me and God.

His tone seemed pleased, and in the gloom he gave the impression of smiling.

—Well, I'm glad our little talk is going the right way, Mick said.

—Yes, he murmured. I've just been thinking in recent days of my schooldays at Clongowes Wood College. Of course it's very silly but suppose I were to become a Jesuit as planned, is it not at least possible —*possible*, I repeat—that I would in my old age be appointed Rector of Clongowes? Could it not happen?

—Of course it could.

Joyce's fingers were at his glass of Martini, playing absently. His mind was at grips with another matter.

—I must be candid here, and careful. You might say that I have more than one good motive for wishing to become a Jesuit Father. I wish to reform, first the Society, and then through the Society the Church. Error has crept in . . . corrupt beliefs . . . certain shameless superstitions . . . rash presumptions which have no sanction within the word of the Scriptures.

Mick frowned, considering this.

—Questions of dogma, you mean? These can be involved matters.

—Straightforward attention to the word of God, Joyce rejoined, will confound all Satanic quibble. Do you know the Hebrew language?

—I'm afraid I do not.

—Ah, too few people do. The word *ruach* is most important. It means a breath or a blowing. *Spiritus* we call it in Latin. The Greek word is *pneuma*. You see the train of meaning we have here? All these words mean life. Life, and breath of life. God's breath in man.

—Do these words mean the same thing?

—No. The Hebrew *ruach* denoted only the Divine Being, anterior to man. Later it came to mean the inflammation, so to speak, of created man by the breath of God.

—I find that not very clear.

—Well . . . one needs experience in trying to grasp celestial concepts through earthly words. This word *ruach* latterly means, not the immanent energy of God but His transcendent energy in imparting the divine content to men.

—You mean that man is part-God?

—Even the ancient pre-Christian Greeks used *pneuma* to denote the limitless and all-powerful personality of God, and man's bodily senses are due to the immanence of that *pneuma*. God wills that man have a transfusion of His *pneuma*.

—Well . . . I don't suppose anybody would question that. What you call *pneuma* is what distinguishes man from the brute?

—As you will, but it is wrong to say that man's possession, charismatically, of *ruach* or *pneuma* makes him part-God. God is of two Persons, the Father and the Son. They subsist in hypostasis. That is quite clear from mention of both Divine Persons in the New Testament. What I particularly call your attention to is the Holy Spirit— the Holy Ghost, to use the more common title.

—And what about the Holy Spirit?

—The Holy Spirit was the invention of the more reckless of the early Fathers. We have here a confusion of thought and language. Those poor ignorant men associated *pneuma* with what they called the working of the Holy Spirit, whereas it is merely an exudation of

God the Father. It is an activity of the existing God, and it is a woeful and shameful error to identify in it a hypostatic Third Person. Abominable nonsense!

Mick picked up his glass and gazed into it in dismay.

—Then you don't believe in the Holy Ghost, Mr Joyce?

—There is not a word about the Holy Ghost or the Trinity in the New Testament.

—I am not . . . much experienced in Biblical studies.

Joyce's low grunt was not ill-natured.

—Of course you're not, because you were reared a Catholic. Neither are the Catholic clergy. Those ancient disputants, rhetoricians, theologisers who are collectively called the Early Fathers were buggers for getting ideas into their heads and then assuming that God directly inspired those ideas. In trying to wind up the Arian controversy, the Council of Alexandria in 362, having asserted the equality in nature of the Son with the Father, went on to announce the transfer of a third hypostasis to the Holy Spirit. Without saying boo, or debating the matter at all! Holy pokey but wouldn't you think they'd have a little sense?

—I always understood that God was of three Divine Persons.

—Well you didn't get up early enough in the morning, my lad. The Holy Ghost was not officially invented until the Council of Constantinople in 381.

Mick fingered his jaws.

—Goodness, he said. I wonder what the Holy Ghost Fathers would think of that?

Joyce noisily rapped his glass and murmured to the server who appeared and took them away. Then he drew expansively at his cigar.

—One thing you *do* know, he asked—the Nicene Creed?

—Sure everybody knows that.

—Yes. The Father and the Son were meticulously defined at the Council of Nicaea, and the Holy Spirit hardly mentioned. Augustine was a severe burden on the early Church, and Tertullian split it wide open. He insisted that the Holy Spirit was derived from the Father *and* the son—*quoque*, you know. The Eastern Church would have nothing to do with such a doctrinal aberration. Schism!

Joyce paid for two new drinks then sat down. His voice had been lively, as if joyous in disputation. Mick's own mind had been awakened sharply by mention of Augustine, and he struggled to get into words a rather remote idea which was forming. He sampled his sherry.

—That word *pneuma*, Mr. Joyce . . .?

—Yes?

—Well, you remember my friend De Selby, whom I mentioned to you?

—I do indeed. Dalkey.

—I told you he was a physicist . . . a theologian also.

—Yes. Fascinating mixture but not incongruous, mind you.

—You will probably laugh in my face if I told you to believe that I met Saint Augustine in the company of De Selby.

Joyce's cigar glowed dimly.

—Faith, now—*laugh?* Certainly not. There are conditions . . . opiates . . . gases—many ways of confuting weak human reason.

—Thank you, Mr Joyce. I'll talk about the Augustine affair another time, but the circumstance of this encounter involved the operation of a formula whereby De Selby claims to be able to stop the flow of time, or reverse it.

—Well, it is a big claim.

—It is. But the phrase he used to describe his work was 'pneumatic chemistry'. You see? That word *pneuma* again.

—Indeed yes. Life, breath, eternity, recall of the past. I must think about this man De Selby.

—I'm glad you are so serious and reasonable. *Pneuma* in its divine aspect seems to have been concerned somehow in the manifestation of Saint Augustine.

—One must not be astonished at a thing merely because it looks impossible.

Mick's thought was occupied with another encounter disclosing a situation which, if not impossible, was certainly unlikely.

—Mr Joyce, he said, I have another unusual experience which seems to have involved this *pneuma* also.

—Oh, I don't wonder. It's a big subject. We call it pneumatology.

—Yes. I know a Sergeant Fottrell, also of Dalkey. He has an involved theory about the danger of riding bicycles, even if they are fitted with pneumatic tyres.

—Ah, bicycles? I never had any love for those machines. The old Dublin cab was my father's first choice for getting around.

—Well, the Sergeant thinks that, *pneuma* in the tyres or not, the rider gets a severe jolting and that there is an exchange or interfusion of bicycle atoms and human atoms.

Joyce quietly drank.

—Well . . . I would not reject the possibility outright. The *pneuma* there might be preserving life, in the sense of preserving the physical integrity of the rider. Half an hour in a laboratory is a thing that would help us here. The interchange of cells of human tissue with elements of metal would seem a surprising occurrence but of course that is merely a rational objection.

—All right. In any case the Sergeant had no doubt of it. He personally knew men whose *jobs* entailed much cycling every day and he regarded some of them as more bicycle than man.

Joyce chuckled dimly.

—There we have a choice. Psychical research or cycle research. I prefer the psychical. Ah, indeed . . . my own little troubles are more complicated than the Sergeant's. I have to get into the Jesuits, you might say, to clear the Holy Ghost out of the Godhead and out of the Catholic Church.

There was a silence. Mick's business seemed almost at an end. It had been a short evening, yet Joyce's disclosures about himself, past and present, had not been inconsiderable. Joyce moved his chair.

—Tell me, he said, how soon could I see Father Cobble?

—How soon? Well, as soon as you like, I suppose. These men are usually accessible enough at any time.

—What about tomorrow?

—Goodness!

—You see, I have three days off from work just now—from work as a curate. Could we strike the iron while it's hot?

Mick pondered this urge for action. All he could think about it was—why not?

—Well, I have an appointment at Dalkey tomorrow night. But provided I could meet you somewhere in town about half-six or so, I suppose we could go along and meet Father Cobble. I could telephone him during the day and make the appointment.

—Excellent. Excellent.

—What time would you say for a meeting? The place I suggest is outside St Vincent's Hospital, on the Green. But at what time?

—Yes. I know the hospital. Would seven in the evening suit?

Mick agreed with this: it would fit neatly into his schedule. They fell silent, finishing their drinks. Was there anything else of a semi-private nature to be asked, Mick wondered, for there would be very little opportunity for confidence the following day. Yes, there was: one thing.

—Mr. Joyce, he said, I know the subject displeases you but I must return briefly to that work *Ulysses*. Do you mind?

—No, no, but it's just a boring, dirty subject.

—I take it you have no literary agent?

—What would I have the like of that for?

—Well, I mean—

—Do you think the Catholic Truth Society are commercial publishers, on the make?

—Never mind. Would you appoint me your literary agent?

—Call yourself that by all means if it pleases you, I can't imagine why.

—Well, it's like this. Notwithstanding your ignorance, there may be money lying to your credit from the sales of *Ulysses* in the accounts of publishers. There may be several thousands of pounds there. There is no reason why you should not claim money which is your due— no reason that I should not claim it on your behalf.

—You would probably be offended if I were to say that you suffer from an obsession, from an excited imagination.

Mick laughed lightly to put him at ease.

—You ought to know, he said, that a person who seems to get a bit light-headed should be humoured.

—Well, yes ... flighty children should be treated that way. It saves trouble. But you're no child, even if the bottle is no stranger to you.

Both of them relaxed.

—There can be no harm in me, as your agent, making inquiries. Now can there?

—There certainly would appear to be no breach of the moral law involved, and that's a sure fire. The only thing you must never reveal is my address—particularly not to any of those lascivious pornographic blackguards.

Mick drank audibly.

—Perhaps you may have something else to say, he said mildly, if it turns out that there is a sum of £8,000 due on foot of *Ulysses*.

Joyce's voice, when it came, was low and strained.

—What would *I* do with £8,ooo? he demanded—a man who is tomorrow taking the first step to join the Jesuit Order?

—As I think I reminded you before, they call it Society, not Order. And I can tell you this. If they take you, they take you as you are, poor or rich. The founder Loyola was a nobleman, remember that. And another thing . . .

—What?

—If sundry scheming ruffians in Paris or elsewhere imputed to you matter you did not write and sought to besmear your good name, would it not look like Divine Providence if their base handiwork were to turn out to do you immense corporal good?

Joyce smoked testily.

—But I tell you I don't want or need money.

—Maybe you do. The Jesuits have a wide choice. It may be that they are not particularly fond of paupers.

The silence which followed possibly meant that Joyce was acknowledging a quite new idea. He spoke at last.

—All right. If eight thousand pounds was in fact earned by that horrible book you mentioned, and can be lawfully got, every penny of it will go to the Jesuits except five pounds, which I will devote to the Holy Souls.

They parted soon after. Mick strolling towards the station, well enough at ease.

He doubted whether the Jesuits would accept a man of his age, other questions apart. Perhaps some other Order would take him as a Brother. Any Order, he hastily warned himself, except the Trappists. He must never mention that community in Joyce's presence. . . .

SELECTED BIBLIOGRAPHY

Flann O'Brien and Myles na Gopaleen are the best-known pseudonyms of Brian O'Nolan, but David Powell suggested that there may be more than one hundred lesser-known pseudonyms. In the present bibliography the title of a work by O'Brien will be followed by the pseudonym under which it was written.

For complete bibliography, including articles by and about Flann O'Brien, reviews of his books, and a list of unpublished material, see David Powell, "The English Writings of Flann O'Brien" (unpublished doctoral dissertation, University of Southern Illinois, 1971), and "A Checklist of Brian O'Nolan" in *The Journal of Irish Literature*, Vol. 3, No. 1 (January 1974), pp. 104–12. Also see Anne Clissmann, *Flann O'Brien: A Critical Introduction To His Writing* (Dublin and London: Gill and Macmillan, and New York: Barnes and Noble Books, a division of Harper and Row, 1975).

BOOKS BY FLANN O'BRIEN

At Swim-Two-Birds. By Flann O'Brien. London: Longmans, Green, 1939; New York: Pantheon Books, 1939; London: MacGibbon and Kee, 1960; London: Four Square Books, 1962; New York: Walker, 1966; London: Penguin Books, Modern Classics, 1967; New York: The Viking Press, Compass edition, 1967.

An Béal Bocht. By Myles na Gopaleen. Dublin: National Press, 1941; Dublin: Dolmen Press, 1964.

— *The Poor Mouth: A Bad Story About the Hard Life.* Translated by Patrick C. Power from the Gaelic. London: Hart–Davis, MacGibbon, 1973; New York: A Richard Seaver Book/ The Viking Press, 1974.

The Best of Myles: A Selection from "Cruiskeen Lawn." By Miles na Gopaleen. Edited and with Preface by Kevin O Nolan. London: MacGibbon and Kee, 1968; New York: Walker, 1968.

Cruiskeen Lawn (selections from *Cruiskeen Lawn, The Irish Times*). By Myles na Gopaleen. Dublin: Cahill, 1943.

The Dalkey Archive. By Flann O'Brien. London: MacGibbon and Kee, 1964; New York: Macmillan, 1965.

Faustus Kelly (a play in three acts). By Myles na Gopaleen. Dublin: Cahill, 1943.

The Hard Life. By Flann O'Brien. London: MacGibbon and Kee, 1962; New York: Pantheon Books, 1962; London: Four Square Books, 1964.

Mairead Gilan (a play by Brinsley MacNamar, translated into Irish by Myles na Gopaleen). Dublin: Stationery Office, 1953.

Stories and Plays. By Flann O'Brien. Introduction by Claud Cockburn. London: MacGibbon and Kee, 1973; New York: A Richard Seaver Book/The Viking Press, 1976.

Contents:
> "Slattery's Sago Saga"
> "The Martyr's Crown"
> "John Duffy's Brother"
> "Thirst"
> "Faustus Kelly"
> "A Bash in the Tunnel"

The Third Policeman. By Flann O'Brien. London: MacGibbon and

Kee, 1967; New York: Walker, 1967; New York: Lancer Books, 1970.

SOURCE MATERIAL

Myles: Portraits of Brian O'Nolan. Edited by Timothy O'Keeffe. London: Martin Brian and O'Keeffe, 1973. (Includes essays by Kevin O Nolan, John Garvin, Jack White, and Niall Sheridan.)

Remembering How We Stood: Bohemian Dublin at the Mid-Century. By John Ryan. Dublin: Gill and Macmillan, 1975.

Also, as this book goes to press a book by Anthony Cronin, an old friend of O'Brien's, is in the works.